Plays for Children
Volume 2

11 Plays

by
Blanche Marvin

A SAMUEL FRENCH ACTING EDITION

SAMUEL FRENCH

FOUNDED 1830

New York Hollywood London Toronto

SAMUELFRENCH.COM

II PLAYS FOR CHILDREN
VOLUME 2

by Blanche Marvin

THE EMPEROR'S NEW CLOTHES
A Mediaeval Morality Play

SLEEPING BEAUTY
Restoration Comedy

CINDERELLA
A Comedy of Manners (styled after Wilde's *THE IMPORTANCE OF BEING EARNEST*)

THE LITTLEST TAILOR
Minstrel Style Theatre

THE ARABIAN NIGHTS
Kabuki Style Theatre

PETER AND THE WOLF
Chekovian (*CHERRY ORCHARD*) Naturalistic Style Theatre

ALICE IN WONDERLAND
Commedia dell'arte Style Theatre

PINOCCHIO
Pirandello (*SIX CHARACTERS IN SEARCH OF AN AUTHOR*) Style Theatre

THE RED DRAGON
Contemporary Miracle Play

MR. EASTER BUNNY
Contemporary Comedy

CROWNING GLORY – THE STORY OF ESTHER
European Classical Style Theatre

SAMUEL FRENCH, INC.

FOREWORD

This collection of plays, mainly fairytales, was written for a particular
company called the Merri-Mimes, and as a result they had an identifiable
style, a signature, that made it a Merri-Mime play in addition to the
theatrical style that differed for each one.

The signature of the Merri-Mimes was the children's participation in each of
the plays. It meant so much to them, that maybe for one of the shows they
would be chosen to go on stage and become part of the story. But
everyone had the chance to participate in some way during each production.

So you will find a continuity of the participation in the Narrator or the Fool
in each of the plays. If you plan a season of children's theatre, the very
young ones will come back and eagerly await that selfsame character, no
matter the change of name or place.

There are three plays that are holiday plays. MR. EASTER BUNNY is a
contemporary comedy based on the play HARVEY (a rabbit). THE RED
DRAGON is again a contemporary drama based on the concept of a miracle
for Christmas, and CROWNING GLORY is a classical Biblical play about Queen
Esther and how her courage evolved so that she eventually saved the Jews
of Persia, creating the holiday of Purim.

Outside of the folk tales of PINOCCHIO, ALICE IN WONDERLAND and PETER
AND THE WOLF, all the other scripts are fairytales, each written in a
specific style of theatre easily defined in the preface to each play. The
style is chosen because it is right for that story. Careful stage directions
have been written in so that the style may be realised by the director.

You may do one or all of these plays, which will entertain yet educate the
children. Professional companies, schools, radio and television may find this
collection of interest. There are no other anthologies as full or as varied
as this.

The sets and costumes are guidelines in understanding the style. They
should be used if they prove helpful. It should not be inhibitive in any
way.

How wonderful if these plays continue to bring such pleasure to future
generations as they have done in the past. I have been privileged to see
children enjoy, be influenced, and grow because of all these theatre
productions. I hope this book continues as a source of nourishment.

BLANCHE MARVIN

OUTLINE OF PLAYS

THE CRICKET THEATRE AND BLANCHE MARVIN
PRESENT:
THE MERRI-MIMES IN

THE EMPEROR'S NEW CLOTHES

BY BLANCHE MARVIN
DIRECTED BY MARIO SILETTI
CHOREOGRAPHY BY RAY HARRISON
SETS AND COSTUME DESIGN BY JOSINE
MUSIC BY CLAIRE BROOK
COSTUMES EXECUTED BY
VICKERY WILLIAMS
STAGE MANAGER-
TINKA CRAWFORD

CAST:

EMPEROR - WILL HAAN
LADY DEIDRE - ELIZABETH WORTH
CRICKET - WILLIAM HAWLEY
LADY CAROLINE - POLLY GARRETT
LORD - BOB SPIVACK
TAILOR DOMER - R.S. DOUGLAS

AT THE CRICKET THEATRE
162 SECOND AVE. (at 10th st.) OR-4-3960
at 1-2³⁰-4 p.m. SAT. OCT. 17, 24, 31, NOV. 7, 14.

ALSO:

CINDERELLA 1-2³⁰-4 pm. SAT. NOV. 21, 28, DEC. 5, 12, 19, 26, MON. DEC. 28, 29, 30, 31. FRI. JAN. 1, & 2
SLEEPING BEAUTY   JAN. 9, 16, 23, 30. FEB. 6th
ALICE IN WONDERLAND   FEB. 13, 20. MON. FEB. 22, 27 MARCH 5, 12.
SINBAD (ARABIAN NIGHTS) MARCH 19, 26. APRIL 2, 9.
PETER AND THE WOLF SAT. APRIL 16, THROUGH EASTER WEEK, APRIL 18
TO SAT. APR. 23, & 30, MAY 7, 14, 21.

JEWELERY COURTESY OF CORO INC. - CANDY COURTESY OF BARTONS.
JOSINE.

THE EMPEROR'S NEW CLOTHES

A MEDIAEVAL MORALITY PLAY

CAST OF CHARACTERS

King Eric, Emperor of Sylvania

Lord

Lady Caroline

Lady Deidre

Cricket, the Jester

Domer, the Merchant-Tailor

Place: Palace of the King

Time: Long Ago

Author's Note:

This play is a parody of a mediaeval morality play ranging
from an elaborate madrigal mocking the Emperor to the
imaginary weaving of cloth by the tailor in front of a
hypocritical Court. The French traditions of comedy are
incorporated from Molliere to Giradoux.

ACT ONE

THE SCENE OPENS ON A PALATIAL THRONE ROOM BEAUTIFULLY
DECORATED IN PASTEL COLOURS. TWO CHANDELIERS HANG FROM
EITHER SIDE AND THE THRONE IS UPSTAGE LEFT. ALL SHOULD BE
ELEGANT AND DELICATE. THE **KING**, IMMACULATELY GROOMED, IS
DANCING WITH A LOVELY LADY OF THE COURT, **LADY CAROLINE**. A
LORD AND **LADY** ARE DANCING ON THE OPPOSITE SIDE OF THE
STAGE. THE **LORD** IS POMPOUS, WELL-GROOMED. THE **LADY** (**LADY
DEIRDRE**) IS SOFT, KIND, NOT SO PRETTY. AS THE CURTAINS OPEN,
WE SEE THE FRIVOLOUS LIFE IN THIS KINGDOM AS THE **COURT
JESTER**, **CRICKET**, SITS CROSS-LEGGED DOWNSTAGE RIGHT. AFTER A
WHILE HE BEGINS TO TALK TO THE CHILDREN. THE MUSIC PLAYS.

CRICKET   Do you see them dancing? That seems to be all they do in this
kingdom. Dance. Vanity ... vanity ... thy name is King Eric. He doesn't
think about anything but his clothes and dancing. He doesn't care about
being king, about the wars, about taxes, about how poor the people are ...
only about clothes. I've never heard of such a King. (POINTS TO KING)
Handsome, isn't he? He's good. He means well, but what can I do to
awaken him? I'm only a fool. Everyone thinks that fools and children
know nothing, but we've great wisdom, haven't we? (WINKS TO CHILDREN)
We don't disguise what we think and feel with layers of other things. No
indeed. We say 'ouch' when it hurts. 'I love you' when we mean it. Don't
you? I do. We're really much better than grown-ups. Now, watch the
King. Look, he's angry. Her Ladyship pulled his cuff a bit. Oh - oh -
she'll lose favour.

KING   My dear, you have creased my cuff.

LADY CAROLINE
         Only by accident, my Lord.

KING   I don't permit such accidents.

LADY CAROLINE   (STRAIGHTENING IT)   There, it's just like new.

KING   Just like new. It is new!

LADY CAROLINE
         I meant just as before.

KING   Almost, but not quite.

LADY CAROLINE
         Mayn't we finish the dance?

KING   No. You never said anything about my new suit.

LADY CAROLINE
         It is beautiful. But then, all your clothes are the most
beautiful in the whole kingdom ... in the whole world.

KING (PLEASED) Yes, I think they're quite the best. You look lovely yourself.

LADY CAROLINE
          Your Highness is kind to say so.

KING   I only dance with the loveliest of ladies.

LADY CAROLINE
          Thank you, your Majesty.

LORD   (HAS STOPPED DANCING) My King, you are very handsome tonight.

KING   Well, then you have a favour to ask of me.

LORD   Not so, your Majesty.

KING   You've never paid me a compliment without asking a favour
afterwards.

LORD   I speak as Minister for the Army. We're in need of money
... for arms.

KING   There are enough arms.

LORD   But sire, we are at war. If we lose, the whole kingdom will
be forfeited.

KING   If we lose, your head will go first.

LORD   We can't fight without weapons.

KING   Enough gold and silver has been given to the Army.

LORD   But that was last week.

KING   Then win and end this war.

LORD   But –

KING   That is a royal command. Win the war.

LORD   Yes, your Majesty.

          THE LADIES HAVE BEEN TOGETHER, FEARFUL FOR THE LORD.

KING   Cricket, sing and dance for me. I'm tired of all the others.

CRICKET   I'm only a poor fool, but I'll do what I can to amuse you,
my King.

          HE DANCES AND MIMES AS HE TALKS, IMITATING EACH ONE'S
          CHARACTER. MUSIC.

                    There is my Lord ...
                    The Minister of War

                    Who dances at Court
                    And for love will explore.
                    Go out to battle,
                    See what's to be done –
                    Or are you afraid
                    Lest the battle be won?
                    Then where would you be,
                    And what would you do?
                    No War Ministry
                    Means no place for you!

LORD   I say, Cricket, enough's enough.

KING   Pay attention, my Lord. Go on, my fool. You're wiser than
the King.

        MUSIC

CRICKET   Lady Caroline, how do you do?
                        Your beauty is all that is real for you.
                        Do you love with a heart that's true?
                        Or is power and fame you pursue?

LADY CAROLINE
            Stop him, your Majesty.

KING   Stay, Lady Caroline, listen to the rest.

        MUSIC

CRICKET   Ah, Lady Deirdre, a woman indeed!
                        For you I would even ride a white steed.
                        Yours is a heart that is loyal and true;
                        Your beauty is inside and outside too.

LADY DEIRDRE (WEEPING)
            Oh, Cricket, how kind.

KING   Come now, Lady Deirdre, it's only a song.

LORD   Well said, Cricket.

        MUSIC

KING   Hear, hear.

CRICKET   And now, my King, with blood so blue,
                        Where is the head that God gave you?
                        Given to lace, and cloth, and rings,
                        Given to unimportant things.
                        Is this how a King of the realm should be?
                        Where are the deeds the world should see?
                        Now is the time you should begin
                        To lead a full life from within,
                        To rule your land, to hold your reign,

                    To lead your subjects through joy and pain.

KING   This is a serious charge, Cricket. Tell me, my Minister of War, do you agree?

LORD   Of course not.

KING   But you did agree only a moment ago!

LORD   Never, Sire. Listen to the mad songs of a fool?

KING   I listen very carefully, but whether I can change, ah well ...

LADY DEIRDRE
There is nothing to change, my King, only to look a little further.

KING   I have always respected your counsel.

LADY DEIRDRE
I offer it with a full heart, Sire.

KING   For that I am grateful.

LADY CAROLINE
I should whip that fool a thousand times for speaking to me in such a way, if I were King.

KING   That's probably why you're not Queen.

LADY CAROLINE
What did you say?

KING   You heard what I said, I think.

LADY CAROLINE
My King ... Eric ... I've known you since we were children, yet each year I know you less and less.

KING   The more you know, the less you know.

LADY CAROLINE
I have been humiliated and my King only encourages it.

KING   Sometimes we need a mirror to see ourselves ... and even then we see only what we want to see. The fool sees us as we are.

LORD   Maybe I should ask the fool for funds for the Army.

KING   You're bitter, my Lord.

LORD   You listen to the fool and not to me. I've worked these many years as Minister to your father, and now to you. You should respect that.

KING   And what do you have to say, my fool?

CRICKET   If the shoe fits, wear it. If I have been right, accept it.

LADY CAROLINE
          Oh, Lady Deirdre, what shall we do?

          SHE RUNS TO **LADY DEIRDRE**. THE TWO WOMEN ARE NOW ON STAGE
          LEFT. THE **KING** SITS ON HIS THRONE, THE **FOOL** AT HIS FEET. THE
          LORD PACES BACK AND FORTH THINKING AND THE TWO **LADIES** IN A
          DANCE PATTERN WALK BACK AND FORTH IN OPPOSITE DIRECTION TO
          THE LORD. THEY DO AN ABOUT-FACE ALL TOGETHER.

LADY DEIRDRE
          There is truth in what Cricket says.

LADY CAROLINE
          About me?

LADY DEIRDRE
          About us all.

LADY CAROLINE
          But I'm unworthy in his eyes. (CRIES)

LADY DEIRDRE
          Do you want to be Queen?

LADY CAROLINE
          Yes.

LADY DEIRDRE
          There, you admit it.

LADY CAROLINE
          Of course I do. Who wouldn't?

LADY DEIRDRE
          Then you'll have to learn how to behave as one.

LADY CAROLINE
          How?

LADY DEIRDRE
          You see – you're much better already.

LADY CAROLINE
          Show me.

LADY DEIRDRE
          You won't do it in one day ... little by little. Wait there a
moment. (SHE EXITS)

LADY CAROLINE
          I wonder what she'll have me do?

          LADY DEIRDRE ENTERS

LADY DEIRDRE

Close your eyes. (FROM BEHIND HER BACK SHE TAKES AN APRON AND PUTS IT ON **LADY CAROLINE**) There you are ... now into the kitchen ... wash some dishes ... help the cook ... he'll show you how.

LADY CAROLINE

But I'm a Lady –

LADY DEIRDRE

In order to command your household you must know it first. Off with you and into the kitchen.

LADY CAROLINE (CRYING)

Oh – oh – oh – will I ever be Queen?

KING   (LAUGHING) Lady Deirdre, what would you suggest for me to do?

LADY DEIRDRE

To be yourself, my Lord. Your true self.

LORD   Lady Deirdre, I'm ashamed of your behaviour. A lady of Caroline's station –

CRICKET   (JUMPS UP SUDDENLY, ALMOST IN AN EVIL WAY TO FRIGHTEN EACH ONE. THE FOOL NEVER WALKS, HE ALWAYS MOVES IN DANCE PATTERNS) Would you put to a test whether each one of you is worthy of your station, including the King himself? Or are you afraid to face it?

LORD   Indeed not. I'm a loyal subject, carrying out the duties of my office as best I can under the circumstances.

KING   A game, Cricket, good. Let's try it. Test me as King.

CRICKET   And you, Lady Deirdre?

LADY DEIRDRE

I have no other station but my birthright. I'm willing to put it to a test.

CRICKET   Very well. I know a merchant tailor who weaves the most beautiful cloth in all the world. This cloth only he himself may cut into clothes. It is so rare, so precious ...

KING   Cricket, where is he?

CRICKET   I haven't finished yet, your Majesty. This cloth is so rare, so precious that only those who are worthy of their station can see it. Those who are not, will never see it.

KING   Bring this merchant tailor here at once. I must have this precious cloth.

CRICKET   But if you do not see it? What then?

KING   A king is born, not made, my Cricket. I'll see it. And you, my

Lord?

LORD   If my King sees it, so shall I.

LADY DEIRDRE
          If there is a cloth at all, I will see it.

CRICKET   Then I'll send for the merchant tailor and may all your eyes be
well-blessed.

          HE JUMPS AND LEAPS OFF STAGE AND EXITS. THE OTHERS STAND
          STARING AT EACH OTHER.

                              CURTAIN

                         END OF ACT ONE

                    ACT TWO

SCENE ONE

          THRONE ROOM AS IN ACT I. THE KING IS SEATED ON HIS THRONE.
          THE LORD AND THE LADY DEIRDRE STAND ON EITHER SIDE.

KING   What's happened to the fool? He should be here by now.

LADY DEIRDRE
          He'll be here at any moment. You're too impatient.

LORD   After he arrives, you probably won't be able to get rid of him.
(THE KING LEAVES HIS THRONE AND STARTS PACING) I hear them. Quickly,
your Highness.

          BACK TO THE THRONE THE KING RUSHES, FEIGNING INDIFFERENCE.
          THE FOOL ENTERS WITH THE MERCHANT TAILOR. THE MERCHANT,
          DOMER, IS A QUIET, SMILING MAN WITH AN AIR OF INNOCENCE. HE
          IS OVERWHELMED AT BEING IN THE PALACE AND MEETING THE KING
          HIMSELF.

CRICKET   Forgive me, my King. I came as quickly as I could.

          THEY ARE ON THEIR KNEES TO THE KING.

KING   Good Cricket, I'm sure you did. Merchant, what is your name?

DOMER (KISSING THE KING'S ROBE) Oh, my King, I am so honoured to be
in your presence!

KING   What is your name?

DOMER   My name? ... Er .. er ... (HE IS SO OVERCOME THAT HE CANNOT REMEMBER) I don't know. (HE IS ALL FINGERS)

CRICKET   King Eric, the merchant is so overpowered by your presence he is speechless. His name is Domer.

DOMER   Domer? (STILL ALL A-FLUSTER)

CRICKET   Yes, Domer.

KING   And his cloth? Can he show it?

CRICKET   Domer, show your King the precious cloth.

DOMER   Oh yes, my King.

SHAKILY HE OPENS ONE BOX AFTER THE OTHER AND FINALLY PICKS UP WITH TENDER CARE WHAT APPEARS TO BE NOTHING. HE BRUSHES IT OFF, HE FOLDS IT OVER AND THEN SHOWS IT TO THE KING. THE KING LOOKS QUICKLY AT THE OTHERS WHO STAND BY IN COMPLETE SURPRISE AT ALL THE DOINGS. EVERYONE PRETENDS TO BE IMPRESSED. CRICKET GRABS THE CLOTH AND DANCES AROUND THE THRONE ROOM SHOWING IT TO EVERYONE.

MUSIC

CRICKET
           Handle it with gentle care –
           Touch it softly here and there –
           Can you see it? Maybe you don't.
           Can you touch it? Maybe you won't.
           This is the cloth of magic hue
           To be worn only, my King, by you.

KING   Well, my Lord, what do you think?

LORD   It's beautiful. But then don't expect me to be enthusiastic over a beautiful piece of cloth.

KING   You did see it?

LORD   Yes.

KING   And you, Lady Deirdre?

LADY DEIRDRE   (LOOKING UP AT THE KING) My Lord ... what can I say?

SHE RUNS OUT.

KING   I wonder if she saw it?

CRICKET   Who knows? Sire, would you care for more cloth, enough to make a complete robe?

KING   Yes. That would be splendid!

DOMER   I am honoured, my King. I myself will weave as much cloth as you need.

CRICKET   May we set the loom here in your throne room?

KING   An excellent idea. Then I can watch as well. Cricket, do it immediately.

KING EXITS, TAKING THE LORD WITH HIM.

CRICKET   Oh, Domer, they say I am the fool. Isn't it a strange world? They're more fools than I. Not one would say he saw nothing.

DOMER   I was trembling in my boots! Someone could have challenged me and said there was nothing. I don't know what I would have done then.

CRICKET   There is no challenge. You must believe it. You must see it.

DOMER   I must believe it, I must see it! I must believe it, I must see it! I must believe it, I must see it!

MUSIC

CRICKET   Say it over and over again to yourself. (LOOKS TO THE CHILDREN AS THEY EXIT) They're all fools ... even Domer.

CURTAIN

SCENE TWO

IN FRONT OF CURTAIN. THE KITCHEN OF THE PALACE. IT IS JUST A SUGGESTION WITH POTS AND PANS, A STOVE, A TABLE AND CHAIR TO GIVE THE IMPRESSION OF A KITCHEN. LADY CAROLINE WITH APRON STILL ON IS TRYING TO FOLD A TABLECLOTH. HER HAIR IS ALL MESSED. SHE IS TIRED AND UNHAPPY.

LADY CAROLINE
    I folded it many different ways and it's still not right. I've washed dishes and only broken three - or was it four? I've been cooking ... oh, I can't bear it any longer.

CRICKET ENTERS THE KITCHEN.

CRICKET   Lady Caroline, I'd forgotten you were here with all the other excitement.

LADY CAROLINE
    Have I been forgotten already?

CRICKET   Oh, no, Lady Caroline.

LADY CAROLINE

Come, help me. The tablecloth has to be folded very carefully.
It's the King's favourite.

CRICKET   How do I begin?

LADY CAROLINE

Take that end ... this way ... now this way ...

CRICKET   This way!

LADY CAROLINE

The way I have it. Now meet your ends with mine.

BY THIS TIME **CRICKET** HAS ROLLED HIMSELF ROUND IN IT. **LADY
CAROLINE** IS BESIDE HERSELF.

LADY CAROLINE

No games, please. Cricket, please. (**CRICKET, ENCASED IN THE
TABLECLOTH, STARTS RUNNING DOWN THE AISLE AWAY FROM LADY CAROLINE.
SHE CHASES HIM**) Come back, I say. Please, Cricket. Stop him – help me,
someone, catch him! (A CHILD HELPS HER BRING **CRICKET** BACK INTO THE
KITCHEN) A fine helper you make. (SHE UNWINDS HIM) Now look at the
cloth. I'll have to iron it all over again!

CRICKET   It's not as fine a cloth as the one Domer is weaving for the
King. His is a cloth of magic.

LADY CAROLINE

You're saying that to change the subject.

CRICKET   Oh, no, it's the truth, Lady Caroline. It's so precious a cloth
that only those who are worthy of their station may see it.

LADY CAROLINE

I mustn't try to look at it now. I've folded the tablecloth as
best I can. I'll dress myself first as becomes a lady of the Court, and then
inspect your magical cloth.

CRICKET   You may see it just as you are now.

LADY CAROLINE

No one must see me now. Not a word to anyone, Cricket. Do
you hear? (**CRICKET** LEAPS AWAY, **LADY CAROLINE** RUNS AFTER HIM
CALLING) Promise me, not a word to anyone. (EXIT)

CURTAINS OPEN ON THRONE ROOM

SCENE THREE

THRONE ROOM. **CRICKET** AND THE **MERCHANT TAILOR** ARE PRETENDING
TO CARRY IN A HEAVY LOOM WHILE THE **KING** SITS ON THE THRONE.

CRICKET   May we put it here, your Majesty?

KING   Yes, of course.

CRICKET   No one would trip on it, would they?

KING   Move it over to the left, just a little.

CRICKET   There is more room. Shall I move it completely to the left?

KING   Yes, you may. I didn't notice the added space.

DOMER   A moment, give me a moment. It's so heavy, I must rest. All
right, one, two, three, up.

CRICKET   (HOPPING) Ow - right on my toe - ow - ow ... you clumsy ...

     HE WINKS TO THE CHILDREN.

DOMER   I beg your pardon. It slipped.

CRICKET   You're forgiven. Isn't it lovely, my King?

KING   Yes, it must be if you say so.

CRICKET   Show the King how it works, Domer.

     MUSIC

DOMER   (GIVING A LOOK OF NOT KNOWING WHAT TO DO TO CRICKET) Let
me find the lever. Here it is.

     GOES UP AND DOWN. LOOKS AT CRICKET TO SEE IF HE APPROVES.
     CRICKET NODS. JUST THEN THE LORD ENTERS AND WALKS RIGHT
     THROUGH WHERE THE LOOM IS SUPPOSED TO BE.

KING   (LAUGHS) You're a great athlete, my Lord Minister of War.
You've just walked through the loom.

LORD   What loom?

     EVERYONE LAUGHS.

KING   Don't you see that enormous loom? The special one to weave the
magic cloth?

LORD   Where? (LOOKS EVERYWHERE)

CRICKET   (POINTING TO THE WRONG PLACE) It's here.

LORD   (PUTTING ON HIS GLASSES) Yes, there it is.

CRICKET   Oh no, my Lord, it's here. (JUMPS TO ANOTHER SPOT)

LORD   (PUTTING ON TWO PAIRS OF GLASSES) Yes, there.

CRICKET   Wrong again. (TO CHILDREN) Shall I show him the right place? (CHILDREN WILL SAY YES AND NO) Let me think ... (SOMERSAULTS OVER TO LORD) It's right here. (POINTING TO THE RIGHT PLACE)

LORD   You wicked Cricket, fooling me. Of course, it's not there.

KING   (LAUGHING BEYOND CONTROL) Is that how we fight our wars, too? Maybe you need a third pair of glasses.

        KING LEAVES THE THRONE AND STARTS WALKING TO THE LOOM.

LORD   You're all making a terrible mockery of my station. I won't have it.

CRICKET   Your Majesty, be careful, you're stepping on the cloth.

KING   My King, don't you see it ... just where Cricket is sitting?

KING   I wasn't looking.

CRICKET   You're standing on it now. (KING STEPS AWAY) You're still on it. (KING STEPS AWAY FURTHER) Still on it.

LORD   Maybe these will help. (HANDS KING HIS TWO PAIRS OF GLASSES)

CRICKET   My Lord, now you're on it.

LORD   So I am.

KING   Do you see it?

LORD   Oh yes.

KING   Then why don't you feel the loom? You're on top of it!

LORD   This is the most dreadful idea you've ever had, Cricket.

        ENTER LADY DEIRDRE AND LADY CAROLINE. THEY GO TO THE KING AND CURTSEY. THE LORD, WHO IS EXHAUSTED FROM THE GAME HE DOES NOT WANT TO PLAY, SPEAKS.

LORD   Ladies, you are both on top of the loom.

LADY DEIRDRE
        What loom? I don't see any.

LADY CAROLINE
        Oh yes, there, near Cricket. And what beautiful cloth.

        EVERYONE STANDS THERE OPEN—MOUTHED AS LADY CAROLINE GUESSES THE PLACE WHERE THE LOOM IS SUPPOSED TO BE. SHE PICKS UP THE CLOTH, THAT ISN'T THERE, AND VERY TENDERLY BRUSHES HER CHEEK AGAINST IT. THEN SHE DOES A DANCE WITH THE CLOTH. SHE HOLDS IT UP TO CRICKET.

LADY CAROLINE
          No, Cricket, it doesn't become you at all. Ah, Lady Deirdre, the
colour is too strong. And you, my Lord, no, it just won't do. Now for my
King — it's just made for you. The gold and green, the blue and silver
filigree, they're royal colours, worthy of a King. (THE KING BEAMS WITH
JOY) And you, my magical cloth, where do you come from?

          SHE DANCES WITH IT. MUSIC.

                    Some far land too enchanted for such as we? —
                    These colours that come from the Sun and Sea,
                    From the grass, the flower, the bird, the bee?
                    It's the fabric of life, all flowing free.

          SHE LOOKS ABOUT HER AS EVERYONE, INCLUDING **CRICKET**, BELIEVES
          HER.
                    What utter fools you all must be.
                    There was nothing here that I could see!

          GOES INTO A PRODUCTION NUMBER OF MADRIGAL A CAPPELLA, AS A
          FINALE.

LADY CAROLINE   (SOLO THROUGH MUSIC)

                    The gold, the green,
                    The silver filigree,
                    Are royal colours, Sire,
                    Especially, especially
                    To see.

(TUTTI)

LADY CAROLINE	**LORD**	**LADY DEIRDRE**
(1)		
The gold, the green,		
The silver filigree,	(2)	
Are royal colours, Sire,	The gold, the green,	
Especially, especially	The silver filigree,	
		(3)
The gold, the green,	Are royal colours, Sire,	The gold, the green,
The silver filigree,	Especially, especially,	The silver filigree,
Are royal colours, Sire,	Are royal colours, Sire,	Are royal colours, Sire,
Especially, especially	Especially, especially	Especially, especially
To see.	To see.	To see.

CRICKET   What fools they all must be!

DOMER   With their silly diddle-dee!

CRICKET &
DOMER   But they cannot fool me,

CRICKET   For there's nothing —

DOMER   No, there's nothing —

CRICKET &
DOMER   No, there's nothing there to see!

KING   The gold, the green

LORD   The silver filigree

TUTTI   Are royal colours, Sire,

KING   Especially for me.

CRICKET &
DOMER   The royal colours, Sire

LADIES   The fi-li-gree

LADY CAROLINE
           The gold

LADY DEIRDRE
           The green

TUTTI   (GRADUAL) Especially ...

           MUSIC, INTERVAL, 3/4S

CRICKET   Fa la la

LORD &
DOMER   And a hey nonny no

LORD   And the gold and green

LADIES   And a tra la la la la

CRICKET   And the fi-li-gree –

KING &
LORD   Fa la la la

CRICKET &
DOMER   Nonny, nonny

LADIES   Trala la la

KING   (VERY BASS) Fiddle [dee] –

TUTTI   Fa la la
           And a nonny, nonny no
           Tra la lá
           Tra la lá LA

           Fa la la
           And a nonny, nonny no
           Tra la lá

22

                    Tra la lá
                    Tra la la la (DIMINISH THROUGH NEXT TWO SPEECHES)

DOMER   FID–DUL–DEE

CRICKET   And there's nothing here to see.

        MUSIC

TUTTI   (GRADUAL CRESCENDO)
               Trá la la lá
               Hey nonny no
               Fá la la
               FID–DUL –

ALL BUT
CRICKET &
DOMER   (SOFTLY)   CRICKET & DOMER
               The gold, the green,   What fools they all must be,
               The filigree –   With a fiddle–faddle–dee –
               Are colours made   But they cannot fool me,
               Especially.   For there's nothing,
               The gold, the green,   No, there's nothing,
               The filigree –   No, there's nothing
               Are colours made   Here to see.
               Especially,
               Especially,
               Especially.

        MUSIC

TUTTI   The GOLD –
               The GREEN –
               The fiiill–iiiii–greeee –

ALL BUT
CRICKET &
DOMER   (VERY SOFTLY ON ONE NOTE)
               The–gold–the–green–especially–the–silver–filigree
               (DIMINISH THROUGH DOMER'S LINE)

                                          DOMER (SPOKEN)
                                          There's nothing here to see.

ALL BUT
CRICKET &
DOMER   (VERY SOFTLY ON ONE NOTE)
               The–gold–the–green–especially–the–silver–filigree
               (DIMINISH THROUGH CRICKET'S LINE)

                                          CRICKET
                                          WHAT FOOLS THEY ALL MUST BE!

LADY CAROLINE
               For there's nothing there to see!

                            CURTAIN

                    END OF ACT TWO

ACT THREE

SCENE ONE

THRONE ROOM. THE **KING** IS SITTING VERY GLOOMILY ON THE THRONE.
THE **MERCHANT** TAILOR IS WEAVING AND THEN PLACING THE CLOTH.
HE IS VERY BUSY. **CRICKET** IS HELPING HIM. IT IS A BALLET–MIME
OF SPINNING, FOLDING THE CLOTH AND PUTTING IT AWAY. INTO THE
QUIETNESS OF THIS SCENE COMES THE **LORD**.

LORD   My King – I've come with curious news.

KING   What is it? Nothing can possibly confuse me more than what's
happened already.

LORD   The representatives of the representatives of the representatives
of the people of the Kingdom have heard of this fabulous cloth, this cloth
of cloths. They wish to see you wear it in your next procession through
the town.

KING   I can't. The procession is next week. There's not time to make
enough cloth for a robe!

LORD   A suit then. It's the cloth they want to see. The whole kingdom
is now involved. You must do so. You have no choice.

KING   Did you hear, Cricket? It's demanded of me to wear a suit made
of the new cloth.

CRICKET Those who are true in heart will see the suit. Those who are
not, won't, but wouldn't dare say so.

   LADY CAROLINE AND LADY DEIRDRE ENTER, EXCITEDLY.

LADY DEIRDRE
    My Lord – my Lord, there's so much excitement outside the
palace walls.

KING   What is it?

LADY DEIRDRE
    I can barely catch my breath.

LADY CAROLINE
    The people, a handful, have tried climbing the palace walls to see
the magic cloth.

LADY DEIRDRE
    No sooner were they turned back when twice as many others
tried.

LADY CAROLINE
Each time there are more and more. The whole kingdom is so
anxious to see this cloth.

LADY DEIRDRE
What will you do? We're not safe.

KING   What decision is there to make?

LORD   Cancel the procession.

KING   Lord Minister of War - would you cancel a battle?

LORD   Of course not ... one's honour is at stake.

KING   What of your King's honour?

LORD   But the King's will ...

KING   The people have a will. Am I King?

CRICKET   You are King ... and kings must act as kings.

KING   Thank you, Cricket.

LADY CAROLINE
Well, does that mean we'll have a procession?

LADY DEIRDRE
Of course there'll be a procession.

KING   I must wear the new suit for the procession next week. Lord
Minister, announce to the whole kingdom that King Eric, Emperor of all
Sylvania, will wear a suit of new clothes made from this magic cloth for the
procession.

LORD   Yes, your Highness.

KING   Domer, can you cut and tailor my suit by next Wednesday?

DOMER   Your wish is my command. I'll work day and night to do so,
your Majesty.

KING   Good. Cricket, you'll help?

CRICKET   Yes, your Majesty.

KING   May God, or at least one of his angels, be with us.

CRICKET   It will be ready.

    THE KING EXITS WITH THE LORD, LADY DEIRDRE AND LADY CAROLINE.

CRICKET   I never thought it would go so far. Domer, sometimes a simple
ripple can create a great wave. Poor King Eric must learn his lesson

before his whole kingdom.

DOMER   Can't we weave a cloth that can be seen?

CRICKET   Then everyone will say it is just an ordinary cloth. We'll pretend we're working hard. Let's finish the cutting.

DOMER   You talk as if there was something to cut.

CRICKET   We must always act as if there is. Start sewing or we won't be ready in time.

DOMER   What shall I sew?

CRICKET   The new suit.

DOMER   But there is none.

CRICKET   Can't you pretend? Now pick up that cloth and sew.

DOMER   I'm a simple man, not an actor. You brought me into this whole thing and now I don't know what will happen.

CRICKET   Just follow my instructions – my plan is what we're really weaving and cutting and sewing ... My wonderful ... wonderful plan.

LIGHTS FADE OUT AND UP

SCENE TWO

    THE **KING** SITS ON HIS THRONE PATIENTLY WAITING FOR DOMER AND CRICKET TO FINISH THE SUIT. LADY DEIRDRE, LADY CAROLINE AND THE LORD ARE WAITING WITH HIM. DOMER AND CRICKET ARE FINISHING THE LAST TOUCHES.

    PLEASE NOTE: MUSIC OF YOUR CHOICE SHOULD BE USED, AS BACKGROUND, THROUGHOUT THE ACT.

CRICKET   Domer! My side is finished.

DOMER   Just a few minutes more – I'll be done in a moment.

CRICKET   You're an excellent pupil ...

DOMER   I'm a master tailor.

CRICKET   As an actor, I mean.

DOMER   Don't say that.

    LADY CAROLINE WALKS OVER TO CRICKET AND DOMER. DOMER MAKES ROOM FOR HER BY STEPPING ASIDE.

LADY CAROLINE
        Careful, Domer, you'll soil the suit.

DOMER   Oh! I forgot.

CRICKET   Now you're the fool. We're ready, your Majesty.

        THE **KING**, **THE LORD** AND **LADY DEIRDRE** MOVE TOWARDS DOMER AND
        CRICKET. MUSIC.

KING   Good, good. Let me see it quickly.

LORD   Yes ... there it is ... all nice and ready.

LADY CAROLINE
        The suit seems to be getting more attention than a lady of high
station. I must say, it's beautiful.

KING   Do you think so?

LORD &
LADY CAROLINE
        Oh yes, your Majesty.

KING   Cricket! I didn't hear you say anything.

CRICKET   How can we, Sire. It would be immodest to boast about our
work.

LADY CAROLINE
        Lady Deirdre, you haven't said a word.

LADY DEIRDRE
        My King! I can't see what's not there. Say that I am unworthy
of my station ... but, I beg you, don't wear this ... nothingness ... for the
procession.

LADY CAROLINE
        How can you, Lady Deirdre! You who've told me that everyone
must be master of their station! How can you tell the King not to wear this
beautiful suit! The whole Kingdom demands it!

LADY DEIRDRE
        I don't know.

LORD   Lady Caroline – you're absolutely right. It's unheard of – that a
lady at Court would humiliate her King.

LADY DEIRDRE
        A humiliation at Court is better than a public humiliation!

LORD   The King is King. The people will see what the King wishes them
to see!

LADY CAROLINE
        Besides it's a beautiful suit. The King will be most elegant.

KING   Lady Deirdre! You're sure you see nothing?

LADY DEIRDRE
        I'm sure.

KING   Then you realise you've admitted being unworthy of your station?

LADY DEIRDRE
        Yes, Sire.

KING   Lady Deirdre, I must ask you to leave the Court. Your brother,
Lord Lansing, will be happy to see you. Are you sure that you don't see
the suit?

LADY DEIRDRE
        I do not see it.

        SHE EXITS IN TEARS.

LADY CAROLINE
        Will she be all right?

LORD   She'll live in the lap of luxury. Lord Lansing has one of the
richest castles ... Ah, that suit is handsome, I must say.

LADY CAROLINE
        Is it?

KING   Well isn't it?

LADY CAROLINE
        It is. (MOVES AWAY TO CRICKET) Oh Cricket ... just a moment
... let me see the suit more closely. (WHISPERS TO CRICKET) Do you
honestly and truly see the cloth?

CRICKET   Do you?

LADY CAROLINE
        I wish I had Lady Deirdre's honesty ... No, I don't see it ... do
you?

CRICKET   Lady Caroline, a King can wear no wrong. I must see what my
King wants me to see.

LADY CAROLINE
        Riddles – all the answers are always riddles.

        THE LORD JOINS CRICKET.

LORD   Lady Deirdre was a bit out of luck, I'm afraid.

CRICKET   I didn't see you stop the King.

LORD   How could I? You with your wicked tongue didn't try to help her.

CRICKET   I don't make the Court rules ... I only break them.

LORD   Do you see the suit?

CRICKET   Didn't I help make it?

LORD   Oh come, Cricket ... what has that to do with it?

CRICKET   If you can judge the truth, then why ask me? We all see just what we want to see ... not even three pairs of glasses can help.

LORD   You impudent, disobedient - fool!

THEY ALL APPROACH THE **KING**, CARRYING THE SUIT THAT ISN'T THERE. MUSIC.

KING   What have I done to Lady Deirdre? I had no choice. Oh Cricket, do you see the suit? Tell me.

CRICKET   I see that the Emperor will wear the most royal suit in all the Kingdom ... for he is Emperor, and all his subjects will see the Emperor.

KING   I hope that means what I think it means. There's no time and no turning back. The hour has come. I must prepare for the procession. Lord Minister, Lady Caroline!

THEY ALL EXIT, LEAVING **CRICKET** AND **DOMER** ALONE. MUSIC.

DOMER   I've never been so nervous in my life. So is everyone else. Only they don't dare say so.

CRICKET   You'd better brush up for the procession.

DOMER   Me?

CRICKET   Yes, you! We'll all march together.

DOMER   What is this, Cricket?

CRICKET   Aren't you happy, Domer?

DOMER   Exuberantly!

CRICKET   I am.

DOMER   Why?

CRICKET   Because everything has gone according to my plan.

DOMER   What plan?

CRICKET   You'll see.

DOMER   Is there more to come?

CRICKET   More is yet to come!

        THEY EXIT.

SCENE THREE

        CRICKET STEALTHILY LEADS LADY DEIRDRE INTO THE THRONE ROOM.
        MUSIC BACKGROUND.

LADY DEIRDRE
        What is happening, Cricket?

CRICKET   Ssh! Someone might hear you.

LADY DEIRDRE
        Then why bring me here? I must finish packing for my journey.

CRICKET   Would you leave the Emperor alone?

LADY DEIRDRE
        But he has ordered me to leave.

CRICKET   He was only following a Court rule.

LADY DEIRDRE
        What should I do?

CRICKET   Break the rule and stay here at Court.

LADY DEIRDRE
        I can't. I must obey the Emperor.

CRICKET   All right! I'll break it for you. I force you to stay ... Ssh ...
the procession is coming.

        CRICKET HIDES LADY DEIRDRE BEHIND THE THRONE. MUSIC.
        ENTER THE PROCESSION LED BY THE EMPEROR. AS HIS ROYAL
        CLOAK IS OPENED WE SEE THAT HE IS CLOTHED ONLY IN HIS
        UNDERWEAR. GENERAL REACTION FROM ALL THE CHILDREN IN THE
        AUDIENCE. THE KING POINTS TO A CHILD IN THE AUDIENCE.

KING   You there ... you. Are you a child?

CHILD   Yes.

KING   Tell me then, my child ... what am I wearing ... am I wearing a
suit?

CHILD   No.

KING   What is it then?

30

CHILD   Your underwear.

KING   Out of the mouths of children will come the truth. And what does my Court have to say? You have all lied to your Emperor ... even you, Cricket!

CRICKET   Sire, I never lied to you. You heard and saw only what you wished to hear and see. The truth is sometimes very difficult.

KING   And yet a child can see and hear the truth, without difficulty.

CRICKET   So can a fool. It was the only way of showing you the truth.

KING   About what?

CRICKET   About yourself!

KING   Did you have to trick me into it?

CRICKET   Forgive me Sire ... but to see one's own vanity is often ...

KING   Since you have shown me, I have very little vanity left.

CRICKET   Sire, will you now look for the truth?

KING   If children can, then so may an Emperor! As for you my Lord ... you deceived me and yourself. How shall I punish you?

LORD   Banish me. I should have enough courage to speak the truth.

KING   You're a good Minister. Now learn to be an honest friend. I will give you one more chance. And you, Lady Caroline – what shall be done with you?

LADY CAROLINE
          Sire, whatever pleases you.

KING   Will you ever want to see the truth?

LADY CAROLINE
          If someone will show me where to look.

KING   Then look to our Minister of War.

LORD   Oh, Lady Caroline ... do you think that you could have a change of heart?

LADY CAROLINE
          Not a change of heart, but certainly a change of hands, if necessary.

          SHE TAKES HIS HAND GENTLY INTO HERS.

KING   Domer, what have you to say for yourself?

DOMER   I meant no harm, Sire. Forgive me. I'll never weave or sell another cloth ... I'll never sew another stitch ...

KING   Oh no, Domer! I condemn you to stitching for the rest of your life ... as my personal and royal tailor.

DOMER   Yes, Sire ... yes, yes.

KING   Oh, how cruel I've been to Lady Deirdre.

CRICKET   Sire, she could be persuaded to return to Court.

KING   Do you think so?

CRICKET   It could be arranged.

KING   How?

CRICKET   Watch. Abracadabra – now close your eyes, and when you open them you'll see Lady Deirdre in place of me.

     A BLINKED BLACKOUT, VERY QUICKLY OFF THEN ON. LADY DEIRDRE
     STANDS IN CRICKET'S PLACE.

KING   Can you ever forgive me?

LADY DEIRDRE
     Sire, there is nothing to forgive.

THE KING MOVES TO LADY DEIRDRE AND TAKES HER HAND.

KING   Lady Deirdre ... my Kingdom ... my Court ... I ... need your eyes to see the truth. Stay with us and be our Queen.

LADY DEIRDRE
     Sire, I will stay ... for ever.

THE KING EMBRACES LADY DEIRDRE.

CRICKET   A wedding – a wedding!

KING   Cricket, be still! I have not yet finished with you.

CRICKET   Will it be my life?

KING   Your entire life. My foolish fool will become my wise Counsellor. Now Cricket, find me four loyal subjects to bear the canopy above our heads.

     CRICKET GOES INTO THE AUDIENCE AND SELECTS FOUR CHILDREN TO
     CARRY THE CANOPY ABOVE THE HEADS OF THE EMPEROR AND LADY
     DEIRDRE DURING THE PROCESSION OUT OF THE THEATRE.

CRICKET   Bow to the King and Emperor of us all.

HE INTRODUCES THE CHILDREN TO EVERYONE ON STAGE. AND HELPS THEM PREPARE THE CANOPY.

KING   Come here my little ones. Tell me, do you have imagination? Then imagine my new suit. It's as beautiful as you want it to be. Whatever colour you choose. What colour do you choose? (CHILDREN WILL CHOOSE A COLOUR) Very well, then it is a kingly colour. I shall wear it just for you.

LADY DEIRDRE
          My love, clothes do not make the Emperor. You are Emperor because of what you are and not because of what you wear.

     THEY EMBRACE.

CRICKET   Three cheers for the Emperor. Long live the Emperor.

     THE CHILDREN CARRY THE CANOPY AS THE KING AND HIS COURT EXIT THROUGH THE THEATRE TO FANFARE MUSIC.

CURTAIN

END OF PLAY

CRICKET, THE JESTER
DONNER
LADY CAROLINE
KING ERIC
LORD
LADY DEIRDRE

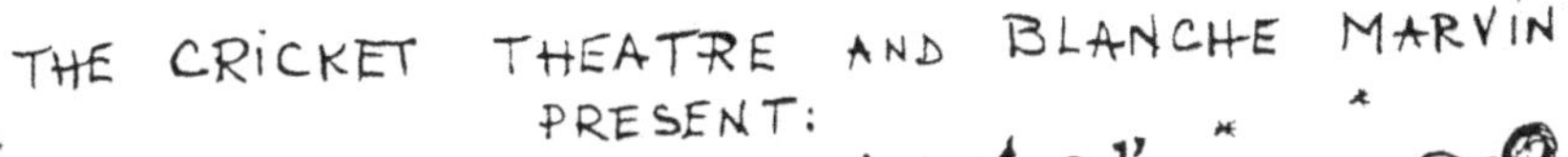

THE CRICKET THEATRE AND BLANCHE MARVIN
PRESENT:
"THE MERRI-MIMES"
in
Sleeping Beauty

by BLANCHE MARVIN

DIRECTOR - CHOREOGRAPHER -
• IGOR YOUSKEVITCH •

SETS - JOSINE   LIGHTS - STEVE MILLER
STAGE MANAGER - CHUCK HOVER

CAST:

PRINCE CHARMING - JAMES McDONALD
BEAUTY - JANET COMSTOCK
KING - DINO LAUDICINA
QUEEN - ANNA TARLOV
CRICKET - RALPH ROBINSON
BARBEL - JAMES McDONALD
GOOD FAIRY - MARIA YOUSKEVITCH
LINDA WATSON
LORD - STEVEN MILLER
FIRST LADY - VALERIE GAIL
SECOND LADY - JOAN DURR

AT THE CRICKET THEATRE
162 SECOND AVE (AT 10TH ST)
OR 4-3960
PERFORMANCES AT 1, 2:30 + 4 P.M. SAT.
MAR. 23, 30 APR. 6, 13, 20 + 27
SPECIAL ON MON - THURS APR. 8, 9, 10, 11
AT 9:45 A.M 11:15

JOSINE.

Across the Footlights
By Frances Herridge

'Sleeping Beauty' is Fun at Cricket

An enchanting and amusing "Sleeping Beauty" is delighting children for three performances each Saturday at the Cricket Theater, Second Av. and 10th St. It is Blanche Marvin's English-pantomine version with dance, dialogue and music. And although it is artistically graceful, it doesn't forget that its audience is young. It keeps a sense of humor about itself, and what's better, lets the youngsters take part in the show.

THE SLEEPING BEAUTY

A RESTORATION COMEDY

CAST OF CHARACTERS

King

Queen

Princess Beauty

Prince Charming

Court Jester, Cricket

Queen of the Fairies

Fairies (2)

Wicked Fairy, Barbel

Ladies-in-Waiting (2)

Lords (2)

Cook

Cook's Boy

Emelia (doubles with Lady-in-Waiting)

Soldiers and Pages (optional)

Place: Palace of the King

Time: Once upon a time

Author's note:
This version is a story based on the accompaniment from
Tchaikowsky's SLEEPING BEAUTY BALLET SUITE. Music cues are
given in the script.
The Restoration comedies, THE WAY OF THE WORLD or THE SCHOOL
FOR SCANDAL, which satirised Court life and gossip are
reflected in the Lords and Ladies in SLEEPING BEAUTY.
The foppish gents of that time are portrayed by the Lords
here. Their concern for substantial marriage which allowed
domination over women by controlling their money are also
mocked in this play. The absent-minded Prince is commanded by
a forceful Beauty. The humour and pacing is styled on this
period.

ACT ONE

(THE CHRISTENING, THE BLESSING, THE CURSE)

A FAIRYTALE PALACE DIVIDED INTO THREE STAGE AREAS.

CENTRE STAGE IS THE LARGEST AND MAIN PLAYING AREA. IT IS THE
BALLROOM – GOLD DROPS ARE THE MAIN SOURCE OF DECORATION. A
SLIGHTLY RAISED PLATFORM HOLDS THE **KING'S AND QUEEN'S**
THRONES. THE ROOM IS DECORATED WITH PINK AND BLUE RIBBONS
WITH LACE EFFECTS. THE **ROYAL CRADLE** COVERED WITH RIBBONS
AND BOWS AND FRILLS IS ON A SMALL PLATFORM ON STAGE LEFT.

THE **LADIES-IN-WAITING** ARE PRESENT. THE **FIRST LADY-IN-WAITING**
IS A BUXOM OVERDRESSED WOMAN WHOSE DRESS IS BURSTING AT THE
SEAMS. THE **SECOND LADY-IN-WAITING** IS VERY THIN; HER DRESS
FALLS THIS WAY AND THAT, NOTHING SEEMS TO STAY IN PLACE. SHE
KEEPS LOSING HER FEATHERED STOLE OR IT SLIPS OFF HER
SHOULDERS; AFTER RETRIEVING IT SHE GETS IT ENTANGLED IN HER
HAIR AND THROUGHOUT THE SCENE SHE IS STRUGGLING TO UNDO IT.

AT STAGE CENTRE A **SOLDIER** STANDS GUARD UNDER AN ARCHWAY
WHICH IS THE MAIN ENTRANCE TO THE BALLROOM. THE **COURT JESTER**
SITS CROSS-LEGGED AT THE FOOT OF THE THRONE AS IF HE WERE A
STATUE – NOT AT ALL ALIVE. THE **KITCHEN** ON THE STAGE LEFT, IS
HALF LIGHTED. WE SEE BABY'S NAPKINS (DIAPERS) HANGING TO DRY.
THE **BOY** IS DILIGENTLY WASHING AS THE **COOK** SHOWS HIM WHERE
TO HANG THE WASH. IT IS ALL DONE IN SLOW SMALL MOVEMENTS.
THE **COOK** IS IMPATIENT, THE **BOY** AT A LOSS AS TO HOW ANYTHING IS
DONE.

THE **LADIES-IN-WAITING** MOVE TO A DOLL-LIKE DANCE IN A MIME AND
DANCE SEQUENCE WHICH IS DISTANT AND UNREAL. IN THIS MIME
SHOULD BE THE SUGGESTION OF JOY AT THE CRADLE.

FROM STAGE RIGHT, COMPLETELY OUT OF THIS MOOD AND AWAY FROM
THE SET, OUR **PRINCE CHARMING** APPEARS. HE IS DRESSED IN A
WHITE PAGE-BOY WIG, KNEE-LENGTH RED TROUSERS WITH BRASS
BUTTONS, WHITE HOSE, THE SLIPPERED LOUIS XIV HEELED SHOE, A
DOUBLE-BREASTED JACKET WITH BRASS BUTTONS AND LACE CUFFS.
HE WANDERS ON TO THE STAGE AS IF HE SHOULD NOT BE THERE.

PRINCE   Am I really here? Well I must be. (LOOKING CLOSELY AT THE
AUDIENCE) I see so many happy faces. You can't imagine what I am
looking for. Can you? What was it I was looking for? Ah well ... I'll find
a good excuse. (WINKS AT AUDIENCE) Now let me see ... ah yes ... my
father's crown. You know a Prince, even a Prince Charming, can't be
crowned without a crown ... and my father will one day want to crown me.
We retire early in our Kingdom. We don't wait to die before we hand down
the crown. Such an adventure just for a missing crown. Maybe we should
not be crowned. Maybe we should have golden shoes put on our feet
instead. Now that's an idea. You could call it getting 'footed' ,,, 'Golden
Footed'. (LAUGHS TO CHILDREN) Good joke for a fellow like me. Don't you

think? Well let's hear one laugh anyway. Good ... that's more like it! If
you don't laugh, I'll become shy. Then I won't be able to go on with my
story. You do want to hear the story of Prince Charming. Of course you
do! Come now, just one little 'Yes'? (STRONGER) One 'Yes' I said!
(SWEETLY) I wouldn't want to coax you. (SHOUTING HIS COMMAND) Say
'Yes'! That's better. Now where was I before you all shouted 'yes'?
(FROM THE AUDIENCE SOMEONE SAYS 'YOU LOST YOUR FATHER'S CROWN')
Oh no, I didn't lose it. He did. I'm trying to find it - and that's why
you've come to hear my story. It began way back ... so many years ago
I'm ashamed to admit it. But it did begin.

          APPLAUSE. MUSIC.

Yes, it began when a baby was born to the King and Queen of a very
happy kingdom. She was a beautiful Princess with raven hair and blue
eyes and fair skin.

          HE STARTS WALKING QUIETLY OFF STAGE. THE LIGHTS COME TO
          FULLNESS IN THE BALLROOM. THE PEOPLE BECOME ALIVE EXCEPT
          FOR THE JESTER, WHO SITS STATUE-LIKE THROUGHOUT.

Sssh ... listen ... the story begins ...

FIRST LADY-IN-WAITING
          At least I may say that I know my Court manners and am
dressed properly for the christening of our lovely new Princess. Which is
more than I can say for some people I know.

SECOND LADY-IN-WAITING
          Pardon. Are you suggesting my manners are not courtly?
Just look into your mirror, you'll see a sight or two ... ha-ha ...

FIRST LADY-IN-WAITING (HER NOSE TOUCHING 2ND LADY'S NOSE)
          Anyone who can't keep themselves together, doesn't belong in
Court.

SECOND LADY-IN-WAITING
          And anyone whose clothes keep bursting doesn't belong in
Court.

FIRST LADY-IN-WAITING (STANDING ERECT AND HAUGHTY)
          You can't even speak correctly.

SECOND LADY-IN-WAITING
          I talk well enough to make you mad. (FINALLY HAS HER
STOLE IN PLACE)

FIRST LADY-IN-WAITING (FEIGNING INDIFFERENCE)
          Sticks and stones may break my bones, but names will never
hurt me.

SECOND LADY-IN-WAITING
          It would take a boulder not a stone. Anyway you started it ...
on a day of rejoicing too. (SHE TRIPS OVER HER STOLE)

FIRST LADY-IN-WAITING
Clumsy! I did not! And don't think for a moment that the christening of the baby Princess will soften my feelings towards you.

SECOND LADY-IN-WAITING (KEEPING HER PLUMES TOGETHER IN HER HAIR)
I certainly don't need your kindness. I can do very well without you.

FIRST LADY-IN-WAITING
Good. Then why don't you go to the other side of the ballroom. There's so much more room there. Besides, I'm hot.

SECOND LADY-IN-WAITING
I'll go where I please and as I please. You don't have to order me about. Only the Queen can do that.

SOLDIER (HE HAS BEEN STANDING EXPRESSIONLESS UP TO NOW, AND SUDDENLY CALLS OUT)
Calm yourselves! The King and Queen are arriving! (MUSIC) Attention!

> THE TRUMPETS SOUND, THE **SOLDIER** QUICKLY DRAWS HIS HEELS TOGETHER AND IS BACK IN HIS RIGID POSITION. THE **LADIES** GO TO THEIR PLACES AND TAKE THEIR POSITIONS. WHEN THE TRUMPETS FINISH PLAYING, THE **PAGE** MAY OR MAY NOT BE SEEN, ACCORDING TO THE PRODUCTION. TWO HANDSOME **LORDS**, ELEGANTLY DRESSED, ENTER IN A PAGEANT-LIKE FORMATION ... THEN THE **KING**, AND THE **QUEEN** HOLDING THE BABY IN HER ARMS, FOLLOW. THEY COME TO CENTRE STAGE AND THE BABY IS PUT INTO THE CRADLE. THE **LADIES-IN-WAITING** GO TO THE CRADLE.

KING   Are we not fortunate in Rainbow Kingdom with such a beautiful Princess?

QUEEN   My sweet darling.

1ST LADY   Isn't she adorable!

2ND LADY   Adorable!

QUEEN   Adorable!

1ST LADY   Isn't she precious!

2ND LADY   Precious!

QUEEN   Precious!

1ST LADY   Isn't she a rarity!

QUEEN   A rarity!

KING   Come now, do I hear echoes? You've said that before. Let us prepare for the feast. We have much on hand. (MUSIC)

THE **KING** AND **QUEEN** GO TO THEIR THRONES. ALL THE COURT WAITS.
THE **KING** AND **QUEEN** SIT DOWN. THE **KING** CLAPS HIS HANDS. TWO
PAGES APPEAR AND IN A MIME-DANCE BRING IN THE TABLES AND
BEGIN TO SET THEM. THE **COOK** AND **BOY** IN THE KITCHEN JOIN IN
THE DANCE AS THEY HELP SET UP THE FEAST. THE **LORDS AND
LADIES** ALSO JOIN IN, WHILE THE **SOLDIER** REMAINS IN HIS PLACE
AND ACCENTUATES THE CLIMAXES BY HIS ROUTINE OF ABOUT-FACE
AND CHANGING HIS GUN FROM ARM TO ARM. THE **JESTER** STILL HAS
NOT MOVED. FINALLY AT THE HEIGHT OF THE GAIETY THE TABLES
ARE SET. EVERYONE GOES BACK TO THEIR ORIGINAL POSITIONS. THE
LIGHTS DIM SLIGHTLY IN THE KITCHEN AS THE **COOK** AND **BOY** GO
INTO A SLOW PANTOMIME OF POLISHING UP THE KITCHEN UTENSILS.
THE **BOY** PLAYS AT BEING A SOLDIER BY PUTTING A SAUCEPAN ON HIS
HEAD AND USING THE ROLLING PIN AS A GUN. THE **COOK**, PEEVED,
GETS HIM BACK WORK. BUT EVEN MOPPING THE FLOOR BECOMES A
GAME FOR HIM ... USING THE MOP AS A JUMPING STICK. MEANWHILE
THE BALLROOM IS ANXIOUSLY IN A STATE OF ANTICIPATION.

KING   All should go well. Our fairy friends should be here at any
moment.

QUEEN   Of course they will. They have never failed us. Why we even
have their special cups and plates.

KING   And such wondrous, delicious things to eat!

QUEEN   Oh what an exciting day.

KING   We are indeed blessed, my Queen, to have so much: such a
beautiful baby and such good friends as the fairies.

QUEEN   This is a day of rejoicing and celebration.

FIRST AND SECOND LADIES AND LORDS
          To the christening of our baby Princess.

THEY HOLD UP SILVER GOBLETS AND DRINK DOWN THE WINE.

KING   Drink and be merry.

HE GOES TO TABLE, THE **QUEEN** AT HIS SIDE. HE TAKES UP HIS
GOBLET, AS DOES THE **QUEEN**, AND THEY ALL DRINK AGAIN.

KING   To the christening once again, and to all our friends.

THEY ALL TAKE A SECOND DRINK AND AD LIB THEIR GOOD WISHES.

1ST LORD   Long may she live!

THEY ALL TAKE ANOTHER DRINK.

2ND LORD   May she be as happy as our King and Queen!

ANOTHER DRINK. EVERYONE IS NOW HILARIOUS.

KING   You know this is the grandest ballroom I've ever seen.

QUEEN   Yes indeed! Two of everything. (SHE HICCUPS) Oh, pardon me!

    EVERYONE LAUGHS AT THIS. THE **FIRST LADY** LAUGHS SO HARD SHE LITERALLY SPLITS HER DRESS.

2ND LADY   Oh my goodness, your dress is opened!

1ST LADY   A blessing ... a blessing in disguise.

2ND LADY   For the Princess?

1ST LADY   No, for me. Now I can breathe. How lovely!

2ND LADY   (COMB IN HER HAIR ALL AWRY) Joy ... oh joy ... now you'll be human again.

    IN HER JOY, SHE LOSES HER STOLE.

KING   Joy!

    HE TRIES PICKING UP THE FEATHER STOLE, AS IF IT WERE A PET.

1ST LORD   Your highness, you mustn't. Allow me. (TRIES, BUT CAN'T SEEM TO CATCH IT) Oh, it seems to slip.

2ND LORD   Allow me.

    HE SUCCEEDS BUT THE FEATHERS MAKE HIM SNEEZE SO HARD HE DROPS IT.

2ND LADY   My, oh my! All because of my feathers. Come here now and behave yourself.

    SHE PICKS IT UP LIKE A KITTEN.

QUEEN   The fairies should be here any moment. I wish I knew which door they'll use.

KING   There's only one door to use.

QUEEN   That's true. But one never knows with fairies.

KING   Let us coax our playful friends. Everyone be seated. It will be comfortable while we wait. Surely if we act as if we are waiting they will come. My arm, Madam. (MUSIC)

    SHAKILY THE **KING AND QUEEN** WALK TO THEIR SEATS. IN A DANCE THE LORDS AND LADIES FOLLOW AFTER THE **KING AND QUEEN**. THEY SEAT THEMSELVES. SUDDENLY ALL THE LIGHTS CHANGE COLOUR AND KEEP CHANGING. THEY SETTLE ON BLUE AND DESCEND. A GOLDEN LADDER APPEARS AND THE **THREE FAIRIES** DESCEND. THE WHOLE SEQUENCE IS A BALLET-MIME TO THE MUSIC. THEY PARTLY FLY

DOWN THE LADDER. THE **QUEEN OF THE FAIRIES** WEARS A CROWN
AND A DRESS WHICH IS MUCH MORE A-GLITTER THAN THOSE OF HER
TWO ACCOMPANYING FAIRIES. ALL THREE ARE DRESSED IN WHITE
AND SILVER COSTUMES WITH IRIDESCENT WINGS. THE **FAIRY QUEEN**
DANCES TO THE HEAD OF THE CRADLE. THE OTHER TWO DANCE TO
EITHER SIDE OF THE CRADLE. THE DANCE ABOUT THE BABY
PRINCESS BEGINS AS THEY ROCK THE CRADLE, AND AT THE CLIMAX
THE **FAIRY QUEEN** USING HER MAGIC WAND LIGHTS THE STAGE. THEY
COME TO THE FOOT OF THE THRONE WHERE THE **COURT JESTER** SITS.
WITH HER WAND THE **FAIRY QUEEN** TOUCHES HIM AND IMMEDIATELY
HE COMES TO LIFE, TUMBLING AND JUMPING WITH THEM IN THEIR
DANCE. THE FOUR OF THEM DANCE TOGETHER, PARTAKING OF THEIR
FOOD AND DRINK. THERE ARE ONLY THREE FAIRY GOBLETS OF GOLD.
THEY DANCE WITH THEIR GOBLETS, TOASTING TO ONE ANOTHER AND
TO THE WHOLE **COURT** AND THE BABY. THE **JESTER** FIRST PARTNERS
THE **QUEEN FAIRY** AND THEN ALL THREE. THE DANCE ENDS WITH THE
JESTER AND **FAIRIES** AT THE BASE OF THE THRONE.

KING   Welcome ... welcome ... welcome. With great joy do we welcome
you today.

QUEEN   The christening of our baby has been fulfilled. What more
could one ask?

FAIRY QUEEN
          Good King and Queen, we have come today because you are
worthy of our visit. We have come with many gifts for the newborn
Princess.

KING   A decree ... a decree. I must send forth a decree. We shall
have a week of festivity ... no work, only play ... dancing and singing ...
making merry ...

          AS HE SAYS THIS THE **BOY** IN THE KITCHEN STOPS WORK
          IMMEDIATELY. THE **COOK** IS AFTER HIM, BUT THE **BOY** REFUSES
          TO WORK. THE **COOK** CHASES AFTER HIM WITH A BROOM.

KING   Yes, we will celebrate for one week the christening of ... of ...
of ..

QUEEN   Oh dear, what shall we name her?

FAIRY QUEEN   (AT THE FOOT OF THE CRADLE) 'Beauty', for so she is.

QUEEN   Yes, 'Beauty'!

KING   Well named, well named. 'Beauty' she shall be.

LORDS AND LADIES
          'Beauty', of course! (MUSIC)

          THE **FAIRY QUEEN** IS AT THE HEAD OF THE CRADLE, WHILST THE
          OTHER TWO ARE ON EITHER SIDE. THE BESTOWAL OF GIFTS NOW
          BEGINS AS THE **FAIRY QUEEN** WAVES BACK AND FORTH HER MAGIC
          WAND.

(SET WITH MUSIC)

FAIRY QUEEN
    She will be fair in face.

1ST FAIRY   Fair in form.

2ND FAIRY   Fair in grace.

FAIRY QUEEN
    She will be fair in voice.

1ST FAIRY   Fair in play.

2ND FAIRY   Fair in choice.

FAIRY QUEEN
    She will be fair in heart.

1ST FAIRY   Fair in mind.

2ND FAIRY   From the start.

    THROUGHOUT THIS THE FAIRIES ARE ON TOE. WITH EACH GIFT THEY
    ROCK THE CRADLE, AND DANCE ABOUT. THE COURT REACTS WITH
    'OOHS' AND 'AAHS' AS THE FAIRIES NAME THE GIFTS. (MUSIC)

FAIRY QUEEN
    She will be fair in dance.

    SUDDENLY ALL IS INTERRUPTED BY A HUGE BLACK CLOUD OF SMOKE
    ... A LOUD CACKLE IS HEARD AND AT THE FOOT OF THE CRADLE
    BARBEL, THE WICKED FAIRY, APPEARS. SHE IS OLD AND WIZENED.
    DRESSED IN BLACK, THE WICKED FAIRY LOOKS LIKE A WITCH. SHE IS
    DIRTY AND IN RAGS.

BARBEL   Fair ... ah, ah, ah ... but for how long? (CACKLES) (MUSIC)

FAIRY QUEEN
    Away with you, Barbel. You shall not harm this child. She
is blessed by us.

BARBEL   And cursed by me!

    EVERYONE AD LIBS 'NO' TO THIS. IT CANNOT HAPPEN.

FAIRY QUEEN
    I do not fear you or your curses.

BARBEL   You will.

KING   Oh Barbel, have mercy. She is our only child.

QUEEN   Why have you come to curse us? We've done you no harm.

BARBEL   No? Why didn't you invite me?

KING   We didn't think you would want to come.

BARBEL   I love christenings! Especially if they cause tears!

KING   I somehow thought your pleasure different from ours. Join us
then, and let there be laughter.

BARBEL   It's too late ... too late. You should have thought of me sooner.
The curse is made. I brewed it myself.

KING   But if you know magic, surely you can change it?

BARBEL   I never change my mind.

QUEEN   (WEEPING) My poor Beauty.

KING   Have no fear my dear. We are still protected. (MUSIC)

BARBEL   (CHASING ROUND THE CRADLE AS THE **FAIRIES** PROTECT THE
BABY. (SET TO MUSIC)

> Blessed as you are
> Cursed you will be.
> When you are sixteen
> Changes you'll see.
> Pricked by a needle,
> Smitten with sleep,
> For ever and ever
> Doomed to my keep;
> All in the Kingdom
> Asleep here as well,
> For ever and ever
> Under my spell.

EVERYONE CRIES OUT AT THIS. THE **QUEEN** FAINTS. THE LADIES-
IN-WAITING RUSH OVER TO HER SIDE AND TRY TO REVIVE HER. THE
SOLDIER WALKS BACK AND FORTH PROTECTING NO ONE. THE
COURT JESTER SUDDENLY CHANGES THE EXPRESSION ON HIS FACE TO
ONE OF SURPRISE AND DISBELIEF. IN THE KITCHEN, THE COOK AND
BOY ARE TERRIFIED, HIDING THEMSELVES IN CUPBOARDS. TO ADD TO
THE FEAR AND HORROR, THE LIGHTS GO ON TO FULL BRIGHTNESS IN
THE BEDROOM OF THE **PRINCESS** AND ALL WE SEE IS A SPINNING
WHEEL.

FAIRY QUEEN
          It is within my power, cruel Barbel, to change your curse,
even though I cannot lift it. (HURRAH FROM EVERYONE) She shall fall
asleep, as you say, but not forever ... only for a hundred years. She shall
awaken, and everyone in the Kingdom with her ... if she is kissed by a
Royal Prince who knows nothing of the curse and kisses Beauty only out of
love.

          COURT REACTS WITH BRAVOS.

IN THE NEXT SPEECHES BARBEL IS FIGHTING THE **FAIRY QUEEN** AND **KING.** EACH SLIGHTLY OVERLAPS THE OTHER IN THEIR SPEECHES.

BARBEL   Love ... hah ... hah ... Curses are stronger.

KING   I will banish every needle in the Kingdom. Even pine needles.

BARBEL   (LAUGHS) Banish every needle! Barbel's curses <u>never</u> fail!

FAIRY QUEEN
              I shall watch over them.

BARBEL   With me by your side.

KING   You will not win.

BARBEL   I've won already.

FAIRY QUEEN
              Do not cross me.

BARBEL   (CACKLES) I'm stronger.

KING   We are as strong as you. Be warned.

BARRBEL   You'd have done better with me.

FAIRY QUEEN
              We shall see.

BARBEL   You're afraid. You're trembling all over. (MUSIC)

       BUILD MUSIC THROUGH NEXT SPEECHES.

FAIRY QUEEN
              I fear no one.

KING   We are not afraid.

BARBEL   Look at your Court.

FAIRY QUEEN
              Have no fear. I shall watch over you.

BARBEL   And so will I ... hah ... hah.

       AS THE **KING** AND **FAIRY QUEEN** CONTEND WITH BARBEL, THE COURT
       STANDS ABOUT IN TERROR, AS THE

                        CURTAIN <u>FALLS</u> ON ACT ONE
                        CURTAIN <u>OPEN</u> ON TABLEAU
                        CURTAIN <u>CLOSES</u>

                        END OF ACT ONE

ACT TWO

(SIXTEEN YEARS LATER)

THE BALLROOM IS SOFTLY AGLOW. A HUGE CHANDELIER HANGS FROM
CENTRE STAGE WITH SMALLER CHANDELIERS ON EITHER SIDE. A
BANQUET TABLE IS BEAUTIFULLY LAID WITH THREE GOLD GOBLETS
DOMINATING THE TABLE. THE WHOLE COURT IS PRESENT .... A SLOW
MOVEMENT OF LORDS AND LADIES IS TAKING PLACE. THE KITCHEN IS
DIMLY LIGHTED ... THE COOK IS BAKING AND THE BOY HELPING. THIS
IS A QUIET PANTOMIME, AS PRINCE CHARMING APPEARS IN FRONT
AGAIN.

PRINCE   Well, you see what fairies can do ... such a to-do. Do you like
Barbel? ('NO' FROM CHILDREN IN THE AUDIENCE) Of course you wouldn't.
She's a mean old thing ... isn't she! ('YES' FROM CHILDREN IN THE
AUDIENCE) I wish I could have wings. (WINGS SUDDENLY APPEAR FOR HIM)
Well, look! Magic! (HE TRIES PUTTING THEM ON BUT HAS SO MUCH
TROUBLE, AS THEY ARE TOO SMALL, THAT HE GIVES UP) I suppose you
have to be a fairy to wear these. Anyway, where would fairies be if
everyone could wear wings? Fairies know how to put them on. I think I'd
look silly in them. ('YES YOU WOULD!' FROM CHILDREN IN THE AUDIENCE) I
like my costume to be just as it is. (HE FIXES HIS WIG) Well now, to get
on with the story. Everything may look the same to you but it is not.
Sixteen years have passed in just ten minutes. Beauty turned out to be
just everything the Fairy Queen said she would be. She is loved by all ...
and here she is sweet sixteen already ... Oh, but I told you that. The ball
is her Birthday Ball and everyone in the Palace is just as nervous as can
be. Will Barbel's curse come true? Or won't it? Will the good fairies win
or won't they? (FORGETS WHAT HE'S ABOUT TO SAY) Where was I? Yes,
yes indeed. I remember now. The King banished every needle from the
Kingdom. Even the pine needles, as he said he would. No one has seen
any kind of needle for years ... sixteen to be exact. No mending or sewing.
(HE STARTS WALKING OFF STAGE) The Court is excited about the ball. At
the same time everyone is watching ... will Barbel come? (MUSIC)

LIGHTS GO ON IN THE PRINCESS'S BEDROOM. WE SEE A BIG BED WITH
A CROWN ON TOP THROUGH WHICH IS LOOPED AND DRAPED AN AWNING
EFFECT, IN AN AIRY FABRIC. THE PRINCESS IS SIXTEEN AND LOVELY.
HER LADY-IN-WAITING, EMELIA, IS HELPING HER DRESS. THE
BALLROOM AND KITCHEN ARE STILL IN SLOW MOTION ..... AS THE
PRINCESS EXCITEDLY TALKS TO EMELIA.

PRINCESS   Quickly ... quickly ... dear Emelia. I mustn't be late for my
own ball.

EMELIA   There is time.

PRINCESS   No there isn't. Oh how exciting to have a ball just for me.

EMELIA   Stand still, Beauty, or I shan't be able to finish.

PRINCESS   (ABSOLUTELY RIGID) Is that better?

EMELIA   Excellent. You're stiff as a soldier. There ... it's done.

PRINCESS   My shoes ... my crown ... goodness we've so much yet to do.

EMELIA   All in good time, all in good time. Ah me, to think you are
already sixteen. You were just a baby and now you're growing up into a
young lady.

PRINCESS   Emelia, I am old enough to be treated as a grown-up. Sixteen
is not to be sneezed at.

EMELIA   I wasn't for a moment sneezing ... (SUDDENLY SNEEZES) Dear
me, I wonder what made me do that?

PRINCESS   Let's hurry ... my shoes ... my crown ... I think I'm a wee bit
afraid.

EMELIA   Afraid of what, dear child?

PRINCESS   You know ... after all it's my sixteenth birthday ... and who
knows what may happen.

EMELIA   Nothing! The fairies will be here to protect us. You know
that.

PRINCESS   Yes, but Mama was crying this morning. I heard her. She
called it 'the fatal day'.

EMELIA   Nonsense. She was crying out of joy.

PRINCESS   I know better. She was afraid.

EMELIA   Utter nonsense.

PRINCESS   You'll see ... but it's all so exciting. Just think, we don't know
what will happen!

        THEY EXIT.

        LIGHTS IN BEDROOM DIM. LIGHTS IN BALLROOM REMAIN THE SAME.
        THE DANCING CONTINUES IN SLOW MOTION. LIGHTS IN THE KITCHEN
        BRIGHTEN FOR THE NEXT SCENE. THE ACTION IN THE BALLROOM
        REMAINS THE SAME THROUGHOUT.

        THE BAKING IN THE KITCHEN IS GOING ON AT A RAPID PACE. THE
        BOY IS NOW ALSO WEARING A COOK'S HAT, WHICH IS EXCEPTIONALLY
        HIGH FOR HIM, SO THAT EVERY TIME HE MOVES HIS HEAD IT SHAKES
        ALL OVER.

COOK   (BENDING OVER THE OVEN AS HE PUTS IN A PIE) That makes
one hundred pies so far. I don't believe I've ever baked so many in my
life. Hey boy ... you done rolling the dough?

BOY   No sir ... (HIS HAT SHAKING BACK AND FORTH) Not yet sir.

COOK   Hop to it!

BOY   But sir, I'm going as fast as I can.

COOK   What a day! Lord, I wonder if Barbel will be here tonight!

HE IS CARRYING A PIE IN HIS HAND AND IS ABOUT TO PUT IT WITH
THE OTHERS WHEN IN HIS NERVOUSNESS HE SLIPS, PULLING THE BOY
DOWN WITH HIM. THEY ARE BOTH COVERED WITH PIE.

COOK   Now look what you've done! I'll box your ears!

BOY   (CLEANING HIMSELF OFF) But sir ... <u>you</u> were carrying the pie!

THE BOY TRIES TO GET UP, THE COOK HOLDS ON TO HIM. BOTH FALL
DOWN AGAIN, PULLING THE DOUGH WITH THEM THIS TIME. THEY CAN'T
CLEAR THEMSELVES OF IT. A WHOLE SEQUENCE FOLLOWS OF THE
PULLING OF THE DOUGH THROUGHOUT THE DIALOGUE.

COOK   Look ... look what you've done!

BOY   Sorry sir. So sorry.

COOK   Sorry? Out of my kitchen!

BOY   But it was an accident ...

COOK   Accident? I can't get it off!

BOY   Let me help.

HE PULLS THE DOUGH AND IT STRETCHES AND STRETCHES AND
STRETCHES, BUT DOES NOT COME OFF. HE LETS GO AND MESSES UP
THE COOK ALL THE MORE.

COOK   I'll make whipped cream out of you! I'll ... (RUNS AFTER THE
BOY TO STRIKE HIM BUT HIS HAND ONLY STICKS TO HIM) Let go.. let go ...

BOY   But sir, I'm not holding you.

COOK   Fool ... help – help!

BOY   Let's pull again!

COOK   I'll do anything, anything! One, two, three .. (THEY PULL
APART BUT THE COOK BACKS INTO THE HOT OVEN) Ow ... ow–ww ... the pie
– it'll burn!

HE GRABS TWO ENORMOUS OVEN GLOVES TO OPEN THE OVEN DOOR, AND
TAKES OUT THE PIE. HE HOLDS IT UP CAREFULLY, TRYING TO HOLD
ON AS BEST HE CAN. HE SLIPS ON THE DOUGH, HIS FACE FALLS INTO
THE PIE.

COOK   (LIFTING HIS FACE COVERED WITH CHERRIES) Well, do
something!!! Don't stand there ... <u>do</u> something!

        LIGHTS DIM.

        THE LIGHTS COME UP ON THE BALLROOM. MUSIC.

        IN THE KITCHEN THROUGHOUT THE BALLROOM SCENE, IN SLOW MOTION
        THE COOK AND THE BOY ARE CLEANING THEMSELVES UP AND THEN
        CONTINUE WITH THE BAKING.

        THE BALLROOM ALL AGLOW, THE JESTER AND SOLDIER IN THEIR USUAL
        PLACES, WE SEE THE LORDS AND LADIES ALL DRESSED IN BRIGHT
        COLOURS DANCING A TRUE MINUET. MUSIC.

1ST LADY   Tonight is the night.

2ND LADY   Every night is a night.

        HER FEATHERED STOLE HAS A HUGE SAFETY PIN ATTACHING IT TO
        HER DRESS.

1ST LADY   You know very well what I mean.

2ND LADY   I think you should say what you mean.

1ST LADY   I mean what I mean.

2ND LADY   I believe you <u>are</u> mean.

1ST LADY   (FURIOUS) You're twisting my words.

2ND LADY   Oh no. That's what I mean.

1ST LORD   (EXPLODING) Never mind!

2ND LADY   I'm going to enjoy the ball tonight and think of nothing else.
I wouldn't spoil the Princess's evening for anything.

2ND LORD   Agreed upon.

2ND LADY   Entirely agreed upon.

1ST LADY   I can't help but wonder.

1ST LORD   Wonder about the stars. You look simply lovely.

1ST LADY   (THRILLED) Do you think so?

1ST LORD   No. But it gives us something to talk about.

1ST LADY   How could you. I can barely breathe in this dress but I wore
it to please you.

1ST LORD   It is lovely. I was only teasing. (LIGHTS DIM SLIGHTLY) What was that? (LIGHTS FULL)

1ST LADY   (FEARFUL) I don't know!

2ND LORD   (PRETENDING COURAGE) Just a change of light.

1ST LADY   I don't suppose anything will happen.

1ST LORD   It must have been the wind.

2ND LADY   (FANNING HERSELF RAPIDLY) I think I shall faint.

2ND LORD   Please don't. You'll spoil the party!

2ND LADY   Very well, I won't then.

1ST LADY   Always looking for an excuse.

1ST LORD   Now let's be gay and cheerful.

2ND LADY   Agreed upon.

1ST LADY   Entirely agreed upon.

THE JESTER, CRICKET, SUDDENLY BREAKS FROM HIS TRANCE AND STATUE-LIKE POSITION AND COMES TO LIFE.

JESTER   Suppose old Barbel's curse came true ...
                        I wonder what would happen to you!

POINTS TO AUDIENCE. MUSIC.

                        Aha! Barbel's sure to be somewhere near.
                        I wonder if I'll fall asleep ... on my ear

ACROBAT'S FALLING ASLEEP ON EAR.

                        Or on my knees (DOES SO) or on my nose (DOES SO)
                        Or maybe even on my toes. (DOES SO)
                        Better still, standing on my head (DOES SO)
                        Or on my back, as if in bed. (DOES SO)
                        Perhaps it will be on my side (DOES SO)
                        Or on my bottom ... no, it's too wide.
                        On my elbow, or my wrist.
                        I say! Maybe I'll be kissed!

THE JESTER MIMES AND DANCES THE WHOLE SONG. EVERYONE LAUGHS AT HIS ACTIONS. HE SUDDENLY GETS UP AND WALKS ROUND IN A FIERCE MENACING WAY.

                        Who knows ... p'raps it's you ... or you in disguise.

POINTING TO EACH.

                        Old Barbel's one that's pretty wise.

Put out your tongue!

LOOKS AT **FIRST LADY'S** TONGUE.

Can't see a thing ...
Let's see your teeth. No - no witch's ring.

(TO 2ND LORD)   And now, my Lord, just jump about.
Click your heels ...

SECOND LORD DOES SO AND HIS TUMMY SHAKES.

My you're getting stout.

SCARING EVERYONE, TUMBLING AS HE GOES.

Now you see me, now you don't.
If I'm Cricket you will, if I'm Barbel you won't.
Am I a fool, or a witch in disguise?
Am I Cricket or Barbel? Look in my eyes.

FIRST LADY STARES, SHAKING ALL OVER.

You silly thing, who do you think I am?
I'm Cricket of course, who else is a ham?

EVERYONE IS RELIEVED. **CRICKET** JUMPS BACK INTO HIS PLACE BY
THE THRONE ... AND SITS.

On with the ball. Now listen to me ...
On with it ... on with it, one two three. (MUSIC)

THE MINUET BEGINS AGAIN. EVERYONE DANCES AS IF THEY ARE
PUPPETS. THEY ARE AFRAID. THE **PAGE** BLOWS THE TRUMPET.
LORDS AND LADIES TAKE THEIR PLACES. THE **KING AND QUEEN**, ALL
BEDECKED, ENTER. BEHIND THEM IS **PRINCESS BEAUTY**. THE LIGHTS
IN HER ROOM HAVE DIMMED FURTHER AND ONLY A CANDLE LIGHT CAN
BE SEEN. NO SOONER HAVE THE ROYALTY ENTERED WHEN SUDDENLY
THE LIGHTS IN THE BALLROOM BEGIN TO CHANGE COLOUR AND THEN
REMAIN ON BLUE AND GREEN.

EVERYONE CHEERS, AND SHOUTS 'The fairies have come! The
fairies have come!'.

KING   They have kept their word. All is well.

QUEEN   Thank goodness we are safe. (MUSIC)

THE FAIRIES DESCEND THE GOLDEN LADDER AND EVERYONE JOINS
INTO A GREAT AND JOYOUS BALLET. THE BALL HAS BEGUN. THE
FAIRIES AND **BEAUTY** DOMINATE THE SCENE. THE **JESTER** PARTNERS
THEM. IT IS A FULL PRODUCTION NUMBER ... THE JESTER FIRST
DANCES WITH THE **FAIRY QUEEN**, THEN WITH **BEAUTY**. THE THREE
DANCE TOGETHER, THEN **BEAUTY** AND THE **FAIRY QUEEN** DANCE. THE
FAIRIES AND **BEAUTY** AND THEN THE **JESTER** LEAD THE WHOLE

COMPANY. BEAUTY DANCES WITH ABANDON. EVEN THE QUEEN IS
HAPPY. THE FAIRIES MAKE A CIRCLE ROUND BEAUTY.

EVERYONE CALLS OUT 'No harm will come to her now'.

KING   All is well.

QUEEN   And all will remain so.

KING   Look how happy Beauty is.

QUEEN   I remember my sweet sixteenth birthday.

KING   It wasn't too long ago, my dear.

THE JESTER AND BEAUTY ARE DANCING, LAUGHING ALL THE WHILE ...
AS EVERYONE JOINS IN. THE FAIRIES FLY OVER EACH OTHER. THE
ENTIRE COMPANY ARE DANCING AS BEAUTY IS BEING LIFTED ON THE
SHOULDERS OF CRICKET. THE CLOCK STRIKES TWELVE. SUDDENLY
THERE IS ABSOLUTE SILENCE. THE FATAL HOUR HAS PASSED.

KING   The witching hour is over. Nothing will happen now.

QUEEN   I am eternally grateful to you, my dearest fairies, for looking
after us.

KING   Happy birthday, Beauty!

EVERYONE   Happy birthday, Beauty.

FAIRY QUEEN
              Happy birthday! We will always be here to protect you.

EVERYONE   Cheers for the Fairy Queen!

KING   And now, dear Beauty, it's time to say goodnight.

BEAUTY   Is it all to end so soon? Just another five minutes. I'm
having such a lovely time.

KING   All good things must come to an end. (MUSIC)

BEAUTY   Ah well then ... goodnight ... goodnight ... I shall never forget
tonight.

SHE BLOWS A KISS TO EVERYONE ... KISSES THE KING AND QUEEN,
MAKING A LONG SLOW EXIT BLOWING KISSES ALL THE WAY. AT THE
SAME TIME A SPINNING WHEEL APPEARS IN HER ROOM AS THE LIGHTS
HEIGHTEN THERE. SITTING AT THE WHEEL IS AN OLD WOMAN.

IN THE KITCHEN, THE COOK, WHO HAS JOINED IN THE BALLET AND
WATCHED THE GOODNIGHT, IS SO OVERWHELMED HE KISSES THE BOY!
THEY GO BACK TO THEIR WORK, FOR THE CELEBRATION IS TO
CONTINUE FOR MANY DAYS.

MEANWHILE IN THE BALLROOM A QUIET MINUET IS DANCED BY THE
COURT. THE **KING AND QUEEN** ARE SEATED ON THEIR THRONES, AND
THE **FAIRIES** FLY AWAY.

BY THE TIME **BEAUTY** REACHES HER ROOM THE LIGHTS IN THE
BALLROOM AND KITCHEN HAVE ALL BEEN DIMMED AS THE LIGHTS IN
THE BEDROOM REACH THEIR FULNESS. **BEAUTY** ENTERS ALL AGLOW,
NOT NOTICING AT FIRST THE OLD WOMAN OR THE SPINNING WHEEL.
GRADUALLY SHE BECOMES AWARE.

BEAUTY   Is this my room?

BARBEL   (DISGUISING HER VOICE AND SPEECH) Indeed it is.

BEAUTY   (FEELING HER BED) Yes, it must be. There's my bed.

BARBEL   I've come to wish you well ... and give you this present for
your birthday.

BEAUTY   How kind of you. My birthday has been full of surprises.
What is it?

BARBEL   Have you never seen a spinning wheel before?

BEAUTY   No, never. I've never even heard the word. What does it do?

BARBEL   Have you never touched one before?

BEAUTY   No, never. Tell me, what shall I do with it?

BARBEL   Oh it's simple, and so delightful.

BEAUTY   (EXCITED) Show me.

BARBEL   Come closer and watch. You see how easy it is. (SHE SPINS)

BEAUTY   May I try?

BARBEL   It's yours to do as you please.

BEAUTY   Oh thank you.

BARBEL RISES FROM THE STOOL AND **BEAUTY** SITS DOWN. SHE COMES
CLOSE TO THE WHEEL. A CHILD FROM THE AUDIENCE BY THIS TIME,
WE HOPE, WILL SHOUT 'No! Don't!'

BEAUTY   Now let me see ... like this?

BARBEL   Quite so.

BEAUTY   How easy. (MUSIC) Oh!

SHE SPINS AND SUDDENLY SHE PRICKS HER FINGER. SHE BECOMES
VERY SLEEPY. SHE LOOKS TOWARDS **BARBEL**.

BEAUTY   Is that what it means to prick one's finger? I can barely see
you. I must rest now. (LIES DOWN)

BARBEL   Ah-hah-my-curse-comes-true! Sleep Beauty!

SHE CACKLES AS SHE LEAVES, TAKING THE SPINNING WHEEL WITH
HER.

BEAUTY   Goodnight everyone. I shall never forget tonight. (FAST
ASLEEP)

AS BEAUTY FALLS ASLEEP, EVERYONE IN THE ENTIRE KINGDOM FALLS
ASLEEP. THE KING FALLS ASLEEP ON HIS THRONE WITH HIS MOUTH
STILL OPEN AS HE WAS ABOUT TO SPEAK. THE QUEEN ON HER
THRONE IS ASLEEP WITH HER HEAD TURNED AS SHE IS LISTENING TO
THE KING. THE LORDS AND LADIES ARE ASLEEP STANDING UP IN
THEIR DANCING POSITIONS WITH OUTSTRETCHED ARMS. CRICKET IS IN
A TUMBLING POSITION. THE COOK IS JUST ABOUT TO BOX THE EARS
OF THE BOY WHO IS RUNNING AWAY. HIS HAND JUST MISSES HIM.
AT THE PRECISE MOMENT OF THE PRINCESS'S SLEEP, THERE IS A
SUDDEN STOPPING OF MOVEMENT EVERYWHERE. THE FACIAL
EXPRESSIONS ARE ALL SET IN MID-ACTION. THE KING IS FORCEFUL,
THE QUEEN AMUSED, THE LORDS AND LADIES SMILING, THE JESTER
SURPRISED, THE COOK FURIOUS, THE BOY ANXIOUS.

THE FAIRIES RETURN TO LOOK AT THEM, AND THEN GENTLY CLOSE
THE CURTAIN. MUSIC.

THE CURTAIN IS LIKE A HUGE SPIDER-WEB AS IT ENCLOSES THE
ENTIRE PALACE.

END OF ACT TWO

ACT THREE

(100 YEARS LATER)

PRINCE CHARMING WALKS IN FRONT OF THE CURTAIN. HE PUTS HIS
FINGER TO HIS LIPS AND SAYS 'Ssh'. TIPTOES LIGHTLY ACROSS THE
STAGE. LIGHTS ARE ON IN EACH PLAYING AREA, BUT ALWAYS MORE
BRIGHTLY WHENEVER PRINCE CHARMING APPEARS. EVERYONE IS
EXACTLY AS THEY WERE AT THE END OF ACT TWO. THE PRINCE IS
TRYING TO SQUEEZE THROUGH THE SPIDER CURTAIN, WITH GREAT
DIFFICULTY.

PRINCE   This is worse than looking for the crown. If I push a little
harder, I can almost manage it. (HE TRIES SQUEEZING THROUGH THE
CURTAIN NEAR THE KITCHEN, TO NO AVAIL) Now what do I do? Hey, boy,
come and help!

THE BOY DOESN'T ANSWER OF COURSE. CHILDREN CRY OUT FROM

AUDIENCE 'He's asleep!'.

Oh well, don't help then. Is anyone there? I say is anyone there! (NO ANSWER) Well, here goes.

    THE CURTAIN/WEB MAGICALLY OPENS. THE SHADOW OF **BARBEL** PASSES AND QUICKLY DISAPPEARS.

PRINCE   (TURNING ROUND) Who was that?

CHILDREN   The witch.

PRINCE   Don't be silly. (LOOKS ABOUT) No one's there.

    BARBEL'S HEAD SUDDENLY APPEARS.

CHILDREN   There she is.

PRINCE   (LOOKING) She's not there ... You're wrong.

    BARBEL APPEARS AGAIN AND THE CHILDREN CALL OUT AGAIN. THE PRINCE KEEPS MISSING HER. IT CAN BE REPEATED SEVERAL TIMES UNTIL THE **PRINCE** FINALLY SAYS:

PRINCE   I don't believe you. Anyway, what can a little old witch do?

    BARBEL LAUGHS AND STARTLES THE **PRINCE** SO THAT HE LEAPS WITH FRIGHT.

PRINCE   Blast that witch ... which way did she go?

CHILDREN   There.

PRINCE   Where?

CHILDREN   There!

PRINCE   Where? Oh, never mind, I'll ask the Cook. (TO COOK) Did you see a witch? (NO ANSWER) All right, but leave the boy alone. Did you hear me? And stop this game. Now tell me, what's going on? (NO ANSWER) Did you hear me! Boy, come here. I'll defend you against this mean fellow. (NO ANSWER) Don't you want help? Come now, what's going on? (SHAKES THE BOY) He doesn't move ... Goodness me ... no one talks, no one walks ... this is a strange palace. (BARBEL LAUGHS AGAIN) I don't know what's worse, the laugh or the silence. (EXPLORES KITCHEN) I don't belong in the kitchen anyway ... on to the main hall.

    BARBEL ENTERS THE BALLROOM WITH HIM. WHENEVER HE TURNS ROUND SHE MANAGES TO HIDE BEHIND EITHER SOMEONE OR SOMETHING. THE **PRINCE** MAKES A GRAND ENTRANCE INTO THE BALLROOM. NO ONE LOOKS, ONLY **BARBEL** LAUGHS.

PRINCE   Go away. (SHE DISAPPEARS) That entrance was wasted. How do you do? (MAKING A GRAND BOW BUT LOOKING AROUND FOR THE WITCH FIRST) Very well, if no one wishes to talk, we'll leave it that way. (GOES

TO **KING** TO SHAKE HANDS) I hope you know how unfriendly you and your
whole Kingdom are. (TURNS TO **QUEEN**) Won't you listen to me? All right.
Don't. Look here, Jester, there are better ways of sitting than that.
(SHOWS HIM HOW TO SIT ... YET NO RESPONSE FROM ANYONE) I say, let's
dance. (RUSHES OVER TO **LORDS AND LADIES**. STARTS HIS DANCE SOLO
SINCE NO ONE DANCES WITH HIM) Thank you one and all for the dance.
Never in my life have I met such people. (WALKS AROUND THE ROOM) I'll
take every precious ornament away with me. Doesn't that bother you?

> HE BEGINS TO TAKE OFF THE **QUEEN'S** CROWN. NO RESPONSE. HE
> TAKES OFF THE **KING'S** CROWN. NO RESPONSE. THEN HE FURIOUSLY
> TAKES OFF JEWELLERY FROM EVERYONE. STILL NO RESPONSE.

This is dreadful. There's no fun in mischief if no one cares.

> THROWS EVERYTHING IN CENTRE OF ROOM.

Take back your diamonds and your crowns. I don't need any of you.

> LIGHTS DIM IN BALLROOM AS THEY COME UP MORE BRIGHTLY IN
> **BEAUTY'S** BEDROOM. THE **PRINCE** APPEARS IN THE BEDROOM.

PRINCE   Oh! What have I come upon? Isn't she lovely? Hello. Hello.
What, you too! You're playing the game. Very well, I'll play too. Maybe
this will wake you. (MUSIC)

> HE KISSES HER ON THE CHEEK. SUDDENLY LIGHTS GO UP
> EVERYWHERE. PEOPLE START MOVING AND ABOVE ALL STRETCH AND
> STRETCH AND STRETCH. BEAUTY AWAKES GRADUALLY, YAWNING AS
> SHE DOES SO.

PRINCE   My goodness ... it did wake her.

BEAUTY   I'm so glad you finally came.

PRINCE   (BEWILDERED) Finally came?

BEAUTY   Yes. I've waited one hundred years for you.

PRINCE   Are you that old?

BEAUTY   Yes and no.

PRINCE   See here ... what goes on? First no one moves and then just
like that everyone is ... alive.

BEAUTY   It must seem strange to you. But you see we were all cursed
with sleep a hundred years ago, until a handsome prince should kiss me.
Then we would all awaken and look exactly as we fell asleep ... no older.
And that's what's happened, thanks to you. I must say you're not quite as
handsome as I thought you would be. Still you did come and you did
awaken us. We must be grateful for that.

PRINCE   I must say! Not as handsome as you expected! What more
could you expect? After all I did save you. What else?

BEAUTY   There, there. You're right. You are such a dear.

PRINCE   (PLEASED) At last a kind word.

BEAUTY   You do have a sweet face, like a teddy bear. Yes, you are a
Prince Charming. I'm Beauty. Princess Beauty.

PRINCE   Princess Beauty ... ah, Beauty, you have waited a long time to
see me. I feel very flattered.

BEAUTY   One hundred years is a long time. But I can't remember. It
seems like only yesterday I fell asleep.

PRINCE   How old are you?

BEAUTY   Sixteen years old, plus a hundred years asleep which if you
subtract because they don't really count as I was asleep and nothing could
happen because the fairies protected me and I still have a whole lifetime
you can see then that I'm really only sixteen so you needn't worry about
my old age really.

PRINCE   Well ... I mean ... I wasn't worried about your old age. I mean
... what concern is it of mine.

BEAUTY   You're going to marry me. And since I know you will ask and
since you know I'll say yes, well, it's very simple for you to ask that now
isn't it?

PRINCE   How do you know I want to marry ... anyone?

BEAUTY   Because that's the way all fairytales end and that's the way
Prince Charmings are supposed to be ... so ask me now, quick ... so we can
ask Papa.

PRINCE   I'm too shy.

BEAUTY   Course you're not. You really don't have to ask, since I know
what you intend.

PRINCE   No, I'll do the asking. You're going to be my bride.

BEAUTY   Yes, of course. But first let's find Mother and Father.

PRINCE   (SWEEPING HER UP IN HIS ARMS) On to the ballroom!

          MUSIC. THE BALLROOM IS ALL EXCITED AND ANIMATED. EVERYONE IS
          COMPARING NOTES, CLOTHES, ETC. THE KING AND QUEEN ARE STILL
          ON THEIR THRONES. LORDS AND LADIES SURROUND THE ROYAL
          COUPLE. BEAUTY AND THE PRINCE APPEAR. UTTER SILENCE
          PREVAILS AS ALL GAZE UPON THE PRINCE WITH APPROVAL. HE MAKES
          A GRAND ENTRANCE AND THIS TIME IS NOTICED.

KING   Don't say a word. You may marry my daughter with my
blessing.

QUEEN   With both our blessings.

PRINCE   (MOUTH OPENED, ABOUT TO ASK THE QUESTION) Yes ... ah ...
thank you.

BEAUTY   Where will the wedding be, Prince Charming?

PRINCE   Here and now, Beauty. By the way, you may call me Charming.

BEAUTY   Charming, isn't that a wonderful name. You are wonderful,
Charming.

PRINCE   I'm Charming, my darling.

BEAUTY   Wonderful too.

PRINCE   <u>You</u> are wonderful, Beauty, beautiful wonder. We will be so
happy.

KING   The wedding.

QUEEN   Oh my yes, the wedding.

KING   Beauty, off with you. Prepare yourself for your wedding.

        BEAUTY EXITS.

Prince Charming, you'll need help. Choose your Court. (HE POINTS TO THE
AUDIENCE)

PRINCE   An excellent idea. (HE CHOOSES TWO OR THREE CHILDREN FROM
THE AUDIENCE) I have an ideal Court, your Majesty.

        THE CHILDREN ARE DRESSED ON STAGE BY THE LORDS AND LADIES.
        IN GRACEFUL MOVEMENTS, HATS AND CLOAKS ARE PUT ON THEM.

KING   Now, courtiers, help your Prince dress.

        A CLOAK OF GOLD IS PUT UPON THE PRINCE'S SHOULDERS, A HAT OF
        GOLD UPON HIS HEAD. LORDS AND LADIES HELP WHERE NECESSARY.

KING   Blow, bugles, blow. Places everyone. The wedding! (MUSIC)

        THE KITCHEN HAS BEEN BUSY WITH THE BAKING AND AN ENORMOUS
        CAKE IS READY. LORDS AND LADIES TAKE THEIR PLACES. KING AND
        QUEEN MARCH HAND IN HAND TO THE REAR CENTRE DOORS OF THE
        BALLROOM. THE PRINCE FOLLOWS. PROCESSION STARTS, HEADED BY
        KING AND QUEEN, THEN PRINCE AND BEAUTY (WHO MAKES A SPECIAL
        ENTRANCE), TUMBLING JESTER, LORDS, LADIES AND CHILDREN. KING
        AND QUEEN REACH THEIR THRONES AND STAND IN FRONT OF THEM.
        PRINCE AND BEAUTY KNEEL BEFORE THEM. THE KING PERFORMS
        CEREMONY, WHICH ENDS IN CROWNING OF PRINCE AND BEAUTY.

KING   Let us be merry! The wedding cake!

COOK ENTERS WITH AN ENORMOUS CAKE, BOY BEHIND HIM. PUTS IT IN
CENTRE OF BALLROOM. MUSIC. DANCE AROUND THE CAKE BY THE
ENTIRE COMPANY. GREAT GAIETY. LIGHTS START CHANGING COLOURS,
THEN SETTLE ON BLUE AND GREEN. THE FAIRIES FLY IN. JOYFUL IS
THE DANCE AROUND THE PRINCE, BEAUTY AND THE CAKE. THE KING
CAN BE HEARD SAYING:

KING   And they all lived happily ever after.

MUSIC, AS THE ENTIRE COURT MARCH DOWN THE CENTRE AISLES.

CURTAIN

END OF PLAY

BARBEL,
THE WICKED
FAIRY

FAIRIES

QUEEN
OF THE
FAIRIES

KING   QUEEN

LORDS
A.G
PRINCE CHARMING.
SECOND LADY-IN-WAITING
FIRST LADY-IN-WAITING
COOK'S BOY
COOK
COURT JESTER CRICKET
PRINCESS BEAUTY

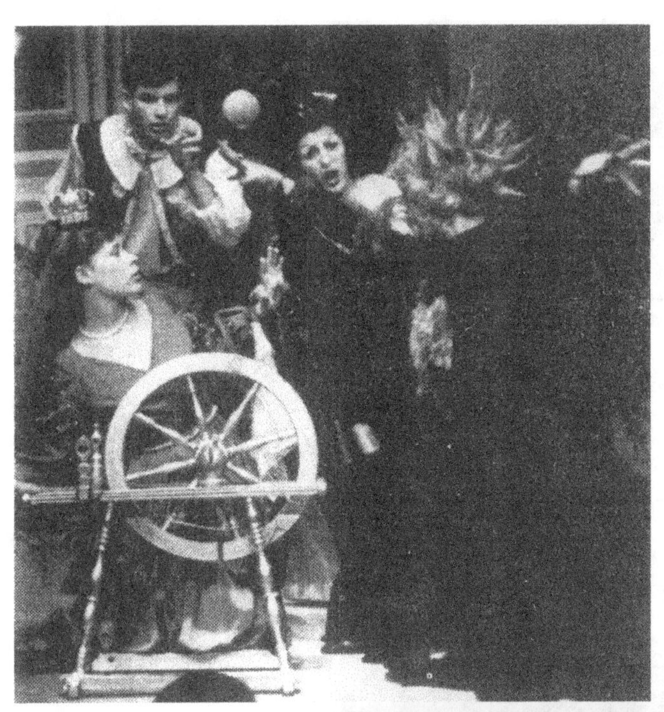

THE CRICKET THEATRE
AND BLANCHE MARVIN
PRESENT:
THE MERRI-MIMES'

Cinderella

by Blanche Marvin

DIRECTED BY MARIO SILETTI

CHOREOGRAPHY- RAY HARRISON   COSTUMES-CONNIE BAXTER
LIGHTS-RICHARD NELSON   SCENERY-ROBERT JEFFORDS

CINDERELLA	-BETTY SCHWARTZ
STEPMOTHER	-MARY WATSON
MINERVA	-BRUCE VALE
ANGELA	-RUSSELL DOUGLAS
FAIRY GODMOTHER	-DOROTHY RUSSELL
CHAMBERLAIN	-JAMES S. TOLKAN
PRINCE	-WILLIAM HAWLEY

STAGE MANAGER-ROBERT JEFFORDS

AT THE CRICKET THEATRE
162 SECOND AVE.   OR 4-3960
FEB. 21, 28, MARCH 7, 14, 21 also
FEB. 23 WASHINGTON'S BIRTHDAY
ALSO:
MEET MR. EASTERBUNNY- on
MARCH 28, 30, 31, APRIL 1, 2, 3, 4th
ALICE IN WONDERLAND on
APRIL 11, 18, 25, MAY 2, 9, 16
SEE GATE THEATRE SERIES!

CINDERELLA

A COMEDY OF MANNERS

Styled after "THE IMPORTANCE OF BEING EARNEST" by Oscar Wilde

<u>CAST OF CHARACTERS</u>

Cinderella

Prince

Stepmother, Lady Letitia

Angela, stepsister (male part)

Minerva, stepsister (male part)

Chamberlain, Lord Horatio

Fairy Godmother, Britannia

Place: ACT I and ACT III - Stepmother's Cottage
           ACT II   - Prince's Palace

Time: Edwardian days, 1900's

Author's Note:

This is a comedy of manners based loosely on the characters of
Wilde's play. CINDERELLA is a warm and giving girl, sensitive
and capable of love. The PRINCE is spoiled and bored by life
until he meets love, when he makes a complete change in his
surrender to it. He is EARNEST. The STEPMOTHER, mocking LADY
BRACKNELL, is a snobbish social climber, dominant but feminine
and feathery. Angela, satirizing CECILY, is aggressive,
belligerent and egotistical with no social graces. MINERVA,
exaggerating Gwendolyn, is the near-sighted older sister
attempting the polish of sophistication. The CHAMBERLAIN is
the typical Country Squire with an ease of the landed gentry.
The FAIRY GODMOTHER is the essence of English eccentricity,
haughty but kind, absent-minded but shrewd in the use of her
magical power. She may be an amateur with magic but is
representative of the English amateur professional who knows
exactly how to exert power. As Britannia, she rules the waves,
but her cousin, Columbia seems far more secure.

ACT ONE

OVERTURE.

LIGHTS UP IN FRONT OF CURTAIN. BRITANNIA, DRESSED LIKE THE
SYMBOL OF BRITANNIA, IS ACTUALLY THE FAIRY GODMOTHER.

BRITANNIA   (ENTERS FROM STAGE LEFT AUDIENCE) Good afternoon, boys
and girls. I am very glad to see all of you here. Do you mind if I put
these down for a moment. They are the Scales of Justice, and a bit
unbalanced I'm afraid. So if you don't mind ... ah, there! (PUTS THEM
DOWN) How do you do. I am Britannia. You may not know me. I rule the
waves, waves and waves and waves. (LAUGHS) Ah well! Perhaps you are
better acquainted with my cousin, Columbia, the Gem of the Ocean? Well,
what's an ocean compared to waves. Cousin Columbia's such a braggart.
Anyway I really detest water. However, I do prefer my other cousin, from
my father's side. She's such a dear and I'm sure you all know her. The
Statue of Liberty! Her blood's a bit mixed you know ... born in France and
bred in New York. She stands for the United States and I stand for the
United Kingdom. Oh my – the poor thing, standing for years with her arm
up in the air. But what would people say if she ever put it down. You
have no idea how difficult it is to hold one's arm up in the air indefinitely.
I'd like you all to try. Everyone's arm up. Way up! That's it. Now I am
going to count and see how long you can keep your arms up in the air.
One, two, three ... heavy isn't it? You can all put your arms down now.
You did very well for amateurs. I shall keep you in mind when she goes
on holiday.

Well now, I must let you know why I came to visit you. You'll never guess.
You couldn't possibly imagine that I might be able to do such a thing. I
practise magic!! Of course I only use it to help good people who are in a
great deal of trouble. Would you like to see the power of my magic right
now?

    AUDIENCE: 'YES!'

Very well. Abracadabra ... one, two, three!

    CURTAINS OPEN ON A FAMILY TABLEAU – STEPMOTHER SEATED AT
    TABLE, STEPSISTERS MAKING THEIR ENTRANCE, CINDERELLA SERVING
    TEA AT TABLE. THE SET IS THE HOME OF THE STEPMOTHER – IN
    EDWARDIAN STYLE. THERE IS A FIREPLACE, PLANTS, TABLE AND
    CHAIRS, AND A PIANO.

    BRITANNIA SPINS CENTRE STAGE.

BRITANNIA   Here we are ... in the story of Cinderella ... as it was told to
me when I was a little girl in London. This is Cinderella, her two
stepsisters, Lady Angela and Lady Minerva, and her stepmother Lady
Letitia, going to have their morning tea. Now I must go and they will tell
their story. Au revoir, mes chéries – as my cousin Liberty would say.
Abracadabra ... one, two three!

SHE SPINS OFF.

BREAK TABLEAU AS CHARACTERS COME TO LIFE. THE **UGLY SISTERS**
(PLAYED BY MALE ACTORS) WALK TO TABLE AND SIT DOWN TO
BREAKFAST. **CINDERELLA** IS DRESSED IN RAGS, WHILE THE
STEPMOTHER AND **STEPSISTERS** ARE DRESSED IN NIGHTGOWNS AND
CAPS.

ANGELA   One lump or none?

MINERVA   None, Angela. A lady always has her tea without sugar.
Besides – you're the one with the sour disposition. You need the
sweetening. Cinderella, bring the jug.

CINDERELLA Yes Minerva.

IN THIS SCENE **CINDERELLA** DASHES IN AND OUT, SERVING.

ANGELA   And be quick about it.

STEPMOTHER My tea has cooled. Fetch some more hot water.

SHE IS READING THE MORNING MAIL.

CINDERELLA Yes Mama.

ANGELA   And don't forget to butter the scones.

CINDERELLA Right away, Angela.

MINERVA   And fill my plate with crumpets.

CINDERELLA At once, Minerva. (AS SHE EXITS SHE WHISPERS TO THE
AUDIENCE) Scones and crumpets should be eaten at teatime, and not for
breakfast!

MINERVA   Angela, my ownest, pass me the jam.

ANGELA   Here you are dearest. (SHE ALLOWS **MINERVA** ONE SPOONFUL
AND RETRIEVES THE JAM)

STEPMOTHER Girls, do listen. Dear Lady Harbury writes to say that she
attended the Chamberlain's reception.

ANGELA   (SLAPPING **MINERVA'S** HAND, AS SHE'S BEEN TRYING GENTLY TO
STEAL THE JAM) Social climber.

STEPMOTHER Never speak disrespectfully of people in Society, Angela.
Besides, I knew Horatio well.

ANGELA &
MINERVA   Horatio???

STEPMOTHER Yes, Horatio – he is now Chamberlain to the Prince.

ANGELA   Oh, Mama, it is not the Horatio?

MINERVA   The man who regarded you with love when you were a girl!

STEPMOTHER Yes, the very same.

ANGELA   Regard yourself Minerva, you are spreading jam on your hand
and not on the crumpet.

MINERVA   Am I really?

ANGELA   Yes, you foolish frump.

MINERVA   Foolish frump! Really, you ... you ... old maid.

ANGELA   People in stone houses shouldn't throw glass.

MINERVA   It's people in glass houses shouldn't throw stones.

ANGELA   I must remember to respect my elders. I'm only an old maid
after you.

CINDERELLA Here you are Angela, ten scones.

ANGELA   Goodness, what took you so long?

MINERVA   Quickly, my crumpets.

STEPMOTHER You have been so long about it my tea has grown cold.

CINDERELLA (AGAIN DASHING BACK AND FORTH) This water is hot, Mama.

ANGELA   Minerva, you are pouring tea all over the table and not in the
cup.

MINERVA   Am I really? Oh, Mama, why can't I wear glasses?

STEPMOTHER What, and spoil your face, my pretty dove? Utter nonsense.
Cinderella, clean the table at once.

ANGELA   Look, you've spoilt my satin slipper. Cinderella, clean it off at
once.

MINERVA   And my skirt, Cinderella.

STEPMOTHER More tea.

ANGELA   More butter.

MINERVA   Another serviette.

CINDERELLA But ... but ... but ...

STEPMOTHER Don't stammer, child.

ANGELA   What can you expect from a cinder maid?

        CINDERELLA EXITS.

MINERVA   (AS ANGELA TRIES STEALING MINERVA'S TOAST) More than
one can expect from one's own sister. I see through you.

ANGELA   And when I see a spade, I call it a spade.

MINERVA   Exactly! You are stealing my toast!

ANGELA   You can't see me stealing your toast, much less see through
me, even if you wore four pairs of glasses.

MINERVA   Mama, she's always picking on me. Just for that you won't
wear my pearls. (SHE PULLS OFF ANGELA'S PEARLS)

ANGELA   Give them back to me. A bargain is a bargain. (SHE TRIES
TO GET THE PEARLS BACK)

MINERVA   (AS SHE IS BREAKING THE PEARLS OFF ANGELA'S NECK) You
broke your bargain.

ANGELA   Indian giver!

        A BATTLE ROYAL ENSUES OVER THE PEARLS.

STEPMOTHER Girls ... girls ... bicker, bicker, bicker – where are your
manners? We must set a good example for Cinderella. (BELL RINGS) The
bell? Cinderella!

CINDERELLA I know Mama. Answer it. (EXITS)

ANGELA
        La bell so soon?

ANGELA &
MINERVA   Postman at ten – postman at noon.

CINDERELLA (AS SHE CARRIES IN A LETTER) A registered letter, Mama.

STEPMOTHER (GRABBING LETTER AND OPENING IT WITH FURIOUS RAPIDITY)
Good heavens, it's from Horatio!

ANGELA &
MINERVA   Horatio??? The 'I-knew-him-well' one?

STEPMOTHER Oh my ... it brings back my youth.

MINERVA   Horatio, Horatio, Horatio.

        STEPSISTERS IMITATE STEPMOTHER IN HER YOUTH.

ANGELA   Letitia, my very own. (KISSING MINERVA'S ARM UP TO THE
NECK)

MINERVA   Saucy fellow. (HITS ANGELA WITH FAN)

ANGELA   And you have a wicked tongue - a sharp weapon.

MINERVA   But what else can I do. I am betrothed to another. We must
say goodbye.

ANGELA   Is there no hope?

MINERVA   It is goodbye forever, Horatio.

ANGELA   Letitia, fare thee well.

STEPMOTHER Girls, girls - hearken to this. 'My dear Letitia' ... dear ... my
dear. How beautiful, how heartbreaking, how informal.

ANGELA   Do go on.

STEPMOTHER 'My dear Letitia. Though years have stood between, I trust
you will remember me.' Do you hear that, girls, do you hear that?

ANGELA, MINERVA AND CINDERELLA   We hear.

STEPMOTHER 'It is my pleasurable duty, as Chamberlain of the realm, to
invite you and your daughters to a Royal Ball to be given in honour of the
Prince ...'

CINDERELLA Oh the Prince.

ANGELA   Oh a ball.

MINERVA   Oh Horatio.

STEPMOTHER '... this Saturday night at 9 p.m. P.S. Please do come.
Yours, Horatio.' How simply divine.

CINDERELLA How lovely.

ANGELA   How smashing!

MINERVA   How ... Horatio.

STEPMOTHER At last, at long last good fortune has come our way. Oh,
girls, I see it all. This is what I've waited for. A higher rung on the
social ladder for you, my dears. The Prince is bound to be captivated by
one of you - to fall desperately, madly, hopelessly in love with one of you -
to make a bride of one of you.

ANGELA &
MINERVA   Which one?

STEPMOTHER Never tempt the Fates, my dears, it only brings misfortune.
Ah but ... the Chamberlain will be there. Perhaps we will recapture the old
times (READING LETTER) sooner than I thought. Oh dear - it's tonight!

MINERVA   What is?

STEPMOTHER   The ball!

ANGELA   Cinderella, quickly, my gown.

MINERVA   My jewels, my fan.

STEPMOTHER   Not now, not now. First you must practise your dance.
Practice now, perfect later.   Oh Cinderella, we'll be the men and lead.

ANGELA   It really doesn't matter - when I can't follow, I lead.

STEPMOTHER   That's just what I mean, Angela. You must always give a man
the impression that he leads ... even if you do.

MINERVA   That would be the eighth wonder of the world.

ANGELA   I don't see you following the men.

MINERVA   Mother really - will you tell Angela to mind her Ps and Qs?

STEPMOTHER   Angela ... that was very rude.

ANGELA   But that's what you just said.

STEPMOTHER   I didn't mean for anyone to actually go and follow a man. I
meant that when you are with a gentleman you allow him to lead and in that
way you follow.

ANGELA   Which way?

MINERVA   That way.

ANGELA   There is always this way or that way. But then ... then you
couldn't see the difference anyway.

MINERVA   My eyes may not be perfect but my manners are.

ANGELA   Then how could you see if you were following or leading.

STEPMOTHER   Girls, we must practise our dance. Angela, darling, dance
deliciously!

     MUSIC. ALL FOUR DANCE. DANCE OVER.

Well, I'm afraid it will have to do. Time is pressing.

CINDERELLA   Oh, Mama, how marvellous to go to the ball with the Prince.
To dance all evening in silks and satins. Oh Mama, mayn't I go too?

STEPMOTHER   You?

MINERVA   A cinder maid at the ball?

ANGELA   Ridiculous ... social climber.

STEPMOTHER   What would you wear?

MINERVA   What would you do?

ANGELA   What would you say?

STEPMOTHER   You're much too young yet. You'd be out of place with the Chamberlain and the Prince.

ANGELA   Really my dear, your position is too low.

CINDERELLA   But I don't understand.

STEPMOTHER   When your sisters are well taken care of and married they will help you on to the ladder of success. They are the keepers of your key to Society.

     MUSIC.

TRIO (SING)   We are the keepers of the key
                      To all of good Society
                      And we must rudely, crudely scorn
                      Unless you're to the manner born,
                      Precisely to the manner born.

                      If your blood isn't royal blue
                      We are afraid it just won't do,
                      For dancing with the Prince, you see,
                      Is for the aristocracy,
                      Only the aristocracy.

                      You can perceive by now, we trust,
                      That you are just not upper crust.
                      This ball you want to go to, lass,
                      Is strictly for a higher social class,
                      For the higher, very higher, very higher,
                      Ever higher social class.

STEPMOTHER   We're wasting precious time. Quickly girls. Cinderella, clear the dishes, sweep the floors, ready our gowns. We must prepare for the ball.

ANGELA &
MINERVA   The ball!

     EXIT STEPMOTHER AND STEPSISTERS. MUSIC.

CINDERELLA   The tea's gone cold, the butter's melted and they've spilt the jam. All these dishes ... (AS SHE READS THE INVITATION) 'It is my pleasurable duty to invite you to the Royal Ball in honour of the Prince.' I wish ... oh, I wish ...

     FADE OUT. CURTAINS CLOSE. THE FAIRY GODMOTHER COMES OUT IN

FRONT OF CURTAIN.

GODMOTHER   I wish ... I wish that I could dry her tears.

SHE USES THE DRAPERY OF HER DRESS TO DRY HER TEARS, BUT IT
GETS CAUGHT ON HER CROWN AND COVERS HER EYES. AS SHE TRIES
TO UNTIE IT, SHE CALLS OUT:

Now you know why Justice is blind ... my poor Cinderella ... But maybe I
will, one day. Oh dear ... you can see why I decided to leave my cousins
and practise magic. People do need Fairy Godmothers. Now, whilst we've
been talking ... a miracle just took place. TIME marched on without me.
He's an old man but he can run very fast when he wants to. You may be
sitting in your seats ... but Time has run right past you too. Indeed
Time has run so much that it's almost night time. Time for the ball, and
Minerva and Angela are still upstairs getting ready while Cinderella waits
on them hand and foot. There they are squeezing into dresses, squashing
feathers into their hair, dangling jewellery round their necks, covering
themselves with frills, and frivolities, fripperies and furbelows fatuously
foolish. And the arguments have gone round and round just like a circle
without an end. Listen, you can hear them from here. They're coming
down now, I think. Yes. Lights – lights – if you please. Oh I forgot –
ABRACADABRA with all my might. From magic dark, come magic light!

EXITS.

CURTAINS OPEN AS **STEPSISTERS** MAKE THEIR ENTRANCE. THEY ARE
OVER-DRESSED TO A POINT OF STUFFED DOLLS, COMPLETELY
RIDICULOUS IN THEIR WIGS AND GOWNS.

MINERVA   (HOLDING HAND MIRROR) My, I look divine. If I could only
see. (CINDERELLA STARTS TO BRUSH **MINERVA'S** DRESS) Don't brush my
dress with your cinder hands.

CINDERELLA I'm sorry ... it's so lovely.

ANGELA   Cinderella, fix my collar. After I have married the Prince you
may have this old rag. Yes, when I have married the Prince ... I shall have
a dozen dresses ... each more beautiful than the last. Then you shall all
beg for my company. (CINDERELLA JABS HER) Ouch! Clumsy fat fingers!

CINDERELLA I'm so sorry.

MINERVA   Cinderella, my fan, my fan – hurry.

ANGELA   It's on your wrist, you owl.

STEPMOTHER ENTERS, BEAUTIFULLY GOWNED.

STEPMOTHER We do look lovely. Come now – we mustn't be late for the
ball. Good night.

EXIT ALL THREE. MUSIC.

CINDERELLA Good night, mother, good night, sisters. Have a lovely time.

Good night. I so want to go to the ball. My stepsisters may never be married and then I shall never go. Oh, how unhappy I am. I wonder how many beautiful ladies there will be at the ball? What dress will they wear? Will the Prince dance with them all? (MUSIC) ... all dressed in satins and silks and velvets and laces, whilst I must be in my rags. I can dance ... I can dance so much better than they. I'm not ashamed of my manners. I'm well-born and yet I must sit by the cinders and ashes, never to dance with the Prince. Will I be faced with rags all my life? I can't bear it.

FAIRY GODMOTHER ENTERS.

GODMOTHER   Good evening, child.

CINDERELLA   Good evening. Oh, who are you?

GODMOTHER   I can't tell you all my secrets.

CINDERELLA   I'm sorry, you frightened me.

GODMOTHER   Frightened you, indeed. You called for me when you were weeping, and I came!

CINDERELLA   I did? But who are you?

GODMOTHER   I am your Fairy Godmother.

CINDERELLA   How do you do?

GODMOTHER   What can I do for you, child, and why were you weeping?

CINDERELLA   I wanted so much to go to the Prince's ball.

GODMOTHER   If you want to go to the ball that much, then go.

CINDERELLA   I can't. I don't have a dress. I'm in rags.

GODMOTHER   Oh, yes, you do look rather shabby, but your good heart and character with your lovely face decorate your rags.

CINDERELLA   But the Prince and the Court may not see it.

GODMOTHER   Oh, yes they shall. You'll go to the ball clad as a Princess.

CINDERELLA   How shall we do it?

GODMOTHER   With this!

CINDERELLA   What do I do?

GODMOTHER   Nothing. Now, here is a table with a lovely cloth. I shall say Abracadabra, touch it with my magic wand, and voila, as Cousin Liberty would say, here is your dress for the ball. ... Upon my word. I wonder what happened? Perhaps the cloth was soiled. Help me blow it clean first. Now, Abracada - oh yes, I forgot to turn around three times. One ... two ... three, and, voila, here is your dress for the ball!

MUSIC. THE DRESS MAGICALLY APPEARS.

CINDERELLA   Oh, is it mine? Is it really and truly mine? May I touch it?
May I wear it?

GODMOTHER   Of course. It's yours for the ball.

CINDERELLA   But I never had a dress for a ball before. Is it really mine?

GODMOTHER   It is yours, that is, until twelve o'clock. For at the last
stroke of twelve it will no longer be. My magic power lasts only till the
hour of midnight. I'm just a part-time Fairy Godmother.

CINDERELLA   How lovely, how absolutely lovely!

GODMOTHER   And now for your shoes. Golden slippers for a golden heart.
Abracadabra, and I won't forget to turn around three times, and, Ricky-
ticky, here are your shoes for the ball!

MUSIC. THE SHOES MAGICALLY APPEAR.

Good heavens, they're not gold at all, they're made of glass. My magic is
a little off-colour today. At least no one else will have glass slippers.
Here you are, Cinderella.

CINDERELLA   Oh, glass slippers! I'll have magic feet to dance away the
night.

GODMOTHER   No, no! Remember, no later than twelve o'clock, for then you
will be back in your rags.

CINDERELLA   Yes, yes, I'll remember. But ... how will I get to the ball?

GODMOTHER   That is simplest of all. Go quickly into the garden and fetch
me a pumpkin.

CINDERELLA   A pumpkin? Why a pumpkin?

GODMOTHER   Just fetch one. My magic wand is magic because it can do
anything, I trust.

CINDERELLA   What size should it be?

GODMOTHER   Cinderella, you are a good girl. The size does not matter.
Any pumpkin will do. But quickly, before the ball is over.

CINDERELLA   Oh, yes, Fairy Godmother. I'll return in an instant.

EXITS. MUSIC.

GODMOTHER   (DANCES AND SINGS)

> Pumpkin, pumpkin, you shall be
> A golden coach for all to see,
> Glittering like the stars that shine.

Remember you are always mine.

CINDERELLA ENTERS.

> Tra-la-la, pumpkin;
> Tra-la-la, pumpkin;
> Tra-la-la-la-la-la-la-la, pumpkin - COACH!

(STAGED BUSINESS OF TRANSFORMING PUMPKIN TO COACH)

And now, Cinderella, you are ready for the ball. Remember you must return at the stroke of twelve.

CINDERELLA   Oh, Fairy Godmother, I had no idea I would have such an elegant coach, or that all these wonderful things could possibly happen to me.

GODMOTHER   Good gracious, even I am excited! We don't know what will happen tonight. Should you see your stepmother and sisters, don't let them know who you are. Away with you. Your coach awaits. TALLY HO!

MUSIC.

CURTAIN

END OF ACT ONE

ACT TWO

FOYER TO THE BALLROOM.

WE SEE THE BACKGROUND OF THE PALACE ON A BACKDROP. THERE ARE THREE COLUMNS IN THE FOYER AND A CLOCK. STAGE RD, ONE COLUMN; UPSTAGE SECOND COLUMN; STAGE LD, THIRD COLUMN. CLOCK CENTRE STAGE. REGENCY ELEGANCE MUST BE THE EFFECT, WITH A MINIMUM OF SCENERY.

MUSIC. ANGELA, MINERVA, STEPMOTHER ENTER THROUGH AUDIENCE.

STEPMOTHER   The ball! We mustn't stop now. I hear the music.

MINERVA   It was for our arrival.

ANGELA   To be sure. There are the Pickering girls, all six of them. My, they look ridiculous.

MINERVA   Oh, where? Let me see.

ANGELA   Put on your glasses. You are looking at the column, not the door.

MINERVA   Am I really?

ANGELA   Really.

STEPMOTHER Are we ready for our entrance to the ball? Let's practise
our curtsey for the Prince.

MINERVA   Mama, really, we are old enough to go to a ball on our own.

STEPMOTHER One is never too old to practise.

ANGELA   (A QUICK CURTSEY) There, we've practised.

STEPMOTHER Oh, very well. It's your ball.

          ALL EXIT. PRINCE AND CHAMBERLAIN ENTER.

CHAMBERLAIN
          What am I to do with you, my Prince? This is the ball of
your lifetime, when you are to choose your bride, and you haven't danced
one dance.

PRINCE   I have looked and looked and not one Princess has appeared at
the ball with whom I care to dance.

CHAMBERLAIN
          There are ladies from several different countries who seem
rather interesting, not to mention some fair English roses.

PRINCE   Enjoy yourself, Chamberlain.

CHAMBERLAIN
          You make no attempt.

PRINCE   There is no one here with whom I care to dance.

CHAMBERLAIN
          But it is your duty as Prince of the realm on the night of
the Grand Ball to dance with every maiden in the Kingdom who is attending
the ball. You cannot avoid your duty.

PRINCE   I'll choose my own duties, Chamberlain. I shall rule this
kingdom, and rule my own heart.

CHAMBERLAIN
          I am not overruling, I'm just advising. It has been
difficult enough for me to help you rule. If you wish to do so alone, I'm
willing to retire to the country this very moment.

PRINCE   Please don't. You know that I am unhappy.

CHAMBERLAIN
          Yes, a country squire ... a manor or two of my own,

shooting, riding to hounds ... that's the life I look forward to. So whenever you're displeased with me, I shall be only too happy to retire.

PRINCE   Listen please, dear Chamberlain. You know I need you desperately. You must not leave me. Why don't you dance with all the pretty maids?

CHAMBERLAIN
             No, no. But I've seen one woman, and she is a dream.

PRINCE   Go and find her.

CHAMBERLAIN
             I shall.

PRINCE   I envy you. I wish I could find the one for me. Maybe she'll never be.

CHAMBERLAIN
             She will, if you look for her.

PRINCE   Maybe so.

CHAMBERLAIN
             There, there, don't despair. The evening has just begun.
Oh, that beautiful woman, if only I could see her now ... alone.
(STEPMOTHER AND STEPSISTERS ENTER AND PRESENT THEMSELVES TO THE
CHAMBERLAIN) Letitia!

STEPMOTHER I am honoured, Chamberlain ... Horatio. My daughters, Lady Angela and Lady Minerva.

CHAMBERLAIN
             Honoured, ladies. (HE PRESENTS THEM TO THE PRINCE) Your Royal Highness, the Lady Letitia and her daughters.

PRINCE   Charmed, ladies.

STEPMOTHER Oh, your Royal Highness, we are greatly honoured.

CHAMBERLAIN
             The Fates have been kind to bring you here, Letitia.

STEPMOTHER The Fates and the Prince's gracious invitation. My daughters have so looked forward to this moment.

CHAMBERLAIN
             I'm sure.

ANGELA   Excuse me, Prince, but my programme has it that you're now to dance with me.

MINERVA   Did I see right, or did you drop your fan?

        MINERVA MANOEUVRES ANGELA OUT OF THE WAY.

CHAMBERLAIN (WHISPERS TO PRINCE) Dance with her.

PRINCE   (WHISPERS) Only if you dance with the mother.

CHAMBERLAIN
          Delighted.

PRINCE   I'll try. (DANCES WITH MINERVA)

ANGELA   Excuse me, Prince, I'm ready now.

          SHE GLARES AT MINERVA, WHO'S DANCING WITH THE PRINCE. ALL
          THREE DANCE TOGETHER - PRINCE AND TWO STEPSISTERS.

CHAMBERLAIN
          Letitia, may I have this dance?

STEPMOTHER I think so. (MUSIC. THEY DANCE) They are a
handsome couple, aren't they?

CHAMBERLAIN
          Of sorts.

STEPMOTHER Do you think the Prince is taken with them?

PRINCE   Not with them, but he is certainly taken with something.

          DANCE ENDS.

PRINCE   Chamberlain, what's happened? Why has the music stopped?

CHAMBERLAIN
          It seems a very beautiful Princess has arrived. She is so
beautiful that even the musicians have stopped playing and are just
looking. She's coming this way.

PRINCE   Are you sure?

CHAMBERLAIN
          Yes, here she is now.

          CINDERELLA ENTERS. SHE TOUCHES HANDS WITH THE PRINCE.
          MUSIC.

PRINCE   Where did you come from?

CINDERELLA From a distant land, but not too far away.

PRINCE   What is your name?

CINDERELLA Whatever you prefer.

PRINCE   Are you a Princess?

CINDERELLA Yes, of many realms.

PRINCE   You're mysterious, yet I know you.

CINDERELLA You know me, as I know you.

PRINCE   Yes, I do, but from where?

CINDERELLA From a lifetime.

PRINCE   I won't ever let you go.

CINDERELLA What would you think of me if I were not a Princess? If I
were a very humble person who was so poor that I had only rags to wear?
Would you dance with me then?

PRINCE   I would dance with you in rags or riches. I only ask that you
love me. Do you?

          THEY DANCE AWAY.

MINERVA   I tell you, Angela, it's disgraceful. Mama's been dancing all
night with that man.

ANGELA   I must say, Minerva, Mama has disappointed me. The food has
disappointed me. I wouldn't mind going home. My feet hurt.

MINERVA   No, we won't. Not until we've danced with the Prince again.
Mama, Mama! Oh, really, she doesn't even see me.

ANGELA   We can't ask the Prince to dance a second time, can we? It
wouldn't be etiquette.

MINERVA   What would you know about etiquette? Let's dance. You lead.

ANGELA   No, you lead. You're older.

MINERVA   Don't raise your voice. You lead.

ANGELA   You lead!

MINERVA   Oh, very well. But warn me so that I don't bump into things.

ANGELA   I will.

          EVERYONE IS NOW DANCING.

ANGELA &
MINERVA   Hello, Mama.

STEPMOTHER Hello, my dears. What are you doing?

ANGELA &
MINERVA   Dancing, we think.

CHAMBERLAIN
          Look at that beautiful Princess.

STEPMOTHER   The Prince is in love. I wonder who she is?

CHAMBERLAIN
            I don't know. I've never seen her before.

STEPMOTHER   (TO STEPSISTERS) Did you see the lovely Princess?

ANGELA &
MINERVA   (TEARFUL) Yes, we did!

CHAMBERLAIN
            What's the matter?

ANGELA   He'll never look at us now.

MINERVA   He may look, but with indifference.

STEPMOTHER She is lovely.

CHAMBERLAIN
            Yes, she is.

CINDERELLA Is it twelve o'clock?

THE CLOCK LIGHTS UP EACH HOUR TILL IT REACHES 12.

PRINCE   Why yes.

CINDERELLA I must go.

SHE EXITS, DROPPING HER SHOE DOWN THE AISLE AS SHE RUNS OUT
THROUGH THE AUDIENCE.

PRINCE   Wait! Tell me your name. Will I ever see you again? She's
gone. I must find her.

HE RUNS AFTER CINDERELLA.

CHAMBERLAIN
            My Prince!

HE RUNS AFTER THE PRINCE DOWN CENTRE AISLE.

STEPMOTHER Don't worry, Prince. The course of true love, they say,
never does run smooth.

MINERVA   I wish I had said that.

ANGELA   You will, Minerva, you will.

MINERVA   Oh, let's go home.

ANGELA   Yes, let's! Mama, do come!

ALL EXIT. PRINCE AND CHAMBERLAIN RE-ENTER.

PRINCE   She's gone. I couldn't find her.

CHAMBERLAIN
          Nor could I. All I saw was a maid weeping on the steps of
the Palace. She was in rags, but a strangely beautiful light encircled her.
She wept bitter tears whilst a pumpkin rolled away down the steps. It was
utter magic.

PRINCE   What can I do? How shall I ever find her? (TO CHILDREN IN
THE AUDIENCE) Can any of you help me? (CHILDREN POINT OUT SLIPPER)
Here is my weapon, stronger than any sword of steel. I will search every
house in the kingdom until I find the maiden who fits this shoe.

CHAMBERLAIN
          I'll join you, less fully perhaps, but none the less I'll join.
I, too, am in search of love.

PRINCE   We start tonight.

CHAMBERLAIN
          Tonight?

PRINCE   Tonight! Aren't we men of action?

CHAMBERLAIN
          Well, yes. Action of sorts, but it's too rash ... too ill-
advised ... too ... too.

PRINCE   Does it matter when our cause is just?

CHAMBERLAIN
          Indeed not.

PRINCE   To our successful search.

PRINCE &
CHAMBERLAIN To victory!

          MUSIC. BOTH EXIT.

CURTAIN

END OF ACT TWO

ACT THREE

SAME SET AS ACT ONE. CURTAIN GOES UP ON **FAIRY GODMOTHER** ALONE ON STAGE.

GODMOTHER   (TO AUDIENCE) I was afraid for a while that my magic wand wouldn't work at all. I must really practise. I used to be so very good. Now let me see, is everything put away? (SHE LOOKS AROUND AND PUTS THINGS INTO PLACE) It's after twelve and there really isn't much I can do. I wonder whether Cinderella did dance with the Prince? (TO MAGIC WAND) The ball will be over shortly and Cinderella is still not here ... oh dear, oh dear ... what can I do ... but wait. Oh magic wand, there are times when I wish I could do better.

(CINDERELLA COMES RUNNING IN)

Thank goodness, you're back.

CINDERELLA   Oh Fairy Godmother – you're still here.

GODMOTHER   I haven't gone anywhere else. You're late.

CINDERELLA   I'm sorry but I ran all the way.

GODMOTHER   Well ... did you dance with him?

CINDERELLA   (IN A DREAM) With the Prince?

GODMOTHER   Who else? Tell me quickly, child.

CINDERELLA   (EXCITED) Oh yes, I danced with him.

GODMOTHER   And is he handsome?

CINDERELLA   Terribly handsome.

GODMOTHER   Is he terrible or is he handsome? He can't be both!

CINDERELLA   He's handsome.

GODMOTHER   Then why didn't you say so in the first place?

CINDERELLA   I did.

GODMOTHER   Children of today ... they just don't speak clearly. Tell me more. Did he like you?

CINDERELLA   I think so. Oh, Fairy Godmother, you have been so kind to me.

GODMOTHER   Never mind the kindness. Tell me about the Prince!

CINDERELLA   And I thank you for everything tonight.

GODMOTHER   Tell me about the Prince!!!

CINDERELLA   It's been the most wonderful evening of my life and I have
this (SHE TAKES OUT THE GLASS SLIPPER) to remember it always.

GODMOTHER   Jolly good. There are times when my magic not working is
better than when it does. Keep that slipper and don't lose it. It's the key
to your kingdom.

CINDERELLA   I shall never lose it.

GODMOTHER   Better hide it before your stepmother and sisters arrive.

CINDERELLA   What will happen next?

GODMOTHER   Ah ... ah ... that's telling. Wait and see.

CINDERELLA   Will I ever see the Prince again?

GODMOTHER   You may ... and now I must go. I have a pressing
appointment.

CINDERELLA   Please Fairy Godmother, just tell me if I'll ever see the Prince
again.

GODMOTHER   Have patience, child ... my scales are still a bit unbalanced. I
must leave. Goodbye ...

     EXITS.

CINDERELLA   Goodbye, dear Fairy Godmother, and come back soon.

     FROM OFFSTAGE WE HEAR THE STEPMOTHER.

STEPMOTHER   Come along, girls ... we've only a few more steps. (THEY
ENTER. THE SISTERS ARE ANGRY BUT THE STEPMOTHER IS NOSTALGIC)
Well ... we're home.

ANGELA   At last. My feet will never recover.

MINERVA   I wish your tongue could be that tired.

     ANGELA GIVES HER AN ILL LOOK.

CINDERELLA   Didn't you enjoy the ball?

MINERVA   Of course we did.

STEPMOTHER   I thought you would be asleep by now.

CINDERELLA   I couldn't wait to hear about the ball.

STEPMOTHER   It was beautiful ... beautiful. But it ended too soon.

ANGELA   Go off to bed, Cinderella, before Mother starts telling you
everything.

STEPMOTHER   Don't you realise what happened, girls?

MINERVA   We do. You danced all night with the Chamberlain.

STEPMOTHER   You should be happy for me.

ANGELA &
MINERVA   What about us?   (THEY WEEP)

CINDERELLA   But tell me, wasn't the Prince there?

ANGELA   Of course he was.

MINERVA   And we danced with him.

ANGELA   Until a beautiful, mysterious Princess arrived.

MINERVA   Who danced with him all night.

ANGELA   The Prince fell madly in love with her.

MINERVA   But at twelve o'clock ... she disappeared.

CINDERELLA   Then what happened!

ANGELA   We decided to go home.

CINDERELLA   (DISAPPOINTED) Oh. ... What was the Prince wearing?

ANGELA   Blue and white.

CINDERELLA   And the Princess?

MINERVA   She was in blue ... no, green ... no, blue ... grey ... no, she
was in mauve.

CINDERELLA   I thought she was in white. (REALISES HER MISTAKE AS
EVERYONE LOOKS AT HER)

TRIO   What?

STEPMOTHER   How would you know?

CINDERELLA   I only thought a Princess would be in white.

MINERVA   Yes, well she was in blue.

ANGELA   And she wore glass slippers ... did you ever hear of anything
so ridiculous?

STEPMOTHER They were beautiful.

CINDERELLA Was she lovely?

ANGELA Not really.

MINERVA But the Prince thought so.

STEPMOTHER Here we talk about the Prince and the Princess ... when we should be thinking about the Chamberlain.

ANGELA Oh, Mama, really!

STEPMOTHER But girls ... it's your future, too.

MINERVA Oh I'm going to bed. (READY FOR BED BY NOW)

STEPMOTHER We should all go to bed. Tomorrow will be a very busy day.

MINERVA Where's the door?

ANGELA Oh very well. I'll show you. This way ...

ALL THREE GIRLS STAGGER OFF.

STEPMOTHER Forward march!

SHE EXITS.

THE SOUND OF THE PRINCE'S BUGLE IS HEARD. **STEPMOTHER** AND **GIRLS** COME RUSHING BACK.

ALL FOUR Trumpets! (WITH STAGED BUSINESS)

STEPMOTHER It's the Chamberlain. I knew he'd come for me. Cinderella, are you here? Off to bed, all of you, and stay in your rooms until I call you.

SISTERS &
CINDERELLA Yes, Mother.

THEY EXIT AS **STEPMOTHER** PREENS HERSELF. WE HEAR A KNOCK ON THE DOOR.

STEPMOTHER Who is it ... at this time of night?

CHAMBERLAIN
        It is I, the Prince's Chamberlain. I order you to open the door by the Royal Command of the Prince himself. (HE ENTERS) Letitia! (COMPLETE CHANGE OF VOICE AND MANNER) I didn't know ... that is ... at this time of night ... I wasn't sure, just where we were going ...

STEPMOTHER Of course you didn't. Won't you come in?

CHAMBERLAIN (EMBARRASSED) Honoured, Lady Letitia. Please forgive the

intrusion ... but the Prince has ordered me to look for a Princess ... at this
time of night.

STEPMOTHER Your presence was never an intrusion. Do sit down.

     THEY LOOK AT EACH OTHER ... TRY TO SAY SOMETHING AND NEITHER
     KNOWS WHAT TO SAY.

CHAMBERLAIN
     Er ... lovely weather we're having.

STEPMOTHER Is it? I mean ... yes it is. There's a beautiful moon.

     SILENCE.

CHAMBERLAIN
     I ... sorry ... it's a bit late.

STEPMOTHER Is it? Er ... maybe it is. (CROSSES TO PIANO AND PLAYS)

CHAMBERLAIN
     I ...

STEPMOTHER Yes? You were saying?

CHAMBERLAIN
     It was easier in our early days when you were never short
of words.

STEPMOTHER I was a foolish girl.

CHAMBERLAIN
     Oh no ... just a spirited one.

STEPMOTHER I suppose ... (SILENCE) You have a message for me from
the Prince?

CHAMBERLAIN
     No ... I have a shoe ... (HE LOOKS AT IT AND FEELS
FOOLISH)

STEPMOTHER Oh ... a glass slipper.

CHAMBERLAIN
     Yes ... everyone who attended the ball must try it on.
Whoever fits this slipper will marry the Prince. Would you ...

STEPMOTHER (CROSS - FORGETTING HERSELF) No, it isn't mine, Horatio.

CHAMBERLAIN
     Oh, Letitia ... you know what I want to say.

STEPMOTHER Yes, but you don't say it!

CHAMBERLAIN (WITH COURAGE) At last we've found each other again. (HE

HURRIEDLY KISSES HER) I don't know why I waited so long.

STEPMOTHER But this is so sudden.

CHAMBERLAIN
          It is not ... (STERNLY) I've waited thirty years.

STEPMOTHER I'm honoured, my Chamberlain ... my Horatio.

CHAMBERLAIN
          Letitia!

     TRUMPET SOUNDS.

BOTH   Trumpets! (STAGED BUSINESS)

CHAMBERLAIN
          The Prince is arriving. Is there anyone here who can try
on the slipper?

STEPMOTHER My daughters ... Girls! Girls, the Prince is arriving.
Quickly, come down ... he's looking for his Princess.

GIRLS (OFFSTAGE)   What did you say?

STEPMOTHER I said, come down here at once. The Prince himself is here,
looking for a Princess.

GIRLS   Anon.

STEPMOTHER I hope the shoe will fit one of them. Let's try to make it fit.

CHAMBERLAIN
          Dear Letitia.

     ANGELA ENTERS – DISHEVELLED BUT EAGER.

ANGELA   I'm here – where's the Prince?

STEPMOTHER Angela, curtsey to the Chamberlain.

ANGELA   But Mama, I thought you said the Prince ...

STEPMOTHER Curtsey, dear, England Expects!

ANGELA   (AS SHE CURTSIES) Honoured, Lord Chamberlain.

     MINERVA FEELS HER WAY INTO THE ROOM AND GOES TO THE
     CHAMBERLAIN AND CURTSIES.

MINERVA   I'm honoured, my Prince.

CHAMBERLAIN
          I'm only the Chamberlain.

MINERVA   Oh ... excuse me ...

        TRUMPETS SOUND.   THE PRINCE ENTERS.

CHAMBERLAIN
            Ladies of the Kingdom, the Prince.

        EVERYONE BOWS.

STEPMOTHER   Honoured, your Royal Highness.

PRINCE   (TAKING ONE LOOK)   I'm sure the slipper will not fit anyone
here.   (STARTS TO EXIT)

CHAMBERLAIN (URGED ON BY STEPMOTHER)   Oh, but we must try.

PRINCE   Very well – you do it.

CHAMBERLAIN (TO MINERVA)   My dear ...   (SHE SITS DOWN AND ALMOST
MISSES THE SEAT OF THE CHAIR.   SHE TRIES THE SHOE)   I'm afraid it
doesn't fit.

MINERVA   Oh, it tickles.   Let's try again.   Mama, Angela!

CHAMBERLAIN
            (HE TRIES THE SHOE AGAIN)   There, you see ... it just
doesn't fit.   Does it?   (TO CHILDREN, WHO SAY, "NO")   I'm sorry.

ANGELA   My turn now.   Arise, Minerva – that means remove your
posterior from the exterior of that seat.   (SHE JUMPS INTO THE CHAIR WITH
GREAT VIGOUR)   Oh it does tickle!   Let's just twist it a bit.   (IT STILL
DOESN'T FIT, NO MATTER HOW HARD SHE TRIES)

CHAMBERLAIN
            Be careful.   You'll break the shoe.

ANGELA   Twist it again.

CHAMBERLAIN
            It just doesn't fit.

ANGELA   (STILL TRYING)   Oh, my ankle ... Cinderella ...   (EVERYONE REACTS
TO HER SLIP)

PRINCE   Cinderella?   Is there someone else here who might try on the
slipper?

STEPMOTHER   Not really ... only a cindermaid.

PRINCE   (WITH A TEASING JEST IN MIND)   Send her here at once.

CHAMBERLAIN
            But my Prince ...

PRINCE   (ASIDE TO THE CHAMBERLAIN)   Hush ... I'll teach them a lesson.

STEPMOTHER   Cinderella ... please come down.

CINDERELLA   (ENTERING)   Did you call me, mother?

STEPMOTHER   Yes, dear.

CINDERELLA   Oh, the Prince.   (SHE CURTSIES)

STEPMOTHER   Yes, dear.

PRINCE   You may try on the slipper.   (AGAIN HE DOES THIS TO SHOW
THE GIRLS AND **STEPMOTHER** HIS GRACIOUSNESS)   A Prince's proclamation
must be honoured by all.   (TO CHILDREN)   Isn't that so?   (CHILDREN SAY,
"YES")

CHAMBERLAIN
            True ... true.   Now, won't you sit down?

PRINCE   No, Chamberlain.   I'll try this myself, my dear.

     CINDERELLA SITS DOWN.   THE GIRLS ARE FURIOUS, **STEPMOTHER**
     APPEASING A SIMPLE-MINDED **PRINCE** ... SO SHE THINKS.   **CINDERELLA**
     DRAMATICALLY PUTS HER FOOT INTO THE SLIPPER AND EVERYONE
     LOOKS UP IN SURPRISE.

STEPMOTHER   Oh no.

     SHE FAINTS.   THE **CHAMBERLAIN** CATCHES HER.   THE GIRLS CRY ON
     EACH OTHER'S SHOULDERS.   BUT IT IS THE **PRINCE** WHO IS MOST
     STARTLED.   FOR WHAT HE THOUGHT WOULD BE A JEST HAS TURNED
     INTO A TRUTH.

ALL   It fits!

PRINCE   (HE CANNOT BELIEVE IT)   You are the Princess ... the
mysterious Princess?

CINDERELLA   Yes, I am.   You don't recognise me in my rags.   Here ... here
is the other slipper.   (SHE TAKES IT OUT TO PROVE HERSELF TO THE
PRINCE ... HURT BY HIS FAILURE TO RECOGNISE HER)

PRINCE   (WITH LOVE FOR THE FIRST TIME)   You are my Princess.

ANGELA   She's the Princess.

MINERVA   Now she'll marry the Prince.

     THE **FAIRY GODMOTHER** APPEARS.

GODMOTHER   Hear! Hear!

ALL   Hail, Britannia!

CINDERELLA   Oh, Fairy Godmother ... what shall I do. My Prince has seen
me in rags, and didn't know me.

GODMOTHER   Go up to your room and dress yourself.

CINDERELLA   But I have no other clothes.

GODMOTHER   You'll find your dress all prepared for you. Go now.
(CINDERELLA EXITS) As for you ... (VERY STERNLY) ... my Prince. You
did not live up to your promise.

PRINCE   (SLIGHTLY FEARFUL, AND TO KEEP THE HUMOUR OF THE
MOMENT) Forgive me, Fairy Godmother, for not knowing my Princess even
in her rags.

GODMOTHER   Then this is the wedding day?

PRINCE   It is, and I'm the most fortunate of men.

GODMOTHER   Let this be a lesson to you, Stepmother and haughty sisters,
who lived with a Princess and never knew it. To you, Prince, to look
beyond the rags to see the riches of the heart. Chamberlain, proclaim the
Wedding Day. We will have a march through the town.

CHAMBERLAIN
             Your Highness ... may I ... that is ... can there be ... Is it
possible ... to have a double proclamation ... for me as well?

STEPMOTHER   Oh, Horatio.

CHAMBERLAIN
             You must have guessed.

ANGELA   Guessed ... she plotted the whole ruddy thing.

STEPMOTHER   Angela.

MINERVA   She means Cinderella, I'm sure.

PRINCE   It doesn't matter if the Victory is Love. (LAUGHINGLY SAID TO
THE FAIRY GODMOTHER)

GIRLS   Love ... Oh, Father. (THEY TAKE HIS ARMS)

CHAMBERLAIN
             Oh, my. I will be your father.

GODMOTHER   Now I must choose a few maids and lads of honour for the
new Princess. Let me see. I think you ... (CHILDREN IN THE AUDIENCE)
and you ... and you ... and you. There, we have enough now. You must
stand in a straight line and when our new Princess Cinderella enters ... you
must all bow and curtsey. (SHE ASKS EACH CHILD ITS NAME AND THEY ARE
INTRODUCED TO EACH CHARACTER)

PRINCE   Fairy Godmother, I think we are ready for the Wedding!

(**CINDERELLA** ENTERS ALL AGLOW) Here is my Princess. You may all wish us happiness and long life.

CHILDREN FROM AUDIENCE CHEER.

GODMOTHER Then God bless you all.

MUSIC. **CINDERELLA** TAKES THE **PRINCE'S** HAND AS THEY BEGIN THE MARCH DOWN THE AISLE, TO BE FOLLOWED BY EVERYONE ELSE INCLUDING THE CHILDREN.

THE WEDDING MARCH AND THE FINALE DANCE IS DONE.

> Land of hope and glory,
> Ne'er our prayer forget,
> God who made thee mighty
> Make thee mightier yet;
> God who made thee mighty
> Make thee mightier yet.

REPEAT AND FLAGS FLY.

CURTAIN

END OF PLAY

STEPMOTHER'S HOUSE

FOYER TO THE BALLROOM

ANGELA
MINERVA
CHAMBERLAIN
STEPMOTHER

CINDERELLA
PRINCE
FAIRY GODMOTHER
CINDERELLA
AT THE BALL

THE CRICKET THEATRE AND BLANCHE MARVIN

PRESENT:

THE MERRI MIMES'

THE LITTLEST TAILOR

BY BLANCHE MARVIN

DIRECTED & STAGED - RICHARD MAZZA

LIGHTS & STAGE MANAGER- STEVEN MILLER

COSTUMES- LOHR WILSON   SCENERY- JOE STELL

CAST

LITTLEST TAILOR- PAT McKENNA
CASSY   - KATHY KELLY
PRISCILLA   - JANET NIGHTINGALE
UNCLE BEN   - BURT HEYMAN
GIANT FORK   - BOB SHIARELLA
GIANT KNIFE   - TONY RISTOFF

AT THE CRICKET THEATRE
162 SECOND AVE (at 10th st.
OR-4 3960
Performances : 1, 2:30, 4 pm

THE LITTLEST TAILOR IS A MUSICAL DONE AS A
MINSTREL SHOW IN THE TYPICAL VAUDEVILLEAN
MANNER. IT POKES FUN AT THE POST-CIVIL WAR
PERIOD.... WHAT HAPPENS TO EACH OF THE
CHARACTERS IS SHEER FUN - SO LAUGH ALONG WITH
US - IN THIS FARCICAL STORY.

LITTLEST TAILOR

Minstrel Style Theatre

CAST OF CHARACTERS

Ashley   - Tailor

Cassy   - Creole Girl

Uncle Ben - Plantation Owner

Priscilla - His Daughter

Giant Fork

Giant Knife

Place: Deep South, USA

       Act 1   - Crumbling Plantation,
               Veranda and Garden

       Act 11 - The Swamp

Time: Post Civil War, USA

ACT ONE

SCENE ONE

> SCENE OPENS ON A TYPICAL SOUTHERN MANSION VERANDA...AND GAR-
> DEN. IT HAS THE FADED ELEGANCE OF THE POST CIVIL WAR ERA.
> THE GARDEN FURNITURE IS OVERTURNED. THE GENERAL FEELING IS
> CHAOS ADDED TO THE SHABBY GENTILITY. THE GARDEN HAS A BIG,
> SWEEPING CYPRESS WHICH OVERHANGS THE VERANDA. A CREOLE GIRL
> NAMED **CASSY** APPEARS. IT IS EARLY MORNING. **SHE** IS A SWEET
> YET MYSTERIOUS CREATURE. **SHE** LOOKS ABOUT AND SIGHS AS **SHE**
> SEES THE OVERTURNED CHAIRS AND TABLE. **SHE** STARTS TO PUT
> THINGS RIGHT.

CASSY   Just look at this. Poor, poor Uncle Ben...Priscilla
has had one of her temper tantrums again. Some gentleman caller
didn't propose last night. If only...only someone would marry
her, Uncle Ben would have one problem less. Oh, life is very
hard for him. The spirits are making trouble for us. I know it.
(MUSIC) If I could only speak to them and make it right again.
Swamp Spirits do you hear me...if you do...listen...listen. (SHE
DOES A VOODOO-KIND OF POSITION AND INCANTATION) Uncle Ben is a
good...good man. A Born Gentleman! It's hard...so hard for
him...to keep this house going...and you haven't tried to help
him. He needs your help. You've played mischief with him...too
long...what with stealing the chickens. We ain't got no field
help to plant cotton no more. We need the chickens... to sell.
So please, please stop. And maybe send us some good, too. Help
us marry Priscilla even though she's no dowry.

> UNCLE BEN COMES IN AS HE SEES AND HEARS **CASSY** PRAYING. HE
> IS A TRUE SOUTHERN GENTLEMAN...SOFT, KIND, HUMANE.

UNCLE BEN   Cassy...that is very good of you...to pray for us.
But spirits won't help. We need more than that.

CASSY   They can change your luck.

UNCLE BEN   (HOLDS **CASSY**) Cassy, I've raised you like my own
daughter...since you were a baby and still you believe in
spirits. There are none, child.

CASSY   (SWAMP POSITION) There are...I tell you. We Creoles
know. They live in the cypress swamp. And when night
falls...they come out...creeping to where you least suspect.
(BACK TO **UNCLE BEN**)

UNCLE BEN   Oh Cassy. Someone's been stealing the chickens but
it's those darn Yankee Carpet-Baggers. If I catch one...I'll
make him pay.

CASSY   Ain't no Carpet-Baggers...I tell you it's those
monster swamp spirits.

UNCLE BEN   They steal from the poor South, those demons. Oh, if
I could only put my hands on whoever it is.

CASSY   (TAKES CARDS FROM POCKET, SQUATS, THEN PLACES THEM ON

FLOOR) I'm going to trap them.

UNCLE BEN   Why don't you.   Then let me decide whether it's the spirit or the flesh.

CASSY   (LOOKING AT ONE CARD) Oh...I see, I see...a man...a little man...and he will lead us to the swamp.

UNCLE BEN   I wish that little man would want to marry Priscilla. What with saving the house...the chicken stealing...and Priscilla not being married...I'm fighting my own Civil War...all over again. (SITS)

CASSY   (BEHIND TABLE) This little man...will save us, I'm sure.

UNCLE BEN   Will he marry Priscilla...without a dowry?

CASSY   No...it'll be more than that. He'll lead us to where we'll all find the answers. (PUTS CARDS ON TABLE)

UNCLE BEN   That doesn't help, Cassy.

CASSY   (SITS AT TABLE LOOKING AT CARDS) Oh! I see, I see...

        PRISCILLA ENTERS...A BIG, AWKWARD, UGLY GIRL. ALL THE
        THINGS THAT A SOUTHERN BELLE SHOULD NOT BE.

PRISCILLA   Will I ever see...a wedding ring?

UNCLE BEN   (CROSSES TO PRISCILLA) Oh, good morning, Priscilla.

PRISCILLA   What's good about it?

UNCLE BEN   It's warm...the sun's shining.

PRISCILLA   (POINTS TO FLY OFF LEFT. SHE FOLLOWS FLIES. SWATS. MISSES) And we're surrounded by flies...

UNCLE BEN   What happened to your gentleman caller...last evening? (FOLLOWING PRISCILLA)

PRISCILLA   (TURNS SHARP) He left.

UNCLE BEN   I guessed that. But isn't he going to call again?

PRISCILLA   I don't guess so. (SEES FLY. FOLLOWS. SWATS. MISSES) A girl without a dowry isn't very interesting.

UNCLE BEN   (FOLLOWING PRISCILLA) Honey, you wait and see. Mr. Right will come along and want you with or without a dowry. Maybe you're too anxious.

PRISCILLA   (TURNS SHARP) What would you be at my age? (SEES FLY AND SWATS. LOOKS TO FLOOR) I got him! (BOTH **UNCLE BEN AND PRISCILLA** ARE JUBILANT OVER FLY KILLING) About all I can catch round here are flies.

UNCLE BEN   I don't know about that. Cassy's been looking at the cards and she sees something very good for you.

CASSY   (READING CARDS ALL THIS TIME SHE SUDDENLY STANDS UP) Oh, Priscilla...I see the answer...here in the cards. It tells me to leave...now.

PRISCILLA   (RUNS TO TABLE) To where?

CASSY   Ah...I mustn't say. But I will follow directions and go. The cards have unfolded a plan...a plan which I must follow...all'll be well. (SHE PUTS THE CARDS AWAY AND STARTS WALKING OFF STAGE)

UNCLE BEN   (TO **CASSY**) Are you really going?

CASSY   Yes...right now... Remember no-one must follow me.

UNCLE BEN   When will you be back?

CASSY   By tonight or tomorrow. Goodbye.

PRISCILLA   (RUNS TO **CASSY**) She means it. Cassy, just give me an idea 'bout the plan. Do I have to do anything?

CASSY   No...honey...you stay here and look pretty. I shall return. (EXITS)

PRISCILLA   Well, at least it's exciting... (SHE STARTS HICCOUGHING. WALKS TO **UNCLE BEN**) Frighten me!

UNCLE BEN   Why?

PRISCILLA   (IN **UNCLE BEN'S** FACE) I can't stop hiccoughing.

UNCLE BEN   Some Yankee will marry you.

PRISCILLA   (HICCOUGHING STILL) That don't frighten me.

UNCLE BEN   (FOLLOWS **PRISCILLA**) You'll never marry.

PRISCILLA   (TURNS TO **UNCLE BEN** AND STARTS CRYING) Oh, I can't bear that! (SHE STARTS TO THROW PILLOWS OFF CHAIRS. PICKS UP CHAIR)

UNCLE BEN   (STOPPING HER) I was only frightening you. See, you've stopped hiccoughing. (PRISCILLA PUTS CHAIR DOWN ON HER FOOT ACCIDENTALLY INSTEAD OF FLOOR) Why are you limping?

PRISCILLA   (REFUSING TO BLAME HER CLUMSINESS) These shoes are too tight. I can only wear them for a little while.

UNCLE BEN   Why don't you have a proper fit?

PRISCILLA   I have fits all the time but it don't help. See! (SHE GOES INTO A TIRADE)

UNCLE BEN   I mean for your shoes.

PRISCILLA   (STOPS CRYING. CROSSES TO **UNCLE BEN**) Buy me a new pair. I've had these for months.

UNCLE BEN   You've only worn them now and then.

PRISCILLA   (THROWS ARMS AROUND **UNCLE BEN**. HE BENDS OVER. **SHE HELPS HIM** UP) But Daddy, I'm a growing girl.

UNCLE BEN   Yes, of course. We'll get new ones for your wedding.

PRISCILLA   (CRYING) I shall have holes in the soles by then.

UNCLE BEN   Do stop this carrying on. After all...no daughter of mine will remain an old maid. (**PRISCILLA** laughs) I hope.

PRISCILLA   (ANGRY) You're afraid I might be. I knew it...I knew it! (**SHE STARTS CRYING, HICCOUGHING, FOLLOWED BY TANTRUMS**)

UNCLE BEN   (**SLAPPING HER**) Stop it. This instant. After all, Cassy should return with some plan or other.

 MUSIC. THEY STAGGER WITH EACH OTHER. PRISCILLA'S TANTRUM AND HICCOUGHING CONTINUE AS SHE PICKS UP A CHAIR, ABOUT TO THROW IT.

FAST CURTAIN

SCENE TWO

 MUSIC. SAME AS SCENE ONE. ONLY IT IS DARK. A LIGHT GRADUALLY BRIGHTENS ONE CORNER. CASSY ENTERS ON TIP-TOE HOLDING A LANTERN. SHE IS FOLLOWED BY A POOR-LOOKING YOUNG MAN. SHE KEEPS SHUSHING HIM. THEY SNEAK DOWN THE AISLE. THE YOUNG MAN IS CASSY'S INTENDED HUSBAND, A TAILOR, NAMED ASHLEY.

CASSY   (ON FORSTAGE - LOOKING AROUND) No-one must hear us yet.

TAILOR   We meet in secret...part in secret. Let's stop this pretending. Marry me now!

CASSY   How can I when I keep telling you the trouble Uncle Ben is in.

CURTAIN OPENS

TAILOR   Then why did you bring me all this way to the house?

CASSY   (PUTS LANTERN ON TABLE) I have a plan to capture those evil monster spirits in the cypress swamp. Then everything'll be fine again. We'll stop the stealing and Uncle Ben can save enough money to take care of the house and marry off Priscilla too.

 MUSIC. THEY TANGO DANCE TO FLY SWATTING AS THEY TALK.

TAILOR   Why don't you forget about Spirits, Uncle Ben and

Priscilla. Just marry me. Flies! I hate flies! (BRUSHES OFF A FLY)

CASSY   If Uncle Ben knew I loved you, he'd want me to marry you. (DANCE STOPS) But I can't leave Uncle Ben. He needs my help.

TAILOR   So do I. (**HE** BRUSHES AWAY ANOTHER FLY)

CASSY   Then capture the Swamp spirits.

TAILOR   How?

CASSY   Sew them up in a bag.

TAILOR   Why?

CASSY   Then I'd give them a good scare and make them change Uncle Ben's luck. (SWATS FLY)

TAILOR   And after that?

CASSY   I'd let them go and get to work.

TAILOR   And they wouldn't change their mind?

CASSY   Oh no...not to me, they wouldn't.

TAILOR   Think of our future. (BRUSHES OFF A FLY)

CASSY   I'm too worried.

TAILOR   (NOW JUST SWATTING FLIES) I'll catch this...by golly. (JUMPS ON CHAIR)

CASSY   Oh, Ashley...now someone is sure to hear us. If Uncle Ben finds you, he'll know about us. Go hide.

TAILOR   (STANDING ON CHAIR) Not till I kill this group here. Look 1,2,3,4,5,6,7... (HE HITS FLIES WITH SUCH FORCE HE PRACTI-CALLY BREAKS HIS WRIST) Oh, my hand...but I caught them. Seven at one blow! Imagine. (VERY LOUD) I killed seven at one blow!

CASSY   Please go before they catch you. (**BOTH** START OFF)

UNCLE BEN   (OFF STAGE) Who's there?

  MUSIC. TOO LATE...LIGHTS GO ON. **UNCLE BEN** COMES OUT WITH LANTERN AND RIFLE IN HAND. FINDS **ASHLEY**. HE AIMS TO SHOOT. SEES **CASSY**. STOPS.

UNCLE BEN   Cassy! I'm so glad it's you. Son, I heard you when you called out, "Killed seven with one blow".

CASSY   (HESITANT) Yes, Uncle Ben, this is...

UNCLE BEN   (STILL DISBELIEVING AND SLIGHTLY AMUSED) So you're the little man in the cards.

CASSY   Yes, the little man in the cards.

          PRISCILLA ENTERS. TAILOR LOOKS AT UNCLE BEN, PUZZLED.

PRISCILLA   Man! Did I hear someone say, "Man"... Oh, there he
is.

CASSY   (TO TAILOR) Ah, yes...there he is.

UNCLE BEN   And to think for a moment I thought you were a darn
Yankee Carpet-Bagger. (SLAPS TAILOR ON BACK PUSHING HIM TO
PRISCILLA).

PRISCILLA   A man!

UNCLE BEN   (TAILOR GOES BACK TO UNCLE BEN) Seven at one blow.
Now all you have to do is one at seven blows.

TAILOR   I'm sure...I could kill one...with seven blows.

UNCLE BEN   (HAND ON TAILOR'S SHOULDER) I knew it. They didn't
happen to be Yankees, did they?

TAILOR   Oh no...they were Southern.

UNCLE BEN   They must have been pretty terrible.

CASSY   They were.

UNCLE BEN   Well, you're a brave man.

TAILOR   Not really.

UNCLE BEN   Anyone that can kill any seven of any kind at one
blow is a brave soldier.

TAILOR   (CROSSES TO CASSY) I'm not a soldier...only a tailor
from town.

CASSY   It don't matter, if you have courage. (HOLDS TAILOR
TAKING FIRM STAND) The cards have chosen you... (TO TAILOR) to
go to the Cypress Swamp.

TAILOR   OOOOOOh!!!

UNCLE BEN   (GRABS TAILOR'S RIGHT ARM) Don't be humble...I know
you can do it. (TAILOR IS PULLED BACK AND FORTH BY UNCLE BEN AND
PRISCILLA)

PRISCILLA   (GRABS TAILOR'S LEFT ARM) You can't do this, Cassy!

UNCLE BEN   (PULLS TAILOR) Why not?

PRISCILLA   (PULLS TAILOR IN TEARS) Why he might never come
back.

UNCLE BEN   (PULLS TAILOR) Never you mind. Cassy knows what
she's doing.

PRISCILLA   (STARTS OFF) I do mind. I'll run away...that's what I'll do.

TAILOR   (STARTS TO FOLLOW **HER** BUT TURNS BACK TO **CASSY**) I'll go with you! No...better the swamp.

UNCLE BEN   (STOPS **TAILOR**) You are the man in the cards that Cassy saw?

TAILOR   (TO **CASSY**) Oh, but you don't quite understand... Cassy...

UNCLE BEN   No, I don't. I don't know where or how she found you.

TAILOR   Well sir... (**HE** LOOKS TO **CASSY** FOR HELP BUT NO HELP OFFERED) It's a long story.

UNCLE BEN   But Cassy brought you here...for whatever reason!

PRISCILLA   (POINTING TO **HERSELF**) For me!

    CASSY, TAILOR AND **UNCLE BEN** STAND IN STRAIGHT LINE FACING AUDIENCE.

CASSY   (PLEADING TO **TAILOR**) I have brought you here to help Uncle Ben.

TAILOR   But...But...But...

UNCLE BEN   Is there another reason?

PRISCILLA   (CROSSES TO **UNCLE BEN**) For me! (PRISCILLA STILL KEEPS ON SAYING "ME". NO ONE LISTENS)

TAILOR   (LOOKS TO **CASSY** WHO GOES INTO HYPNOTIC TRANCE. TAILOR IS CAUGHT) BBBu...

CASSY   (HYPNOTICALLY) There is no other reason.

PRISCILLA   For me!

CASSY   He'll capture the monster spirits and win!

UNCLE BEN   No Cassy, not the spirits...but those darn Yankee Carpet-Baggers, those chicken stealers. May the best man win. (SHAKES **TAILOR'S** HAND)

PRISCILLA   (SHAKES **TAILOR'S** HAND) May I win the best man.

TAILOR   And I don't know what or who or where there is to win anything!

    MUSIC: RIGOLETTO QUARTET - SONG AND DANCE - EVERYONE

SONG - TO THE SWAMP

TAILOR   Must I go to the swamp?
It is so cold and damp

                        Why do I have to tramp
                        Off to that muddy swamp?

UNCLE BEN   Here is your lighted lamp
                   For your trip to the swamp

CASSY   Don't let your spirits damp
                   Remember that you're the champ

PRISCILLA   Oh but I want him
                   Oh but I need him
                   Oh but I love him

                             <u>QUARTET</u>
PRISCILLA & TAILOR   UNCLE BEN & CASSY
          No no don't let him go   Yes yes off he
                                                     must go
          No no don't let him go   Yes yes off he
                                                     must go
          Noooooooooo don't let   Yeeeeeeeeees he
                    him go   must go

TAILOR   You two go to the swamp

CASSY   Remember that you're the champ

PRISCILLA   Why look he's got a cramp

UNCLE BEN   Don't talk just take the lamp

TAILOR   Oh but she wants me
                   Oh but she needs me

PRISCILLA   Oh but I love him.

                   <u>DUET OF PRISCILLA & TAILOR</u>
TAILOR   Don't let me go

PRISCILLA   Don't let him go

                             <u>QUARTET</u>
PRISCILLA & TAILOR   UNCLE BEN AND CASSY
          No no don't let me go   Yes yes off he
                                                     must go
          No don't let him go   Yes yes off he
                                                     must go

              - END OF SONG AND DANCE -

**TAILOR IS PUSHED OFF TO THE SWAMP AFTER BEING GIVEN SOME
CHEESE, A LAMP, A ROPE AND A GUN. ALL THE OTHERS WAVE
GOODBYE.**

                        FAST CURTAIN

                        END OF ACT ONE

ACT TWO

TAILOR   (COMING DOWN AISLE TO MUSIC) All that talk of my
capturing a swamp spirit...or a Carpet-Bagger and then everything
will be just dandy. All I'll do is get good and wet...and tired.
About the most I'll catch is a cold. I don't know about Cassy
and her crazy plan.   If she's not afraid of the swamp
spirits...why didn't she come? But no. It was a little man she
saw in the cards, so I have to do it!!

          MUSIC. CURTAINS OPEN ON MUSIC CUE AS **ALLIGATOR** CROSSES IN
          FRONT OF CURTAINS, TERRIFYING THE **TAILOR**. THE **ALLIGATOR**
          DISAPPEARS. CURTAINS HAVE OPENED. THE SCENE IS A CYPRESS
          SWAMP IN THE BAYOU. IT IS DARK AND EERIE. ANIMAL SOUNDS
          ARE HEARD. THE FOG CAN ALMOST BE FELT. OUR LITTLE **TAILOR**
          HAS BEEN WALKING A LONG TIME. ON STAGE, THERE ARE TWO
          TREES, A STONE BENCH AND A TREE STUMP. THERE ARE TWIGS ON
          THE BENCH. THERE ARE STONES BEHIND THE STUMP AND A CUT-OUT
          BIRD ON THE TREE. THE **ALLIGATOR** CAN MAKE A QUICK APPEARANCE
          AND DISAPPEARANCE, ONCE AGAIN, FRIGHTENING THE **TAILOR**. HE
          IS EXHAUSTED AND AS **HE** SETTLES DOWN...

TAILOR   I'm tired, but I'm afraid to go to sleep. I wish I
were home by a nice, warm fire with music playing. Maybe if I...

          HE STARTS TO DROWSE. MUSIC. MOON SPOTLIGHT COMES ON. HE
          FALLS ASLEEP DESPITE THE NOISES WHICH FRIGHTEN **HIM**. AS HE
          SNORES A **GIANT** APPEARS. HE IS A BIG MAN DRESSED IN A DERBY,
          LOOSE JACKET, SHARP VEST AND TROUSERS. TAKING A BRANCH OF
          LEAVES **HE** TICKLES THE **TAILOR'S** NOSE. THIS CAUSES THE **TAILOR**
          TO LAUGH AND LAUGH. EVERY ONCE IN A WHILE HE GRABS OUT IN
          HIS SLEEP. **TAILOR:** "FLIES ALL OVER THE PLACE." FINALLY HE
          REALISES THAT THIS IS NOT A FLY. HE TURNS SLOWLY, DOES A
          DOUBLE-TAKE AS **HE** SEES THE **GIANT**. HE LOOKS UP...AND
          UP...AND UP. HE FEELS THE **GIANT'S** LEG. HIS HAND MOVES
          CAUTIOUSLY UP AND DOWN. HE GULPS OUT, "HELP!"

GIANT KNIFE (LAUGHS) I'm quite a fly, eh?

TAILOR   (PRETENDING TO LAUGH) Well, I must say, I thought it
was a fly tickling me. But you look like...just a very big man.

GIANT KNIFE I am...I'm a giant!

TAILOR   Ain't you a Yankee Carpet-Bagger?

GIANT KNIFE No...I'm a giant.

TAILOR   Well, maybe a giant Carpet-Bagger!

GIANT KNIFE Now get this straight. I'm a plain giant... (TO
AUDIENCE) in hiding.

TAILOR   Well, you look like a giant. Only I thought they
were in story books. You're not a swamp spirit?

GIANT KNIFE (FRUSTRATED) No...I'm a giant!!!

TAILOR   I wasn't prepared for this. I thought it'd be a Yankee...or a spirit...or the truth of the matter...a snake... (**GIANT** BEGINS STALKING HIM AS **TAILOR** CROSSES TO STUMP) but now that I've found you...well...I don't know anymore. You sure look like a giant.

GIANT KNIFE You look like a good supper for me. Not the main course, just as a starter.

TAILOR   (SITTING ON STUMP) I'm not very tasty. Wouldn't you like some of my cheese? (TAKES OUT CHEESE)

GIANT KNIFE (Laughs) No!

TAILOR   No. I'm skin and bones.

GIANT KNIFE Well now, that's very interesting, Mr...what's your name?

TAILOR   Mr. Bones.

GIANT KNIFE (LAUGHS. CROSSES TO **TAILOR** AND TICKLES **HIM**) Mr. Bones, that's what you are, skin and bones.

TAILOR   Don't laugh at me, please. (STEPS DOWNSTAGE IN MINSTREL STYLE) What's your name?

GIANT KNIFE Knife...Mr. Knife.

TAILOR   Mr. Knife? Like a knife that cuts?

GIANT KNIFE Never touch the stuff.

TAILOR   Why not?

GIANT KNIFE Because I use my hands.

BOTH   Very funny, very funny!

GIANT KNIFE Now tell me, Mr. Bones, what shall we do with you?

TAILOR   (TO AUDIENCE) I know this routine. It's like the minstrel show I once saw on the Showboat. Watch me. He'll fall for it and let me go free! (MUSIC) Now tell me, Mr. Knife, have you any plans?

GIANT KNIFE Yes, Mr. Bones.

TAILOR   What is it, Mr. Knife? Elucidate. Elucidate.

GIANT KNIFE Eat you, Mr. Bones.

TAILOR   Without a fork and knife?

GIANT KNIFE We can always try.

DANCE COMBINATION PERFORMED HERE.

TAILOR   What was that dinner I saw you with last night?

GIANT KNIFE That was no dinner, that was my knife. (HE LAUGHS)

TAILOR   Very funny...very funny!   (**HE HAS A SUDDEN THOUGHT**)
If I can prove I'm stronger than you, will you let me go free?
(**TAILOR CROSSES TO STUMP**)

GIANT KNIFE If you can prove that, I'll let you go free. Look at
Mr. Bones trying to be stronger than a giant.

TAILOR   (PICKING UP STONE)   Take this stone and squeeze it
until it breaks, Mr. Knife.

GIANT KNIFE Very well, Mr. Bones.   (**HE TAKES THE STONE AND
SQUEEZES...NOTHING HAPPENS. MUSIC**)   Look at that...blood out of
a stone. (LAUGHS AT HIS JOKE)

TAILOR   (CROSSES TO STUMP)   Not a dent, Mr. Knife. Watch me.
(WHISPERING TO AUDIENCE) I'll use my cheese. (**HE TAKES THE
CHEESE IN PLACE OF THE STONE AND SQUEEZES**) Look a'here, Mr.
Knife. (**MUSIC. TAILOR THROWS CHEESE AWAY**)

GIANT KNIFE (SHOCKED)   Well, I'll be a monkey's uncle. You're a
tough little feller. By the way, do you know the story of the
three waters. (**HE TURNS TO AUDIENCE**) Do you?

TAILOR   No, I don't know the story of the three waters.

GIANT KNIFE Well, well, well! (LAUGHS)

TAILOR   Very funny...very funny!   Shall we continue, Mr.
Knife.

GIANT KNIFE Yeah, Mr. Bones.

TAILOR   (**TAILOR PICKS UP STONE AND GIVES IT TO GIANT KNIFE**)
Take that stone, Mr. Knife, and see how high you can throw it.

GIANT KNIFE Very well, well, well, Mr. Bones. (**MUSIC. HE THROWS
STONE INTO AIR WHICH THEN FALLS AT HIS FEET. IT CAN BE A MIMED
ACTION**)

TAILOR   Now watch me, Mr. Knife. (**MUSIC. HE EXCHANGES THE
STONE FOR THE BIRD. HE THROWS THE BIRD INTO THE AIR AND IT FLIES
AWAY. THE CUT-OUT BIRD IS ON A WIRE SO THAT IT CAN FLY. THE
TAILOR STANDS ON THE TREE STUMP TO DO THE TRICK**) What do you
think of that, Mr. Knife?

GIANT KNIFE Great, great, great, Mr. Bones.

TAILOR   Now that I've won, will you let me go free as you
promised?

GIANT KNIFE (TO TAILOR)   I can't exactly break a promise. But
first let's go to my brother's house and if you prove you're
stronger than he is, why then, I'll let you go.

TAILOR   But a bargain's a bargain.

GIANT KNIFE (PUSHES TAILOR) Let's get going, or I might change my mind and eat you here all by myself.

TAILOR   (WEEPILY) Seven at one blow.   Seven at one blow.

GIANT KNIFE What did you say?

TAILOR   I said, "Seven at one blow".

GIANT KNIFE What for?

TAILOR   I don't know. I just killed them.

GIANT KNIFE You did?

TAILOR   Yes, I did.

GIANT KNIFE Why didn't you tell me that before?

TAILOR   You didn't ask.

GIANT KNIFE Wait till my brother hears that.

TAILOR   (AS THEY ARE MARCHING) What's your brother's name? (GIANT KNIFE LAUGHS SO HARD HE CAN'T SAY THE NAME) Don't tell me, then.

GIANT KNIFE It's... (HE LAUGHS)

TAILOR   I know, Mr. Fork.

GIANT KNIFE It is...Fork!

TAILOR   Your house's name is Diner, I suppose.

GIANT KNIFE No, that was my Mother's name.

TAILOR   Well, where are we going?

GIANT KNIFE To Diner's house. (GRABS HIM HARD)

TAILOR   (STARTS OFF BUT GIANT KNIFE CATCHES HIM) Oh, no! What else can I do?

   MUSIC. THEY DO A SHUFFLE DANCE AS THEY WALK. THE TAILOR IS TERRIFIED, GIANT KNIFE, FEROCIOUS. THEY COME UPON A TREE AND WALK IN.   THIS MAY BE DONE IN SEVERAL WAYS...EITHER BY DRAWING CURTAINS WHICH THEY WALK THROUGH AND START THE NEXT SCENE OR COMICALLY SEEING THE STAGE MANAGER SET UP A SIGN THAT SAYS, "DINER'S HOUSE" ON THE BIG TREE. DANCE ENDS.

GIANT KNIFE Fork, Fork, where are you?

GIANT FORK (OFFSTAGE) I'm out here.

GIANT KNIFE What are you doing?

GIANT FORK Practising my giant steps. (**TAILOR** LAUGHS. **GIANT FORK** ENTERS FROM BEHIND A TREE, BELLIGERENTLY. HE SHOULD BE MORE RIDICULOUS IN **HIS** CLOTHES THAN **HIS** BROTHER. HE CROSSES TO **TAILOR**) You think I was joking?

TAILOR (SHAKILY) Yes.

GIANT FORK Who asked you? Who is he?

GIANT KNIFE Someone I picked up along the way.

GIANT FORK Which way?

GIANT KNIFE Any way.

GIANT FORK That's no way! (BOTH GIANTS SLAP **TAILOR**) Let's do Giant Steps. Noway, you call. (**TAILOR** FALLS TO THE GROUND AND STARTS TO CRAWL AWAY BUT **GIANT FORK** CATCHES HIM)

TAILOR Mr. Bones is the name.

GIANT KNIFE Mr. Skin and Bones. (HE LAUGHS)

TAILOR You may take two steps... But why are we playing Giant Steps?

GIANT FORK (STALKS **TAILOR** TO STUMP) Playing? Who dares to call it play?

TAILOR I don't know. I mean...why do you...we...do it?

GIANT KNIFE (CROSSES TO STUMP) You tell him, Fork.

<u>**KNEE SLAPPING ROUTINE**</u>

GIANT FORK Tell him what?

GIANT KNIFE About the...you know what.

GIANT FORK What, <u>what</u> do you mean?

GIANT KNIFE About the ceremony, that's what.

GIANT FORK You mean <u>the</u> ceremony?

GIANT KNIFE Yeah...<u>the</u> ceremony.

GIANT FORK Very well, Gentlemen, be seated! (ALL SIT) "Take a Giant Step" is the most important ceremony that giants have.

TAILOR (CHEWING HIS NAILS) Ceremony for what?

GIANT KNIFE You tell him, Fork.

GIANT FORK Ceremony before cooking.

TAILOR You mean cooking for eating?

GIANT KNIFE Tell him more, Fork.

GIANT FORK   Ceremony before cooking for eating...you!

TAILOR   (FALLS TO GROUND THEN RUNS TO CENTER STAGE)   That's
what I thought you meant.   But you see, Knife made a bargain with
me.

GIANT FORK   (CATCHING **TAILOR**)   But I didn't.   Now start calling.
(HE PLACES **TAILOR** ON STUMP THEN FACES AUDIENCE AND CALLS OUT FOR
"MUSIC")

TAILOR   You may take two steps.

GIANT FORK   Who may?

TAILOR ·   You may.

GIANT FORK   May I?

TAILOR   Yes, you may...not.

GIANT FORK   Why you...

TAILOR   Ah! Ah! Temper! Temper! You may take two baby
steps, Mr. Knife.

GIANT KNIFE May I?

TAILOR   Yes, you may.   (**GIANT KNIFE** TAKES TWO STEPS WHILE
GIANT FORK STANDS FUMING.   THE STEPS TAKEN ARE ENORMOUS)   My,
those are giant steps.

GIANT KNIFE What other steps can a giant take?

BOTH   Very funny...very funny!

    GIANT FORK GROWLS AND CALLS OUT FOR "MUSIC! MUSIC!".

TAILOR   You may take two giant steps, Mr. Fork.

GIANT FORK   (ANGRILY)   May I?

TAILOR   Yes, you may.   (HE DOES SO)   They're certainly the
biggest giant steps I ever saw.

GIANT FORK   And what other kind of steps can the biggest giant
you ever saw, take?

TAILOR   But that's not the game according to the rules.

GIANT FORK   We play the game according to the rules, don't we,
Knife?

GIANT KNIFE Yes, we do.   The rules, Mr. Bones, are of Fork and
Knife.

GIANT FORK   When you play with Fork and Knife they make the rules, Mr. Bones.

TAILOR   (COUNTING THIS OUT ON HIS FINGERS)   But we haven't finished the game.

GIANT FORK   (MENACINGLY)   No need to.

GIANT KNIFE You tell him, Fork.

TAILOR   Why don't I show you my ceremony.   Then we...you can have diner...er, dinner.

GIANT KNIFE Shall we, Fork?

GIANT FORK   Why not?   Keep him busy while the water boils.

TAILOR   Oh, but you'll have to join me.

GIANT FORK   Get going.

TAILOR   (STARTS OFF)   That way.   (HE POINTS TO THE EXIT)

GIANT FORK   No.   I mean your ceremony.

TAILOR   Oh, that old thing.   Yes.   Well, it starts this way.

> MUSIC.   THE **TAILOR** DOES A SOFT SHOE NUMBER.   THE **GIANTS** SMILE AT ONE ANOTHER.   THE **TAILOR** TAKES HEART AND BECKONS THEM TO JOIN HIM.   THEY DO...FIRST SLOWLY.   THEN THE THREE OF THEM DANCE A SOFT SHOE NUMBER TOGETHER, HAVING FUN WITH THE SUZZY-CUE.   THEY PICK UP CANES AND ADD IT TO THE DANCE, HOLDING EACH OTHER.   EVERY TIME THE MUSIC STOPS, THE **TAILOR** CALLS OUT, "ONCE MORE".   HE CONTINUES UNTIL THE **GIANTS**, ALTHOUGH THOROUGHLY PLEASED, ARE SO TIRED THAT **THEY** FALL DOWN DOGGED TIRED AND DRIFT INTO SLEEP.   THE LIGHTS DIM AND THE **TAILOR** SPEAKS TO THE CHILDREN IN THE AUDIENCE.

TAILOR   I'm not sure what to do.   Should I outwit the giants and run away never to see my Cassy again, or should I capture the giants and try to marry Cassy?   How will that help Uncle Ben?   I have it.   I'll kill the giants, so I'm sure Cassy will be safe and then I'll run away, because she won't marry me.   I'm going to kill the giants! (**TAILOR** PICKS UP GUN AND GOES TO **FIRST GIANT**. AIMS.   MUSIC)   I can't.   I can't.   I just can't.   Cassy, I'm coming to get you.   Cassy!

> THE **TAILOR** RUNS OFF AS **GIANTS** SUDDENLY WAKE UP, ROARING, WHEN **THEY** REALISE THE **TAILOR** HAS GONE.

FAST CURTAIN

END OF ACT TWO

ACT THREE

SAME AS ACT TWO.   WE SEE CASSY, UNCLE BEN AND PRISCILLA TRUDGING THROUGH THE SWAMP.   IT IS DARK.   THEY MARCH DOWN THE AISLE.

PRISCILLA   Why are we doing this, father?   It's so dark...and wet...I don't see how we could possibly be of any help.

UNCLE BEN   Just do as Cassy says.   She knows best.

    CURTAINS OPEN.

UNCLE BEN   Where are we going, Cassy?

CASSY   The cards said to keep north...that we would find him ...there.

PRISCILLA   Well, why couldn't he come back on his own?   Why do we have to come here?

CASSY   The cards said to find him. He might be hurt.

    LIGHTS BEGIN TO COME UP VERY SLOWLY.

PRISCILLA   Yes...but all this mud and swamp!!

UNCLE BEN   Priscilla, stop talking and keep walking.

    LIGHTING EFFECT WITH MUSIC.

CASSY   What was that? I heard something.

PRISCILLA   Where? (SHE HIDES. MORE LIGHTING EFFECTS)

UNCLE BEN   Cassy...quickly hide...

    ALL HIDE BEHIND TREES, PRISCILLA BEHIND THE STUMP. THE
    TAILOR APPEARS.

TAILOR   Cassy...Cassy...I'm coming home.

CASSY   (FROM HIDING PLACE) Shush!

PRISCILLA   There he is...our hero.

TAILOR   (TO STUMP) Who's there?

PRISCILLA   It is I...your intended bride.

TAILOR   Cassy...

PRISCILLA   No...Priscilla.

TAILOR   (RUNNING BACK) Better the giants to devour me.

PRISCILLA   (COMING OUT OF HIDING...DISBELIEVING) Did you say giants? Did you see giants?

UNCLE BEN
& CASSY   (COMING FROM HIDING) You're safe, thank goodness!

PRISCILLA   (PATRONISING...APPEASING WHAT SHE THINKS IS MADNESS)

Did you capture the giants?

TAILOR   I captured them...but at the last moment I couldn't kill them. I couldn't!

PRISCILLA Oh, never you mind about the giants. (SHE GRABS **TAILOR**) You can still be mine.

UNCLE BEN Never you mind, Priscilla. Tell us about what you saw! Did they carry any bags that look like carpets.

TAILOR   No sir. I saw really and truly ferocious beasts who devour humans. They cook them in a pot, first. You might say they are civilised cannibals. We must leave the swamp at once and run for safety. (HE TRIES TO MOVE **THEM** ALL IN THE OPPOSITE DIRECTION)

CASSY   (TO **TAILOR**) There are only spirits here. No giants. Maybe the spirits disguised themselves.

UNCLE BEN There are <u>no</u> spirits. There are <u>no</u> giants. Only darn Yankee Carpet-Baggers.

TAILOR   Run for your lives...I hear them! Quick...we must hide.

     ALL RUN EXCEPT **UNCLE BEN** WHO REFUSES. **TAILOR** GRABS HIM.
     THEY ARE ALL NOW HIDING.

UNCLE BEN There are <u>no</u> giants! There are <u>no</u> giants! (**TAILOR** SILENCES **UNCLE BEN**)

     THE **TWO GIANTS** APPEAR SEARCHING THIS WAY AND THAT. MUSIC.

GIANT KNIFE Watch out! Stupid!

GIANT FORK Who you callin' stupid?

GIANT KNIFE (STOPS SUDDENLY) I smell human flesh!

GIANT FORK Well, he sure disappeared. (THEY KEEP SEARCHING. MUSIC)

GIANT KNIFE We were stupid to go off to sleep.

GIANT FORK You don't have to be stupid, stupid. Just tired, and we were tired. Let's keep on. He couldn't have gotten very far.

GIANT KNIFE You've said that for the last hour.

GIANT FORK Keep quiet and just look.

     TAILOR THROWS A STONE AT **GIANT KNIFE** FROM BEHIND A TREE.
     MUSIC.

GIANT KNIFE Stop Fork.

GIANT FORK Stop what? (**TAILOR** THROWS A STONE AT HIM)

GIANT KNIFE You threw something at me.

GIANT FORK I didn't. Just look! (MUSIC. HE IS HIT BY A STONE)
Now look here. Do you want trouble?

GIANT KNIFE No...but you do. (CROSSES TO GIANT FORK. MEET,
GROWL, TURN BACK TO POSITIONS, THEN GIANT FORK IS HIT AGAIN.
MUSIC) That's it...

> THE TWO GIANTS START HITTING EACH OTHER. THIS SHOULD AGAIN
> BE DONE WITH HUMOUR. THEY MISS EACH OTHER EACH TIME. THEY
> DO A FIGHTING BOUT...LIKE THE GAY NINETIES. THE TAILOR,
> MEANWHILE, STARTS LAUGHING AT THEM. BY THE TIME THEY HAVE
> FINISHED FIGHTING, THEY ARE BOTH WORN OUT AND ON THE GROUND.
> THE TAILOR TAKES SOME ROPE FROM HIS WAIST THAT HOLDS UP HIS
> TROUSERS AND TIES THEM. THEY ARE TOO WEAK TO RESIST.

TAILOR   Well, that takes care of you two!

GIANT FORK   What are you going to do with us?

GIANT KNIFE You can't prove anything.

UNCLE BEN   (COMING OUT OF HIDING) I can. (DOUBLE TAKE WHEN HE
SEES THEM) My...you are giants! You have done terrible things
and everyone knows that. Our hero will take you to gaol.

GIANT KNIFE We haven't done anything but scare people away.

UNCLE BEN   Didn't you steal my chickens?

GIANT FORK   Yeah, but, we don't have any money to buy meat.

GIANT KNIFE You get tired of fish and berries.

TAILOR   But you were ready to cook and then eat me.

GIANT KNIFE No, we wasn't. We'd just get you good and wet.
Teach you a lesson and then you'd never come to this swamp again.

GIANT FORK   We have a reputation to live up to. After all, you
came to us. We didn't go to you.

GIANT KNIFE Yeh, what would people think if we didn't try to act
like giants?

GIANT FORK   Exactly. They wouldn't believe in our act.

ALL   Act!

TAILOR   (PULLING GIANTS UP) You mean to tell me it's an
act?

UNCLE BEN   Then what are you doing here in the swamp?

GIANT FORK (GIANTS STILL TIED, TURN TO UNCLE BEN) We missed the
Showboat and planned catching up with it later...on its way back.

UNCLE BEN   So...you're actors!   Better the Yankees!!   (HE PULLS THE ROPE)

GIANT KNIFE We thought we'd like to take a nice quiet vacation ...away from people.

GIANT FORK   It's hard work making people laugh all the time.

GIANT KNIFE Besides, you get tired of people staring at you and asking, "Are you a giant or something"?

UNCLE BEN   (BEWILDERED, TO **CASSY**) Now that we've caught the culprits in the swamp, we're no better off. You read in the cards...about our being saved. What have you to say now?

CASSY   (TAKES OUT CARDS, PLACES THEM ON THE GROUND, AS **ALL** STAND BEHIND **CASSY**) The cards are never wrong. Here's the answer, right here.

UNCLE BEN   How?

CASSY   No one'll steal your chickens any more. They'll grow and grow and grow. You'll sell them and everything will be fine again.

UNCLE BEN   Fine enough to pay for the house?

CASSY   Yes indeed.

TAILOR   Cassy, my sweet, now will you marry me?

ALL   Marry!!

PRISCILLA   What about me? Don't you all just stand there.

GIANTS   And what about us?

PRISCILLA   You're mine. (PULLS **TAILOR**)

CASSY   (PULLS **TAILOR**) Now that the house will be saved, he's mine. I'll admit it.

PRISCILLA   (PULLS **TAILOR**) I'm bigger than you and I say he's mine.

CASSY   (PULLS **TAILOR**) All my life I've given you every-thing. But now...he's mine.

    MUSIC. A BATTLE ENSUES. THE **TAILOR** IS TRAPPED THEN FREES HIMSELF. BUT HE'S GRABBED BY **PRISCILLA**, THEN BY **CASSY**. THEY TOSS HIM BACK AND FORTH. FINALLY, **THEY** END UP PUNCHING EACH OTHER. THE **TAILOR** DUCKS AND THE **GIRLS** HAVE A GO AT ONE ANOTHER CRYING OUT, "HE'S MINE"! **GIANT FORK** HAS BEEN ROOT-ING FOR **PRISCILLA** DURING THE FIGHT. **GIANT KNIFE** FOR **CASSY**. THE **TAILOR** HELPS **CASSY**. THE BATTLE ENDS.

GIANT FORK   Good girl, Priscilla, that was very good.

PRISCILLA   Thank you, Mr...

GIANT FORK   Mr. Fork. Pleased to meet you.

PRISCILLA   (LOOKING AT HIM) Likewise, I'm sure.

UNCLE BEN   Come children, help pull the rope. Let's take care of these giants first. (**THEY PICK UP THE ROPE. MUSIC**) Forward march!

GIANT FORK   We're not moving.

> BY THIS TIME **EVERYONE** IS HANGING ONTO THE ROPE. **THEY DO A DANCE MARCH OF GOING OFF. THE DANCE ENDS AS THE GIANTS REFUSE TO MOVE.**

UNCLE BEN   Forward march, I say!

GIANT FORK   No.

UNCLE BEN   Yes!

GIANT KNIFE   You're taking us to gaol and we don't belong there.

GIANT FORK   You untie us and we'll go back to the swamp, until our boat comes.

GIANT KNIFE   We'll never touch another chicken. We promise.

TAILOR   You belong on the Showboat... (PUZZLED AT WHAT TO DO) but... (**THEY** END THE TUGGING ON THE ROPE AS **UNCLE BEN** AND THE **TAILOR** BRING THE **GIANTS** TO CENTRE STAGE)

GIANT FORK   We know that...I told you that before. We belong on the Showboat.

UNCLE BEN   What are we to do?

TAILOR   Take them to the courthouse and let the judge decide.

UNCLE BEN   But how?

PRISCILLA   Oh! Forget the courthouse, I want to get married.

ALL   Married...   Married...

TAILOR   Mr. Knife, do you have any ideas?

> MUSIC. GIANT STEP ROUTINE DANCE BEGINS.

GIANT KNIFE   Yes, I do, Mr. Bones.

TAILOR   Well, elucidate, Mr. Knife, elucidate.

GIANT FORK   Let's all stay here.

TAILOR   Let's not. Mr. Fork, you may take six giant steps.

GIANT FORK   May I?

TAILOR   Yes, you may. (GIANT FORK TAKES IT) Now, Uncle Ben,
it's your turn.

UNCLE BEN   Mr. Knife, you may take ten giant steps.

GIANT KNIFE May I?

UNCLE BEN   Yes, you may. (HE TAKES IT) Mr. Fork...

PRISCILLA   Father, you forgot all about me. I want the same
number as Mr. Fork.

UNCLE BEN   (FINALLY DAWNS UPON HIM) Priscilla, you may take six
giant steps. (AS SHE DOES SO, SHE STANDS ALONG THE SIDE OF GIANT
FORK WHO TAKES HOLD OF HER HAND. SHE LAUGHS FLIRTATIOUSLY)
Giant Fork, you may take two giant steps.

GIANT FORK   (NO ANSWER AS HE LAUGHS WITH PRISCILLA)

PRISCILLA   Say, "May I", Fork.

GIANT FORK   May I? (HE SAYS THIS TO PRISCILLA)

PRISCILLA   Yes, you may.

GIANT FORK   Priscilla... (DANCE ENDS)

PRISCILLA   Fork. (TO CASSY) Cassy, I need the cards, to tell
my future.

CASSY   (GIVING CARDS TO PRISCILLA) With all my blessings,
I give them to you...forever. (SHE TURNS TO TAILOR. THEY
EMBRACE)

PRISCILLA   (CROSSES TO FORK) Pick a card... (FANNING THEM)
any card.

GIANT FORK   Any one?

PRISCILLA   Yes.

GIANT FORK   (PULLS OUT CARD...LOOKS AT IT) It's a Jack of
Hearts.

PRISCILLA   (THROWING CARDS UPSTAGE) Then you are _the_ one.

GIANT FORK   Am I? How do you know?

PRISCILLA   The cards say so.

GIANT FORK   (NOSE TO NOSE) But I'm a giant.

PRISCILLA   (STRONG) Oh, no you're not.

GIANT FORK   (SOFTLY) Why not?

PRISCILLA   Because I say so.

GIANT FORK   Then it must be so.

PRISCILLA   (GRABBING **GIANT FORK'S** ARM)   We'll go to the courthouse.

GIANT FORK   Do the cards say so?

PRISCILLA   Yes, they do.

GIANT FORK   Where?

PRISCILLA   With the Jack of Hearts.

GIANT FORK   How come?

PRISCILLA   Didn't you ever hear of "This is the house that Jack
built"?

GIANT FORK   Very funny...very funny!   She belongs in our act,
Knife.   (THE **GIANTS** ARE UNTIED AS **PRISCILLA** HANGS ON TO **GIANT
FORK**)

GIANT KNIFE Wait till I teach her a few routines.   She'll wow
them.

UNCLE BEN   Then we're all off to the courthouse.   Priscilla has
met her match.   If she chooses the giant comedian, then you,
Cassy, may choose your tailor.   Let the judge arrange it.

        GIANT FORK AND PRISCILLA, CASSY AND THE TAILOR ARE TOGETHER.
        GIANT KNIFE AND UNCLE BEN LOOK AT ONE ANOTHER.

ALL   To the courthouse.

TAILOR   To the Judge.

GIANT FORK   To get married.

TAILOR   At last, I'll marry you.   What a wonderful end.

CASSY   End?   It's only the beginning!   Only the beginning!

TAILOR   Uncle Ben, I have another idea.   Let's have a
showhouse wedding.

UNCLE BEN   A what?

TAILOR   A showhouse wedding, instead of a showboat wedding.
At your plantation.   We'll make the show ourselves for the
guests.

UNCLE BEN   That's the best idea yet.   Why we'll have the most
famous wedding in the county.   Instead of a courthouse wedding, a
showhouse wedding.   But how will we do it?

TAILOR   I'll sew the costumes.

CASSY   I'll read the cards.

UNCLE BEN   I'll be the host.

GIANTS   And we'll do our act.

       MUSIC - SONG AND DANCE - EVERYONE SINGS AND DANCES.

                    <u>SONG - SHOWHOUSE WEDDING</u>
TAILOR   I'll make the costumes nicely
             I'll sew with many a stitch
             With silks and satins and sequins
             There'll never be a hitch.

CASSY TO   I'll be a fortune teller
TAILOR   Don't need a crystal ball
             I'll wear a gypsy costume
             And read the cards for all.

GIANTS   We'll dance and sing and chatter
             We'll play the trumpet tunes
             It really doesn't matter
             We're the greatest of buffoons.

PRISCILLA   Tra la la la la la la la la la la la
             I'll be the prima donna
             You'll bill me at the top
             For I can reach the highest C
             Just listen, watch me...

ALL   Stop!

GIANTS   We'll dance and sing and chatter

PRISCILLA   I'll sing the greatest tunes

GIANTS &   It really doesn't matter
PRISCILLA   We're the greatest of buffoons.

UNCLE BEN   I'll roast the chickens lightly
             I'll play the part of host
             I'll serve mint juileps sprightly
             So to the Weddings' toast
             To the Weddings that we love the most.

ALL   A toast!
                    - END OF SONG -

                    FAST CURTAIN

THE DANCING OF THE **ENTIRE CAST** IS DONE WITH THE SINGING.
THE BURLESQUE MOMENTS OF MIME WITH THE DANCING ARE IN-
TEGRATED THROUGHOUT. **CURTAINS** CLOSE QUICKLY AFTER THE
TOAST. THE **TAILOR** RE-APPEARS AS **CAPTAIN** IN FRONT OF THE
CURTAINS. MUSIC.

CAPTAIN   And now our curtain call. (CURTAINS OPEN WITH ALL
THE ACTORS ON STAGE. **CAPTAIN** NAMES **EACH ACTOR** AS EACH ONE TAKES

A SINGLE BOW.   THEN A **COMPANY BOW** FROM THEM **ALL** IN DANCE
FORMATIONS)

GIANT FORK You've been a great audience...just for that you can
all come to my Wedding. Let's give them a hand.

CAPTAIN   Give tham a hand and they take a foot.

ALL   Very funny...very funny!

CAPTAIN   All ashore that's going ashore. Let's go!

THEY ALL EXIT DOWN THE AISLE AS **THEY** SAY GOODBYE TO THE
AUDIENCE ON THEIR WAY OUT. LIGHTS FADE ON MUSIC.

FAST CURTAIN

END OF PLAY

CRUMBLING PLANTATION,
VERANDA & GARDEN

TREE CUT-OUTS, VINES AND 'CREEPERS' (CAN BE EASILY MADE FROM ROPE & MATERIAL) IN FRONT OF SWAMPY BACKDROP

TREE
Stump
'STONE'
BENCH
Floor scattered
with leaves and debris

THE SWAMP

ASHLEY,
THE TAILOR
CASSY
PRISCILLA
UNCLE BEN

GIANT KNIFE
GIANT FORK

THE CRICKET THEATRE AND BLANCHE MARVIN
PRESENT:

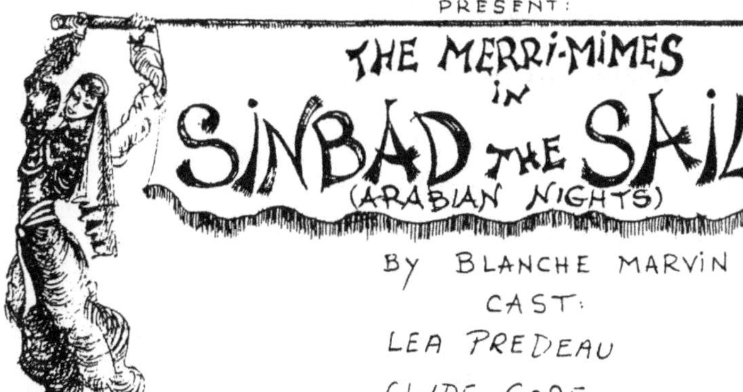

BY BLANCHE MARVIN

CAST:

LEA PREDEAU

CLYDE GORE

SANDRA NYARY

JOHN GAUDRY

WILLIAM WENDT

WILLIAM HAWLEY

RHODA CARROLL

STAGE MANAGER – JOE STELL   ADDED CHOREOGRAPHY – CLYDE GORE

AT THE CRICKET THEATRE   at – 1 – 2:30 – 4 pm. MARCH. 19, 26
162 SECOND AVE. (at 10th st.)   OR-4 3960   APRIL. 2, 9.

ALSO: PETER AND THE WOLF: SAT. APRIL 16 THROUGH
EASTER WEEK, APRIL 18 TO SAT. APR. 23, & 30 MAY 7, 14, 21

SEE CRICKET THEATRE SERIES!

ARABIAN NIGHTS

KABUKI STYLE THEATRE

<u>CAST OF CHARACTERS</u>

(ACTOR 1)	(ACTOR 2)
Narrator	King Shahryar of Arabia
Fisherman	Prince of Persia
Indian Prince	
Sinbad the Sailor	

(ACTOR 3)	(ACTOR/DANCERS)
Vizir	2 Dervishes
King Katschei	2 Sinbad's Friends

(VOICE ONLY)	(ACTRESS 1)
Jini	Scheherezade

(ACTRESS 2)	(ACTRESS 3)
Queen Fata Morgana	Princess of Bengal
Beggar Woman	Enchanted Bird

Place: Palace of the King of Arabia and Distant Lands

Time: Long ago

ACT ONE

IN FRONT OF THE CURTAINS THE **NARRATOR** AND CAST OF ACTORS
STAND IN ARRANGED POSITIONS.   EACH ACTOR STEPS FORWARD ON
CUE FROM THE NARRATOR.   MUSIC.

NARRATOR   My good children, today will be
A kind of theatre done orientally.
Here are the gracious actors who'll play
Many characters on stage today.
Don't look to the actor in his part
Search the character from your mind to the heart.
There are so many stories we will tell
And you, my children, come under my spell.

Once upon a time in an Arabian town
Lived a humble Vizir who feared the Crown
For this most noble King would wed
A new bride daily who then lost her head.
Listen now our story begins
Like the many webs a spider spins.

CURTAINS OPEN ON THE THRONE ROOM OF THE **KING** IN HIS PALACE.
THE SET HAS A THRONE WITH A FEATHERED BACK TO REPRESENT THE
THRONE ROOM WHICH IS EASILY REMOVED OR SET TO ONE SIDE.
PILES OF PILLOWS WITH A FEATHERED CANOPY IS SCHEHEREZADE'S
PLACE, AGAIN EASILY LEFT TO ONE SIDE OF THE STAGE.   THE
STORIES AND THEIR SETTINGS ARE CHANGED BY THE USE OF TWO
LONG PIECES OF SILK WHICH TWO OF THE ACTORS USE TO MAKE THE
SEA, THE SMOKE AND **JINI**, THE SKY, THE SHIP'S SAILS, THE
HORSE, THE TRAVELLING...ALL BY THE MOVEMENT OF THE TWO
PIECES OF SILK WHICH CAN BE TWIRLED VERTICALLY OR HORIZON-
TALLY BILLOWED OR RIPPLED.   BUT FOR NOW WE ARE IN THE THRONE
ROOM.   THE **KING** IS SEATED ON HIS THRONE AND **SCHEHEREZADE**
SITS IN HER CORNER UNSEEN BY THE AUDIENCE AS HER SPACE IS
UNLIT.   THE ACTORS DISPERSE TO THEIR GIVEN TASKS AND ASSUME
THEIR ACTING ROLES AS SOON AS THE CURTAINS OPEN. THE VIZIR
PACES BACK AND FORTH.

VIZIR   (AN OLD **MAN** IN FLOWING ROBES, PACING DESPERATELY) Oh,
most gracious King, we are soon to come to an end of the young
women in our city. I cannot find you a new bride.

KING   You are my Vizir and my slave. My command is yours to
obey. If there are no women left in Baghdad then look elsewhere.

VIZIR   I have searched all of Arabia.   But mothers now hide
their daughters for fear of their lives.

KING   I am King of the highest. My subjects will follow as I
say. I demand my new bride for tomorrow.

VIZIR   Most noble of noble Kings...most kindly, generous King
of Kings...when shall we stop this madness?   There will be no
young women left.

KING   Vizir, your life is at stake, should you fail me tomorrow. I shall have a new bride! (EXITS)

VIZIR   What shall I do? I must speak with Scheherezade.

MOVEMENT IS DESIGNED TO GIVE THE EFFECT OF TRAVELLING. HE
ARRIVES HOME. **SCHEHEREZADE** IS SEATED ON A COLLECTION OF
PILLOWS.

VIZIR   Scheherezade, Scheherezade, where are you?

SCHEHEREZADE
          (SHE SITS ON HER PILLOWS SURROUNDED BY BOOKS) Father
dear, I'm here, amongst my books!

VIZIR   Oh my daughter, may your wisdom help me today! Help
me, Scheherezade, help me!

SCHEHEREZADE
          (RISING FROM THE PILLOWS, SHE RUNS TO HER FATHER AND
PUTS HER HEAD ON HIS SHOULDER) What is it, my father, that up-
sets you so?

VIZIR   The King, I fear, is mad. He marries a young girl one
day and has her put to death the next. Now, I cannot find him a
new bride and so he threatens my life.

SCHEHEREZADE
          He was once kind and just. He must become so again.
Father dear, he believes that all women betray love and therefore
cannot be trusted. All because his Queen was unfaithful. But if
I prove to him that there is good and evil and that he must
choose for himself the good, he'll stop these mad marriages and
deaths.

VIZIR   You have so much faith, Scheherezade, but as your
father, I forbid you to give yourself to the King and chance a
terrible death.

SCHEHEREZADE
          I must go to the King. You'll see that he will listen.
I will persuade him.

VIZIR   How?

SCHEHEREZADE
          I have a plan which will save all the women of Arabia!

VIZIR   I beg you, my precious daughter, don't do this rash
thing, we have greater need of you than the King.

SCHEHEREZADE
          Listen to the story I tell
          Of the Fisherman and Jini
          And why all came out well
          How changing the Jini's evil plan
          Made good fortune come to the Fisherman

EACH TIME **SCHEHEREZADE** BEGINS HER STORY THE TWO ACTORS AP-
PEAR WITH THE TWO PIECES OF SILK. THEY WAVE THE SILK TO
MAKE THE LAKE. THE **FISHERMAN** APPEARS FROM BEHIND. THE

STORY IS ENTIRELY CHOREOGRAPHED IN MIME AND DANCE...TO THE SPOKEN LINES OF **SCHEHEREAZADE**, **FISHERMAN** AND **JINI**. THE MUSIC ALWAYS ACCOMPANIES THE STORIES THROUGHOUT.

SCHEHEREZADE
He was a poor fisherman and every day he cast his net four times into the same waters...carrying home whatever fish he caught. One day after he had cast his net three times, to no avail, he feared that there would be nothing to eat for his little ones. Determined to catch something he threw his net the fourth time. This time it was so heavy he could barely lift it. He pulled and pulled and finally saw his catch...a brass jug which was firmly capped by a lead stopper.

MUSIC.

FISHERMAN Ah, I will take this to the market and receive enough gold to last all my life. I will no longer have to fish.

SCHEHEREZADE
As he lifted the jug, he wondered at its weight.

FISHERMAN Surely it must be its contents which make it so heavy.

SCHEHEREZADE
So he tried and tried and tried to pull out the cap and finally succeeded. Suddenly out of the jug came a huge black ring of smoke which formed itself into a tremendous Jini. He rose and rose up to the sky.

THE TWO ACTORS TWIRL THE SILK INTO SMOKE AS LIGHTS BLACKEN THE COLOUR. THE <u>VOICE</u> OF THE **JINI** IS HEARD AS THE SMOKE TWIRLS IN RHYTHM TO THE **JINI'S** WORDS. THE **FISHERMAN** MIMES THE ACTIONS.

JINI   Ha, ha!   Good Fisherman, you are indeed blest. You will never have to worry again. You will prepare yourself... for death.

FISHERMAN Would you kill me after I have saved your life?

JINI   Silence, Fisherman. And hear my story! Know then that I was a sinner who would not accept the Law. I was imprisoned in this jug and thrown to the depths of the sea. After the first one hundred years of imprisonment, I swore I would enrich forevermore whosoever would release me. For the next hundred years of imprisonment, I swore to my rescuer I would open the hoards of the earth. Still no one came. For four hundred years, my fury has been so aroused that I swore I would give only a choice of death to whoever should release me from hereon.   So choose now...and be quick!

THE DANCE CONTINUES.

SCHEHEREZADE
The Fisherman pleaded for his life, but soon saw it was useless. Then he thought to himself.

FISHERMAN I must outwit the Jini. (TO THE AUDIENCE) Evil spirits think only of themselves and therefore can be outwitted by greater thoughts and plans. (TO JINI) Oh Jini, since I am about to die, at least grant a dying man his last wish.

JINI   Granted.

FISHERMAN How can it be that so big a Jini as you could fit into such a small jug? Why your hand alone is bigger than the jug! Are you certain that you came out of this object?

JINI   What Fisherman! Do you doubt my story and my word? I will show you.

SCHEHEREZADE
          That instant the evil spirit shook itself and turned into black smoke once again, entering the jug little by little 'til all was inside. Then as fast as lightning the Fisherman put the stopper back.

FISHERMAN Ha, ha! Now, Jini, tell me by what way you would die! I will throw you back into the sea and stand here to warn off all others.

JINI   Please, Fisherman, do not do so. I have learned a lesson. I was evil and you are a good man. I promise to reward you well.

SCHEHEREZADE
          The Fisherman realised the fright of the Jini and that the Jini now believed in the power of the good Fisherman. He, therefore, released the Jini again.

JINI   Ho, ho! Now I am free forever!

SCHEHEREZADE
          Then he cast the jug far out to sea. The Fisherman suddenly feared the Jini would destroy him. But the Jini had learned his lesson and he laughingly called out:

JINI   Fisherman...follow me, for I will lead you to waters unknown. There you will find fish fit for the King and so will you fulfil your fortune when you present the fish to him.

SCHEHEREZADE
          And so it was that the Jini led the Fisherman to the unknown waters where the Fisherman cast his net and there found four fish...blue, red, white and yellow in shapes and colours so glorious. The Jini told the Fisherman that the King would give him 400 pieces of gold, and then he disappeared into the centre of the earth. The Fisherman became a prosperous man who had only to cast his net into the unknown waters and there be rewarded each time.

          THE ACTORS EXIT WITH THE SILK PIECES. THE **FISHERMAN** CHANGES
          HIS HAT AND BECOMES THE **NARRATOR**.

SCHEHEREZADE
So dear Father, will I teach the King...as the Fisherman taught the Jini of the good as well as the evil that is here...cast in the net of life.

VIZIR So be it my daughter. I will present you to the King. May Allah have mercy on you.

NARRATOR Scheherezade was led this way
To the King of Arabia for her Wedding Day.
The Wedding Feast was held for all
Where her very life was at beck and call.

MUSIC. THE CEREMONY IS A CHOREOGRAPHED DANCE OF THE WHOLE COURT. THE **KING** IS VERY MUCH TAKEN WITH **SCHEHEREZADE**, THE **VIZIR** IS TERRIFIED AND **SCHEHEREZADE** ENJOYS THE PLEASURE OF THE WEDDING.

KING Enjoy this day, the Wedding Day, for who knows how long life lasts!

BLACKOUT

END OF ACT ONE

ACT TWO

PALACE OF THE KING. THE THRONE ROOM. **NARRATOR** WALKS ON TO SIDE OF STAGE. **SCHEHEREZADE** SITS AT THE **KING'S** FEET AS HE SITS UPON HIS THRONE.

NARRATOR That night the spinning of the web began
All according to Scheherezade's plan. (EXITS)

SCHEHEREZADE
Oh, King, I shall sing you a tale of true love.
Of a woman whose choice changed the Heaven's above.
Her faith was strong, her love was true
But we must never forget that there was evil too.
The Enchanted Horse is the story's name
And it was the saving of so much pain.

MUSIC. THE **PRINCE** AND **PRINCESS** ENTER.

SCHEHEREZADE
Many years ago there was a beautiful Princess from Bengal who was betrothed to the handsome Prince of Persia. Their love was known throughout Persia and all rejoiced in its beauty. One day as they walked through the palace gardens, the Princess showed the Prince a flower.

PRINCESS Oh, my love, look at the beauty of this flower.

PRINCE It is beautiful, my love, but not as beautiful as you.

PRINCESS Oh, my Prince, beware of this flower. Do not touch it, ever, for its beauty is evil.

PRINCE   A flower, evil? Beauty, evil?

PRINCESS   Sometimes evil is so well disguised we cannot recognise
it.

PRINCE   And what is the evil of this flower?

PRINCESS   If anyone should pierce its heart, an evil spirit will
appear...impossible to capture.

PRINCE   Come now. Do you believe in magic?

PRINCESS   Oh, yes. Magic is an unseen power.

PRINCE   You must not believe in such things!

     HE PRESSES THE FLOWER AND THE EVIL SPIRIT OF AN INDIAN
     PRINCE APPEARS OUT OF A CLOUD. THE ACTORS WITH THE TWO
     PIECES OF SILK HAVE ENTERED AND WAVE THE SILK AS A CLOUD.

INDIAN PRINCE
          Laugh, would you, Prince of Persia, at a great Indian
Prince like myself? I will put a curse upon you. There, you
cannot move.

PRINCE   Stop, evil Prince.

INDIAN PRINCE
          I will take your betrothed Princess away with me and
she will be mine.

PRINCESS   Great Prince of India, I've done you no harm. Let me
remain with my Prince.

INDIAN PRINCE
          No...it's too late!

     THEY DISAPPEAR. THE SILK PIECES COVER THEM.

SCHEHEREZADE
          The Prince of Persia, now able to move, tried to catch
the evil spirit and bring back his love, but they had disappeared.

PRINCE   I shall never return to these gardens until my Princess
has been found.

SCHEHEREZADE
          And so it was that the Prince searched for many years,
but could not find his bride-to-be. He crossed many lands of
valleys and mountains, rich and dry, green and grey but still
could not find her. At last he came upon a desert. He thought
all was lost.

PRINCE   I've little water left and less heart...and still not
found my love.

SCHEHEREZADE
        As the Prince stood thus, a blind Beggar Woman suddenly
appeared and touched his royal robe.

A BLINDING LIGHT IS SPOTTED ONTO A DARK STAGE AREA WHICH
CREATES THE BEGGAR WOMAN'S SUDDEN APPEARANCE.

BEGGAR WOMAN
        Oh, gentle Prince, help a blind beggar. I thirst for
my life.

PRINCE   Where have you come from? I never saw you approach!

BEGGAR WOMAN
        It's the sun that blinds you. I beg water.

PRINCE   I have little...but you may share it with me.

BEGGAR WOMAN
        You are kind and shall be blessed.

PRINCE   May Allah be praised. I only ask to be led to my
Princess.

BEGGAR WOMEN
        For your kindness, I will give you a wooden horse. But
this is an enchanted horse. You've only to press the jewelled
peg forward and it will take you to wherever you wish.

PRINCE   Old woman, Allah, himself, shall reward you!

BEGGAR WOMAN
        I am well rewarded Prince. I was sent to the desert to
test you. Go now!

TWO ACTORS APPEAR WITH A PIECE OF SILK AND MOVE IT AS A
HORSE.

SCHEHEREZADE
        The Prince mounted the horse and just as the Beggar
Woman promised...he had only to press forward the jewelled peg
and he flew. He passed countries and cities, houses and palaces,
and then suddenly as they passed a strange palace the horse began
to descend.

PRINCE   Is my Princess here? Surely the horse was meant to
bring me to her. But it is such a strange palace!

HE DISMOUNTS FROM THE HORSE. THE TWO ACTORS LEAVE WITH THE
PIECE OF SILK. THE PRINCE WALKS UNTIL HE COMES UPON THE
PRINCESS AND THE INDIAN PRINCE. HE HIDES AND WATCHES.

PRINCESS (FEIGNS MADNESS) I heard the birds talking. (PRETENDS
TO BE A BIRD)

INDIAN PRINCE
        We'll have time to wed, when you're free of your mad-
ness.

PRINCESS (LAUGHS) Oh, pretty birds, I shall surely be one too. Chirp...chirp.

INDIAN PRINCE
        I have found a new Doctor, a special one.

PRINCESS I am a bird...I am a bird.

INDIAN PRINCE
        I've sent for him from Greece. Oh my precious Princess, he will surely cure your madness.

PRINCESS He must cure my birds. (SHE FLIES) Oh, oh, my birds.

PRINCE   (SUDDENLY BREAKS FORWARD) I am a Doctor and can treat the Princess immediately.

INDIAN PRINCE
        Doctor? No, it's you my Prince of Persia, just in time.

PRINCE   So it would seem.

INDIAN PRINCE
        Prepare yourself, my Prince.

PRINCE   For what?

INDIAN PRINCE
        For your death!

PRINCE   No...for yours!

        MUSIC.   THEY BEGIN THE SWORD BATTLE, A CHOREOGRAPHED DANCE FULL OF SUSPENSE.   THE **INDIAN PRINCE** FALLS, THE **PRINCE OF PERSIA** WINS.   THE **BEGGAR WOMAN** SUDDENLY APPEARS.

BEGGAR WOMAN
        You have won your battle fairly, oh, Prince. You may now reclaim your bride.

INDIAN PRINCE
        Do not think I'm defeated, old woman. I'll yet win.

BEGGAR WOMAN
        Silence, evil spirit! Once you disguised yourself into a beautiful flower that someone would pluck. You shall be cursed once again into a flower but one so ugly that none will touch you. As the thistle, you shall be.

SCHEHEREZADE
        With these words of the Beggar Woman the evil Indian Prince disappeared and in his place stood a thistle so full of thorns that none would touch. The Beggar Woman blessed the Prince and Princess, then vanished. As for the Prince and Princess...

PRINCE   Without the magic horse and the Beggar Woman I could never have found you, my love. (THEY EMBRACE)

PRINCESS A <u>magic</u> horse? Does my Prince believe in magic?

PRINCE   I've come to know its unseen power. I believe, and now we must fly home.

THE TWO ACTORS ENTER WITH THE TWO PIECES OF SILK WHICH THEY MOVE LIKE A HORSE. THE **PRINCE** AND **PRINCESS** MOUNT THE HORSE. THEY MIME THE CONCLUSION OF THE STORY AS **SCHEHEREZADE** TELLS IT.

SCHEHEREZADE
        The Prince and Princess mounted the magic horse and pressed the jewelled peg. Away they flew back to the gardens of the palace where they were wed. The Princess danced for joy and everyone bathed in the sunshine of her happiness. They lived to be King and Queen for many years. Their reign was a happy one never to be forgotten by the people of Persia. As for the magic horse, it was made into a statue in the palace gardens. The jewelled peg was removed so that it would not fly. But it would always remain in the garden as a symbol of love. So, true love conquered the workings of evil and evil destroyed itself. Oh King, there are many such tales I could tell you if you would give me my life to do so.

NARRATOR   The King enjoyed the tale of love
           But not even the Heavens above
           Could change his hardened heart of stone
           Scheherezade's life was still on loan
           Yes, he would let her tell once more
           A tale she had never told before
           Then after that who knows the end?
           The King's will might never bend.

BLACKOUT

END OF ACT TWO

ACT THREE

THRONE ROOM AT THE PALACE, **NARRATOR** WALKS ON TO SIDE OF STAGE. THE **KING** IS ON THE THRONE. **SCHEHEREZADE** ENTERS AND KNEELS.

NARRATOR   So comes this day, now we must see
           How kind or cruel the King will be
           Will Scheherezade yet live?
           Or can her tales make the King forgive? (EXITS)
KING   Today your life should really end
           But only for you does my will bend
           One more tale will I hear,
           Then after that, the end is near.

SCHEHEREZADE
           My King, My Lord, you must learn well
           The hand of fate is hard to tell.

The unfaithful Queen whom you did love
Was given to you by Allah above
That you may now enjoy full score
Your faithful Queen forevermore.

Oh, King, I will tell a tale today
Of **Sinbad**, the Sailor, who lived his own way
For here was a man who laughed at life
And lived his old age without any strife.

LIGHTS FADE ON **KING** AND **SCHEHEREZADE**. **SINBAD** AND **FRIENDS** ENTER.

SINBAD   Friends... (AS HE SPINS ROUND AND ROUND SINBAD STUMBLES AND FALLS ON THE GROUND. HE'S BEEN DRINKING WINE FROM A CUP)

FIRST   Sinbad, what is the matter?

SINBAD   I drink because I am sad.

SECOND   Tell us, why so sad! Aren't we good friends? Tell us!

SINBAD   You don't understand, my friends.   I must leave Baghdad. Go to sea and seek my fortune. (WEEPING) I've wasted all my money on this. (SHOWS CUP)

SECOND   Don't go to sea. Seek your fortune elsewhere.

SINBAD   I can't seek my fortune except at sea. Let's say goodbye, for now. I must leave.

BOTH   Goodbye, Sinbad, the Sailor!

SCHEHEREZADE
     And so it was that Sinbad set sail to seek his fortune.

MUSIC. SHIP FORMS AROUND **SINBAD**.   THE **TWO ACTORS** HAVE ENTERED ON THE MUSIC CUE WITH THE TWO PIECES OF SILK.   THEY BECOME THE SEA AND THE SHIP, TWIRLING THE CLOTH AS HUGE WAVES, TWISTING THE VERTICAL SAIL INTO THE SEA THEN UP AGAIN.

SCHEHEREZADE
     For three days and three nights the little vessel sailed through a calm sea and little by little Sinbad found that he and the sea could make friends. Suddenly a storm broke, the winds roared, the waves crashed about the ship. Finally a huge wave covered the boat and **SINBAD** was hurled into the sea, as the ship disappeared into the storm. **SINBAD** swam with all his might. He swam and swam and swam...'til he thought he would drown. At last when he thought he could swim no longer, the waters stilled and a great wave washed him onto dry ground.

MUSIC AND ACTION END.

SCHEHEREZADE
     As Sinbad lay asleep on the sand, a bird appeared and gently tapped him.

SINBAD   Where am I? Who are you? Allah be praised! I'm dead
and have gone to heaven!

BIRD   No, my shipwrecked sailor, you were washed ashore by
the waves and I came upon you by accident. But, you must now be
warned.

SINBAD   Warn me? Who are you?

BIRD   I am the most precious bird on this island of the
wicked King Katschei and his evil Queen Fata Morgana. There is a
curse here which touches all who set foot on this isle.

SINBAD   (CRAWLS AWAY) A curse on this island?

BIRD   Many years ago I was stolen from my kingdom and brought
here, never to be free because of the curse, the curse of the
three oranges.

SINBAD   Have the fates washed me ashore to save you?

BIRD   Many have tried to save me only to lose their own
lives.

SINBAD   Oh, most precious bird, in order to win your safety, I
would conquer monsters. (HE TAKES OUT HIS SABER AND MAKES A PRE-
TENDING GESTURE)

BIRD   I beg you, escape with your life before it's too late.

SINBAD   Have no fear, my fair bird.   I have battled the seas.
I can battle this land.

   HE GOES ON WITH HIS MOCK BATTLE, SWORD IN AIR, AS **THE DER-
   VISHES** APPEAR THROUGH **SCHEHEREZADE'S** SPEECH.   HE IS SUR-
   PRISED TO SEE THEM AND STOPS SHORT.

SCHEHEREZADE
   While the **BIRD** stood thus pleading before **SINBAD**, two
WHIRLING DERVISHES, servants of **KATSCHEI** and **MORGANA,** appeared
brandishing their swords.

DERVISH 1 Aha, there is the captive bird.

BIRD   May Allah save us, it's too late!

DERVISH 2 King Katschei has commanded me to find you. You'll
never escape his power. And who is this stranger?

BIRD   Run, run for your life...

SINBAD   No, never. I am Sinbad, the Sailor from Baghdad and
have come to try my fortune in saving the life of the most precious bird in the world. Take me to your oranges! I mean your
majesties.

DERVISH 1 You're brave enough now Sinbad, the Sailor, but in a
little while we'll see.

DERVISH 2 The King waits for us.

    THE DERVISHES MOVE THE BIRD AND SINBAD IN A CHOREOGRAPHED
DANCE WHICH GIVES THE IMPRESSION OF TRAVELLING TO THE COURT.
AS THEY MOVE TO THE COURT **KING KATSCHEI** AND **QUEEN MORGANA** IN
DANCE-LIKE MOVEMENTS ENTER.   THE DERVISHES PLACE THEIR
THRONES ON STAGE.

SCHEHEREZADE
    The **BIRD** and **SINBAD**, the Sailor, were whirled away by
the **DERVISHES**.   They came before a large hall where **KING KATSCHEI**
and **FATA MORGANA** were seated on their thrones.

    BIRD AND SINBAD ARE THROWN TO THEIR KNEES BY THE WICKED DER-
VISHES.

KATSCHEI Well, my Queen, what a pleasant sight we have here
before us. Another sailor to add to your collection.

MORGANA   Oh handsome one, your head will be worthy of my collection.

    SINBAD LOOKS AROUND TO SEE TO WHOM THE **QUEEN** IS TALKING.
SUDDENLY HE REALISES IT IS HE.

SINBAD   Am I handsome?

MORGANA   Most handsome!

SINBAD   Thank you, my Queen.

MORGANA   Thank my collection.

SINBAD   Collection of what?

MORGANA   Of heads.

    SINBAD IS TAKEN ABACK.

BIRD   I beg you, spare him...spare him.

KATSCHEI Who are you stranger, and what power do you possess?

MORGANA   Are you perhaps the reigning Prince of a distant land?

SINBAD   I'm only Sinbad, a sailor from Baghdad...but I claim
the right to try my fortune at any test you would care to put me
to.

MORGANA   You, a commoner?

KATSCHEI Do you know it is a horrible death if you fail?

SINBAD   (KNEES SHAKE) I'm willing. What must I do?

KATSCHEI
You will be blindfolded
The bird will be hidden
inside one of them.

If you cut open the right
orange your life will be
spared.

MORGANA
and led before three huge oranges.

You will have only one choice to
decide in which orange she is
hidden.

And I will have to find a new head!

KATSCHEI But if you should choose wrongly, then our sport will
begin and your end will be at hand.

BIRD   Oh, Sinbad, no one has ever been able to choose the
right orange. Consider your choice, I beg of you.

KATSCHEI The bird is right, foolish sailor. Come away my Queen
and let him decide for himself what to do.

        THE COURT RETIRE LEAVING **SINBAD** ALONE.

SINBAD   Oh, this is a sorry adventure. I wish I knew what to do
or had someone here to help me decide. (TO AUDIENCE) Ahoy! Can
you hear me? (AUDIENCE..."YES") Do you like Katschei and
Morgana? (AUDIENCE..."NO") No, I should think not, they're a
wicked lot. And I guess I'm a rather brave fellow! Well, aren't
I? (AUDIENCE..."YES") Thank you. I was beginning to doubt myself
for a moment. Now, let me think. (PAUSE) Ah yes, you can help
me! (AUDIENCE..."HOW"?) I'll tell you but you must promise to
keep it a secret. Do you promise? (AUDIENCE..."YES") Oh, no
it's a secret, so we must all whisper it. (WHISPERS) Do you
promise? (AUDIENCE WHISPER..."YES") If I decide to challenge
the King for the Bird's safety and if they should blindfold me
will you promise to clap your hands, when I stand over the <u>right</u>
orange? Remember say nothing...only clap your hands and then
I'll know. If you use your voices the secret will be broken and
the wicked King and Queen will surely behead me! Let's practise.
(CHILDREN CLAP THEIR HANDS) Good! The King and Queen must not
see us practising. It would be very dangerous. Remember it's a
secret and no one must know...Shhhhhh. (THE COURT RETURNS)

KATSCHEI Well Sinbad, what is your decision?

SINBAD   I'll try choosing the oranges.

MORGANA   Good, at least you're brave.

KATSCHEI Dervishes, blindfold our brave fool and bring in the
oranges.

        THEY DO AS THEY ARE BID IN A MIME RITUAL. THE ORANGES ARE
        HUGE. **SINBAD** IS BLINDFOLDED ON STAGE, THEN LEAD OFF STAGE.

MORGANA   (TO MUSIC)
          Bird of the enchanted isle
          Vanish for a little while
          Into one of the oranges go
          Let no-one but me know

                    Which of the oranges it will be
                    And so you shall remain with me.

          AT THE END OF THE CURSE A LOUD CLAP OF THUNDER IS HEARD AND
          THE **BIRD** VANISHES INTO THE ORANGE NEAREST THE THRONE. **SIN-
          BAD** IS USHERED IN.

KATSCHEI Now let the Sailor choose.

MORGANA Young man, remember you have only one choice.

KATSCHEI Should you cut open the wrong orange you will die.

SINBAD (SWAYING WITH FRIGHT) I have a natural sway! I'm a
sailor. You may think that I'm shaking, but it's the swaying of
the sea in me.

MORGANA Choose!

SINBAD Now let me see... (APPROACHES THE FIRST ORANGE) I
wonder if she would be in here. (NO CLAPPING) Maybe some in-
spiration will come to me.

          HE APPROACHES THE SECOND ORANGE, STILL NO CLAPPING. **SINBAD**
          GOES TO THE THIRD ORANGE...APPLAUSE! ONE MAY VARY **SINBAD**
          STARTING FROM THE RIGHT OR THE LEFT, ACCORDING TO CHOICE OF
          THE DIRECTOR. **SINBAD** CAN ACT HESITANT, PRETEND HE DOESN'T
          HEAR THE APPLAUSE, ETC. IF THE CHILDREN CLAP STRONGLY THEN
          HE MUST CHOOSE IMMEDIATELY. IT IS BEST TO USE THE <u>THIRD</u>
          ORANGE BUT THE RIGHT CHOICE MUST BE NEAREST THE THRONE.

SINBAD I have had a sign, Your Majesties. THIS is the orange
I choose!

          HE SLASHES THE ORANGE WITH HIS SWORD. THE **BIRD** APPEARS,
          MORGANA SCREAMS.

BIRD Sinbad, you've won.

MORGANA He has won! He has won!

KATSCHEI We are undone!

SCHEHEREZADE
          With the freeing of the bird, the wicked power of King
Katschei and his Queen Fata Morgana were destroyed and disappeared from the face of the earth forever.

BIRD Sinbad, you have freed the island from the magic en-
chantment of Katschei and Morgana.

SINBAD Just with one stroke of my sword. And with the help of
my friends! Now, how are we ever going to leave this island?

BIRD Your ship wasn't destroyed by the storm. It lies
safely in the harbour on the other side of this island.

SINBAD   Then we'll set sail! But first I must say goodbye to
my good friends. Goodbye! Remember our secret.

BIRD   Goodbye?

SINBAD   Not to you...to them. (POINTS TO AUDIENCE) Goodbye!!!

     THEY EXIT THROUGH AUDIENCE.

SCHEHEREZADE
     So Sinbad and the Bird returned to Baghdad, where Sin-
bad was rewarded richly for his bravery and lived to a ripe old
age. Now my King if there is hope, you will save my life. For a
thousand and one tales I can tell if you would listen and
believe.

KING   Oh, wise and noble Queen, for a thousand and one <u>nights</u>
I will listen! Your worthy life shall be saved for <u>everyone</u> to be
blest in its light. Come celebrate! (CAST COMES OUT) Bow before
this most beautiful Queen...toast her long life.

     MUSIC.   DANCE FINALE.   AT THE END OF THE DANCE, EVERYONE
     FREEZES INTO A TABLEAU AS THE **NARRATOR** COMES FORTH AND
     SPEAKS TO THE AUDIENCE. PLEASE NOTE, THE ACTORS ARE IN THE
     SAME POSITION AS THE OPENING.

NARRATOR The King listened and the King had learned,
             For a thousand and one nights as Scheherezade had
                                        yearned
             And when she had finished he laid to rest
             All his cruel desires and thought only the best
             So happily ends this tale of woe.
             And now, my children, it is time to go.

                         CURTAIN

                    END OF PLAY

THE VIZIR
THE KING
SCHEHERAZADE

FISHERMAN

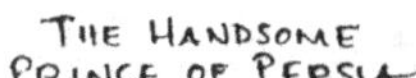

THE HANDSOME
PRINCE OF PERSIA

THE PRINCESS
OF BENGAL

THE EVIL INDIAN
PRINCE

THE BIRD
SINBAD THE SAILOR
THE ORANGES:
FREE-STANDING DISCS, BIG
ENOUGH TO HIDE BEHIND —
CHICKENWIRE OVER FRAME.
KING.
KATSCHEI AND
QUEEN FATA MORGANA

BLANCHE MARVIN PRESENTS:
THE MERRI-MIMES
PETER and the WOLF
BY BLANCHE MARVIN
PRODUCTION OF MARIO SILETTI
DIRECTED & CHOREOGRAPHED
RHODA CARROL + ARNOLD HRUSHKA
CAST
GRANDPA   MICHAEL MONTEL
PETER   PAT McKENNA
DUCK   MIRIAM SCHWARZ
BIRD   KATHY KELLY
WOLF   ED CHIARO
CAT   RICHARD MAZZA
HUNTER   JOSEPH SICARI
LIGHTS, SETS, + STAGE MANAGER
JOSEPH STELL
AT THE CRICKET THEATRE
162 SECOND AVE.
AT 1, 2:30, + 4PM — OR 4-3960
ALSO:
ALICE IN WONDERLAND
THE FIREBIRD
LITTLEST TAILOR
SLEEPING BEAUTY

PETER AND THE WOLF

CHEKOVIAN NATURALISTIC THEATRE

CAST OF CHARACTERS

Grandpa   - Narrator

Peter

Wolf   - Druskha

Cat   - Doctor

Bird   - Anya

Duck   - Marya

Hunter   - Ivan

Place: The Home of Peter and the Forest

Time: Not so long ago

ACT ONE

THE SCENE OPENS ON THE INTERIOR (LIBRARY) OF A RUSSIAN ARIS-
TOCRATIC HOME...SUMMERTIME...IN THE COUNTRY.   ONE CAN SEE
THE FOUNTAIN...THE TREES.   THE SCENERY SHOULD BE SLIGHTLY
SATIRICAL...AN ENORMOUS SWING CAN BE SEEN IN THE GARDEN.
INSIDE **IVAN**, THE TUTOR, AN EAGER AND EXCESSIVELY SENSITIVE
ROMANTIC, (POKING FUN AT THE TYPICAL RUSSIAN TUTOR OF
CHEKOVIAN DAYS) IS SEATED. HE SPEAKS WITH A STUTTER. HE'S
DRESSED IN TAN WITH A TOUCH OF GREEN.   PLEASE NOTE THE
COLOURS OF THE COSTUMES ARE IMPORTANT AS THEY ARE THE
COLOURS OF THE ANIMALS THEY BECOME IN ACT **TWO**. PLEASE NOTE
SET CAN BE AS SIMPLE A ROOM AS ONE PLEASES. A BACK DROP CAN
GIVE US THE GARDEN.

PETER   (TO AUDIENCE) Grown ups...I don't understand them.   I
just don't.   There's my tutor...he's my teacher...he talks all
day and says nothing. My name's Peter. What's yours? And
yours? And yours? I mean everybody. (EACH CHILD CALLS OUT HIS
NAME AND **PETER** SMILES AND GREETS THEM BY NAME WHEREVER POSSIBLE)

IVAN   P-P-Peter...P-P-Peter...Where are you? W-W-We haven't
done our lessons.

PETER   Here I am! No, here! Wait, here! (**PETER** HIDES FROM
ONE PLACE TO THE NEXT. THE **TUTOR** IS UP AND DOWN AND ALL AROUND
IN SEARCH OF HIM. FINALLY, AFTER CHASING HIM, **IVAN** GRABS **PETER**
BY THE HAND AND FIRMLY SEATS HIM WITH HIS LESSON BOOK. HE SITS
BESIDE HIM NODDING DREAMILY WITH BOOKS IN HAND)

IVAN   Y-Y-Y-Yes.   Y-Y-Y-Yes.

PETER   Yes what?

IVAN   To w-w-w-what you... (HITS HIS CHEEK) s-s-s-said.

PETER   What did I say?

IVAN   D-D-D-Does it m-m-m-matter?

PETER   Doesn't it matter?

IVAN   Y-Y-Y-Yes. I s-s-s-suppose it d-d-d-does.

PETER   Matter to whom?

IVAN   W-W-W-Why to y-y-y-you?

PETER   And not to you?

IVAN   Oh y-y-y-yes.

PETER   Yes what?

IVAN   M-M-M-Matter to me!

PETER   What does?

IVAN   (EXASPERATED) Anything you w-w-w-were... (HITS HIS
CHEEK) th-th-th-thinking th-th-that happened to m-m-m-matter.

PETER   What was it?

IVAN   H-H-How do I know? Y-Y-Y-You m-m-m-must tell m-m-m-me.

PETER   But you're the teacher. You're to tell me.

IVAN   (OUT OF CONTROL HE DROPS ALL THE BOOKS) T-T-T-Tell you
w-w-w-what?

PETER   Whatever matters.

        MOTHER ENTERS FROM THE GARDEN DRESSED IN BROWN AND TUR-
        QUOISE. SHE IS BEAUTIFUL...BORED...A WOMAN OF THE RUSSIAN
        ARISTOCRACY, ESCORTED BY THE DOCTOR. HE'S DRESSED IN A
        LINEN SUIT WITH WHITE SHIRT AND BLACK TIE. IVAN IS PRACTI-
        CALLY SITTING ON PETER, BY NOW.

DOCTOR   Anya...I tell you...you must keep up with the times.
If you don't watch out they'll take this house from you and the
orchard.

ANYA   (VERY AGITATED) Take this house! Oh, the orchard...my
beautiful apple orchard. (SHE SNEEZES)

PETER   (TO AUDIENCE) That's my Mother...and the Doctor. She
loves the apple orchard. That's all she talks about. As for the
Doctor, I never know what he talks about.

DOCTOR   You must take care. Put on your shawl.

ANYA   I'm not cold. It's my allergy.

DOCTOR   I'd forgotten. You should go to the sea. The hay is
bad for you.

ANYA   It's not the hay...it's the apple blossoms...the whole
orchard is blooming. I love it here...I don't like sea air.

PETER   (TO CHILDREN) You see. First he says go to the sea,
then she says she'll stay here.

ANYA   (SHE SNEEZES AGAIN) I do love the apple blossoms.

DOCTOR   Anya dear, are you crying?

ANYA   No...it's my allergy.

DOCTOR   Sniff this...it will help. (HE FUMBLES FOR A DISPENSER
IN ALL HIS POCKETS AND FINALLY FINDS ONE) You must do something
about the house. Do as Drushka said. Let them make apple cider
from the apples. It will at least pay the mortgage.

ANYA   Apple cider from my beautiful orchard... (SNEEZES)
Drushka knows about such things. I should do as he says. But
father will never let me. He couldn't bear to see the orchard

changed. Think of all those bottles of cider. What shall we do?

IVAN   (UP TO NOW HE HAS PRETENDED STUDYING WITH **PETER**)   Oh d-d-d-dear lady d-d-d-don't b-b-b-uild factories on this an-n-n-ncestral estate. S-s-sell the f-f-forest.

DOCTOR   Be quiet. Our life is passing by us like the stream flowing at the foot of the hill.

PETER   Where is it going to?

ANYA   Oh, my darling...it doesn't have to go anywhere.

PETER   Then why did Doctor say it was? (TO CHILDREN) See what I mean?

ANYA   He only meant that the life I had when I was your age is gone.

PETER   I should hope so. It was a long time ago.

ANYA   No, it wasn't.

DOCTOR   Of course, it wasn't.

PETER   But Mama...you're old...

DOCTOR   Your mother will never be old.

PETER   She's my mother and she's old.

DOCTOR   She is young. I am old...and foolish...and will always love her. (**ANYA** SMILES AT THE **DOCTOR**)

PETER   I can't count how old you are.

IVAN   F-F-Forgive me M-M-Madame...I can assure you I c-c-c-can't teach P-P-P-Peter n-n-n-not to s-s-speak his m-m-mind. One s-s-s-says s-s-such th-th-things when one is young. (HE WALKS OUT IN CONTROLLED ANGER. WE HEAR, AFTER HE'S GONE, A LOUD CRASH COMING FROM THE KITCHEN)

ANYA   I don't know why I keep Ivan.

PETER   For me? Anyway I love you, Mama, because you're beautiful...but old.

ANYA   And you're impossible.

PETER   What's that?

DOCTOR   That's being young. Come into the garden, Anya...we must discuss what has to be done.

ANYA   Oh dear Doctor, what can we do...nothing! (DRUSHKA ENTERS. HE IS A PEASANT TURNED ENTREPENEUR. FULL OF TREMENDOUS ENERGY AND ENTHUSIASM. HE IS DRESSED IN BROWN)

DRUSHKA   Who said nothing can be done...who?

DOCTOR   (SURPRISED) Drushka, good afternoon! I didn't know you were coming!

ANYA   Good afternoon, Drushka, such a surprise. Why have you come? To see me, I hope. (SHE IS SHY BUT HAPPY TO SEE HIM)

DRUSHKA   (HE LOOKS AT HER) It's always warming to see you.

ANYA   And the orchard! (SHE SNEEZES AND LAUGHS)

DRUSHKA   Ever since my boyhood...I've loved the orchard...this house...and everything in it. (ANYA AND DRUSHKA LOOK AT EACH OTHER)

DOCTOR   Do you remember the curtains in the library when your father was steward?

DRUSHKA   They were wine woven with pink roses. I remember the summer they were changed. I was almost a man. Sixteen.

ANYA   You love this house...this orchard, so much, yet you want me to change it all...to sell the orchard.

DRUSHKA   Times have changed. I'm not the same as my father. He was your servant and I'm your friend who advises you on business matters.

DOCTOR   (SARCASTIC) True...true. Times have changed.

DRUSHKA   Doctor, I've urgent news. That's why I came un- invited.

ANYA   (FRIGHTENED) Good or bad...(EVERYONE BECOMES TENSE AND SURROUNDS DRUSHKA. IVAN RETURNS)

DRUSHKA   The house is to be auctioned next week.

     ANYA FAINTS. DRUSHKA CATCHES HER AND DOCTOR CALLS, "Water, Water!" PETER ASKS IVAN, "What's an auction?" IVAN WEEPS, "A sale!...A sale!" AND INTO ALL THIS COMES GRANDPA.

GRANDPA   And what is all this nonsense that's going on?

DRUSHKA   The house...

GRANDPA   What about the house?

DOCTOR   Prince Peter Petrovitch, the house is to be auctioned next week. What do you intend doing?

GRANDPA   No one will buy my house, do you hear...no one.

DRUSHKA   The Bank won't hear you. Something has to be done.

GRANDPA   We will <u>not</u> sell the orchard!

ANYA   (RECOVERED) Drushka is only trying to help.

GRANDPA   We don't need his help. He's like a wolf waiting to devour us.

DRUSHKA   It's not I who'll devour you but the BANK! You won't face the disaster.

DOCTOR   Anya...Drushka...let's discuss these things in the garden. They're not stories to be told in front of children. (THEY EXIT. **IVAN** EXITS TO KITCHEN)

PETER   Why did you call Drushka a wolf, Grandpa? Are animals people and people animals? That's pretty silly.

GRANDPA   There are some people who behave like animals.

PETER   What kind of animal is Ivan?

GRANDPA   (SARCASTICALLY) He's not clever enough to be an animal. He's a hunter.

PETER   Then Mama?

GRANDPA   She's like a bird.

PETER   And the Doctor?

GRANDPA   He's a cat, a cunning cat.

PETER   And...me...and you!

GRANDPA   We are ourselves. The old and the young always are themselves.

    IVAN ENTERS HAVING OVERHEARD THEM.

IVAN   I b-b-beg your p-p-pardon...but...I'm not a h-h-hunter.

PETER   Catch me, hunter. (HE STALKS LIKE A WOLF BUT **IVAN** REFUSES TO PLAY. **PETER** GIVES UP ON **IVAN**. **IVAN** IS STILL ANGRY AND TRYING TO STOP **PETER** FROM MISBEHAVING) Oho, Grandpa, you're the oldest.

GRANDPA   (PREOCCUPIED AND WORRIED) Yes, I am.

PETER   You're older than this house and the orchard.

GRANDPA   No, it's much older than I.

PETER   How old is the oldest thing that ever was.

GRANDPA   Time itself is the oldest thing that ever was.

PETER   How old is that?

GRANDPA   Timeless.

PETER   Oh...and what age is timeless?   Is it as old as...let me think...

IVAN   (WHO HAS BEEN TRYING TO STOP PETER ALL ALONG) The s-s-sky...the air you b-b-breath...the earth you w-w-walk on is the oldest.

GRANDPA   That keeps changing in time. There's new soil...new grass each year...new air.

IVAN   Y-y-yes there is...b-b-but d-d-deep d-d-down the s-s-soil is old. Way up high the air is old.

GRANDPA   Beyond the gate is the forest. That forest is very old.

PETER   It is? Then I'll go there.

GRANDPA   No, you will not! In that forest is a wolf and that wolf is very dangerous.

PETER   Oh good, maybe it's Drushka. Then I'll capture him.

GRANDPA   No!

PETER   Why not?

GRANDPA   Because there's a real wolf in the forest.

IVAN   B-b-besides one must kn-kn-know how to h-h-hunt before one can c-c-capture a w-w-wolf.

PETER   Show me how.

IVAN   (STRONGLY) I'm not a h-h-hunter!

PETER   You are, Grandpa. Show me. I'm a wolf. See...I'm going to eat you up. (HE STALKS GRANDPA WHO PLAYS THE GAME OF HUNTER AND THE WOLF WITH PETER. THIS IS A MIME-DANCE IN WHICH THE TUTOR KEEPS RUNNING OUT OF THE WAY...JUMPING ON CHAIRS ETC. IN THE MIDST OF ALL THIS MARYA THE MAID DRESSED IN BLACK, YELLOW AND WHITE ENTERS WITH THE BIG SAMOVAR FOR TEA. SHE IS CHASED ROUND AND ROUND. SHE MANAGES TO PUT THE SAMOVAR ON THE TABLE AND FINALLY COLLIDES WITH PETER. BOTH FALL ON THE FLOOR. SHE GETS UP QUICKLY BRUSHING HERSELF OFF, FIXING HER CAP. WITH A LONG LOOK AT PETER AND DISHEVELLED HAIR, SHE ANNOUNCES)

MARYA   The tea is ready! (SHE GOES TO THE DOOR AND SHOUTS) Tea is ready! (ANYA, DRUSHKA AND DOCTOR COME IN FROM THE GARDEN. MARYA STANDS PREPARED WITH TEA CLOTH ON HER ARM NEATLY FOLDED. THIS IS HER INSIGNIA. SHE USES IT FOR EVERYTHING, AS A HANDKERCHIEF...RAG...ANYWAY YOU WISH TO USE IT FOR FUN)

ANYA   Marya, where have you been?

MARYA   Excuse me, but I was caught in the forest between the hunter and the wolf.

ANYA   What?

MARYA   Yes, here in the library.

ANYA   What is wrong with you?

GRANDPA   She was almost caught. (EYEING DRUSHKA) I was the
hunter, so I know.

PETER   I was the wolf. I swallowed her.

ANYA   Peter, stop this at once. Father, you're not helping
the boy with such stories.

PETER   It wasn't a story, it was a game.

ANYA   How will you grow up with everyone spoiling you?

DOCTOR   One does...one always does. Let's have some of that
delicious tea. (ANYA SERVES TEA FROM THE SAMOVAR) One thing will
never change, and that is tea.

PETER   It's not the same tea as yesterday. Or is it, Marya?

MARYA   (TEARFUL) It is freshly-made tea. (SHE RUNS TO THE KIT-
CHEN)

ANYA   (CALLING AFTER HER) The child is only teasing, Marya.

ANYA   Yes, this is what I'll always remember...sitting here
and drinking tea...the samovar, the library, the (SNEEZES) gar-
den. (SHE HAS SPILT THE TEA) Oh look at my dress. Marya!
Marya! Quickly a cloth. (MARYA COMES RUNNING IN WITH THE TEA
CLOTH, DRIES ANYA'S DRESS IN DESPERATION. SHE GOES SKIRTING
ROUND THE ROOM AND DRIES EVERYONE'S LAP. SHE LOOKS TO IVAN FOR
HELP) What are you doing? Enough...enough. (SHE EXITS) What
has gone wrong with that girl.

DRUSHKA   Poor Marya, she's afraid.

PETER   She's still in the forest. (HE STALKS)

ANYA   Father, look what you've done to my Peter.

IVAN   P-P-Peter, come s-s-sit beside me.

PETER   No. I'm a ferocious wolf. Drink your tea. (IVAN CLAT-
TERS HIS CUP AND SAUCER WITH PRETENDED FRIGHT)

IVAN   B-B-B-Behave yourself, P-P-Peter, else everyone will
think you're a p-p-peasant.

GRANDPA   A peasant! The next Prince Peter Petrovitch, a peasant!

DRUSHKA   There's nothing wrong with being a peasant. One day,
the peasants will drink tea in such cups and saucers. (HE PUTS
HIS DOWN FURIOUSLY)

DOCTOR   (TO GRANDPA) Be careful, Peter Petrovitch, all peasants
are no longer serfs. Some are very rich.

ANYA   (LAUGHING) Who knows...Marya might one day own this
house and I might be making the tea. Ah well, my beautiful
memories.

        TEA IS FINISHED. **MARYA** ENTERS AND CLEARS THE TABLE. SHE
        LOOKS AT **IVAN** WHO SHYLY GLANCES BACK AT HER. QUICKLY SHE
        FIXES HER TEA CLOTH AND EXITS.

DOCTOR   Now for a good game of chess. Anya, let's go over to
Nicholai's. He's alone today. And you, Drushka, how is your
chess today?

DRUSHKA   What difference does it make? You already said that
Nicholai plays a better chess game than I.

DOCTOR   Nonsense, Drushka, I have a game going with Nicholai.

DRUSHKA   Let me show you how to play, dear Doctor. (HE IS FUR-
IOUS. HE TEARS INTO PIECES A PAPER HE FINDS IN HIS POCKET. HE
GETS DOWN ON HANDS AND KNEES PUTTING THE PIECES OUT LIKE ON A
CHESS BOARD...PIECES ON BOTH SIDES.   HE STANDS UP PLACING HIS
FEET ON BOTH SIDES OF THE CHESS BOARD AND SHOUTS) My King has
won! (HE PULLS FROM HIS POCKET ANOTHER PAPER WAVING IT AS HE
SHOUTS) My King has won! (HE LEAPS WITH TRIUMPH AS HE WAVES THE
PAPER WHICH IS A LETTER. HE OPENS IT. HE LOOKS AT THE PAPER AND
IT'S NOT WHAT HE THINKS IT IS. HE'S DEVASTATED. HE TRIES PUT-
TING THE LETTER BACK IN HIS POCKET. HE DOESN'T SEE THAT IT
SLIPPED. PETER QUIETLY PICKS IT UP AND PUTS IT IN HIS POCKET)

DRUSHKA   My lease...I've torn my lease!

DOCTOR   A good game of chess will help. (**DOCTOR** DRAGS **DRUSHKA**)
Coming Anya. (THEY LEAVE AS **DRUSHKA** KEEPS REPEATING)

DRUSHKA   I've torn my lease! I've torn my lease! (THEY EXIT)

GRANDPA   Go, go to Nicholai and play chess. We'll save your
pieces of paper! Peter and I will solve the auction of the house
and orchard. Won't we?

PETER   Oh yes, Grandpa, we will.

GRANDPA   Ivan, gather these pieces. (**PETER** AND **GRANDPA** EXIT TO
GARDEN)

        IVAN IS LEFT ALONE ON STAGE. HE GOES ON A RAMPAGE OF COL-
        LECTING ALL THE PIECES. HE PUTS THEM INTO A CUP. **MARYA** EN-
        TERS, HOPING TO BE ALONE WITH **IVAN**.

IVAN   I won't t-t-teach any longer. I h-h-have the soul of a
p-p-poet. I'll l-l-leave this house!

MARYA   Ivan, what have you done!

IVAN   I've d-d-done n-n-nothing. It's D-D-Drushka.

MARYA   Leave this house...and where will you go?

IVAN   P-P-Paris.

MARYA   Just when we're all in trouble!   What will happen to
us? (SHE USES THE TEA CLOTH TO DRY HER EYES)

IVAN   You'll get swallowed up...by the wolf.

MARYA   Don't you start that game.

IVAN   You're a d-d-d-duck...that's what you are.

MARYA   (WEEPING) Why?

IVAN   Because you w-w-w-waddle.

MARYA   (TEARFUL) I do NOT! Oh you wicked, wicked man.

IVAN   No...I'm a H-U-N-T-E-R of p-p-pieces of p-p-paper.

MARYA   (FLOODING TEARS) Stop. You play games when everything
is crumbling! (SHE RUNS OUT WITH IVAN CHASING AFTER HER CALLING
OUT)

IVAN   M-M-Marya, wait, M-M-Marya. I didn't m-m-mean w-w-what
I s-s-said!

        PETER COMES RUNNING IN.

PETER   Ivan? Ivan Ivanovitch, did you call me? No one's
here. Good, now I can read Drushka's letter. (TO AUDIENCE) Oh,
if you tell anyone...I'll surely be spanked. Maybe I better not
say anything. Should I? Do you want me to tell you? (CHILDREN
SHOUT, "YES") Well now, let me find it. (HE SEARCHES INSIDE ONE
POCKET AND THEN THE OTHER, BACK AND FORTH FROM ONE CHEST POCKET
TO THE OTHER UNTIL HE FINALLY FINDS THE LETTER) Here it is.
(OPENS AND READS THE LETTER) It's a love letter...from Drushka
to Mama. Oh...oh, here comes Grandpa.

        GRANDPA ENTERS LOOKING FOR PETER.

GRANDPA   Aha, so there you are.

PETER   Here I am.

GRANDPA   And what are you hiding in your hand.

PETER   I'm not hiding anything. I'll prove it. (HE KNOCKS ON
GRANDPA'S SHOULDER LIKE A DOOR. GRANDPA STANDS THERE WITH FEET
SLIGHTLY APART WAITING TO BE SHOWN)

GRANDPA   (AS PETER KNOCKS ON HIS SHOULDER) What is it?

PETER   May I come in ?

GRANDPA   Now, what are you doing?

PETER   You'll see.   (HE JUMPS DOWN BETWEEN GRANDPA'S LEGS.
HIS HEAD AND HANDS SHOWING THROUGH, WAVING THE LETTER) See I've

nothing to hide.

GRANDPA   What are you waving?

PETER   A love letter.

GRANDPA   Whose?

PETER   Drushka's.

GRANDPA   (SURPRISED) Whose?

PETER   Drushka's.

GRANDPA   You go this minute and put the letter back from
wherever you took it.   (HE PULLS HIM FORWARD FROM BETWEEN HIS
LEGS AND STANDS HIM UP) Wait. To whom did he write?

PETER   To Mama.

GRANDPA   To whom?

PETER   It says here Dearest Anya!

GRANDPA   What more did it say?

PETER   That he'll buy the house and orchard back for her.

GRANDPA   He will what? Never mind, we'd better return the letter. (HE HESITATES) I'll hold it 'til he returns. (HE HESITATES)
But first, I'll read...just a bit of it.

PETER   You mustn't read other people's letters, Grandpa.

GRANDPA   (FINISHES LETTER...FOLDS IT AND THEN PUTS IT IN HIS
POCKET. GRANDPA SITS DOWN TO THINK AS PETER COMES AND SITS BE-
SIDE HIM) Hush, I'm holding it for Drushka. (PETER NESTLES INTO
GRANDPA AS HE PUTS HIS HEAD IN GRANDPA'S LAP)

PETER   Grandpa, is there really a wolf in the forest?

GRANDPA   Yes, there is.

PETER   And is he very dangerous?

GRANDPA   Yes, he is very dangerous.

PETER   How do you know?

GRANDPA   Everyone talks of him.

PETER   Why don't they capture him?

GRANDPA   Because he's outsmarted all of us...even the hunters.

PETER   He has!

GRANDPA   Yes, he has.

PETER   I'll capture the wolf, Grandpa. I'll capture the wolf.
(HE DOZES OFF AS LIGHTS DIM AND GRANDPA SMILINGLY LOOKS AT PETER.
HE TAKES OUT DRUSHKA'S LETTER AND SAYS)

GRANDPA   So shall I.

CURTAIN

END OF ACT ONE

ACT TWO

THE CHARACTERS SET IN THEIR COLOURS OF ACT ONE BECOME THE
ANIMALS IN THE <u>SAME</u> COLOURS IN ACT TWO SO THAT YOU IDENTIFY
EACH OF THE ANIMALS FROM ACT ONE BY COLOUR AS WELL AS
CHARACTERISATION. **GRANDPA** BECOMES **NARRATOR**.

FIRST FANFARE: HOUSE LIGHTS DIM
SECOND FANFARE: CURTAINS PART
THIRD FANFARE: **NARRATOR** ENTERS
FOURTH FANFARE: SPOT LIGHTS **NARRATOR** AT HIS ROSTRUM PLACED
                 AT SIDE END OF STAGE.

THE CURTAINS OPEN ON A HALF LIGHTED STAGE IN THE MEADOW, THE
ORCHARD BORDERING ON THE FOREST. IT IS FILLED WITH TREES, A
BIG ONE DOMINATES THE STAGE. SIDE STAGE THE **NARRATOR** TELLS
THE STORY AS WE SEE THE DREAM. THE MUSIC OF PETER AND THE
WOLF IS PLAYED THROUGHOUT. THE DIALOGUE IS TIMED EXACTLY TO
IT. THE * INDICATES THE SPECIAL MUSIC.

NARRATOR Once there was a boy named **Peter** (HE AWAKENS) and that
is Peter's music played by the strings.* He lived with his
Grandfather, that is my music played by the basoon,* in a big
house. The house had a beautiful orchard bordering the forest.
Now **Peter** had some friends whom he played with all day. One was
a **Bird**, that's the Bird's music played by a flute.*
(**ANYA** APPEARS AS THE **BIRD**)
The next was a **Duck**, that's the Duck's music played by the oboe.*
(**MARYA** APPEARS AS THE **DUCK**)
and finally the **Cat**, the Cat's music is played by a clarinet in
the lower register.*
(THE **DOCTOR** ENTERS AS THE **CAT**)
And just so that you will know their music...listen to the sound
of the **Wolf**, played by the horns,*
(**DRUSHKA** ENTERS AS THE **WOLF** AND DISAPPEARS)
and finally the **Hunter** played by the kettle drums.*
(**IVAN** ENTERS AS THE **HUNTER** AND DISAPPEARS)

MIME-DANCE AND MUSIC. EACH OF THE CHARACTERS (ANIMALS)
SPEAKS HIS LINES. ONE CAN LET THE NARRATOR SPEAK ALL THE
LINES IF THE WHOLE SEQUENCE IS DONE IN DANCE WITHOUT ANY
INTERRUPTION!

NARRATOR While **Peter** was in the orchard with his friends, the
Duck who was very fond of **Peter**...decided to go for a swim.
Peter told her to be careful because there was a **Wolf** in the
forest. Hadn't Grandpa told him that over and over again.

Meanwhile as the **Duck** swam and **Peter** looked about for the **Wolf** he
could not find, the **Bird** fluttered her wings round **Peter**, for she
loved him. "Oh, there's the **Duck**", she chirped. "What kind of a
Bird are you, if you can't fly?" "What kind of **Bird** are you, if
you don't swim?" answered the **Duck**.   "But flying is much more
fun", responded the **Bird**.   And round **Peter** she flew.   Suddenly
...quietly...out crept the **Cat**...cautiously looking this way and
that way.   What was he looking for?   Perhaps the **Wolf**...no.   It
was for the **Bird**.   Just as he was upon her, **Peter** shouted, "Watch
out!"   And away to the tree she flew.   "Oh, oh, I'm here", called
the **Bird**.   "Where?" asked the **Cat**.   "Look for me", teased the
Bird.   The **Cat** stalked about.   "I don't like playing
games...you're probably in the tree hiding".   He curled up his
tail and decided to wait under the tree where the **Bird** tweeted,
gleefully.   He pretended to sleep...for who knows, maybe the **Bird**
might fly down and then what a treat.   **Peter** looked at the **Cat**.
He knew he was up to something.   "Are you sleeping?" asked **Peter**
of the **Cat**.   There was no answer.   "I said, are you sleeping?"
asked **Peter** again.   "Yes", shouted the **Cat** and back to his position he went...waiting...just waiting.   Out of the water came the
Duck.   She shook and shook to dry herself off.   "I can lick myself
clean", bragged the **Cat**.   "I don't have to swim.   My feathers are
always clean", cooed the **Bird**.   "I have to bathe myself in a
tub", said **Peter**, "I wish I could jump into the pond".   The Duck
shook herself again and back to the pond she waddled.   The **Cat**
saw his chance and stealthily crept after the **Bird**.   The **Bird**
watched and waited.   Just as the **Cat** was about to jump...the **Bird**
flew off mocking the **Cat**.   The **Cat** was just not quick enough for
the **Bird**.   "Oh, you did try to catch the **Bird**.   Remember what I
said.   Let's stay friends...and catch the **Wolf** instead", warned
Peter.   Just then **Grandpa** came out, "Peter, didn't I tell you not
to go into the meadow.   There is a **Wolf** in the forest who prowls
these meadows.   Now back to the house with you".   And off he went
taking **Peter** firmly by the hand.   Just as he left...the **Wolf**
stole over the edge of the orchard into the meadow.   The **Bird**
flew quickly into the tree, the **Cat** jumped to safety.   The **Wolf**
stalked the ground, **he** missed his good pickings.   But **he** would
outsmart them.   He would be gallant, and friendly and then take
them by surprise.   "Quack, quack..."   His ears perked.   The **Duck**,
in her excitement, left the pond.   **He** hadn't seen her at first.
Round and round **he** chased, finally pouncing upon the **Duck** and
swallowing her whole.   He was so pleased with himself...a good
meal at last.   He sat beaming.   But meanwhile, **Peter** had returned
with a rope in hand.   "Fly around the **Wolf**", **Peter** commanded.
The **Bird** flew about the **Wolf**. "Come play with me", she taunted.
The **Wolf** chased her but away she would fly each time.   Then back
again round and round the **Wolf**'s head 'til he was dizzy.   **Peter**,
meanwhile, twirled his rope.   Before the **Wolf** knew what had happened, his tail was tied in knots.   The harder the **Wolf** pulled,
the tighter the knots became.   "We've captured the **Wolf**", cried
Peter.   "So did I", reminded the **Bird**.   "We both captured the
Wolf".   As they stood triumphantly, the **Hunter** appeared with his
guns, knives and magnifying glass.   He looked and looked and
looked, closer and closer 'til he suddenly jumped back.   It was
Peter's nose.   "Oh, but where's the **Wolf**?"   "We captured him.
He's here", **Peter** proudly announced.   "But I am the **Hunter** and I
should have done it", whispered the **Hunter**, sadly.   "How did you
find him?"   "He came here", murmured **Peter**, "then I tied him with

my rope. Come see!" "It is the **Wolf**! All nicely captured!"
sighed the **Hunter**.   Suddenly, **Peter** heard a booming voice.
"Peter, Peter, where are you? Did you go into the meadow?
Peter, answer me, I say!"   "Grandpa, I'm here.   Come see how we
captured the Wolf".   "But he might have eaten you", scolded
Grandpa. "He didn't though. Just look", **Peter** cried out. How
happy and triumphant they all were pulling the **Wolf** behind them.
Peter first, of course, then the **Hunter** holding the **Wolf**, followed by the **Cat**. The **Bird** flew back and forth, twittering, "Oh
what a fine pair we are, **Peter** and I. We caught the **Wolf**". As
the procession marched one could hear the quacking of the
Duck...for the **Wolf** in his haste had swallowed her alive and
whole. And that was how **Peter** captured the **Wolf**. (ALL EXIT DOWN
THE AISLE. END OF MUSIC)

END OF ACT TWO

EPILOGUE

WE FIND **PETER** AND **GRANDPA** AS IN THE END OF ACT ONE. PETER
AWAKENS RUBBING HIS EYES.

GRANDPA   You had a pleasant dream?

PETER   Grandpa, honestly and truly, I captured the Wolf!

GRANDPA   Didn't the Bird help you at all?

PETER   How did you know?

GRANDPA   Because, you talked while you were dreaming. But just
the same she did help you.

PETER   It wasn't a dream. I really did it.

GRANDPA   (TAPPING THE LETTER OF **DRUSHKA**) Maybe you did.

PETER   (EXCITED) You mean you believe I really and truly captured the Wolf. Oh, Grandpa, I fooled you. I only dreamt I did.

GRANDPA   Your dream is coming true then.

PETER   How?

GRANDPA   I shall return the letter to Drushka with my blessings...and so we will have captured the Wolf.

PETER   You've mixed me all up.

GRANDPA   If Drushka's the Wolf and your Mother is the Bird, and
I consent to Drushka's marrying your Mama, then the Wolf is captured...for life.

PETER   And we have saved the orchard.

GRANDPA   We will have saved the orchard.

PETER   And captured the Wolf. I shall have a wolf for my
father...well...a captured wolf...no...a tamed wolf.

GRANDPA   Peter, that will be our secret. We have all captured
the Wolf. But we must never let Drushka know.

PETER   No...never. No one will ever say a word. (HE LOOKS TO
CHILDREN)

BLACKOUT

END OF PLAY

THE FOREST

THE LIBRARY

GRANDPA
PETER
BIRD ~ ANYA
CHARACTERS
COSTUMES ALTER
AS THEY BECOME
ANIMALS, BUT
THEIR COLOURS
STAY THE SAME
COLOUR →
TURQUOISE and BROWN

DRUSHKA — WOLF
COLOURS ~ BROWN

MARYA — DUCK
Costume colours ~ Black, yellow, white,
same after transformation.

IVAN — shown as HUNTER
TAN COSTUME

DOCTOR — CAT
BLACK & WHITE COSTUME

THE CRICKET THEATRE
AND BLANCHE MARVIN
PRESENT:

THE MERRI-MIMES'
ALICE in WONDERLAND

ADAPTED by MARIO SILETTI
ARNOLD HRUSHKA AND RHODA CARROLL
DIRECTED by MARIO SILETTI
CHOREOGRAPHY - WILLIAM HARAHAN
MUSIC by CLAIRE BROOK
STAGE MANAGER AND LIGHTS : JOSEPH STELL
CAST :
ALICE — ELIZABETH TANNER
WHITE RABBIT - LEA PREDEAU
MAD HATTER, HUMPTY AND DUCHESS - BOB SPIVAK
MOCK TURTLE AND CHESHIRE CAT - R. S. DOUGLAS
COOK AND GRYPHON - ROBERT PARNELL
WHITE QUEEN - POLLY GARRETT
QUEEN AND DOORMOUSE - RHODA CARROLL

———

AT THE CRICKET THEATRE
162 SECOND AVE. (at 10th st.) OR-4 3960

PERFORMANCES: 1 - 2:30 - 4 PM

ALSO:

PETER AND THE WOLF
CINDERELLA
THE FIREBIRD
SLEEPING BEAUTY
THE LITTLEST TAILOR

ALICE IN WONDERLAND

COMEDIE DEL ARTE THEATRE

CAST OF CHARACTERS

Alice

White Rabbit

Duchess

Cheshire Cat

Hatter

Dormouse

Gryphon

Mock Turtle

Red Queen

White Queen

Humpty Dumpty

Cook

Place: Alice's Sitting Room and Wonderland

Time: Forever and ever

ACT ONE

SCENE ONE

IN FRONT OF THE CURTAINS THE **WHITE RABBIT** ENTERS ON TIPTOE.

WHITE RABBIT
          Sshh, quietly now. She mustn't hear. She mustn't know I'm here.

          A MINIMUM SET PIECE. THERE'S A TABLE WITH A VERY LONG COVER TUCKED UNDER. THE TOP OF THE TABLE IS A SEPARATE PIECE. THE TABLE CLOTH IS STAPLED TO THE TOP. A LARGE BOTTLE IS ON THE TABLE. ALICE IS SITTING ON THE FLOOR, PLAYING WITH HER KIT-TEN.

ALICE   Oh, you wicked, wicked little thing! Really, Dinah ought to have taught you better manners! Imagine playing with Mamma's best wool! When I think of all the mischief you've been doing lately, I really think you need a good talking-to. Now, my mischievous darling, I'm going to tell you all your faults. Fault number one: you pulled Snowdrop's tail just as I set her three o'clock milk down before her. Now don't deny it, kitty; I heard you. Fault number two: kitty, you mustn't giggle when I talk to you...it isn't polite at all...giggle? Cats can't giggle, can they? Why, cats can't even laugh, or at any rate, I've never heard of any that do. How very curious!

WHITE RABBIT
          Oh my ears and whiskers...I'll be late, I'll be late!

ALICE   Goodness, a rabbit with gloves, a waistcoat and a pocket watch.

WHITE RABBIT
          Too late, too late to explain. Today is the Coronation of the new Queen of Wonderland and I'm late. Oh dear, oh dear!

ALICE   A Coronation! Wonderland! (**RABBIT EXITS**) Mr.Rabbit, take me with you. Oh, he's gone! It would have been such fun to go to Wonderland. (TO AUDIENCE) Hello, do any of you know how I can find the rabbit? This bottle? It most distinctly says, "Drink me" on it. Do you think I should try a drop? I do believe I'm a wee bit afraid. (DRINKS FROM BOTTLE, AFTER CHILDREN SHOUT "YES") Oh my, oh my! Oh dear, oh dear, I seem to be shrinking.

          AS SOON AS **ALICE** DRINKS FROM THE BOTTLE, THE TABLE TOP RISES UP AND UP; THE CLOTH GROWS WITH IT. UNDERNEATH HAS BEEN AN ACTOR WHO STANDS UP BIT BY BIT 'TIL HE IS STANDING ERECT. HE THEN RAISES HIS HANDS ABOVE HIS HEAD HOLDING THE TABLE TOP. WE NEVER SEE THE ACTOR BUT THE TABLE IS NOW WAY ABOVE **ALICE** AND SO SHE LOOKS SMALLER.

ALICE: What do I do now? Oh, here are instructions, "Close your eyes and dream of your wish as you turn round and round and round." (**ALICE** CLOSES HER EYES AND TURNS ROUND) Close your eyes and dream of your wish...I wish I were in Wonderland, I wish I were a Queen, I wish I were in Wonderland, I wish I were a Queen...

        MUSIC. BLACKOUT

SCENE TWO

        LIGHTS. THE CURTAINS OPEN ON A SET PIECE OF WONDERLAND. A TREE AND CHESS BOARD FLOOR OF HUGE DIMENSIONS DOMINATE THE STAGE. MUSHROOMS ARE STOOLS TO SIT ON OR USED AS TABLES.

ALICE   Curiouser and curiouser...how queer everything is! Yesterday, things went on as usual, but today I'm sure I must be someone else. I do believe I am in Wonderland. Oh, how lovely! It's marked out like a huge chess game being played all over the world. But how am I ever to get to the Coronation? (**RED QUEEN FLIES IN**) Oh my, look! It's the **RED QUEEN**.

RED QUEEN Where did you come from and where are you going? Look up, speak nicely and don't twiddle your fingers.

ALICE   You see I've lost my way.

RED QUEEN I don't know what you mean by your way, all the ways about here belong to me...but why did you come out here at all? Curtsey while you're thinking what to say. It saves time.

ALICE   I'll try that when I go home, the next time I'm a little late for dinner.

RED QUEEN It's time for you to answer me now. Open your mouth a little wider when you speak and always say, "Your Majesty".

ALICE   I came to go to the Coronation of the new Queen, Your Majesty.

RED QUEEN You may call me "Queen". Oh, here comes the wind! (**WIND BLOWS**) Run, run! Faster, faster!

ALICE   Where are we?

RED QUEEN Don't try to talk! Faster! Faster!

ALICE   Are we nearly there?

RED QUEEN Nearly there, we passed it ten minutes ago. Faster! (**WIND STOPS**) There, you may rest now.

ALICE   Why, I believe we've been in the same spot all the time. Everything's just as it was. Oh look, here is somebody's shawl!

RED QUEEN It must have been blown in by the wind.

WHITE QUEEN
        (**DRIFTS IN**) Bread and butter, bread and butter. (**THEY COLLIDE**) Oh!

ALICE   Am I addressing the White Queen?

RED QUEEN You most assuredly are!

WHITE QUEEN
           I don't know if I'd call that a dressing. It isn't my
notion of the thing at all.

ALICE   Every single thing is crooked!

RED QUEEN And she's opening all over...poor dear!

ALICE   If Your Majesty will only tell me the right way to
begin, I'll do it as best I can.

WHITE QUEEN
           But I don't want it done. I've been addressing myself
for hours.

ALICE   May I put your shawl on straight for you?

WHITE QUEEN
           I don't know what's the matter with it! It's out of
temper I think. I've pinned it here, and I've pinned it there,
but there's no pleasing it.

ALICE   (FIXING SHAWL) There! You look rather better now.

WHITE QUEEN
           But what brings you out here, child?

ALICE   I wanted to see the Coronation of the new Queen. Who
is she, please?

RED QUEEN Oh, that would be telling.

WHITE QUEEN
           It is all a wonderful surprise!

ALICE   A surprise! How wonderful! But how does one get
there?

RED QUEEN In order to see the Coronation of the Queen you must
first visit all eight squares in Wonderland. (SHE PULLS OUT
SEVERAL PLAYING CARDS OF ONLY KINGS, QUEENS, JACKS AND JOKERS
FROM HER POCKET)

WHITE QUEEN
           I shall lead you on your journey and introduce you to
everybody.

RED QUEEN When you have finished meeting everybody you will
have arrived in the eighth and final square where the Coronation
will take place and it's all feasting and fun.

WHITE QUEEN
           Would you like to try the journey with me? You can be
my pawn.

ALICE   Yes, oh yes, Your Majesties!

RED QUEEN Very well, I shall write the instructions down for you.
(SHE WRITES A LIST ON THE PLAYING CARDS) A pawn as you know
starts in the second square.

WHITE QUEEN
          The second square.

RED QUEEN And you are there now. A few yards later you'll be in
the third square where you will meet the Duchess...

WHITE QUEEN
          Her Cook...

RED QUEEN And her Cat. A few yards later you'll be in the fourth
square and you'll have a tea party.

WHITE QUEEN
          With the very best bread and butter, you know.

RED QUEEN Then there's the fifth square. That belongs to the Mock
Turtle. A few yards later you'll be in the sixth square which
belongs to the White Queen.

WHITE QUEEN
          We'll be able to rest in my square, my dear.

RED QUEEN The seventh square...

WHITE QUEEN
          You'll get there in leaps and bounds...

RED QUEEN Belongs to Humpty Dumpty. The eighth square is the end
of your journey.

WHITE QUEEN
          And we shall arrive for the crowning of the new Queen.

RED QUEEN Here is your list of instructions. (GIVES ALICE CARDS)
You are both ready to start your trip through Wonderland. Speak
in French when you can't think of the English for a thing, turn
out your toes when you walk, and remember who you are.
Goodbyeeeee! (EXIT)

     MUSIC.

ALICE   She can run very fast, can't she?

WHITE QUEEN
          Are we ready to start? Are we hungry, child?

ALICE   Well, yes.

WHITE QUEEN
          Come, child, I smell soup cooking at the Duchess'
Square.

MUSIC. DUCHESS AND CAT ENTER.

ALICE   Oh please, I'm looking for the Duchess.

DUCHESS   I'm the Duchess, child. More pepper...

SHE SNEEZES, COOK SNEEZES, ALICE SNEEZES, CAT "MEOW!"

ALICE   Excuse me, but there's too much pepper in that soup.

DUCHESS   And the moral of that is, be what you would seem to be, or if you would like to put it more simple, never imagine yourself to be otherwise than what you might have it appear to others that what you were or might have been was not other than what you had been or would have appeared to them to be otherwise. More pepper?

SHE SNEEZES, COOK SNEEZES, ALICE SNEEZES, CAT "MEOW!"

ALICE   Please, would you tell me why your cat grins like that?

DUCHESS   It's a Cheshire Cat, child, that's why.

ALICE   I didn't know Cheshire Cats could grin. I didn't know cats could grin at all.

DUCHESS   All of them can, and most of them do.

ALICE   I don't know of any that do.

DUCHESS   You don't know much, and that's a fact. More pepper!

ALICE   If I were a Duchess, I'd never have pepper in my kitchen. Soup tastes fine without it. And I do believe that pepper makes people hot-tempered.

DUCHESS   Your're thinking about something, child, and that makes you forget to talk, and the moral of that is, if people would mind their own business, the world would go around a great deal faster than it does.

ALICE   Which would do little good. It takes the earth twenty-four hours to turn on its axis.

DUCHESS   Talking of axes, chop off her head!

ALICE   Oh dear!

DUCHESS   I speak roughly to my little boy
          And beat him when he sneezes
          He only does it to annoy
          Because he knows it teases.
Goodbye, child. Cook and I are off. We have to go and play croquet with the Queen. (EXIT)

ALICE   Well, they're gone. My, what a rude Duchess! However, I must hurry on to the next square. Let me see that list of directions. I can't seem to make much sense of this list, it seems to be written backwards. Oh, Cheshire puss, would you tell me please which way I go from here?

CAT   That depends a good deal on where you want to get to.

ALICE   I don't care much where I go.

CAT   Then it doesn't matter which way you do go.

ALICE   So long as I get somewhere.

CAT   Oh, you're sure to do that if you only walk long enough.

ALICE   Well, what sort of people live about here?

CAT   In one direction lives a Hatter, in the other lives a March Hare. Visit either you like. They're both mad.

ALICE   But I don't want to go amongst mad people.

CAT   We're all mad here. I'm mad. (DISAPPEARS)

ALICE   Oh dear, he's gone. Cheshire Cat?

CAT   (SUDDENLY APPEARS) Meow.

ALICE   How do you know you're mad?

CAT   To begin with, a dog's not mad. Right?

ALICE   That's true.

CAT   Well, a dog growls when it's angry and wags it's tail when it's pleased. I growl when I'm pleased and wag my tail when I'm angry. Therefore, I'm mad. I don't mind. I'm going to see the Hatter. I know what he looks like. (EXITS)

ALICE   I do wish he would stop appearing and disappearing. It makes me quite giddy. Do you know where he is?

WHITE QUEEN
        Dear child, he came to the end of his tale and there-fore he is no more. We still have more squares to visit.

ALICE   But I didn't get any soup and I'm still quite hungry, thank you.

WHITE QUEEN
        Well then, are we ready for tea?

ALICE   Oh, I adore tea! But is it time for tea yet?

WHITE QUEEN
        It's always tea time in Wonderland. Six o'clock. Now ...here is the fourth square with the White Rabbit, the Mad Hat-ter, the Dormouse and the Tea Party.

MUSIC. ALL CHARACTERS ENTER AND SET TABLE FOR TEA.

ALL   No room...no room!

ALICE   There's plenty of room.

WHITE RABBIT
           Have some wine.

ALICE   I don't see any wine.

WHITE RABBIT
           That's because there isn't any.

ALICE   Then it wasn't very civil of you to offer it.

WHITE RABBIT
           It wasn't very civil of you to sit down without being
invited.

ALICE   I didn't know it was your table. It's laid for a great
many more than three.

HATTER   Your hair needs cutting.

ALICE   You should learn not to make personal remarks. It's
very rude.

HATTER   Why is a raven like a writing desk?

ALICE   Oh, a riddle! I believe I can guess that.

WHITE RABBIT
           Do you mean you think you could find out the answer to
it?

ALICE   Exactly so.

WHITE RABBIT
           Then why don't you say what you mean?

ALICE   I do. At least, at least I mean what I say. That's
the same thing, you know.

HATTER   Not the same thing at all. Why you might just as well
say that "I see what I eat" is the same thing as "I eat what I
see".

WHITE RABBIT
           You might just as well say that "I like what I get" is
the same thing as "I get what I like".

DORMOUSE (SLEEPILY) You might just as well say that "I breathe
when I sleep" is the same thing as "I sleep when I breathe".

HATTER   It is the same thing with you.   (TO ALICE) Have you
guessed the riddle yet?

ALICE   No. I give up. What's the answer?

HATTER   I haven't the slightest idea!

WHITE RABBIT
          Nor I.

ALICE   I think you might do something better with the time
than wasting it in asking riddles that have no answers.

HATTER   If you knew time as well as I do, you wouldn't talk
about wasting "it"!   It's a "him"!   Besides, we quarrelled last
March just before he went mad. (INDICATES WHITE RABBIT WITH
SPOON) It was at the great concert given by the Duchess and I had
to sing.
          "Twinkle, twinkle little bat
          How I wonder what you're at..."
You know the song perhaps?

ALICE   I've heard something like it.

HATTER   It goes on,
          "Up above the world you fly
          Like a tea-tray in the sky"

DORMOUSE (IN SLEEP) Twinkle, twinkle, twinkle, twinkle...
(CONTINUES UNTIL PINCHED)

HATTER   Well, I'd hardly finished the first...I'd hardly
finished the first verse. (LOUDER) I'd hardly finished the first
verse... (PINCHES DORMOUSE) when the Duchess bawled out, "He's
murdering Time. Off with his head!"

ALICE   How dreadfully savage!

HATTER   And ever since then, he won't do a thing I ask. It's
always six o'clock now.

ALICE   Is that the reason for so many tea things put out here?

HATTER   Yes, that's it. It's always tea time and we've no time
to wash the things between whiles.

ALICE   Then you keep moving around, I suppose.

HATTER   Exactly so. As the things get used up.

ALICE   But when do you come to the beginning again?

WHITE RABBIT
          Suppose we change the subject.   I'm getting tired of
this. I vote the young lady tells us a story.

ALICE   I'm afraid I don't know one.

WHITE RABBIT
          Then the Dormouse shall. (PINCHING HIM) Wake up, Dor-
mouse.

DORMOUSE   I wasn't asleep.   I heard every word you chaps were
saying.

WHITE RABBIT
          Tell us a story.

ALICE   Yes, please do!

HATTER   And be quick about it or you'll be asleep before it's
done.

DORMOUSE Once upon a time, there were three little sisters,
and their names were Elsie, Lacie, and Tillie; and they lived at
the bottom of a well.

ALICE   But why did they live at the bottom of a well?

DORMOUSE It was a treacle well.

ALICE   Treacle is very much like molasses. They'd have been
very ill and besides there's no such...

HATTER   Shhhhh!

DORMOUSE If you can't be civil, you'd better finish the story
yourself.

ALICE   No, please go on! I won't interrupt again. I daresay
there may be one.

DORMOUSE One, indeed! And so, these three little sisters...they
were learning to draw, you know.

ALICE   What did they draw?

DORMOUSE Treacle.

ALICE   But I don't understand. Where did they draw the
treacle from?

HATTER   You can draw water out of a water well, so I should
think you could draw treacle out of a treacle well...

ALICE   But they were in the well!

DORMOUSE Of course they were...WELL in!   (GETTING SLEEPIER) So
they were learning to draw and they drew all manner of things;
everything that begins with an 'M'.

ALICE   Why with an 'M'?

WHITE RABBIT
          Why not?

     THE **DORMOUSE** IS FALLING ASLEEP, THE **HATTER** PINCHES HIM.

DORMOUSE (SHRIEKING) That begins with 'M', such as mousetraps and moon and memory and muchness...you know you say things are much of a muchness...did you ever see such a thing as a drawing of a muchness?

ALICE   I don't think...

HATTER   Then you shouldn't talk.

ALICE   Really! Well, I'll never come here again. (SHE RISES AND STARTS TO LEAVE) It's the stupidest tea party I ever was at, in all my life!

DORMOUSE And so the three little sisters... (TRAILING OFF AS THEY ALL FALL ASLEEP) Twinkle...twinkle...twinkle...

ALICE   Oh, White Queen, what am I ever going to do? They're all fast asleep and I'm still quite, quite hungry.

WHITE QUEEN
     Ah, child, they were all in that state of mind where they wanted to deny something, only they didn't know what to deny ...nasty, vicious tempers. But come, we're off to the next square.

MUSIC.   CURTAIN

END OF ACT ONE

ACT TWO

SCENE ONE

     THE MAIN SET AS IN ACT ONE OF WONDERLAND. IT'S THE GRYPHON AND MOCK TURTLE SQUARE. THEY ENTER, UNSEEN BY ALICE AND QUEEN.

ALICE   Now let me see...according to these instructions, I should be in the next square by now. (SHE LOOKS UP) Oh dear, I beg your pardon.

GRYPHON   It's not polite to beg. Could you tell me who and what you are?

ALICE   My name is Alice and I think I'm a child. And who or what are you?

GRYPHON   I know I am a Gryphon.

ALICE   Impossible!   I always thought Gryphons were fabulous monsters.

GRYPHON   Impossible!   I always thought children were fabulous monsters. But now that we've met, if you'll believe in me, I'll believe in you. Is that a bargain?

WHITE QUEEN
     It's easy to believe in impossible things.

ALICE   But who is that, Mr. Gryphon?

GRYPHON   Why, that's the Mock Turtle, child.

ALICE   Curiouser and curiouser. I've never heard of a Mock
Turtle before.

GRYPHON   It's the thing Mock Turtle soup is made from. This
here lady wants to meet you, she do.

ALICE   Hello, Mock Turtle.

MOCK TURTLE
          Hello.

ALICE   Please, Mr. Mock Turtle, why are you so sad?

MOCK TURTLE
          Sit down both of you quietly, and don't speak a word
till I've finished. Once I was a real turtle. When we were
little we went to school in the sea. The master was an old
turtle. We used to call him tortoise.

ALICE   Why did you call him tortoise if he was a turtle?

MOCK TURTLE
          We called him tortoise because he taught us. Really
you are very dull.

GRYPHON   You ought to be ashamed of yourself, asking such a
simple question. Continue old fellow.

MOCK TURTLE
          We went to school in the sea, though you may not be-
ieve it.

ALICE   I never said I didn't.

MOCK TURTLE
          You did!

GRYPHON   Quiet!

MOCK TURTLE
          We had the best of educations. Our drawling master was
an old conger-eel that used to come once a week. He taught us
drawling, stretching, and fainting in coils.

ALICE   What was that like?

MOCK TURTLE
          Can't show you myself...too stiff. And the Gryphon
never learned it.

ALICE   And how many hours did you do lessons?

GRYPHON   Ten hours the first day, nine the next, eight the
next...

MOCK TURTLE
And so on , and so on, and so on.

ALICE   What a curious plan!

GRYPHON   That's the reason they're called lessons. Because
they lessen from day to day.

ALICE   Then the eleventh day was called a holiday!

MOCK TURTLE
Of course it was.

ALICE   What did you do on the twelfth?

GRYPHON   That's enough about lessons. Tell her something about
the games now.

MOCK TURTLE
You may not have lived under the sea, so you have no
idea what a delightful thing a Lobster Quadrille is.

ALICE   No, indeed. What sort of dance is it?

MOCK TURTLE
Would you like to see a little of it?

ALICE   Very much indeed.

MOCK TURTLE
(TO GRYPHON) Come, let's try the first figure. We can
do it without the lobsters. Who shall sing?

GRYPHON   Oh, you sing. I've forgotten the words.

MUSIC - SONG AND DANCE WITH GRYPHON AND MOCK TURTLE.

<u>SONG - LOBSTER QUADRILLE</u>
"Will you walk a little faster!",
                    said a whiting to a snail,
There's a porpoise close behind us,
                    and he's treading on my tail.
See how eagerly the lobsters
                    and the turtles all advance!
They are waiting on the shingle -
                    will you come and join the dance?

Will you, won't you, will you, won't you, will you
                              join the dance?
Will you, won't you, will you, won't you, won't you
                              join the dance?

"You can really have no notion
                    how delightful it will be
When they take us up and throw us,
                    with the lobsters, out to sea!"
But the snail replied, "Too far, too far!",
                    and gave a look askance -

                  Said he thanked the whiting kindly,
                                but he would not join the dance.

                  Would not, could not, would not, could not, would not
                                        join the dance.
                  Would not, could not, would not, could not, could not
                                        join the dance.
                          - END OF SONG -

ALICE   What a monumental dance! If I were the whiting in the
quadrille I would have said to the porpoise, "Stand back, please.
We don't want you with us".

MOCK TURTLE
             Oh, they had to have him. No wise fish would go
anywhere without a porpoise.

ALICE   You mean purpose, don't you?

MOCK TURTLE
             I mean what I say!

ALICE   Oh dear! Mock Turtle!   I think I've hurt his feelings. Would you care to dance the quadrille again? Please don't
cry, Mock Turtle. Oh, Mr. Gryphon, what shall I do?

GRYPHON   Ask him to sing "Turtle Soup".

MOCK TURTLE
             It's "Beautiful Soup". Would you really like to hear
it?

ALICE   Oh yes, if the Mock Turtle would be so kind.

GRYPHON   No accounting for people's taste.

        MUSIC - MOCK TURTLE SINGS.

             MOCK TURTLE SONG - BEAUTIFUL SOUP
             Beautiful Soup, so rich and green
             Waiting in a hot tureen!
             Who for such dainties would not stoop?
             Soup of the evening, beautiful Soup!
             Soup of the evening, beautiful Soup!
             Beau...ootiful Soo...oop!
             Beau...ootiful Soo...oop!
             Soo...oop of the e...e...evening,
             Beautiful, beautiful Soup!
                  - END OF SONG -

ALICE   Oh what fun, White Queen! Shall we continue?

WHITE QUEEN
             You must be tired from all this travelling.

ALICE   I am, just a little.

WHITE QUEEN
        Then come. The next square is my square. We can rest
there a little while.

ALICE   How are we to get there?

WHITE QUEEN
        March over to that spot and the wind will blow us.

        MUSIC. WIND BLOWS.

WHITE QUEEN
        Here we are!

ALICE   It's so pleasant and so very quiet.

WHITE QUEEN
        Oh! Oh! My finger's bleeding! Oh! Oh!

ALICE   What is the matter? Have you pricked your finger?

WHITE QUEEN
        I haven't pricked it yet, but I shall soon. Oh! Oh!

ALICE   When do you expect to do it?

WHITE QUEEN
        When I fasten my shawl again; the brooch will come un-
done directly. Oh! Oh!

ALICE   (QUEEN REACHES FOR SHAWL) Take care, you're holding
your shawl all crooked. Oh, look out!

WHITE QUEEN
        (AS **SHE** HOLDS SHAWL **SHE** IS STABBED WITH THE PIN)
There, you see. That accounts for the bleeding. Can you understand the way things happen here?

ALICE   But why don't you scream now?

WHITE QUEEN
        Why, I've done all the screaming already. What would
be the good of having it all over again?

ALICE   I'm glad it's getting lighter. I thought it was the
night coming on.

WHITE QUEEN
        I wish I could manage to be glad! Only I never can
remember the rule. You must be very happy living in this wood...
and being glad whenever you like.

ALICE   Oh dear, it's so very lonely here! (SHE STARTS WEEPING)

WHITE QUEEN
        You mustn't go on like that. Consider what a big girl
you are. Consider what a long way you've come today. Consider
what o'clock it is. Consider anything, only don't cry.

190

ALICE   Can you keep from crying by considering things?

WHITE QUEEN
          That's the way it's done. Nobody can do two things at
once. Let's consider your age to begin with. How old are you?

ALICE   I am seven and a half exactly.

WHITE QUEEN
          You needn't say, "exactually". I can believe it
without that. Now I'll give you something to believe. I'm just
one hundred and one, five months and a day.

ALICE   I can't believe THAT!

WHITE QUEEN
          Can't you? Try again. Draw a long breath and shut
your eyes.

ALICE   There's no use trying. One can't believe impossible
things.

WHITE QUEEN
          I dare say you haven't much practice. When I was your
age, I always did it for half an hour a day. Why sometimes, I'd
believe as many as six impossible things...often before breakfast.

ALICE   Talking of breakfast, I didn't have any tea.

WHITE QUEEN
          Are you still hungry?

ALICE   Oh, yes!

WHITE QUEEN
          Do you like eggs?

ALICE   Very much, thank you. But what size are they in
Wonderland? Are they this small or are they that big?

WHITE QUEEN
          You'll see...when we get to the seventh square...

     MUSIC. THE SEVENTH SQUARE HAS A WALL BROUGHT ON BY **HUMPTY
     DUMPTY. WHITE QUEEN** QUIETLY EXITS.

ALICE   I beg your pardon.

HUMPTY   Don't just stand there, child. State your name and
business.

ALICE   My name is Alice, and I'm looking for...for...why you
must be the seventh square!

HUMPTY   Seventh square indeed! You mean you can't tell who I
am. My name is the shape I am.

ALICE   His name is the shape he is. (TO AUDIENCE) Boys and
girls, can you guess who he is? Of course, it's Humpty Dumpty.
How very like an egg he is!

HUMPTY   It's very provoking to be called an egg, very.

ALICE   I said you looked like an egg, sir, and some eggs are
very pretty.
              Humpty Dumpty sat on the wall
              Humpty Dumpty had a great fall
Oh, do be careful, Sir Humpty, you may fall.

HUMPTY   Well, let me tell you, if I ever did fall...which
there is very little chance of...but if I did fall, the King has
promised to send...

ALICE   I know...to send all his horses and all his men.

HUMPTY   Now that's not fair. You've been listening at doors and
down chimneys.

ALICE   Oh, no, sir! You see, it's in a book.

HUMPTY   In a book?

ALICE   In a book.

HUMPTY   IN A BOOK! Well, they may write such things in books.

ALICE   Why do you sit there all alone?

HUMPTY   Then come sit with me. That's my girl.

ALICE   My, that's a very pretty belt. No...cravat. No ..it's
a very pretty...oh dear, I can't tell where his neck begins and
his waist leaves off.

HUMPTY   It's a cravat, child! It was given to me by the White
Queen as an unbirthday present.

ALICE   Unbirthday present?

HUMPTY   That's what I said child...an unbirthday present.

ALICE   I like birthday presents best.

HUMPTY   No, you are wrong. Let me explain. How many days are
there in a year? Answer me that.

ALICE   Three hundred and sixty-five.

HUMPTY   Right! And how many birthdays do you have?

ALICE   One!

HUMPTY   Right again! And if you take one from three hundred
and sixty-five, how many have you left?

ALICE   Three hundred and sixty-four.

HUMPTY   Still righter!   So you see, you have one day to get
birthday presents.

ALICE   And three hundred and sixty-four to get unbirthday
presents.

HUMPTY   Yes child!   And a happy unbirthday to you.   There's
glory for you!

ALICE   Is that all?

HUMPTY   That's all.   Goodbye, child. (**HUMPTY** TAKES HIS WALL
WITH HIM)

ALICE   Oh, please Sir Humpty Dumpty, the White Queen seems to
have gone and there's only one square left to get to the Coronation.   I do so much want to know who the new Queen is to be.
Won't you take me to the eighth square?

HUMPTY   Why yes, child.   I was waiting for you to invite me.
We're off, my dear, to the eighth square.

     MUSIC.   CURTAIN

SCENE TWO

     IN FRONT OF CURTAINS.   EACH CHARACTER RUNS ACROSS STAGE.

RED QUEEN Run, run, run, we can't be late you know.

WHITE QUEEN
          Bread and butter, bread and butter, bread and butter.

GRYPHON   The Coronation's beginning, the Coronation's beginning,
the Coronation's beginning.   Do hurry, old fellow.

MOCK TURTLE
          (SINGS)   "Twas brillig and the slithy toves..."

RED QUEEN Where is the Rabbit?   We can't begin without the Rabbit.

WHITE RABBIT
          Oh dear, late again.   I've dropped my gloves.   Oh dear,
no time.   I'm late.

HUMPTY   Here we are at last...the eighth square.

ALICE   Sir Humpty, how am I to get in?

ALL   To get into the eighth square, you turn and turn and
stare and stare.   (ALL EXIT AS **ALICE** BEGINS TO TURN)

ALICE   Turn and turn and stare and stare.   Turn and turn and
stare and stare.

SCENE THREE

> THE CURTAINS OPEN. THE SET IS THE SAME BUT THE GAME OF
> CROQUET IS BEING PLAYED ON THE CHESSBOARD. A FEW MALLETS
> ARE SCATTERED ABOUT.

ALICE   Oh dear, it's not a Coronation at all. It's a game of croquet.

RED QUEEN Oh, there you are, you sweet thing. Do you play croquet? Here's your mallet. Fore!

ALICE   But I don't want to play croquet. I came to see the Coronation.

WHITE QUEEN
    My, you play very well. I'm sure I'll hire you ...tuppence a week and jam every other day.

ALICE   But I don't feel like eating jam today.

WHITE QUEEN
    Oh, but you couldn't have it even if you wanted it. The rule is jam yesterday and jam tomorrow, but never jam today.

ALICE   Oh dear, oh dear, how confusing this all is.

HUMPTY   I sent a message to the fish
    I told them, this is what I wish
    The little fishes answer was
    We cannot do it, sir, because...Your turn!

ALICE   Things are much of a muchness.

GRYPHON   Batter up, play the game!

ALICE   But you're not playing with the ball.

GRYPHON   I hit everything within reach...whether I see it or not. And when I'm very excited, I hit only things I see. Stand back!

ALICE   Oh, Red Queen, please help me. Where can I find the Coronation?

RED QUEEN In the eighth square, child. I daresay you haven't had many lessons in manners. It's my turn to play.

ALICE   Manners aren't taught in lessons. Lessons teach you to do reading and spelling and adding.

WHITE RABBIT
    Add 1 and 1 and 1 and 1 and 1 and 1...

ALICE   I'm afraid I've lost count.

ALL   She can't add sums at all!

ALICE   Stop! This is all very unsatisfactory. I came to the
eighth square to see the Coronation and see the new Queen, and
everyone's playing croquet. Please, who is the new Queen?

RED QUEEN But, my dear, it's you.

ALICE   ME? I'm the new Queen...Queen Alice of Wonderland!!!

        THEY CROWN ALICE IN A CEREMONIALLY-STAGED MOVEMENT, WITH
        MUSIC. THEN FORM A CIRCLE ROUND ALICE AND TOAST TO HER.

RED QUEEN Queen Alice's health!

ALL   Queen Alice's health!

RED QUEEN You ought to return thanks in a neat speech.

WHITE QUEEN
            We must support you, you know.

        MUSIC. ALICE AND COMPANY SING

                        SONG - QUEEN ALICE
ALICE   To the Looking Glass Wonderland
             'Twas Alice that said
             "I've a scepter in hand
             I've a crown on my head
             Let all you creatures whatever you be
             Come dine with Red Queen, White Queen and me"

ALL   (SING)
             Then fill up the glasses with treacle and ink
             And everything else that is pleasant to drink
             Mix sand with the cider and wool with the wine
             And welcome Queen Alice with ninety times nine.
                        - END OF SONG -

        EVERYONE QUIETLY DRIFTS AWAY LEAVING ALICE ALONE. MUSIC
        CONTINUES.

            SLOW FADE OUT   CURTAIN   SLOW FADE IN

        ALICE IS ON THE FLOOR IN FRONT OF CURTAINS, ASLEEP. SHE
        GRADUALLY AWAKENS, RUBBING HER EYES.

ALICE   Oh, oh, they've gone and now I'm alone. Oh dear, I'm
afraid it was all just a dream. (MUSIC ENDS) But it was a
wonderful dream, wasn't it?

                        CURTAIN

                        END OF PLAY

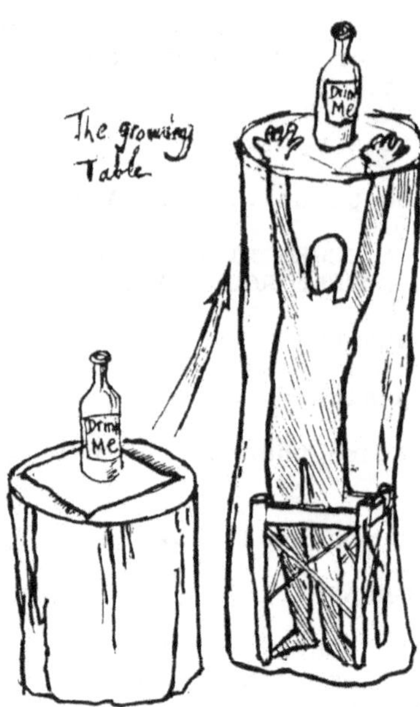

Wonderland Set.

White Rabbit
Alice
Red Queen
White Queen

Cheshire Cat
Cook
Duchess.

Dormouse   Hatter   and White Rabbit

One way.
of doing
Humpty

Humpty

Gryphon and Mock Turtle

THE CRICKET THEATRE AND BLANCHE MARVIN
PRESENT
THE MERRI-MIMES'

Pinocchio

BY BLANCHE MARVIN

DANCES + STAGED — RICHARD MAZZA
COSTUMES + SCENERY — LOHR WILSON
LIGHTS — STEVEN MILLER
STAGE MANAGER — DOLORES FRIEDMAN

CAST:

HOST + PINOCCHIO — DICKSON SHAW

ACTOR I + GUEPPETTO + SEGNOR FIRE EATER + COACHMAN — BOB SHIARELLA

ACTOR II + CANDLEWICK — STEVEN MILLER

ACTRESS + BLUE FAIRY — NAN WILSON

AT THE CRICKET THEATRE
162 SECOND AVE (AT 10TH ST.)
OR 4-3960

PERFORMANCES AT 1, 2:30 + 4 P.M. SAT. OCT 20, 27
NOV. 3, 10, 17, 24
AT 2:30 + 4 P.M. ONLY ON DEC. 1 + 8

SAT. DEC 15, 22, 29 WED-FRI DEC. 26, 27, 28
SAT. JAN 5, 12 + 19
SPECIAL: MON-THUR 9:45, 11:15 + 1:00 DEC 17, 18, 19, 20

— ALSO —

PIED PIPER > SAT. JAN 26, FEB 2, 16, 23
FRI. FEB 22, MAR 2, 9, 16
SLEEPING BEAUTY > SAT. MAR 23, 30 APR 6, 13, 20 + 27
SPECIAL: MON-THUR 9:45, 11:15 + 1:00 APR 8, 9, 10 + 11

WE ARE USING THE MODERN IMPROVISED THEATRE FOR PINOCCHIO BECAUSE PINOCCHIO IS A STORY TRUE TODAY. THE TIME IS NOW AND FOREVER. THIS MODERN FORM OF THEATRE IS FUN — FULL OF AUDIENCE PARTICIPATION — AND GIVES THE CHILDREN AN IDEA OF HOW AN ACTOR GETS INTO HIS PART. THE CHILDREN CAN LEARN QUICKLY WHERE THE MAGIC OF THEATRE BEGINS — WHAT IS REAL — WHAT IS FANTASY. HE IS BEING LET IN ON A BIG SECRET. THE RESULT OF THE STYLE IS THAT OF IMPROVISATION. WE WANT YOU TO FEEL THIS —— BUT THE TRUTH WILL OUT THAT IT IS A REHEARSED SHOW

— ARTISTIC ADVISOR FOR THE MERRI-MIMES — MARIO SILETTI —

PINOCCHIO

based on Pirandellor's style in

"SIX CHARACTERS IN SEARCH OF AN AUTHOR"

CAST OF CHARACTERS

Narrator - Pinocchio

Actor 1   - Gueppetto, Signor Fire-Eater, Coachman

Actor 2   - Candlewick

Actress   - Blue Fairy

Place: Theatre Stage - Italy

Time: Whenever

ACT ONE

WORK LIGHT ON A BARE STAGE. STAGE **MANAGER** OF THE TROUPE OF
ACTORS RUNS DOWN THE AISLE OF THE THEATRE AND LOOKS ROUND
... NO ONE IS THERE.

STAGE MANAGER
> It's late. Where are they?

LOOKS ROUND. WE HEAR A COMMOTION AT THE DOOR OF THE THEATRE
AS THE **ACTORS** TROOP IN. THEY COME DOWN THE AISLE TALKING
AWAY AND FULL OF EXCITEMENT. THEY HAVE COME TO A NEW CITY
AND ARE SETTING UP THE STAGE QUICKLY BECAUSE OF THEIR LATE-
NESS. AS SOON AS THEY ARE FINISHED SETTING UP THEY ALL BE-
COME DEJECTED AS THEY LOOK UP AND SEE NO LIGHTS. THE LEADER
OF THE GROUP IS THE **NARRATOR**.

NARRATOR   (LOOKS AT THE **ACTORS** AND MIMES OUT WHAT IS WRONG. THE
ACTORS LOOK SADLY UP AT THE LIGHTS. THE **NARRATOR** CALLS OUT)
Lights! Stage Manager! (HE COMES IN) Lights! (**NARRATOR** SENDS
THE **STAGE MANAGER** BACKSTAGE. AS BLUE LIGHTS COME ON **ACTORS** MIME
SADNESS. AS RED COMES ON **ACTORS** MIME SADNESS AND FINALLY WHEN
FULL LIGHTS COME ON **ACTORS** ARE HAPPY)

NARRATOR   (COMES FORWARD TO AUDIENCE) Good afternoon ladies and
gentlemen and children of all ages. You have come here today to
see a play...whose name is? That's right...Pinocchio! Our
famous Merri-Mimes troupe have just arrived for your pleasure
carrying with us, in a trunk, our entire show. Props (**ACTOR**
PULLS ONE OUT OF TRUNK), Costumes (**ACTRESS** PULLS ONE OUT OF
TRUNK) and Sound (**ACTOR** PULLS OUT WHISTLE). And is there anything else? (THE THREE **ACTORS** COME FORWARD) Of course...the
ACTORS...who, along with their simple make-up, act with mind, (TO
ACTOR 1) with heart (TO **ACTRESS**) and with stomach (TO **ACTOR** 2).
And last but not least our **STAGE MANAGER**. (WALKS ON)

STAGE MANAGER
> Anytime you're ready, I'm ready! It's past curtain
time. (GRABS PROPS AND COSTUMES RETURNS THEM TO TRUNK)

MUSIC - SONG AND DANCE - EVERYONE SINGS

SONG - THE MERRI-MIMES

Good afternoon, we're here today, from having
> travelled far
To bring to you a simple play in which I'll be the
> star.

We'll sing, we'll dance, we'll act, we'll mime
Before we're through with you
You won't forget the lovely time
And what the actors do.

The Story of Pinocchio and all the things he found
Happened a long time ago and yet its truth is sound.
We now present our simple play and hope that you will
> see
How up-to-date and timely The Merri-Mimes can be.

NARRATOR   But first we must cast the show to get it on the way;
And after that is done we will begin the play.
                    - END OF SONG -

ACTOR 1   I am Signor Roberto and I play Gueppetto.

NARRATOR   This is Signorina Nanena and can you guess who she
will play? That's right, the Blue Fairy. (THE ACTRESS CAN BE
FAT AND CHILDREN MAY PROTEST SHE CAN'T BE THE BLUE FAIRY. NAR-
RATOR MAY HAVE TO JUSTIFY AN ACTRESS TO CHILDREN)

ACTOR 2   I am Signor Stephano and I will play Pinocchio.

NARRATOR   (POLITELY COVERING UP) No, Signor, not today. Today
I play Pinocchio.

ACTOR 2   But you said I would play Pinocchio.

NARRATOR   No, not in......(NEW YORK, LONDON, MANCHESTER, WHER-
EVER IT IS BEING PERFORMED) only on tour. (AD LIB...BATTLE OF
WORDS)

ACTOR 1   I am Signor Roberto and I play Pinocchio.

ACTRESS   Quarrels...always quarrels. Nobody plays what they
want to play. (STAGE COMIC QUARREL) (TO AUDIENCE) We are really
a happy cast!

STAGE MANAGER
          (COMES IN) Anytime you're ready, I'm ready. It's
past curtain time.

NARRATOR   Signor Roberto will play Gueppetto. Signorina
Nanena will play the Blue Fairy and I will play Pinocchio. Signor Stephano will appear in the next Act.

     ACTOR 2 WALKS OFF UPSET AS HE COLLIDES WITH THE **STAGE MAN-
     AGER** AND EXITS.

NARRATOR   Costumes, please.   (EVERYONE PUTS ON A SUGGESTION OF
A COSTUME: **GUEPPETTO** AN APRON, WIG AND GLASSES; **PINOCCHIO** TROU-
SERS AND FALSE HAIR; **BLUE FAIRY** HER CROWN AND SPARKLING CAPE)

STAGE MANAGER
          (EXITS AS HE SAYS) Places please!

     BLUE FAIRY GOES OFF. LIGHTS COME ON. **PINOCCHIO AND GUEP-
     PETTO** GO TO THEIR PLACES AS PLAY BEGINS.

GUEPPETTO   I'm Gueppetto. It is dark and all the town is sleeping, while I am busy working on a puppet. (**PINOCCHIO AND GUEP-
PETTO** ARE IN FULL CHARACTERISATION OF THEIR PARTS. **PINOCCHIO**
SITS HIDDEN ON A BOX LOOKING LIKE A PUPPET. **GUEPPETTO** PICKS UP
AND CARVES A WOODEN DOLL-PUPPET) Little wooden head...that's all
you are...I make you with these two hands, but only God can make
a human. Oh, maybe God would help make you human so that I
wouldn't be alone. What a foolish wish from a foolish old man.
Why do you shake so? Are you trying to speak? Speak then, my

little boy, my little Pinocchio. (NO ANSWER) I'm tired now but tomorrow I'll finish you...nose and all. (YAWNS) Goodnight, my Pinocchio.

PINOCCHIO RESTS ON FLOOR IN HALF LIGHT. THE **ACTRESS** PLAYING THE **BLUE FAIRY** COMES ON. SHE IS WEARING THE SAME CROWN AND SPARKLING CAPE OVER TIGHTS. THERE IS A BLUE LIGHT ON HER. AS THE <u>MUSIC</u> STARTS SHE DANCES ROUND **GUEPPETTO**. THE BLUE LIGHT FOLLOWS HER.

BLUE FAIRY Gueppetto, Gueppetto, you ask of me
To breathe life into a cherry tree
Though the tree has a puppet's head
You wish it were a real boy instead.
If I make your wish come true
This is what you must do.
Teach the boy right from wrong
Give him love his whole life long.
(**GUEPPETTO** SAYS, "YES", TO THE **FAIRY** IN HIS SLEEP)
With that promise I will now try
(SHE GOES ROUND **PINOCCHIO** IN A CIRCLE)
To give Pinocchio life as the crows fly.

BLUE FAIRY DANCES ROUND AND ROUND **PINOCCHIO**. FASTER AND FASTER. **GUEPPETTO** SLEEPS. THE DAWN BREAKS AND WITH IT LIGHTS CHANGE FROM DARK TO LIGHT. WHEN THE LIGHT BRIGHTENS WE SEE **PINOCCHIO, THE BOY,** STANDING THERE, INSTEAD OF THE DOLL. HE DOES NOT MOVE. HE STANDS AT FIRST LIKE A STATUE.

BLUE FAIRY Be a good boy, little wooden head. (SHE DISAPPEARS)

PINOCCHIO Blue Fairy...come back...just a moment. She's gone. Am I a boy? No...not really. I'm still a puppet. (FEELING THROAT) Oh...but I have a voice... (STARTS TO WALK. HE WALKS AND TALKS LIKE A WOODEN PUPPET) and look I can walk. (MUSIC. STAGED DANCE) I suppose that's what she meant by life. Oh...what's this? (HE LOOKS AT **GUEPPETTO**) He looks very funny to me. (**GUEPPETTO** MOVES) He does move! (**GUEPPETTO** THEN RESTS QUIETLY) He doesn't move. (SNORES) I think he's a man. I think he's supposed to be my father. (**PINOCCHIO** IS TRYING TO THINK AND HAS WALKED TO THE BOXES) I think I'm supposed to think. (HE LIFTS THE BOX TO DROP IT ON **GUEPPETTO** WHEN **GUEPPETTO** MOVES IN HIS SLEEP AND THEN HALF AWAKE SPEAKS) Oh, what's this?

GUEPPETTO Did I hear something? No it must be my imagination.

PINOCCHIO It was I. (PUTS BOX DOWN)

GUEPPETTO Pinocchio? It's you. My little wooden head, are you ...a boy? A <u>real</u> boy?

PINOCCHIO Not yet. But the Blue Fairy said to be a good boy. What's that?

GUEPPETTO A good boy is a boy who knows right from wrong.

PINOCCHIO That's even harder to understand.   What is right? What is wrong?

GUEPPETTO Now let me see. How is it best to let you know? Oh, first...you must call me Father.

PINOCCHIO Why?

GUEPPETTO Because I am your father.

PINOCCHIO Is that right? Or is that wrong? (TAKES **GUEPPETTO'S** GLASSES)

GUEPPETTO No, no Pinocchio, (TAKES BACK HIS GLASSES) that was wrong. Wait...just a moment and I will explain. If you call me Father, because I am your father, then you must do as I say and that will be right.

PINOCCHIO But will I always remember what you say?

GUPPETTO That's true. Let me think...I know! We'll make a list of what is right for a little boy. If you follow the list you'll be a good boy.

PINOCCHIO What is a list?

GUEPPETTO We must make it first. Children, can you help me make a list? (TO AUDIENCE) I need your help because it's been a long time since I was a boy.

> THIS BECOMES AN AD LIB SITUATION BUT **GUEPPETTO** MUST PUT SCHOOL DOWN AS NUMBER 1. HE CAN KEEP ADDING THINGS AS AN INCENTIVE TO THE CHILDREN. HE WRITES ON AN IMAGINARY PAD AND READS OFF.

GUEPPETTO
 1. Go to school
 2. Never lie
 3. Eat your food
 4. Love your mother and father
 5. Be polite and kind
 6. Be obedient
 7. Go to bed on time
 8. Don't say bad words
 9. Never steal
10. Take a bath
Now we have 10 rules!! Isn't that wonderful?

PINOCCHIO That's a lot to learn!!! Do you think I can?

GUEPPETTO Of course you can. Tell him, children. You're all learning. Help Pinocchio. Do you think you can do it? (AUDIENCE WILL CALL OUT, "YES") You see if they can do it, so can you.

PINOCCHIO But they've been learning longer.

GUEPPETTO Don't be afraid. Just look at the list when you forget.

PINOCCHIO But I can't read.

GUEPPETTO (LOOKING AT LIST) I'll help you.   Number 1...go to
school! Now that's a good idea!

PINOCCHIO What's school?

GUEPPETTO It's a place to learn.   Here's a book (GIVES HIM A
REAL BOOK)

PINOCCHIO But I can't read.

GUEPPETTO You have got to have a book when you go to school and
they teach you to read.

PINOCCHIO Like this. (HE FLOPS ON THE FLOOR FEET UP IN THE AIR
WITH THE BOOK UPSIDE DOWN)

GUEPPETTO No! You must sit upright on the chair... (HE PUTS HIM
ON THE BOX SEATED IN A PROPER MANNER) and keep the book this way.

PINOCCHIO But I like it this way. (HE TURNS BOOK AROUND) No,
this way...this way...this way. (HE KEEPS SPINNING BOOK AROUND.
THEN, PUTTING IT ON HIS HEAD LIKE A HAT, HE JUMPS UP ON THE
BOXES. UP AND DOWN HE KEEPS JUMPING TWIRLING THE BOOK AS WELL
AND LAUGHING ALL THE TIME)

GUEPPETTO No...no...no...Pinocchio...that's _wrong_. Sit down
like a _good_ boy. (**PINOCCHIO** IS NOW TEARING UP THE BOOK AND GUEP-
PETTO IS RUNNING AFTER HIM. IT IS A CHASE IN A CIRCLE. PINOC-
CHIO KEEPS TEARING THE BOOK AS HE CHASES ROUND, LAUGHING ALL THE
TIME. **GUEPPETTO** CAN'T CATCH HIM AND KEEPS CALLING) I'm your
father and I'm telling you...no...no...it's wrong. You need the
book for school.

PINOCCHIO Why?

GUEPPETTO To learn your A B C.

PINOCCHIO Why?

GUEPPETTO Once you know your A B C then you'll learn to read.

PINOCCHIO Why, Father?

     MUSIC - GUEPPETTO SINGS

                    SONG - A B C
          A B C is taught at school
          Learn that well, it's a very big tool.
          You ask me why the sky is blue?
          The book will answer that for you.

PINOCCHIO From the A B C taught at school
          Can such a little book make such a big tool?
          Will it tell me why I wear a shoe?

GUEPPETTO The book will answer that for you.

PINOCCHIO Can one book answer all the "whys"?

GUEPPETTO   My wooden head, there'll be many tries.

PINOCCHIO   I'll go to school but just for you
Though it sounds hard for me to do.

GUEPPETTO   My boy, that's being wisely good
Now off to school just as you should.
                    - END OF SONG -

PINOCCHIO GOES OFF DOWN CENTRE AISLE CARRYING HIS BOOK AS GUEPPETTO WAVES GOODBYE.

CURTAIN

END OF ACT ONE

ACT TWO

SAME AS ACT ONE.   THE **NARRATOR** STILL WEARS **PINOCCHIO'S** COS-
TUME.

NARRATOR   Well, here we are for Act Two...and as all of you saw, poor Gueppetto is going to have a long way to go before Pinocchio can really learn anything.   You know when you start from so high, (GOES WAY DOWN) your parents are always there to show you and then you learn step by step.   But when you start from so high, (POINTS TO HIS HEIGHT) why then there's so much more to learn <u>all at one time</u>.   Poor Pinocchio.   However, our story continues.   Gueppetto has given Pinocchio a new book for school and this book he will not tear because he knows now that he mustn't tear books.   (REST OF CAST ENTER AND INTERRUPT)

ACTOR 1   Stop the talking and get on with the play.

NARRATOR   But we haven't cast Act Two.

ACTOR 1   In this Act, I play Fire-Eater and Coachman.

ACTOR 2   (COMES FORWARD AND FORGETS)

NARRATOR   In this Act, you play Candlewick!   Remember?

ACTRESS   (TO **NARRATOR**)   And who do I play in this act?

NARRATOR   The Blue Fairy, of course.

ACTRESS   What again!   (TEARFULLY GOES OFF TO A CORNER)

NARRATOR   (GOING TO HER)   What's wrong?

ACTRESS   I'm tired of playing Fairies and Princesses and Queens. I want to play a Witch.   I want to be mean.   (STAGED BUSINESS)

NARRATOR   But Signorina Nanena, Blue Fairies are beautiful.

ACTOR 1   Charming.

ACTOR 2   Blue Fairies are... (EVERYONE EXPECTING PEARLS OF
WISDOM) ...blue.

ACTRESS   Yes, but can I be mean?

EVERYBODY No!

ACTRESS   Then I'm through. (EXITS)

     THE THREE ACTORS GO INTO A HUDDLE AS TO WHAT TO DO. THEY AD
     LIB, "WE NEED HER. WE NEED A BLUE FAIRY". ETC.

NARRATOR   There's always one thing that will bring back an actress...applause. So if you all clap loud enough she might come
back. (THEY CLAP ON STAGE AND ENCOURAGE AUDIENCE BUT BLUE FIARY
DOES NOT RETURN) We can always cast another Blue Fairy. (TO
AUDIENCE) You there. Would you come play our Blue Fairy? You
can do it.

ACTRESS   (COMING BACK HURRIEDLY) I shall play the Blue Fairy.

     BLUE LIGHT COMES ON AS THE ACTRESS COMES ONTO STAGE AS BLUE
     FAIRY IN CHARACTER AND BOWS. THE ACTORS APPLAUD HER ON STAGE
     AND ENCOURAGE THE AUDIENCE.

NARRATOR   On with the play.

STAGE MANAGER
          (ON STAGE) Places please...Act Two. (EXITS)

     THE NARRATOR WALKS LIKE A PUPPET AND TALKS LIKE A PUPPET
     WHENEVER HE PLAYS PINOCCHIO. WHEN HE IS NARRATOR AND ACTOR
     HE ACTS HIMSELF.

NARRATOR AS PINOCCHIO
          (SKIPPING WITH A BOOK IN ONE HAND) School...school
...now I'll see, what Father keeps telling me. (HE SKIPS AS HE
SWINGS HIS BOOK AND SINGS) School...school...now I'll see, what
Father keeps telling me.

     CANDLEWICK, PLAYED BY ACTOR 2, IS LEANING AGAINST A POLE
     WATCHING PINOCCHIO. HE THEN FOLLOWS PINOCCHIO INDICATING TO
     THE CHILDREN NOT TO LET PINOCCHIO KNOW HE'S THERE. HE KEEPS
     TAGGING HIM UNTIL SUDDENLY HE COMES FACE TO FACE WITH PINOC-
     CHIO. BOTH ACTORS ARE NOW FULLY IN COMMAND OF THEIR CHARAC-
     TERS.

CANDLEWICK Hey there. And what makes you so happy about school?
You must be joking.

PIOCCHIO   Joking? No, I'm Pinocchio.

CANDLEWICK (LOOKS AT HIM PUZZLED) My name is Candlewick.   Are
you really going to school?

PINOCCHIO Yes. I'm going to school to learn to read.

CANDLEWICK On a beautiful day like today.

PINOCCHIO Why? Where else should I go?

CANDLEWICK Come with me. (SHOWS HIM TWO TICKETS TO THE THEATRE)
Cut the work and have some fun.

PINOCCHIO But my father said I should go to school.

CANDLEWICK You can go to school anytime. But the theatre is special.

PINOCCHIO It is?

CANDLEWICK For sure. Anyone can tell you that.

PINOCCHIO But what would my father say?

CANDLEWICK He'd think it was a treat.

PINOCCHIO Does that mean yes?

CANDLEWICK 'Course it does!

PINOCCHIO And would I go to school later?

CANDLEWICK You don't have to. You can miss a day.

PINOCCHIO Then why did my father send me?

CANDLEWICK Mums and Dads always send boys and girls to school.

PINOCCHIO Are you a live boy?

CANDLEWICK (LAUGHS AND LAUGHS) I've been called all sorts of
names but that's a winner. I'll show you how live I am.

> **CANDLE-WICK** PUSHES **PINOCCHIO** BUT **PINOCCHIO** BEING A PUPPET
> DOES NOT GET HURT. INSTEAD **PINOCCHIO** KICKS **CANDLEWICK** BACK
> AND ENJOYS IT. **CANDLEWICK** STOPS WHEN HE REALISES **PINOCCHIO**
> WILL WIN. THE FIGHT SHOULD BE STAGED.

PINOCCHIO Is that what real boys do?

CANDLEWICK Don't you know anything? Are you coming with me or
not?

PINOCCHIO To the theatre?

CANDLEWICK Yes!

PINOCCHIO If that's what real boys do.

CANDLEWICK Then let's go.

> MUSIC. THEY DO A DANCE TOGETHER OF GOING OFF TO THE THEA-
> TRE. **PINOCCHIO** DANCES LIKE A PUPPET. THE LIGHTS GO WITH
> THEM SO THAT WE HAVE A FEELING OF MOVEMENT TO ANOTHER PLACE
> AND FINAL ARRIVAL. AT THE ARRIVAL POINT WE SEE **SIGNOR FIRE-
> EATER**, (ACTOR 1 WHO PLAYED **GUEPPETTO**) A BIG, FAT, JOVIAL

BUT EVIL MAN WHO IS AN IMPRESARIO AND THEATRE OWNER. **ACTOR
1** DOES NOT CHANGE COSTUME. HE MOVES LIKE A FAT MAN RATHER
THAN PADDING HIMSELF. HE MAY WEAR A HIGH HAT, A BLACK
CLOAK AND MOUSTACHE, IF NECESSARY, WHICH HE PUTS ON IN FRONT
OF THE AUDIENCE. BUT HE MUST HAVE A FLAMBOYANT QUALITY. HE
SEES **CANDLEWICK** AND **PINOCCHIO**.

FIRE-EATER Ah, my good friends and what are you doing this fine
day?

CANDLEWICK Hello, Signor Fire-Eater. My name's Candlewick and
this is Pinocchio.

FIRE-EATER Ah, what a fine young boy.

PINOCCHIO How do you do, sir.

FIRE-EATER No school today?

PINOCCHIO No, not today. We're going to the theatre.

FIRE-EATER You have arrived. You are here at the theatre.

PINOCCHIO Really? How do I know?

FIRE-EATER Why just look and you will see. There's your audience. (POINTS) Here is the stage and you are on it.

CANDLEWICK Well I never! I thought we'd see actors on stage.

FIRE-EATER You are the actors. Now...perform! Let's see what
you can do. (CLAPS HANDS)

PINOCCHIO Perform what?

FIRE-EATER Fool! (FEROCIOUSLY ANGERED) Sing! Dance! You have
an audience waiting.

CANDLEWICK Well, goodo.

PINOCCHIO What do we sing?

CANDLEWICK Just follow me. Music please.

   MUSIC. **PINOCCHIO** AND **CANDLEWICK** SING AND DANCE.

<u>SONG - ANYONE</u>
CANDLEWICK Anyone can sing a song.

PINOCCHIO Anyone?

CANDLEWICK Anyone. Anyone can hum along.

PINOCCHIO Anyone?

CANDLEWICK Anyone. La la la la la la la la la

FIRE-EATER Move...move!

CANDLEWICK Anyone...can run away.

PINOCCHIO Anyone?

CANDLEWICK Anyway.

CANDLEWICK Anyone can take a stance.

PINOCCHIO Anyone?

FIRE-EATER Dance...dance!

CANDLEWICK Anyone. Anyone can learn to dance!

PINOCCHIO Anyone?

CANDLEWICK Anyone, oh, anyone. I don't know what to do.

PINOCCHIO Then anyone...anyone...we are through. (THEY BOW)
                - END OF SONG AND DANCE -

FIRE-EATER That was terrible. The audience hardly applauded. They
paid for tickets and you were terrible.

PINOCCHIO We were?

FIRE-EATER You have a lot to learn. You'll have to come with me.

PINOCCHIO Oh, no. I must go home. My father will worry.

FIRE-EATER I shall make you into a very big star. Your father
would be very proud of you.

PINOCCHIO You think so?

FIRE-EATER What does your father do?

PINOCCHIO He's a wood carver.

CANDLEWICK Stick with him and your father will be carving diamonds.

PINOCCHIO Diamonds?

CANDLEWICK Diamonds! Real ones!

FIRE-EATER Of course, if you don't want diamonds you can always
go home, now.

PINOCCHIO I think I'll stay with you. I'll become a star and
then bring my father diamonds.

FIRE-EATER Good! Now that we have decided to be in the theatre
we must begin our training.

CANDLEWICK What! Work? No siree. I'm busy at the moment. (HE
SLIPS AWAY FROM FIRE-EATER'S GRASP AND EXITS)

212

FIRE-EATER But you my boy...you wish to become an actor?

PINOCCHIO Oh, yes.

FIRE-EATER Good. Now, I count to three. One, two, three! (HE PICKS UP **PINOCCHIO** AND PUTS HIM ON A BOX STAGE LEFT. **SIGNOR** TIES HIM UP WITH A ROPE SO THAT HE CAN'T MOVE. THE ROPE DOES NOT HAVE TO BE REAL. IT CAN BE DONE IN MIME) If you move I make firewood of you.

PINOCCHIO Help, help, help! Untie me!

FIRE-EATER Oh, but that's part of your training. Bad boys who run away from home and don't listen to their parents cannot be trusted. We tie them up so that they will stay in one place and then teach them. Hah, hah, you foolish boy. I'll teach you how to become an actor...the hard way. Ha-ha-ha-ha! (LAUGHS AND LAUGHS) And now for my exit. Arrivaderci!! (TWIRLS HIMSELF OFF)

PINOCCHIO (ALONE ON STAGE) To be or not to be...what a question? I want to go home. I want to go home. I want to go home. (**BLUE FAIRY** ENTERS AND UNTIES HIM)

BLUE FAIRY Oh little wooden head, you were to be a good boy. And now look at you. No school...hands tied...and your poor father so worried...not knowing where you are. How could you be so bad?

PINOCCHIO I didn't know. Honestly, I didn't know.

BLUE FAIRY You must begin to know.

PINOCCHIO How?

BLUE FAIRY If you listen carefully, deep within is a voice, and when you hear it you will know when you have done something wrong. It is called conscience.

PINOCCHIO But what happens if I can't hear the voice?

BLUE FAIRY It will speak louder.

PINOCCHIO And what if I hear it and don't obey it?

BLUE FAIRY Then it will keep on talking until you do. Sooner or later.

PINOCCHIO I'll try.

BLUE FAIRY If you try, it will happen.

PINOCCHIO What shall I do now?

BLUE FAIRY You are to go home to your father and after that you must go to <u>school</u> every day! Do you promise?

PINOCCHIO Oh, yes, of course I do.

BLUE FAIRY You must remember your promise.

PINOCCHIO I promise to remember my promise.

BLUE FAIRY You must mean it. A promise is sacred never to be broken.

PINOCCHIO I promise, 'scuse me, I mean, I'll <u>try</u> to be a good boy.

BLUE FAIRY And now, goodbye.

PINOCCHIO Blue Fairy, just a moment, please come back. Will I ever be a real boy?

BLUE FAIRY One day, maybe. You must first love.

PINOCCHIO Love? What's that?

BLUE FAIRY That's something warm you feel inside you.

PINOCCHIO Blue Fairy, I'm only a puppet. I can't feel warm or cold.

BLUE FAIRY You have to know love before you can become a real boy.

PINOCCHIO I'll never be a real boy! There's so much to learn. I can't do it. It's too much.

BLUE FAIRY Pinocchio, listen carefully. There is a great deal to learn but if you learn one thing at a time and really learn it, then before you know it, step by step, you've learned the whole. You can't learn the whole all by itself.

PINOCCHIO One step at a time. One step at a time.

BLUE FAIRY Here we are at this point (STAGE RIGHT) and we want to be at that point. (POINTS TO STAGE LEFT) How do we get there, Pinocchio?

PINOCCHIO I know! Oh, I know! One step at a time.

    MUSIC - BLUE FAIRY AND PINOCCHIO DANCE, <u>ONE STEP AT A TIME</u>.

PINOCCHIO I understand now. Blue Fairy you make it sound so easy.

BLUE FAIRY Your next step, Pinocchio, is to learn love. Then we will see if you can become a real boy. It's dawn. I must go. Goodbye, little wooden head. (SHE EXITS)

PINOCCHIO A real boy! She said...one day maybe...I could be a real boy.

    BLUE FAIRY COMES BACK ON STAGE AS ACTRESS APPLAUDING. ACTORS 1 AND 2 RETURN WITH HER ALSO APPLAUDING.

ACTRESS   You did that beautifully. I could almost cry.

ACTOR 1   Here, here. The best performance you have ever given.
There was real emotion.

ACTRESS   You felt that yearning.

NARRATOR   Why, thank you. I was Pinocchio. I wanted him to
have his dream come true. What did you think, Stefano?

ACTOR 2   Well, I wouldn't act it the way you did.

NARRATOR   What do you mean by that?

ACTOR 2   My Pinocchio...well...I don't see him as stupid as you
do.

NARRATOR   What? I never thought he was stupid.

ACTOR 2   Ah...ah...ah...let me put it this way, then. Maybe you
didn't play him as stupid but I see him as bad because he wants
to be bad.

NARRATOR   He does bad things but he doesn't mean them to be bad.

ACTOR 2   Yes he does. Can I show you what I mean?

NARRATOR   Now?

ACTOR 1   Why not. Let him do that last scene. You know...the
one with Pinocchio and the Blue Fairy

ACTRESS   A brilliant idea. Let the audience judge whether
Stephano's Pinocchio or the Maestro's Pinocchio is what they
want. (TO THE AUDIENCE) Do you agree? ("Yes", FROM THE AUDIENCE)
Good. Then I can play the Witch.

NARRATOR   You mean the Blue Fairy.

ACTRESS   No, I mean the witch. You'll see.

      STAGE MANAGER WALKS ON.

STAGE MANAGER
      Places, please from the end of Act Two. (EXITS)

REPEAT THE SCENE OF **PINOCCHIO** AND **BLUE FAIRY** FROM WHERE
PINOCCHIO IS TIED AND CALLS FOR HELP. **ACTOR 2** PLAYS **PINOC-
CHIO** AND **ACTRESS** DOES **BLUE FAIRY** AS A **WITCH**. NO DIALOGUE
CHANGES. IT ENDS WITH **BLUE FAIRY** AND **PINOCCHIO** DANCE OF
"ONE STEP AT A TIME". SCENE PERFORMED AS A COMPLETE FARCE
OPPOSITE TO THE TENDER ONE WHEN FIRST DONE. THE **NARRATOR**
AND **ACTOR 1** WHO HAD SEATED THEMSELVES IN THE AUDIENCE WHILE
THE **BLUE FAIRY** AND **PINOCCHIO** SCENE WAS BEING PLAYED INTER-
RUPT THE SCENE AFTER THE DANCE BY COMING UP ON STAGE AND AP-
PLAUDING. THEY OBVIOUSLY STOP THE SCENE.

ACTOR 1   (GIVING **ACTOR 2** A WARM PAT ON THE SHOULDER) That was very good, but not Pinocchio.

NARRATOR   Very good, Stefano.   We'll see you in Act Three...as Candlewick.   (HE TURNS TO **BLUE FAIRY** WHO HAS STOOD THERE IMPAT- IENTLY AS NO ONE HAS COMPLIMENTED HER.   **ACTOR 1** SEES A STORM IS ABOUT TO BREW SO HE TAPS **ACTOR 2** AND SIGNS FOR THEM TO LEAVE. THEY DO)

ACTRESS   Did you like my Witch?

NARRATOR   (WITH SINCERE WARMTH)   You are much better as the Blue Fairy.   We want you to be the Blue Fairy, always.   We need you. Tell me... (BECOMING PINOCCHIO) will I ever be a real live boy?

BLUE FAIRY (WITH WARMTH AND SINCERITY)   One day...maybe...when you have learned to love.   Goodbye, little wooden head.

PINOCCHIO A real boy!   One day maybe...she said...I could be a real boy!

CURTAIN

END OF ACT TWO

ACT THREE

SAME AS ACT ONE.   **NARRATOR** COMES OUT TO BEGIN ACT THREE WHEN LIGHTS GO OUT TO A COMPLETE BLACKOUT.

NARRATOR   Stage Manager...Lights!   Lights I say!   (LIGHTS COME UP) Thank goodness. Let's begin Act Three and hope you'll see. (BLACKOUT AGAIN)   Stage Manager! Lights! (LIGHTS COME ON)   What are you doing?   (STAGE MANAGER COMES OUT AND WHISPERS INTO **NARRATOR'S** EAR.   **NARRATOR** LOOKS UPSET.   THEN MIMES FOR THE **STAGE MANAGER** TO GO)   Ladies and Gentlemen, I'm sorry to say that the Stage Manager has just informed me the Fire Department will not let our whale into the theatre for Act Three.   Live whales evi- dently aren't allowed in any theatre.   However, with our own in- genuity we have an emergency whale.   Thank you.

STAGE MANAGER
      (OFF STAGE)   Places please,   Act Three.

   NARRATOR AND **ACTOR 1** BECOME **PINOCCHIO** AND **GUEPPETTO**.   GUEP- PETTO IS SENDING **PINOCCHIO** OFF TO SCHOOL.

GUEPPETTO Now remember...no more theatre...but to school. (GIVES HIM HIS BOOK)

PINOCCHIO Oh, I promise, Father.   (ALMOST TO HIMSELF)   I know a promise is sacred so I have to mean it.   Goodbye...I'm off to school to learn to love.

GUEPPETTO Pinocchio, you little wooden head.   You learn love at home and your A B C at school.

PINOCCHIO Father, will you teach me love?

216

GUEPPETTO I don't teach you love, I love you.

PINOCCHIO Then I love you. But I don't feel warm.

GUEPPETTO You are a funny boy. Hurry now, or you'll be late for school.

> AS HE WAVES GOODBYE, **GUEPPETTO** BACKS OFF STAGE. **PINOCCHIO** MOVES IN MIME MOVEMENT AS **GUEPPETTO** EXITS. MUSIC. WHILE **PINOCCHIO** IS DANCING OFF TO SCHOOL, **CANDLEWICK** COMES ON. HE MOVES IMITATING **PINOCCHIO'S** WALK. IT BECOMES A DUET WITH **CANDLEWICK** HAVING FUN. **PINOCCHIO** DOES NOT PAY ANY ATTENTION TO ANY OF IT.

CANDLEWICK Off to school again?

PINOCCHIO Yes, I promised my father and the Blue Fairy I would go. So please don't speak to me.

CANDLEWICK I wasn't going to. Besides, I was here first. I'm waiting to go to school myself.

PINOCCHIO You are?

CANDLEWICK Do you think there's only one school?

PINOCCHIO Are there more?

CANDLEWICK Of course, there are. Don't you know anything?

PINOCCHIO Which school are you going to?

CANDLEWICK It's a wonderful school. Everyone loves it.

PINOCCHIO <u>Love!</u> That's what I have to learn. Could I learn to love at your school?

CANDLEWICK That's the one place where all the children learn... and you'll love it!

PINOCCHIO Let me try to think. If I learn to love, and if it's a school, I won't be breaking my promise.

CANDLEWICK Well then, let's go.

PINOCCHIO But where is the school?

CANDLEWICK In the Land of Pleasure.

PINOCCHIO How do we get there? (WHIP CRACK IS HEARD)

CANDLEWICK Simple. The Coachman is coming for us.

> WE HEAR THE WHIP AS THE **COACHMAN** ENTERS. **ACTOR 1** IS THE **JOLLY COACHMAN**. HE WEARS THE HIGH HAT. HE IS AGAIN THE EX-PANSIVE LAUGHING VILLAIN.

ACTOR 1   Well...well...well, I see two good boys waiting to come with me to the Land of Pleasure.

CANDLEWICK Yes indeed. (POKING PINOCCHIO) Say, "yes", block-
head.

PINOCCHIO Oh, yes.

COACHMAN Why then, come along. We had best get started now or
it will be very late before we arrive.

  THEY USE THE TRUNK TO SIT ON AND MOVE AS IF THEY ARE IN A
  COACH. THE **COACHMAN** CRACKS A WHIP. THE USE OF MUSIC WILL
  GIVE THEM A CLICKETY-CLACKETY SOUND AND LIGHTS WILL ALL
  PROJECT MOVEMENT. WHEN THE MUSIC STOPS THE LIGHTS AND MOVE-
  MENT STOP WITH IT.

COACHMAN Here we are. Take a look round.

PINOCCHIO There's nothing much to see.

CANDLEWICK We're here to play, not to look. Bray! (HE BRAYS LIKE
A DONKEY)

PINOCCHIO (LAUGHS) What did you do that for? Bray! (HE BRAYS
AND LOOKS SURPRISED)

CANDLEWICK Bray! Because I bray! (HE CAN'T SPEAK TOO WELL)

PINOCCHIO Look! Bray! Your ears are like a donkey. Bray!

CANDLEWICK Your ears...bray... (BOTH   BOYS FEEL THEIR EARS AS
THEIR HANDS GO UP TO SHOW US HOW LONG THEIR EARS HAVE GROWN. THE
COACHMAN LAUGHS AND LAUGHS)

COACHMAN   You're both turning into donkeys. For boys who don't
go to school are donkeys with no brains and must do the donkey's
work. Now get to it!! (HE USES A WHIP ON THEM AS THEY HAVE TO
PULL THE BOXES WHICH ARE TOO HEAVY FOR THEM. HE LAUGHS AND WHIPS
THEM...SHOUTING, "FASTER, FASTER". IT'S DONE TO MUSIC TO IN-
CREASE THE PACE UNTIL BOTH **PINOCCHIO** AND **CANDLEWICK** FALL DOWN.
THE **COACHMAN** LOOKS AT BOTH BOYS THEN DECIDES TO TAKE **CANDLEWICK**
WHO IS BREATHING HEAVIER) I'll take this donkey with me to the
workhouse. And this one...is of no use. He's only a puppet. I
think I'll burn him. No, I'll throw him into the water. (HE
TAKES **PINOCCHIO** BY THE LEGS AND DISPOSES OF HIM BEHIND THE TRUNK.
THEN HE LIFTS **CANDLEWICK** UNDER THE ARMS AND DRAGS HIM OFF STAGE.
THE LIGHTS CHANGE AS **PINOCCHIO** IS ALONE ON STAGE SWIMMING. WE
HEAR HIM MOANING AND MOANING. MUSIC. HE SWIMS TO LAND AND
STARTS WEEPING. THE LIGHTS CHANGE TO BLUE AND THE **BLUE FAIRY**
APPEARS)

BLUE FAIRY Weep, Pinocchio, weep and maybe your tears...being
hurt...will teach you the meaning of love.

PINOCCHIO Oh, Blue Fairy. Help me! Help me! (FOR THE FIRST
TIME PINOCCHIO DISPLAYS EMOTION) I'm so unhappy.

BLUE FAIRY Cry. Be unhappy. Then and only then will you <u>want</u> to be good.

PINOCCHIO Oh yes, I want to be happy. I want to be good. But it's too much. I can't do it by myself.

BLUE FAIRY You must not only prove that you can be good but that you can love. The time has come for me to test you.

PINOCCHIO How?

BLUE FAIRY Your poor father has been so desperate about you... that he went out to sea to find you.

PINOCCHIO Where is he, Blue Fairy?

BLUE FAIRY He's been swallowed by the whale. Don't worry he's alive, but inside the whale.

PINOCCHIO What can I do? A wooden-headed puppet like me!

BLUE FAIRY It's not your <u>head</u> but your <u>heart</u> that we must now use. Go find the whale and save your father. Then I'll know that you love him.

PINOCCHIO Oh, I will. I will. I want my father. I love him. But show me where to find the whale.

BLUE FAIRY He'll come...just wait. And now, goodbye.

> SHE DISAPPEARS. MUSIC OF WATER BECOMES LOUDER AND LOUDER. PINOCCHIO STARTS SHAKING BACK AND FORTH TO GET THE FEELING OF A STORM AT SEA. LIGHTS GO WITH THE MUSIC OF STORM AT SEA. THE **WHALE** APPEARS IN THE GUISE OF **ACTOR 2**. HE WEARS A HUGE BLACK CLOAK WHICH MAKES HIM THE WHALE. IT IS PAINTED AND SHAPED AS A WHALE. HE TWIRLS THE CLOAK. IT IS POSSIBLE TO USE AN ACTOR UNDERNEATH THE CLOAK TO EXTEND IT. IN A DANCED MOVEMENT HE PULLS PINOCCHIO UNDER HIS BLACK CLOAK WHICH INDICATES HE'S SWALLOWED HIM. OR A WHALE CURTAIN CAN BE DRAWN WITH A LARGE HOLE IN THE CENTRE COVERED WITH SCRIM. GUEPPETTO (ACTOR 1) COULD MOVE WITH THE CURTAIN. LIGHTS UP AND WE SEE **GUEPPETTO** AND **PINOCCHIO**. THEY MUST CONSTANTLY ROCK IN THIS SCENE.

GUEPPETTO Pinocchio! Pinocchio! My boy! How did you get here?

PINOCCHIO The Blue Fairy told me where you were. Father, for-give me.

GUEPPETTO We mustn't think of that now. You must escape.

PINOCCHIO So must you. We must both escape.

GUEPPETTO How?

PINOCCHIO I don't know yet. I'm just beginning to think. But we will.

GUEPPETTO You're almost a real boy.

PINOCCHIO I've come to understand so much. But most of all how to love.

GUEPPETTO You give me courage. I was ready to die here.

PINOCCHIO You mustn't. I've only begun to love.

GUEPPETTO My son, I know there is hope. (THE WHALE BEGINS TO SHAKE INTENSELY) What's happening? Is the whale ill? Maybe he's hungry?

PINOCCHIO He sounds like he's sneezing.

> SUDDENLY AS THEY ARE TALKING THE **WHALE** STARTS TO SNEEZE. THEY ARE TOSSED ABOUT INSIDE AS THE **WHALE** ATTEMPTS HIS SNEEZE. WHEN THE WHALE FINALLY DOES SNEEZE **GUEPPETTO** AND **PINOCCHIO** ARE THROWN OUT OF HIS MOUTH INTO THE WATER. BUT AS THE **WHALE** INHALES FOR THE NEXT SNEEZE THEY ARE PULLED BACK IN ONLY TO BE THROWN OUT AGAIN AND PULLED IN AGAIN. THEY ARE EXHAUSTED FROM BEING TOSSED ABOUT. THEY   COLLAPSE ON THE FLOOR OF THE **WHALE**.

GUEPPETTO We were almost free. If only the whale could sneeze again.

PINOCCHIO He can.

GUEPPETTO But how?

PINOCCHIO I'm thinking! We will make the whale sneeze again... with this! (TAKES FEATHER FROM HIS CAP)

GUEPPETTO I forgot all about it.

PINOCCHIO I'll tickle the whale. (HE DOES SO) Hold on tight to me. (THEY ARE THRUST BACK AND FORTH AND FINALLY ESCAPE FROM THE WHALE'S MOUTH)

GUEPPETTO (AS THEY ARE SWIMMING) I can't go any further. I just can't.

PINOCCHIO (HOLDING ON TO GUEPPETTO AS HE SWIMS) Please, please don't die. We've come such a long way. Oh, Blue Fairy, help me! I love my father ! HELP! HELP!

> THE WATERS RECEDE AS THEY COME TO LAND. THE LIGHTS TURN TO BLUE AND **BLUE FAIRY** APPEARS. SHE HAS SAVED THEM.

BLUE FAIRY I am here, Pinocchio. And you are both safe. The journey has ended. You've learned to love. And now for the miracle of life. Up Gueppetto. You must! (SHE TAPS HIM WITH HER WAND) Pinocchio needs you. (**GUEPPETTO** SLOWLY RISES AND SEES EVERYONE ROUND HIM)

GUEPPETTO Blue Fairy, I'm grateful to you for saving my life.

BLUE FAIRY You must also thank Pinocchio.

GUEPPETTO I do. I do. My <u>good</u> little wooden head.

BLUE FAIRY The next miracle is one which was earned.

        Pinocchio, Pinocchio, you asked of me
        To make a real boy from the cherry tree
        Now with this wand, just wait and see
        It's the touch of life! And a real boy you'll be!

    PINOCCHIO SHAKES HIMSELF AND STARTS TO WALK LIKE A BOY AND NOT A PUPPET. MUSIC.

PINOCCHIO Look! Just look! I'm a boy! A real boy!

BLUE FAIRY Remember from now on you know right from wrong
        Remember from now on the place where you belong.
        Remember from now on the things that you must do.
        Remember from now on the love that was given you.
        At last you are real and must grow up on our own
        I'll say goodbye forever, it's yours to do alone.

And now boys and girls would you like a happy ending or a sad ending? (SHE ADJUSTS TO WHATEVER CHILDREN SAY CREATING A DIF-FERENT MOOD WITH SAME WORDS) Then we will have a.........ending.

        But the lessons that I taught you
        You must always use
        For practise will perfect you
        Your age will not excuse
        Goodbye Pinocchio. Remember me.
        Goodbye Pinnochio. Live happily.

    SHE EXITS. **GUEPPETTO** TURNS TO **PINOCCHIO.**

GUEPPETTO You've grown up, my boy. Come with me and I'll show you how to carve the wood. (THEY SIT DOWN TOGETHER)

        SLOW FADE OUT   SLOW FADE UP

    THE **ACTORS** COME ON STAGE FOR CURTAIN CALL. THEN, PACK UP ALL THEIR PROPS AND SCENERY IN THE TRUNK, READY TO LEAVE, CHATTERING WITHOUT STOP. **NARRATOR** ADDRESSES AUDIENCE.

NARRATOR   I hope all of you learned just a little.

ACTRESS   Of how long it takes to grow up.

ACTOR 1   And that growing up means learning from inside you.

ACTOR 2   Don't repeat yourselves. They saw the show. They're not idiots. There's only one word of advice to give. Whatever you do...when you grow up...don't become actors!

    LIGHTS DIM, **ACTORS** PICK UP TRUNK, EXIT DOWN AISLE.

               END OF PLAY

ALL COSTUMES AND PROPS FOR 'PINOCCHIO'
APPEAR FROM THE TRUNK

The End.

GUEPPETTO:
WILD RED WIG
AND APRON
AND GLASSES
SUGGEST
CHARACTER
'PINOCCHIO'
WEARS
SHORT PANTS
AND FALSE
PUPPET HAIR
'WHALE' — SCRIM CUT-OUT OF
WHALE IN CANVAS CLOTH SO GUEPPETTO
AND PINOCCHIO CAN BE LIT AND SEEN
INSIDE THE WHALE

BLUE FAIRY:
SPARKLING FAIRY
CAPE AND CROWN
CANDLEWICK —
JUST A CAP
MIGHT BE
ENOUGH TO
SUGGEST
THIS CHARACTER
School
FIRE-EATER-
-BLACK CLOAK,
MOUSTACHE,
AND HIGH HAT
RED WIG-AND-STOMACH
- NO MOUSTACHE -
FOR
COACHMAN

The Cricket Theatre
and Blanche Marvin
PRESENT

THE MERRI-MIMES

in

THE RED DRAGON

BY BLANCHE MARVIN

DIRECTED BY MARIO SILETTI

SETS BY HELEN POND AND HERBERT SENN

CAST:

JOHN - RUSSELL DOUGLAS
ELLEN - SUZANNE COLONA
MOTHER - POLLY GARRETT
MRS. ELSWORTH - BARBARA DICKENS
SAINT GEORGE - JAMES S. TOLKAN
STAGE MANAGER - WILLIAM HAWLEY

AT THE

CRICKET THEATRE   OR-49305
162 SECOND AVE. AT 10th St.

PERFORMANCES at 1, 2³⁰, 4 pm. on DEC. 23rd,
24th, 26th, 27th, 29th, 30th, 31st, JAN. 1st, 2nd, 3rd
ALSO
PETER AND THE WOLF - JAN. 10th
SLEEPING BEAUTY - JAN. 17th, 24th, 31st
and FEB 7th.

DESIGNED & ILLUSTRATED BY JOSINE-JANCO-KLINE

THE RED DRAGON

Contemporary Miracle Play

CAST OF CHARACTERS

John   - 13 years old. Crippled

Ellen   - 15 years old. His Sister

Mother   - Mother of John and Ellen

Mrs. Ellis   - Neighbour

St. George

Place   House in South London -
        Sitting Room and Garden

Time: The present

ACT ONE

THE SCENE OPENS UPON THE SITTING ROOM OF A MIDDLE CLASS
FAMILY LIVING IN A WORKING CLASS HOUSE TYPICAL IN ENGLAND.
THE GARDEN IS VISIBLE.   THE DRAB VICTORIAN DECOR DOMINATES
THE ROOM.   A MOVABLE WALL SEPARATES HOUSE FROM GARDEN.   WE
SEE SEATED: **MOTHER**, A PALE HARASSED WOMAN, GENTLE BUT
WORRIED; **ELLEN**, HER DAUGHTER, A LIGHT-HEARTED VERSION OF
HER MOTHER; **JOHN**, HER SON, WHO CANNOT WALK.   THEY ARE
HAVING BREAKFAST. IT IS WINTER AND COLD. CHRISTMAS IS ONLY
A WEEK AWAY.

MOTHER   Watch how you pour the tea, Ellen.   We don't need any
more problems.   You could scald yourself.

ELLEN   Mums, don't be so worrisome.   I've poured tea thousands
of times.   Christmas is almost here, so let's be more cheerful.

MOTHER   Oh, Ellen...cheer doesn't come because of Christmas.
We're no better off with or without Christmas.   I just don't see
our way clear of all this.

JOHN   Mums...we'll manage.   One day when I can walk you'll
stay home and never work again.

MOTHER   Oh my darling, I shouldn't make you feel badly.   I
don't mind working.   After all, I'm working for us.   And what
better children could I ask for. It's only that with all the
work...we live so poorly.

ELLEN   Don't forget when I finish school I'll be there to
help. At least we all have each other.

MOTHER   You're right.   I'd best be off now.   (STARTS PUTTING ON
HAT AND COAT TO LEAVE) Shall we take you upstairs, Johnny, or do
you want to stay in the sitting room for the day?

JOHN   I'll stay here...you'd better hurry...bye.

MOTHER   Goodbye.   Ellen get some kippers on the way home for
tea. (SHE EXITS)

ELLEN   Right...bye.

JOHN   What shall we do with Mother?   She's so tired and so
afraid.

ELLEN   I don't know...except we've got to try to   make   you
walk.   Other children like you have learned to walk.   Let's forget that you were ever ill and just think about walking and playing and jumping and running...

JOHN   Elly, I try but it doesn't help.   Br-r-r-r.   I'm so
cold, I'd build a fire, if I could.

ELLEN   We have to save on the electricity bills...for
Christmas, Johnny.

JOHN   I know. You'd better hurry or you'll be late for school.

ELLEN   I'll clear the breakfast dishes first. Do you have all the things you want downstairs? (CLEARS TABLE)

JOHN   Yes, I've my books...paper and pencils.

ELLEN   Better study up on Maths. You've not been doing so well at it. I'll be home early today. Bye, Johnny boy.

JOHN   Bye. (ELLEN EXITS) Well, here it is another day. I don't want to study any of my lessons. Red Dragon come out now ...it's safe...everyone's left. You can play with me and take me on one of your wonderful adventures in Rainbow Land. I do wish you'd start from the beginning. What did you say? Oh, Red Dragon, really, are we friends or are we friends? Well then, tell me where we're going. Here now, I've mounted you. How wonderful to fly like a bird...no need to walk at all. Look ...look there. I see Rainbow Land! What happy faces of children! There...there are the long-nosed elfs and the green-faced dragons. Look! Are they your relatives? You do look alike! We're landing in the green-faced dragon's territory in Rainbow Land! (HE BEGINS TO WALK ON HIS CRUTCHES) How do you do. My friend, the Red Dragon, brought me here. My legs? Oh, this...it's a crutch. Oh no, I couldn't. I could never throw them away. I couldn't walk if I did that. Here comes the Magician! Maybe he can help. Hello, Magician, could you help me walk? I thought maybe a few magic words...I have to help myself. Red Dragon! Over there! Who is he? Please tell me. Aren't you friends? Well, tell me his name anyway. St. George! (A VISION OF **ST. GEORGE** APPEARS IN THE GARDEN. **JOHN** CHASES OUT TO THE GARDEN AFTER HIM) St.George, St. George, please tell me, who are you? (**JOHN**, WHILE RUNNING, FALLS AS **ST. GEORGE** DISAPPEARS. THROUGH THE GATES **MRS. ELLIS**, THE NEXT DOOR NEIGHBOUR, ENTERS)

MRS.ELLIS Here, I say. What do you think you're up to, Johnny, comin' out into the garden on such a cold day with no hat, no cardigan, no coat? What in the world will I do with you? You should know better.

JOHN   Oh, please, Mrs. Ellis, I was fine. You shouldn't have stopped me.

MRS.ELLIS Fine was you...out in the cold...yelling yer head off for St. George. You're loony. Your Mother's asked me to keep me eyes on you and so I shall.

JOHN   I'm old enough to take care of myself. Honestly, I promise to stay indoors.

MRS.ELLIS (STRAIGHTENING UP) Now on to the couch with you and I'll put the covers over you. Stay there. It's so cold in this house I don't know why you don't go upstairs and keep warm in bed like your Mother asks you to.

JOHN   I can't stay in bed all my life. It's lonely up there. Besides when I stay in bed, I feel as if I'm ill.

MRS.ELLIS Now what was all this calling after St. George?

JOHN   I saw him.

MRS.ELLIS You what?

JOHN   I saw him.

MRS.ELLIS Where? Just show me where?

JOHN   There in the garden.

MRS.ELLIS You're really loony, that's what.

JOHN   I'm not, Mrs. Ellis. Word of honour. I saw him.

MRS.ELLIS You know who he is?

JOHN   I know he's our Patron Saint.

MRS.ELLIS Well, they say, now mind you I myself don't believe it, but they say, every once in a while he comes to visit a child whose pure heart calls him. But you have to have so much love inside you, that it lights his way. He performs miracles if you lead a good life...loving all creatures that is...cats, dogs, birds and even people.

JOHN   I know he came to me.

MRS.ELLIS Go on now. Keep quiet and cover up before I tell your Mother about going out in the cold. Want some tea?

JOHN   No thank you. Ellen should be home soon.

MRS.ELLIS As you please. I'll just straighten up a bit.   (ELLEN ENTERS)

ELLEN   Oh, it's so cold out. I wish winter would pass.

JOHN   I'm glad to see you, Elly.

MRS.ELLIS Well now, ain't you early?

ELLEN   Could be.

MRS.ELLIS What's come over you? Want some tea?

ELLEN   No tea, thank you, Mrs. Ellis. (TAKING HER ASIDE) Christmas is coming soon and I would love to surprise Mummy. I don't suppose you could help me with a job for Christmas...with Mr. Pierce? I'd save enough for all of us to have a real Christmas.

MRS.ELLIS Well, as far as I know, Mr. Pierce would hardly pay. You know how miserly he is...a regular Scrooge...a proper tightwad. Besides, it's not fittin', you leavin' your brother alone all day!

ELLEN   It would only be for Christmas.

MRS.ELLIS Ellen, today I found him in the garden...cold and wet
...yelling his head off about St.George. No, I wouldn't leave
him alone.

ELLEN   I'll have a talk with him. He'll be all right. Where
else can I work?

MRS.ELLIS You stay here with him. He needs you. Something only
has to happen once, and that's it. I'll be going. If you need
help, shout. (EXITS)

ELLEN   (BACK TO JOHN) What happened when you were in the garden? Mrs. Ellis said you were shouting after St. George.

JOHN   Elly, I saw him, honestly and truly, I did. Mrs. Ellis
said only the pure in heart see him and I did.

ELLEN   Darling Johnny, I love you. You are a wonderful
brother and one day God will show us mercy and you will walk, but
the miracle of St. George is in your head.

JOHN   I saw him as clear as crystal, shining in a light that
I've never seen before. He belongs to me and I won't fail him.
He's chosen me.

ELLEN   Johnny, you only think you saw him!

JOHN   I did see him. He came to me.

ELLEN   Don't tell Mummy any of this or anyone else. Did you
ask St. George to help you walk?

JOHN   No, I only saw him a moment and then Mrs. Ellis came
and he disappeared. But he was so beautiful. I will see him
again.

ELLEN   If you should, if there is anything like a miracle,
then ask him to help you walk.

JOHN   I can't do that. He would never come again.

ELLEN   Oh, what's wrong with you? Why not ask for help?

JOHN   I must earn it.

ELLEN   How will you do that?

JOHN   You'll see.

ELLEN   Let's practice your walk. A little exercise should
help.

           MUSIC - ELLEN AND JOHN SING

<u>SONG - WALKING</u>

ELLEN   If fish can swim and birds can fly
Then you will walk one day like I.
1, 2, 3, 4, 5...
Once I caught a fish alive
6, 7. 8, 9, 10...
You will walk like me again.

JOHN   It maybe that that is so,
But I must go very slow
1, 2, 3, 4, 5...
Once I caught a fish alive
6, 7, 8, 9. 10...
I will walk like you again.
     - END OF SONG -

    JOHN TRIES TO WALK BACK AND FORTH WITH ALL OF HIS STRENGTH.
REPEAT SINGING AS MANY TIMES AS NECESSARY.

JOHN   Oh, this is difficult. But I must keep trying.

ELLEN   We must. What a wonderful Christmas present it would
be for Mummy if you could walk.

JOHN   I know...

ELLEN   Johnny, I was thinking that if Daddy were alive...what
would he say to you about St. George?

JOHN   He would believe me.

ELLEN   Maybe so. But I know Daddy would never stop trying to
make you walk.

JOHN   I'll keep trying.

ELLEN   Mummy should be home soon. I'd better make the tea.
Sit down now and keep warm. (EXITS)

ST.GEORGE (APPEARS AT THE GARDEN GATE) John! John! I call to
you and you alone. (**JOHN** STARTS TO MOVE TOWARDS HIM) No, don't
move...stay where you are. You called to me and I came with my
sword of truth. It has been with me through many lands, through
time, through love, through hate, through peace, through war,
through tears, through laughter, through life, through death,
through the beginning, through the end. Know then St. George.
See him...believe in him...but let him pass in the night. He
will return... (FADES AWAY)

JOHN   Wait...wait a moment...please let me speak to you just
for one moment...please don't go...don't... (HE IS TRANSFIXED)

MOTHER   (JUST RUSHING IN FROM WORK) Johnny! Johnny, what is
it? Who were you talking to? No one's here except you. Darling, please wake up. (SLAPS HIS FACE) Ellen! Ellen! Quickly,
water! Johnny! I don't know what's happened to him.

ELLEN   Mummy...what is it? Here's some water.

MOTHER   Help me with Johnny. Let's carry him to the couch.

JOHN   (MUMBLING) He passed in the night.

MOTHER   Oh Johnny, are you all right? Are you all right?

CURTAIN

END OF ACT ONE

ACT TWO

CURTAIN GOES UP SOME MINUTES LATER ON **ELLEN**, **JOHN** AND **MOTHER**
IN THE SITTING ROOM. JOHN HAS RECOVERED. EVERYTHING ELSE
REMAINS THE SAME.

MOTHER   Johnny, sweet boy, what was it?   You stood there as if
you had a vision.

ELLEN   Don't get upset. You know what a vivid imagination he
has. It was nothing. (LOOKING AT **JOHN** WARNING HIM NOT TO TALK)

MOTHER   Please, Ellen. Johnny is old enough to speak for himself. What was it that you saw?

JOHN   Nothing...really.

MOTHER   Ellen, what is this all about? You must tell me.

ELLEN   Honestly, Mums, Johnny plays imaginary games. It
doesn't mean anything.

MOTHER   You're holding something back. I want to know.

ELLEN   It seems silly to talk about it.

MOTHER   (BESIDE HERSELF) Silly was it to find him mesmerised?

JOHN   It wasn't quite as bad as all that. I have a friend.
He's a Red Dragon who takes me on all sorts of adventures.

MOTHER   Where is he?

JOHN   In my mind...but he keeps me company when I'm alone in
the house.

MOTHER   I knew I shouldn't leave you alone. What can I do?
What can I do? Johnny, imaginary friends like Red Dragons are
not for grown up boys like you. You should be studying your
Maths, or History, or French. You'll never keep up with your
school work.

JOHN   Don't worry. I study very well. I have to have some
friends.

ELLEN   You're making a storm in a tea cup.

MOTHER   You're always conspiring behind my back, the two of you.

ELLEN   That's not so. We love you. (KISSES HER GENTLY) Let's have our tea. The kippers are ready. (SHE EXITS)

MOTHER   John darling, I don't mean to be picking on you...

JOHN   I know. Ellen and I practised my walk. You'll see, I'll walk one day soon.

MOTHER   I want only the best for you and Ellen. Tell me about your Red Dragon.

JOHN   There isn't much to tell. He takes me on his back and we fly to Rainbow Land. You know Mums...it's such a wonderful light feeling just floating with no crutches to hold you down ...when you fly. I meet all kinds of people. The walls of my room just open up and I travel round the world.

MOTHER   Poor sweet Johnny. I should get you out of the house more often. Wait for Spring. We'll go visiting. In Springtime, everything seems more cheerful. The garden will be beautiful.

JOHN   Things are smashing for Christmas.

MOTHER   For some people.

     ENTER MRS. ELLIS THROUGH THE GATE.

MRS.ELLIS Hello there! I thought I'd pop over and make sure you were home all right.

MOTHER   Thank goodness for you, Mrs. Ellis. What would I have done without you.

MRS.ELLIS Oh love, I've done nothing.

     ENTER ELLEN WITH TEA TRAY.

ELLEN   Hello, Mrs. Ellis. Stay and have some tea with us.

MRS.ELLIS Heavens, no. Me old man'll be home soon. I have to get his tea ready. You know how he is...one foot in the door and it's his tea he wants.

MOTHER   Don't grumble...it's good to have your husband with you.

MRS.ELLIS Oh, I'm not grumbling. Goodness knows I'm blessed to have him...but it's work. There's no denying that.

MOTHER   There's always work...one way or another.

MRS.ELLIS True...true. Well now, I came over to tell you to keep the garden door locked 'til Spring.

MOTHER   Why? (ELLEN AND JOHN LOOK AT EACH OTHER FEARFULLY)

MRS.ELLIS Just so strangers might not get in or out.

MOTHER   What are you trying to say?

MRS.ELLIS I don't like worrying you.   There's no need to worry...not really...er...Johnny...Johnny went out into that cold garden today. He fell. You've no use for the garden in winter and Johnny shouldn't be out there.

ELLEN   But, Mrs. Ellis, how would you come over then?

MRS.ELLIS Through the front door.

ELLEN   That's the long way round.

MRS.ELLIS Look here, Elly, I don't mind.

JOHN   Please, Mrs. Ellis, there's no need to worry Mother, as you said. I didn't go back into the garden again and I promise I won't.

MRS.ELLIS Well, I was only trying to help.

MOTHER   Of course, you were.   I'm sure Johnny will keep his word.

MRS.ELLIS You remember Mrs. Bond's boy.   You know, the one that died of pneumonia. Poor Mrs. Bond. She should have stopped him. Now she's sorry.   But what can you do...it's too late. Pity, but too late.

JOHN   Mrs. Ellis, I told you, I won't do it again.

ELLEN   He's always kept his word.

MRS.ELLIS Well, it isn't that he doesn't keep his word. He might just get carried away again. Calling for that fellow St. George.

    JOHN AND ELLEN LOOK AT EACH OTHER. THEY FAILED IN STOPPING **MRS.ELLIS**.

MOTHER   What do you mean, Mrs. Ellis? When was Johnny calling for St. George.

MRS.ELLIS That's what brought me over. I heard him calling St. George, shaking all over with cold, right out in the garden. No cardigan...no hat...no coat.

MOTHER   Johnny, what is it? Is that what you saw? Tell me.

JOHN   Yes, Mother.

MOTHER   You didn't, you know.   It's just more of your games with your imaginary friends, isn't it? Like Red Dragon. Tell me...Johnny...isn't it?

JOHN   Yes, Mother.

MOTHER   Don't keep saying, "Yes"! Tell me the truth.

JOHN   The truth, Mums, the truth... (ELLEN LOOKS AT HIM) is I
saw St. George. He spoke to me, just to me, with a voice I'll
never forget. Why should I deny I saw him? I did see him...I
did see him...I did see him!

MRS.ELLIS There he goes again.

MOTHER   Johnny, people today don't hear voices or see Saints.
I've left you alone too much. It's my fault.

MRS.ELLIS There now, don't be so hard on yourself. You know
children of today.

ELLEN   Stop it! If Johnny wants to see St. George, he has a
right to. All this commotion over nothing.

MRS.ELLIS Nothing is it, when your brother's loony? Ain't your
Mum got enough troubles? You should try and help...that's what.

MOTHER   Mrs. Ellis, he is <u>not</u> "loony". He's a child with a
vivid imagination.

     AS THE ARGUMENT CONTINUES **ST. GEORGE** APPEARS.

ST.GEORGE John! John! Don't move, just listen to me. There are
many who believe only in what they can see. But you know better.

     JOHN IS LISTENING TO **ST. GEORGE** IN THE GARDEN. **MOTHER** AND
     MRS. ELLIS STOP TALKING AS THEY SEE **JOHNNY**'S FACE.

MOTHER   There, there it is again. Johnny, what is it?

     JOHN DOESN'T ANSWER. HE IS LISTENING TO **ST. GEORGE** AS THE
     OTHERS FREEZE IN POSITIONS OF FEAR AND BEWILDERMENT.

ST.GEORGE We'll not speak now, but look for me on Christmas Eve.
Stay in your room. Believe in miracles, they do happen.

JOHN   'Til Christmas.

MOTHER   Did you see St. George again?

JOHN   Only for a moment.

MRS.ELLIS I'd take him to a Doctor if I was you. No telling what
will happen.

MOTHER   He'll be all right.

MRS.ELLIS I hope so. I'd better get back. Or tea'll be late.
Yours is cold now. Go on all...go have your tea.

     SHE EXITS AS TABLE IS SET AND TEA IS SERVED AND EATEN.

MOTHER   When did you first see him, Johnny?

JOHN   Today.

MOTHER   Where?

JOHN   In the garden.

MOTHER   Did you call him?

JOHN   No. Red Dragon took me to him.

MOTHER   Stop it, Johnny. Stop this madness.

ELLEN   Mother, I remember when I was little, father used to tell us about St. George. He believed in him.

MOTHER   He believed in the spirit of St. George not in a ghost!

ELLEN   Imaginary things can become real and then you can do real things. This tea _is_ cold. I hate cold tea!

JOHN   It's all right.

MOTHER   I'll warm the pot and the kippers. (EXITS)

ELLEN   Johnny, if you say another word about any of your so-called friends I'll never help you with your homework...ever... ever again!

JOHN   But I didn't bring it up. Mrs. Ellis and her snooping nose did. What could I say? I held out for as long as I could.

ELLEN   From now on don't you dare say another word!

JOHN   You think I'm not concerned about Mums as much as you.

ELLEN   'Course you are, but you mess things up. I'm older than you, so I know more.

JOHN   That's not true. I know things you don't know.

ELLEN   Such as...

JOHN   Such as the structure of the earth's surface...distance ...space...

ELLEN   Who cares about that?

JOHN   I want to be a scientist.

ELLEN   That's a laugh! A scientist who believes in St. George and has visions?

JOHN   One thing has nothing to do with the other. When I go off to University, I'll learn all about the scientific experi- ments in rockets and satellites.

ELLEN   I can just see you as a spaceman in St. George's ar- mour. (LAUGHS)

236

JOHN   I don't need armour or a space suit to prove my faith.

ELLEN   (STILL LAUGHING) Which faith?

JOHN   When I'm a scientist, one day, you won't laugh.

ELLEN   Well, you'd better study up quickly if you intend going
to University. Better forget your Red Dragon and start on your
Maths.

JOHN   The more scientific I become the more I'll understand
my Red Dragon.

ELLEN   How's his smoke these days?

JOHN   <u>Filtered</u>...good as a dragon should...

ELLEN   And his scaly tail...does it still wave?

JOHN   It's jet-propelled.

ELLEN   Oh, I see...a mechanical Wizard.

JOHN   Oh, he keeps up with the times. He's quite an intel-
ligent fellow.

ELLEN   He must be or else how could he be your friend?

JOHN   As soon as I can walk, I'll be back to school.

ELLEN   (SUDDENLY UPSET) Oh Johnny, I wish that more than anything else in this world.

JOHN   I'm sorry, Elly, I didn't mean to upset you.

     MOTHER ENTERS WITH TEA AND KIPPERS AS **JOHNNY** IS COMFORTING
     ELLY.

MOTHER   What now?

JOHN   Nothing, Mums.

ELLEN   I'm Alice in Wonderland crying milk tears over spilt
milk.

MOTHER   Come, let's have our tea before it's bedtime.

ELLEN   (PECKING AT HER FOOD) I think it was better cold...the
kippers are dried as toast.

MOTHER   (ELEGANTLY) Let's have our Tea Party with the Mad Hatter and our Alice.

JOHN   It's delicious.

MOTHER   No, it's not. It's dried and burnt, but it will have
to do. Maybe your St. George can miraculously cure the kippers.

JOHN   Poor St. George having to cure burnt kippers!

ELLEN   (SUDDENLY LAUGHING) His torch of truth would probably
burn them to a crisp.

JOHN   Oh, Elly, come off it.

MOTHER   I must say I feel much better about the old boy.

ELLEN   Think of the old boy holding up that sword for so many
years. His arm must be drooping.

MOTHER   (STARTS LAUGHING) I can just see St. George now...

JOHN   Is the joke over?

          MOTHER IMITATES ST. GEORGE. ELLEN JOINS HER. AMIDST THE
          LAUGHTER, MRS. ELLIS CALLS OUT FROM OFF STAGE.

MRS.ELLIS Can I barge in?   Me old man's staying late at the Post
Office because of this Christmas rush.

MOTHER   Come join us. You're most welcome to burnt kippers and
cold tea.

MRS.ELLIS I don't know, Christmas is just a bloody nuisance. My
poor Tom got more work...more late hours.

          AS SHE COMES THROUGH THE GARDEN SHE STOPS TO LOOK AT SOME-
          THING.   IN A PUZZLED MANNER SHE PICKS IT UP. MEANWHILE THE
          LAUGHTER AND JOKING OF THE FAMILY HAS CONTINUED. MRS. ELLIS
          ENTERS WITH A BEWILDERED EXPRESSION ON HER FACE.   HER WORDS
          SILENCE THE LAUGHTER.

MRS.ELLIS Look here.   I found this Spring flower in the garden
near the gate. Imagine, at this time of year?

CURTAIN

END OF ACT TWO

ACT THREE

          CHRISTMAS EVE.   SAME SET.   WE SEE A SMALL TREE BEING DEC-
          ORATED.   TINSLE, HOLLY, BELLS AND CHRISTMASSY EFFECTS HAVE
          BEEN HUNG IN THE SITTING ROOM. JOHN IS SITTING ON THE COUCH
          WHILE ELLEN AND MOTHER ARE BUSY DECORATING THE TREE WITH A
          STRING OF LIGHTS.

MOTHER   Well, the tree may not be up to scratch, but it's ours.

ELLEN   Let's imagine that it's big and beautiful with the most
expensive decorations.

MOTHER   All right. Christmas Tree, you are tall and beautiful
with outstretched branches, dressed in gold and silver and blessed because you are in the home of Ellen and John. (BOWS)

JOHN   I've never seen you like this before, Mums.

MOTHER   I used to be young once. I even believed in St.
George.

ELLEN   Give us a show. I remember how you used to play.

MOTHER   Not now.

ELLEN & JOHN
            I'll bet you've forgotten.

MOTHER   All right, I accept the challenge. (GOES OUT TO HALL
OFF STAGE) I'll be back in a moment. (MAKES AN ENTRANCE WITH
BOWLER HAT) Good evening, folks. (GOES INTO BUSKER ROUTINE WITH
FOLLOWING SONG)

            MUSIC - MOTHER SINGS

            SONG - CHRISTMAS HAT SONG
            Christmas is a coming
            Geese are getting fat
            Will you please put a penny
            In the old man's hat
            If you haven't got a penny
            A ha'penny will do
            If you haven't got a ha'panny
            God Bless You!

        ELLEN JOINS IN WITH MOTHER-BUSKER.   THEY DO A TAP ROUTINE
TOGETHER AND THE SECOND VERSE.

            Christmas is a coming
            Light up the Christmas Tree
            Will you please put a stocking
            On the Christmas Tree for me
            If you haven't got a stocking
            A little sock will do
            If you haven't got a little sock,
            God Bless You!

        THEY FINISH THEIR NUMBER TO JOHN'S DELIGHT.

JOHN   Well, I must say that's more of the Christmas spirit we
should have round here.

MOTHER   (OUT OF BREATH) Dear me, I don't know if I could do
that again.

ELLEN   We could always try.

MOTHER   Maybe you, Elly, not me. Let's finish the decorations.

ELLEN   We're doing very well.

JOHN   Wish I could help.

MOTHER   The best way to help is to be patient.   (THE SNOW

BEGINS TO FALL IN THE GARDEN) Look it's snowing.

JOHN   Snow for Christmas.

ELLEN   All that's missing are the reindeer.

MOTHER   Oh, look...look...the Christmas star.

JOHN   Where? Let me see.

MOTHER   As I remember, I used to think if you saw the Christmas
star, your wish would come true.

ELLEN   What wish?

MOTHER   Any you made up.

JOHN   Is it a sign, then?

MOTHER   Depends on what you mean. It could be a sign.

ELLEN   Just think all over the world, tonight, everyone is doing the same sort of thing. That's what's so super about
Christmas...sharing the same thought with the world.

MOTHER   Before we're through, I'll believe in St. George...and
signs.

JOHN   Faith is something you shouldn't lose, no matter how
old you are.

MOTHER   Well, John-John, as you get older and things don't go
well, for a long time, you do lose faith.

ELLEN   Whatever happened to the Christmas spirit? How did we
lose it? It was here only a minute ago. Christmas spirit, where
are you?

MOTHER   All right, Elly, point taken. Why don't we finish
wrapping the presents.

JOHN   Oh, then I'll see them.

MOTHER   I'll hide behind the tree.

ELLEN   I'll stand on the other side.

JOHN   I'll sit here. Someone throw me paper and ribbons.

MOTHER   Here's some.

     MOTHER GIVES PAPER AND RIBBONS TO JOHN. THEY ALL WRAP THEIR
     PRESENTS SECRETLY. JOHN FINISHES QUICKLY.

JOHN   Ready, there. (HOLDS HIS UP. IT IS NOT VERY WELL DONE)

MOTHER   Mine may look a little sad but at least it's covered.

ELLEN   There, how's mine?

MOTHER   Good enough. Let's put them under the tree. (DOES SO)
That looks rather nice. We're all set for the magic moment.
Turn on the lights! (**ELLEN** PUTS THE PLUG INTO THE SOCKET)

ELLEN   Hold your breath, everyone. (TREE LIGHTS UP) Isn't it
magnificent! (HUGS **MOTHER**) Let's sing, "We Three Kings", to our
tree.

        CHRISTMAS CAROL, "WE THREE KINGS", IS SUNG A CAPPELLA BY ALL
        THREE.

MOTHER   And we all kept in tune! Let's get some sleep. Tomorrow's our big day. Come, John-John.

        MOTHER AND **ELLEN** HELP **JOHN** AS THEY ALL EXIT. ROOM DARKENS.
        LIGHTS GO ON IN **JOHN**'S ROOM.

JOHN   (FROM HIS WINDOW) Please, St. George, you promised to
come on Christmas Eve. Everyone's gone to bed. It's safe.
(NOTHING HAPPENS) You wouldn't break a promise. Maybe you're
waiting for me. Just a moment. I'll be there. Wait, I'm com-
ing. (HE COMES BACK INTO THE SITTING ROOM BY CRAWLING DOWN THE
STAIRS) Red Dragon, quickly where are you? Ah, there you are.
Were you waiting for me? Oh you mustn't feel hurt, I didn't for-
get you.   I do want to see St. George, it's true, but that
doesn't mean I don't want to see you. Let's leave the house.
Let the walls open up. Let the world come in and we'll fly away.
(HE OPENS THE GARDEN BY ROLLING BACK THE WALL, CRAWLING ON HIS
KNEES. THE MOVABLE WALL CLOSES IN THE SITTING ROOM AS IT OPENS
THE GARDEN.

            MUSIC - JOHN SINGS

            SONG - RED DRAGON
        Red Dragon, Red Dragon let's light up the sky
        With laughter and songs as we fly by
        We'll stop in Rainbow Land
        And shake everyone's hand
        Red Dragon, Red Dragon, there'll be company
        And so many friends that we'll just have to see
        So open the walls of this small Sitting Room
        And let in the big world with all things that bloom
            - END OF SONG -

Wait. Now, I've mounted you. Oh, what a beautiful night.
Christmas star, how close you are. You led the way once before,
centuries ago, to the Jesus child. Please lead the way for me.
Else why do you shine? Red Dragon, I can't see him. Won't he
come? Must I stop believing? You're right! I must wait for
him. Well, Red Dragon, let's go home. Turn round. (HE DRAWS
BACK THE WALL CRAWLING ON HIS KNEES) Merry Christmas and long
life, Dragon. Are you leaving? I'll see you tomorrow. Goodnight. (HE CRAWLS UP TO HIS ROOM. LIGHTS GO ON. HE WAITS BY
THE WINDOW AND **ST GEORGE** APPEARS BY THE GARDEN GATE. LIGHTS GLOW
AROUND HIM)

ST.GEORGE John, I have come back as promised. Only children seem to believe in St. George today.

JOHN   St. George, you <u>have</u> kept your word. Are you a child's Saint?

ST.GEORGE Don't you know who I am? I am the St. George centuries old. Great men of all ages have believed in me. I am the same St. George that fought the Battle of Agincourt with King Henry. And when England was torn open by war just yesterday, it was I who spoke of the courage to fight with blood, toil, sweat and tears. You must know that love is made of firmer stuff. St. George has always <u>fought</u> for those he loved. Love is not in the <u>hoping</u> but in the <u>doing</u>. Remember St. George always...as a child...as a man. You must fight for life... (SWORD UP) for Elizabeth, England and St. George. (EXITS AND LIGHTS OUT)

JOHN   Please wait, wait for me. Don't go yet, not yet.

JOHN COMES DOWN FROM HIS ROOM RUNNING THROUGH THE SITTING ROOM TO GARDEN CHASING AFTER ST. **GEORGE** WITHOUT HIS CRUTCHES. THE DAWN IS JUST BEGINNING TO BREAK. **ELLEN** SLEEPILY COMES DOWN TO WITNESS THE MIRACLE OF **JOHN**. SHE STANDS THERE TRANSFIXED AS IF SHE HAD A VISION.

ELLEN   God help us. He's walking!

JOHN   Bless you, St. George.

MOTHER COMES DOWN. OFF-STAGE WE HEAR, "JOHN...JOHN...ELLY!" SHE IS ON STAGE...SEES **JOHN** IN THE GARDEN WITHOUT CRUTCHES AND STOPS. **JOHN** STARTS TO WALK TOWARDS HER.

JOHN   Mums, Mums, Merry Christmas!

CURTAIN

END OF PLAY

HALLWAY TO UPSTAIRS
MOVING 'EMPTY' WALL — MOVES TO MAKE GARDEN AND ROOM BIGGER OR SMALLER AS NEEDED.
GARDEN GATE
St GEORGE

ST. GEORGE
MOTHER
ELLEN
JOHN
MRS. ELLIS

THE CRICKET THEATRE AND BLANCHE MARVIN
PRESENT
THE MERRI-MIMES'

MEET MR. EASTERBUNNY

BY BLANCHE MARVIN

DIRECTED BY   MARIO SILETTI
CHOREOGRAPHY BY KATHERINE LITZ
COSTUMES   BY   MIDGE
LIGHTING   BY   RICHARD NELSON
SOUND AND STAGE MANAGER - NORMAN
                          BLUMENFELD

CAST:

MR. EASTERBUNNY - ARTHUR LEWIS
    HANS   - RUSSELL DOUGLAS
    OLGA   - BETTY SCHWARTZ
    MAYOR - GORDON SPENCE

MAYOR'S WIFE - ADELE REEL

AT THE CRICKET THEATRE
162 SECOND AVE (at 10th st) OR-49
1 - 2³⁰ - 4 pm. during EASTER
SAT MARCH 28, MON 30th, TUES 31, AND
THURS 2, FRI 3, SAT 4th

ALSO: ———
ALICE IN WONDERLAND: APRIL
AND EVERY FOLLOWING SATURDAY

A VERY HAPPY EASTER
            and PASSOVER
FROM THE BARTON CANDY CO.!

MR. EASTER BUNNY

CONTEMPORARY COMEDY

CAST OF CHARACTERS

Mayor

Mother

James

Jane

Mr. Easter Bunny

Place: A village in England

Time: The present

ACT ONE

A SMALL ENGLISH VILLAGE. IT IS THE MAYOR'S HOUSE. WE SEE THE GARDEN AND SITTING ROOM. THE SCENE OPENS ON A STORM. NO ONE IS ON STAGE. THE STORM SUBSIDES. IT IS LATE AT NIGHT. WE SEE TWO HEADS SUDDENLY APPEAR. A BOY AND GIRL LOOK AT EACH OTHER THEN DISAPPEAR. WE HEAR THEIR OFF-STAGE VOICES.

JAMES   The storms's over...let's go.

JANE   No, wait...

JAMES   No one is awake.

JANE   You know what a light sleeper Father is.

JAMES   I've worked this all out. Come on now.

JANE   But you didn't count on a storm. Maybe the storm awakened...

OFF-STAGE WE HEAR THE NOISE OF A WINDOW BEING CLOSED AND OFF-STAGE VOICES.

MAYOR   Is that better, my dear?

MOTHER   Yes, dear...much.

JANE   I told you...

JAMES   Be quiet. It's all right. He's back in bed.

JANE   Let's wait a moment.

JAMES   Shh...now, let's go.

JANE AND JAMES, THE BOY AND GIRL, COME INTO THE SITTING ROOM ON TIPTOE. THEY PROCEED TO HIDE SOMETHING WHICH WE DON'T SEE. THEY DO NOT LET EACH OTHER SEE EITHER AND ARE CON-STANTLY ON GUARD ABOUT THEIR FATHER. THEY GO OUT TO THE GAR-DEN CONTINUING TO HIDE WHAT THEY WERE HIDING. QUIETLY STEALING THROUGH THE AUDIENCE IS AN **EASTER BUNNY** DRESSED IN TOP HAT AND TAILS, VERY DIGNIFIED, OLD AND TIRED. HE COMES UPON **JANE** AND **JAMES**. THEY DO NOT SEE HIM. HE NODS TO CHILDREN IN THE AUDIENCE. HE BOWS THEN TAPS **JANE**. SHE JUMPS WITH FRIGHT.

JANE   Who's that?

EASTER BUNNY
          My name is Mr. Easter Bunny. What are you hiding there, by the way?

JANE   Sh! Mother and Father mustn't hear us.

JAMES   We'll ask questions, not you!

EASTER BUNNY
Oh, very well. I'm tired anyway. Two thousand years of travelling is enough to make anyone tired.

JANE   You couldn't possibly be that old.

EASTER BUNNY
I am. Stop playing games with me, I know what you're hiding.

JAMES   You do not...

EASTER BUNNY
Oh, yes, I do.

JAMES   What is it?

EASTER BUNNY
I'll whisper in your ear. (HE DOES SO) Am I right?

JAMES   Yes, you are. But how did you guess?

EASTER BUNNY
(SPOKEN IN ONE BREATH VERY FAST) Well, when you've travelled as much as I have to as many countries for so many years, met so many people all believing that rabbits go with Easter, celebrating with lots of food and the beginning of Spring, when so many people for so many years believe in you...you believe in yourself, after a while.

JANE   You haven't met Father.

JAMES   That's right. Father doesn't believe that Easter should be full of fun and games. He thinks it's very serious.

JANE   He'd be furious if he saw you here.

EASTER BUNNY
He's never met me. That's why.

JAMES   He mustn't...

EASTER BUNNY
I'm staying...for Easter.

JANE   Oh, but you can't. Where could we hide you?

JAMES   Father might do...anything...if he found you.

EASTER BUNNY
Don't worry. I've lived through far more difficult things. I'll hide myself.

JANE   Please, Mr. Easter Bunny, don't stay. We wouldn't want to see you harmed.

EASTER BUNNY
I'll take care of myself.

248

JAMES   You don't know Father.

EASTER BUNNY
         (GOING TO ALL THE HIDING PLACES)   Here's an egg...and
here...and here...and here.

JANE   Oh, leave our secret alone!   Now everyone knows what
we've been hiding.

JAMES   We wanted to find them ourselves.

EASTER BUNNY
         I want everyone to close their eyes... (TO AUDIENCE)
that means you and you and you. I'll hide the eggs. It's my job
really. Have you kept your eyes shut tight? Good! Now don't
make a sound or we'll wake up the Mayor...then there'll be
trouble. (HE HAS BEEN HIDING EGGS IN THE GARDEN ON STAGE) I'm
almost finished.

         PLEASE NOTE THAT EASTER EGGS HAVE BEEN HIDDEN UNDER SEATS IN
         THE AUDIENCE BEFORE THE SHOW STARTS.

JAMES   Oh, good. Tell me, Mr. Easter Bunny, was it your in-
vention about Easter eggs and hiding them.

EASTER BUNNY
         Do I look like a chicken?   My ears...my tail...just
look at me...Don't I look like a rabbit? (TO AUDIENCE) Don't I?

JANE   Sh!   Quiet, please! Excuse me, Mr. Easter Bunny, I
didn't for a moment think you were anything but a bunny. But I
always thought <u>you</u> brought the Easter eggs.

JAMES   We were always told that.

EASTER BUNNY
         Maybe I'd better explain a few things. The idea about
Easter eggs...just eggs...goes back to when I lived in Pharoah's
Egypt. Why, even then the egg meant the beginning of life. The
phoenix laid the egg in those days. Now the phoenix was the most
beautiful bird and when it died in a blaze of flame at sunset, it
rose again, into life, at the following dawn. Resurrection.

JANE   What happened to the phoenix?

EASTER BUNNY
         The phoenix became the beautiful peacock.   And then
from the peacock it went to a gander, next a swan, finally the
hen. It never was a rabbit. The egg is still the same. But the
idea of Easter...of being reborn...or of new life arising from
old life...comes with Spring when new grass, new flowers, new
leaves, new animals are born. So, if you put eggs and Easter
together...they belong.

JAMES   I must say I never thought of that. But that doesn't
explain the rabbit!

EASTER BUNNY
        Well, I'm sort of a mystery.

JAMES   I think I know.

EASTER BUNNY
        Do you?

JAMES   (DRAMATICALLY) Once you were a bird but the Dawn God-
dess Eostre <u>changed you</u>...into a hare.

EASTER BUNNY
        I must say that was a good try taking me back more
years than I care to remember. But I'm still a mystery.

JAMES   You're pretending.

JANE   Oh, tell us!

EASTER BUNNY
        No one's quite sure. It could be because we rabbits
multiply so rapidly...full of life, you might say. They used to
call the last sheaf of corn, the hare. The corn-spirit was part
of the Spring rites. I just might have begun anywhere.

JANE   You're keeping it secret. You know and won't tell us.

EASTER BUNNY
        If you want to pin me down, I think it was first in
Germany that I gave Easter eggs to the children.

JAMES   Have you seen children all over the world for Easter?

EASTER BUNNY
        Oh, yes.

JANE   And do they all have fun?

EASTER BUNNY
        Mostly, yes.

JAMES   Do they have egg hunts?

JANE   And do they paint Easter eggs?

EASTER BUNNY
        Oh, yes...in most countries they do.

JANE   Then, why doesn't Father let us?

EASTER BUNNY
        Well, maybe he only thinks of Easter as a Christian
holiday.

JANE   What other kind of holiday can it be?

EASTER BUNNY
        But that's what I've been explaining.

JAMES   Sh...You'll wake Father.

EASTER BUNNY
          Excuse me.   But I told you that Easter goes way back
before Christianity.   It is a Springtime festival, celebrated by
many, many, many people in many, many lands...by many, many
names.

JAMES   But Father only celebrates it in church.

EASTER BUNNY
          I'll have to explain it to him then.

JANE   You couldn't teach him. He's the Mayor.

EATER BUNNY
          I'm Mr. Easter Bunny. How do you do.

JAMES   Do you think you can change Father's mind?

EASTER BUNNY
          Maybe.

JANE   Well, why did you come, if you can't help us?

EASTER BUNNY
          I didn't say I wouldn't help you.

JANE   But you didn't say you would.

EASTER BUNNY
          Why don't you wait and see what happens?

JAMES   I wonder whether you could win over Father?

EASTER BUNNY
          I dare say.

JANE   He's a stubborn man.

EASTER BUNNY
          I've met them before.

JANE   Oh, James, maybe we'll have an egg hunt before Easter's
over!

JAMES   Mr. Easter Bunny's the one who can do it.

EASTER BUNNY
          I hope so.

JAMES   Of course you can.

JANE   Well, can you?

EASTER BUNNY
          Maybe.

MAYOR   (OFFSTAGE) James...Jane...where are you?

JAMES   Here comes Father. Where will we hide you...here...
no...here...

JANE   Quickly...behind the gate.

     FRANTICALLY THEY HIDE **MR. EASTER BUNNY** AS **MAYOR** APPEARS.

MAYOR   What are you doing?

CURTAIN

END OF ACT ONE

ACT TWO

     EXACTLY AS END OF ACT ONE.

MAYOR   Explain yourselves.

JAMES   We decided, since it was Easter, that we should...

MAYOR   You're hiding things from me.

JANE   Oh, no.

MAYOR   You are! What is it?

JAMES   Father, we were doing nothing wrong. We were only
hiding Easter eggs.

MAYOR   What! Haven't I told you a thousand times, Easter must
be observed with thought...serious thought. Not with Easter
eggs!

JAMES   But we didn't invent hiding eggs for Easter. There
must be a reason.

MAYOR   (ANGRY) I'll give you a reason...

MOTHER   (ENTERS SLEEPILY) I'm sure we can discuss it after
we've all had a good breakfast. (SHE EXITS)

MAYOR   We certainly shall. (HE WALKS INTO THE GARDEN) I must
say everything smells so fresh in the morning.

     CHILDREN FOLLOW **FATHER** INTO THE GARDEN. **EASTER BUNNY** POKES
     HIS HEAD OUT. THE **CHILDREN** BECKON TO HIM TO HIDE. **JAMES**
     STANDS BEHIND HIM.

MAYOR   Why are you standing there? You look like a statue.

JAMES   I'm just smelling the spring air.

JANE   It's so sweet.

MOTHER   (MOTHER ENTERS WITH BREAKFAST TRAY) It's such a lovely morning after last night's storm. Did you sleep well?

CHILDREN Yes.

MOTHER   Didn't the storm wake you?

JAMES   Only for a moment. (THEY SET THE TABLE AND CHAIRS)

MOTHER   Come, sit down. Breakfast's ready. (THEY ALL SIT)

MAYOR   Delicious eggs, my dear.

JAMES   Yes, Father, they are good.

JANE   Let's call them Easter eggs!

MAYOR   Don't spoil my breakfast...

MOTHER   We'll discuss it all later. Remember, Jane!

JANE   Yes, Mother. (MR EASTER BUNNY COMES OUT AGAIN. SHE MO-
TIONS FOR HIM TO HIDE. MR. EASTER BUNNY SIGNS BACK THAT THE
MAYOR AND HIS WIFE CANNOT SEE HIM)

MAYOR   What are you doing, Jane?

JANE   Fanning myself.

MAYOR   It's not that warm.

MOTHER   Do be still!

JAMES   Can we have a Maypole dance this year?

MAYOR   No!

MOTHER   James, why must we have arguments during breakfast?
Later, dear.

MAYOR   I will not discuss it later. (MR EASTER BUNNY IS NOW IN
FULL SIGHT. JAMES RUNS OVER TO HIM)

JAMES   Go away. Father will have a fit.

EASTER BUNNY
            He can't see me.

JAMES   Oh yes he can.

EASTER BUNNY
            You don't understand...I have on my invisible cloak.
Only you and Jane can see me now.

JAMES   Are you sure?

EASTER BUNNY
            Positive.

MAYOR   What is wrong with that boy?

MOTHER   He's just playful.

MAYOR   At his age?

MOTHER   My dear, don't be too harsh on him.

MAYOR   Oh, very well. Thank you, my love for a delicious breakfast. (**MOTHER** PICKS UP BREAKFAST THINGS. **JANE** HELPS. THEY EXIT) Are you all right, James?

JAMES   I'm very fit.

MAYOR   I didn't want to worry Mother, but you are behaving strangely.

JAMES   In what way? (HE PUTS ON **MR.** EASTER BUNNY'S HAT)

MAYOR   Where did you get that hat? It wasn't there a minute ago.

JAMES   Magic.

MAYOR   This is no joking matter!

JAMES   It's not a joke. Don't you believe in magic?

MAYOR   Here I am Mayor of this town with an idiot of a son.

JAMES   Some people might think...I'm talented!

MAYOR   Talented...for what?

JANE   (**JANE** ENTERS AND SEES THE HAT ON **JAMES'** HEAD) Oh goodness...James...what are you doing with Mr. Easter Bunny's hat?

MAYOR   What did you say?

JANE   Oh...I meant...it looks like a hat in pictures of Easter Bunnies I've seen.

MAYOR   This is too much. I try to raise my children as befits a Mayor and look at them.

MOTHER   (ENTERS) Don't upset yourself. They are only teasing. James take off the hat. (DOUBLE TAKE) Wherever did you get it?

JAMES   From Mr. Easter Bunny.

MAYOR   There he goes again! He is mad!

MOTHER   Now James, we mustn't make up stories.

JANE   He's only joking. Aren't you? (**SHE** STANDS BEHIND **MR. EASTER BUNNY**)

254

EASTER BUNNY
        They can't see me, I'm wearing my invisible cloak.

JANE   I can see you.

EASTER BUNNY
        Yes, I know. So can James, but no one else can.

JANE   Are you sure?

EASTER BUNNY
        Positive.

MAYOR   Now look at Jane! Oh my dear, I think both our children are mad.

MOTHER   Not at all. James...Jane...enough. There's work to be done.

EASTER BUNNY
        Do as they say.

JAMES   If you say so.

MOTHER   Of course, I say so.

JAMES   But Mother, you said we could discuss the Maypole dance after breakfast.

MOTHER   After a while.

MAYOR   There will be no Maypole dance in this town.

JANE   But why!

MAYOR   I don't believe in these foolish Spring festivals for Easter. Maypole dancing means May wine drinking! Wine drinking means drunkards! Drunkards mean trouble!

MOTHER   Do as your father says.

        MR EASTER BUNNY COMES BEFORE THE MAYOR AND BOWS. THE CHILDREN LAUGH. THE MAYOR DOESN'T SEE HIM. HE LOOKS AT THE CHILDREN.

MAYOR   What are you laughing at? Mother, Mother do something about these children.

MOTHER   Stop it, at once! James!

JAMES   Very well...

MAYOR   I must go to the Town Hall now. When I return we'll hear no more of Maypoles or Easter eggs. Is that understood?

JAMES   Yes, Father.

MR EASTER BUNNY PULLS AT THE MAYOR'S SUIT. JAMES IS FAR AWAY FROM HIM. THE MAYOR LOOKS TO SEE WHO COULD HAVE DONE IT.

MAYOR   Madness...plain madness. (EXITS)

MOTHER   Goodbye, darling. (TURNS TO CHILDREN) Enough is enough. I'll have no more of this.

JANE   Mother dear, please listen to us...

MOTHER   I'll not hear another word.

JAMES   Mr. Easter Bunny, remove your invisible cloak so Mother can see you.

EASTER BUNNY
           Very well. Madame, may I present myself to you. I am Mr. Easter Bunny.

MOTHER   (SHE SEES HIM) Oh my, let me sit down. Oh children, what am I to do with you! Now I'm seeing things.

EASTER BUNNY
           No you're not. I'm here.

MOTHER   So it would seem. Why?

EASTER BUNNY
           Because you and the Mayor have forgotten the joy of Easter! Don't you remember your youth?

MOTHER   I suppose I do.

EASTER BUNNY
           Didn't you dance in the Maypole dance?

MOTHER   Why, yes...but we danced the Maypole dance to celebrate the May wine...and the Mayor does not believe in any drinking.

EASTER BUNNY
           The Maypole is a dance of triumph...the triumph of Spring over Winter...with or without May wine.

MOTHER   Oh, I see.

EASTER BUNNY
           Nature is bigger than us all.

MOTHER   That's true.

JANE   Oh, Mother, I'm so glad you agree with Mr. Easter Bunny.

MOTHER   I didn't say I'll agree to a Maypole.

JANE   What shall we do?

MOTHER   I don't know.

JAMES   We can start with the Maypole. A very small one.

MOTHER   Your Father is head of this house and we must do as he
asks.

EASTER BUNNY
          You can blame it all on me.

MOTHER   No, we'll have to try by ourselves...but gently.

JAMES   I knew you'd see it our way!

JANE   What should we do first?

MOTHER   Wait...wait, we may not make out so well. What else
have you planned?

JAMES   An Easter egg hunt.

MOTHER   Oh dear, Father will never forgive us.

JANE   Let's try...

MOTHER   How?

JAMES   Let's get a pole for the Maypole dance.

MOTHER   And where will you put it?

JANE   In the garden.

JAMES   Then Father can see we won't be drinking any wine.

MOTHER   Oh my, he'll never forgive me.

EASTER BUNNY
          Don't worry, we'll help you.

     JAMES DASHES OUT...JANE FOLLOWS.

MOTHER   Where are they going?

EASTER BUNNY
          To get the pole.

MOTHER   What will Father do? A Maypole in our garden but for-
bidden in the town?

EASTER BUNNY
          We'll do it in stages. First the garden, then the town.

MOTHER   You can't just change things overnight!

EASTER BUNNY
          The Mayor was once a boy.

MOTHER   Maybe so. But that was a long time ago. He's a very solemn man now.

EASTER BUNNY
       Did you know that the Church, a long time ago, before so many people confused goodness with gloom...celebrated Easter Sunday with a game played by Clergy and even Bishops. They stood in a circle and played "Catch" with an egg, as part of the Service? (HE DEMONSTRATES AS HE TALKS)

MOTHER   Really?

EASTER BUNNY
       Yes, indeed.

     JAMES AND **JANE** ENTER WITH A POLE.

JAMES   Look, Mother, we found a wonderful pole.

JANE   Even ribbons.

     THEY PUT UP THE POLE ADDING RIBBONS. **MOTHER** SITS THERE HELP-
     LESSLY WATCHING.

EASTER BUNNY
       Beautiful...beautiful.

MOTHER   You don't know what you've done. For goodness' sake, James, give Mr. Easter Bunny back his hat.

CURTAIN

END OF ACT TWO

ACT THREE

     A FEW HOURS LATER. THE **CHILDREN** AND **EASTER BUNNY** ARE FINISH-
     ING THE MAYPOLE.

EASTER BUNNY
       You know in some countries they don't celebrate the Maypole with a pole. They just raise branches as a sign, for the Resurrection.

MOTHER   Mr. Easter Bunny, let's worry about this country, let's narrow it to this town, let's make it smaller, to this house. What do I tell the Mayor when he comes home? Which will be any moment!

EASTER BUNNY
       My dear Madame, I shall take care of everything.

MOTHER   Oh, that's perfect, especially when he can't see you.

EASTER BUNNY
       He will!

MOTHER   No, he won't. Not yet! Let's settle the pole in the garden.

JAMES   Don't worry, Mother, we can handle Father.

JANE   Of course we can.

MOTHER   Oh, we can! Don't hold me responsible for what happens then.

JANE   Don't fret so much.

JAMES   Enjoy yourself.

MOTHER   Oh, I shall, one day.

MAYOR   (OFF STAGE) Mother, what's wrong? The front door is locked.

MOTHER   Just a moment, darling. I'll be there. (TO CHILDREN) Not a word.   I'll see what can be managed. (SHE EXITS AND COMES BACK INTO SITTING ROOM WITH **MAYOR** WHILE **CHILDREN** PRETEND THEY ARE PLANTING FLOWERS)

MAYOR   My dear, I'm so tired. This has been such a difficult day.

MOTHER   I don't doubt it. Why don't you go upstairs and rest?

MAYOR   No, I think I'll go out to the garden. Where are the children?

MOTHER   In the garden. Wait until they finish planting.

MAYOR   I think I shall help them.

MOTHER   Oh, please, darling...they'd love to do it by them- selves. They have a surprise for you.

MAYOR   I want to see it.

MOTHER   Not yet. You look so tired.

MEANWHILE THE **CHILDREN** ARE ON GUARD IN THE GARDEN AS THEY SEE THE **MAYOR** APPROACH THE DOOR. EACH TIME **MOTHER** PULLS HIM BACK.

MAYOR   Do you think so?

MOTHER   Yes, dear. Why don't you rest on the sofa?

MAYOR   Very well, maybe I shall. (HE LIES DOWN AND RESTS)

MOTHER   There now, don't you feel better?

MAYOR   (DROWSILY) Yes.

HE IS ASLEEP AND STARTS SNORING. **MR. EASTER BUNNY** COMES IN

FROM THE GARDEN.

EASTER BUNNY
Now that he's asleep I think I'll lift his shoes.

MOTHER   Oh no, you don't.

EASTER BUNNY
It's a traditional Easter game.

MOTHER   No more Easter games!

EASTER BUNNY
(HE TAKES OFF THE SHOES) He'll sleep better.

MOTHER   Give me the shoes!

EASTER BUNNY
No, you have to chase me for them.

JAMES AND **JANE** LAUGHINGLY WATCH FROM THE GARDEN AS **MOTHER** CHASES **MR. EASTER BUNNY** FOR THE SHOES DOWN THE AISLES AND BACK ON STAGE.   THE **MAYOR** AWAKENS.

MAYOR   What is it, my dear?

MOTHER   (CHASING **MR EASTER BUNNY**) I'm trying to find your shoes.

MAYOR   My shoes? (HE LOOKS AT HIS FEET AND SEES HE'S BARE-FOOTED) My shoes, where are they?

MOTHER   Mr. Easter Bunny has them!

MAYOR   Oh no, now you! (**MAYOR** STARTS CHASING **MOTHER**) Stop! Please stop!

MOTHER   (**MOTHER** IS NOW CHASING **MR. EASTER BUNNY** THROUGH THE GARDEN) I must get your shoes.

MAYOR   Forget the shoes. Will you please come back into the house before all the neighbours see us.

MOTHER   Mr. Easter Bunny, no more pranks. Give me those shoes. (HE DOES SO. **MOTHER** RETURNS TO THE HOUSE)

MAYOR   What is going on?

MOTHER   Oh, what's the use of telling you...you won't believe me. Put your shoes on before we have another chase.

MAYOR   I'll leave home, that's what I'll do.

MOTHER   Nonsense. You have your shoes, don't you.

MAYOR   What happened while I was away?

MOTHER   Nothing...really... (**MAYOR** WALKS TO THE GARDEN. **MOTHER** FOLLOWS)

MAYOR   James...Jane! (SEES MAYPOLE) Nothing. A surprise for me, eh? The whole household has deliberately disobeyed me.

MOTHER   My dear, it's only a little Maypole for the children. You know it's not just May wines that created the Maypole. Oh no, it started with the bearing of branches...the carrying of wood for the joy of the Resurrection.

MAYOR   Oh, so we now give lectures, do we? Well then you be Mayor.

MOTHER   Heavens, no. It's just that it's harmless.

MAYOR   It's not harmless to look like a fool and be Mayor. A Maypole in my own garden when its not allowed in town?

EASTER BUNNY
    Sir, let's have a man to man talk.

MAYOR   Who said that?

JAMES   Mr. Easter Bunny.

MAYOR   Don't you start that again.

JAMES   But it's true.

MOTHER   I'm afraid so.

MAYOR   You are all conspiring against me. There is no such thing as a live Easter Bunny.

EASTER BUNNY
    Yes there is. (**HE** PUTS HIS HAT ON THE **MAYOR**)

MAYOR   Stop this! (**EVERYONE** LAUGHS EXCEPT THE **MAYOR**)

MOTHER   Oh my dear, a little humour can go a long way. (SHE PUTS ON THE HAT. IT IS PASSED ROUND UNTIL IT IS BACK ON **MR. EASTER BUNNY**'S HEAD. THE **MAYOR** NO LONGER SEES IT)

MAYOR   What happened to the hat?

JAMES   The rabbit is wearing it.

MAYOR   Stop this, I say.

JANE   Honestly, Father, he is.

MOTHER   Mr. Easter Bunny, take off your invisible cloak and let the Mayor see you.

EASTER BUNNY
    Very well.

MAYOR   They're all mad. (SUDDENLY HE SEES **MR. EASTER BUNNY**)
I'm mad too! I see him! Or am I seeing things?

EASTER BUNNY
          You see me. Watch carefully. I'll make an entrance.
(GOES TO GARDEN GATE. LIGHTS DIM. FAIRY LIGHTS GO ON ROUND THE
GATE AND **MR. EASTER BUNNY** DANCES IN)

MAYOR   Is that all you do?

EASTER BUNNY
          Oh, there's much more.

JAMES   Mr. Easter Bunny, allow me to introduce you to the
Mayor of Tidbit.

EASTER BUNNY
          Honoured.

MAYOR   Explain yourself. No one else speak.

EASTER BUNNY
          No explanations are required. I have lived for many
more centuries than you can count.

MAYOR   I don't doubt that people have had silly thoughts about
Easter Bunnies but how do I know that you're real?

EASTER BUNNY
          (TO CHILDREN IN AUDIENCE) Tell him who I am! (THE CHIL-
DREN SHOUT, "MR. EASTER BUNNY")

MAYOR   That is not proof. You've convinced the children of
this town, now try and convince me. I'll give you two minutes.

JAMES   Father, what are you planning?

MAYOR   You'll see.

JANE   You won't hurt him, will you?

MOTHER   Of course, Father won't.

MAYOR   Mother, come with me a moment. (THEY EXIT. **JAMES** AND
JANE RUN OVER TO **MR. EASTER BUNNY**)

JAMES   What do you think he's going to do?

EASTER BUNNY
          Get rid of me, of course.

JANE   But how?

EASTER BUNNY
          I don't know. But what can I give him as proof?

JAMES   Your hat!

EASTER BUNNY
      No, that could belong to anyone.

JAMES   That's true.

JANE   Your tail.

EASTER BUNNY
      That would hurt!

JAMES   Do you think you're in danger?

EASTER BUNNY
      Of course.

JANE   Oh, what will we do?

EASTER BUNNY
      Don't worry. You'll help me and so will the other
children, won't you? (CHILDREN FROM THE AUDIENCE CALL OUT,
"YES") Whatever happens...if I'm in trouble...I want you all to
call out, "We <u>want</u> Mr. Easter Bunny!" But only when I tell you
to do so.

      THE **MAYOR** AND **MOTHER** RETURN.

MAYOR   Well, where's your proof?

EASTER BUNNY
      Everyone, except you, believes I am Mr. Easter Bunny.
My proof is in the belief of so many children against you.

MAYOR   But I am Mayor of this town. I'll take you to the village square and there let the people judge for themselves.

JAMES   Why?

JANE   It's not fair!

MOTHER   Children, hush. Let's judge, here, in our own garden!
If Mr. Easter Bunny convinces the Mayor, we'll have our Maypole
celebration. If the Mayor is unconvinced, then Mr. Easter Bunny
will have to leave and there'll be no Maypole dance. Fair
enough?

MAYOR   Eh...yes...if the judges are townspeople.

EVERYONE Agreed!

EASTER BUNNY
      If I can make all those children happy will you be con-
vinced, Mayor?

MAYOR   There are so many children. Hm, let me think. Yes,
I'll accept that as a challenge.

EASTER BUNNY
        Very well. (TO CHILDREN IN THE AUDIENCE) Children,
look under your seats. Every one of you. We're having an egg
hunt. Did you find any? Good. Now for those that didn't find
any...James and Jane take my basket and give the Easter eggs to
all the children. **(JAMES AND JANE** TAKE THE BASKET AND GO INTO
THE AUDIENCE) Whom do you want, children, Mr. Mayor or Mr.
Easter Bunny? Say it, children, "We <u>want</u> Mr. Easter Bunny".
("WE WANT MR. EASTER BUNNY", IS SHOUTED BY THE CHILDREN. THE
EASTER EGGS ARE BEING GIVEN OUT, EATEN, DISCOVERED. IT'S CHAOS)

MAYOR   All right...all right...I want order. I say let's have
order. Children, be seated! Sit down! Oh my, someone do
something! I believe in you, Mr. Easter Bunny. Please, make the
children behave.

EASTER BUNNY
        Hurry up, everyone, sit down so we can convince the
Mayor. If you don't sit down, I'll have to leave. (EVERYONE BY
NOW IS SEATED)

MAYOR   Thank goodness for Mr. Easter Bunny!

MOTHER   I'm so pleased you said that.

JANE   Will you dance with us, round the Maypole?

MAYOR   It's been such a long time. I'm not sure I know how.

JANE   I'll show you.

    MOTHER, MAYOR AND JANE WALK TO MAYPOLE.

JAMES   To the Maypole!

EASTER BUNNY
        Shall we dance! (TO THE AUDIENCE) I think I'll choose
you...and you...and you...and you...and you to join us. (MUSIC)

    AS SOON AS **MR. EASTER BUNNY** HAS COLLECTED THE CHILDREN FROM
    THE AUDIENCE WITH **JAMES'** HELP THEY ALL BEGIN THEIR DANCE
    ROUND THE MAYPOLE INCLUDING THE **MAYOR, MOTHER** AND **JANE**.
    WHEN THE DANCE FINISHES THEY TAKE THEIR CURTAIN CALL WITH
    THE CHILDREN WHO ARE THEN ESCORTED BACK TO THEIR SEATS. AS
    THE AUDIENCE LEAVES THE MAYPOLE DANCE CONTINUES 'TIL THE
    AUDITORIUM IS EMPTY.

                         CURTAIN

                       END OF PLAY

SUGGESTIONS OF PERIMETERS OF ROOM.
MINIMAL FRAME TO SUGGEST 'INSIDE' — 'OUTSIDE WALL'
PAINTED BACKDROP OR CUTOUTS.
3d plants AT FRONT
SLOT IN 'LAWN' FOR MAYPOLE
BREAK-FAST TABLE & CHAIRS
INSIDE THE MAYOR'S HOUSE
THE GARDEN.

MAYOR
MAYOR'S WIFE
JANE
JAMES
MR EASTER BUNNY

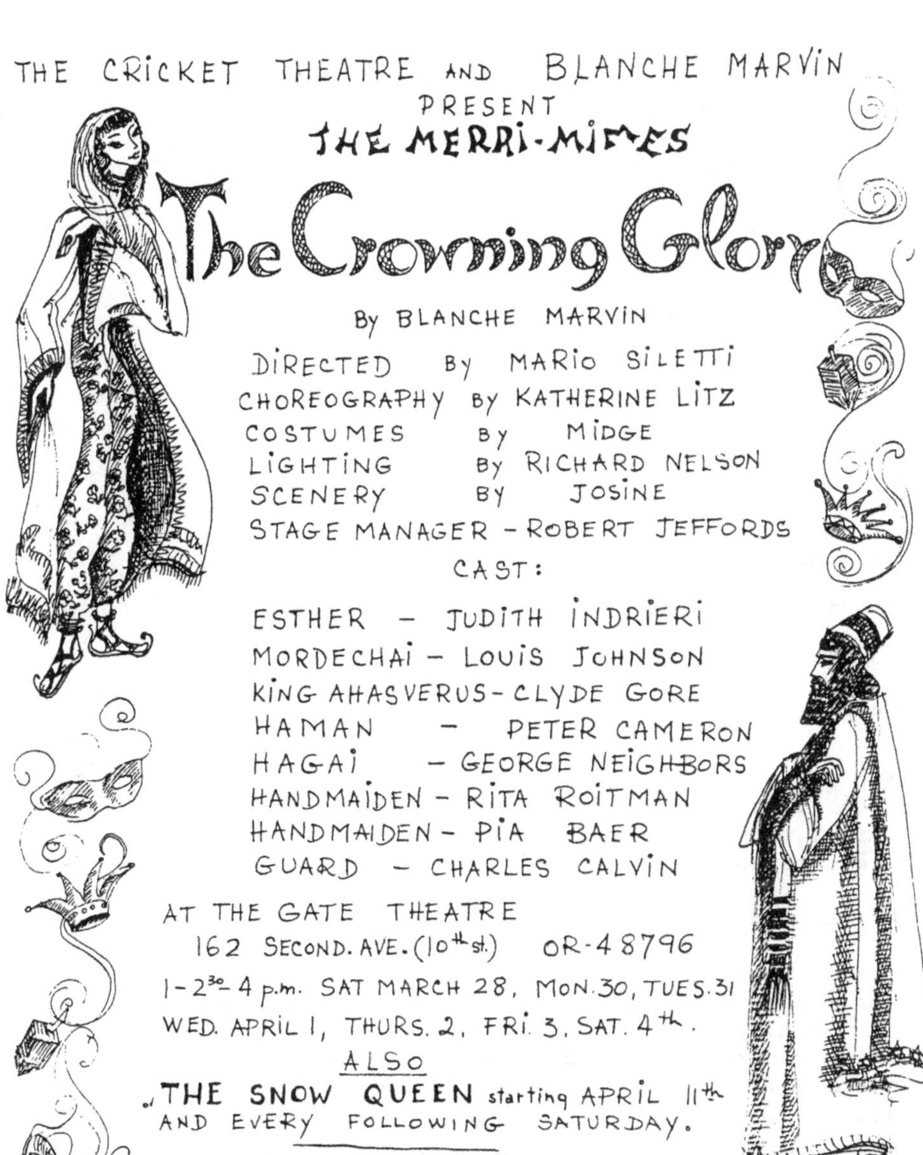

THE CRICKET THEATRE AND BLANCHE MARVIN
PRESENT
THE MERRI-MIMES

The Crowning Glory

BY BLANCHE MARVIN

DIRECTED BY MARIO SILETTI
CHOREOGRAPHY BY KATHERINE LITZ
COSTUMES BY MIDGE
LIGHTING BY RICHARD NELSON
SCENERY BY JOSINE
STAGE MANAGER - ROBERT JEFFORDS

CAST:

ESTHER — JUDITH INDRIERI
MORDECHAI — LOUIS JOHNSON
KING AHASVERUS — CLYDE GORE
HAMAN — PETER CAMERON
HAGAI — GEORGE NEIGHBORS
HANDMAIDEN — RITA ROITMAN
HANDMAIDEN — PIA BAER
GUARD — CHARLES CALVIN

AT THE GATE THEATRE
162 SECOND. AVE. (10th st.) OR-48796
1-2³⁰-4 p.m. SAT MARCH 28, MON. 30, TUES. 31
WED. APRIL 1, THURS. 2, FRI. 3. SAT. 4th.
ALSO
THE SNOW QUEEN starting APRIL 11th
AND EVERY FOLLOWING SATURDAY.

HAPPY PURIM!
FROM THE BARTON CANDY CO.

THE CROWNING GLORY
The Story of Esther
EUROPEAN CLASSICAL THEATRE
(First Prize Winner at Lexington Avenue YMHA)

CAST OF CHARACTERS

King Ahasuerus

Esther

Mordecai

Hamen

Hegai

2 Handmaidens

2 Dancing Girls (May also double as Handmaidens)

2 Heralds

2 Guards

Place:
Palace of Shushan, Persia. Costumes should be robes worn in
Biblical times in Persia, with the exception of Mordecai
whose robes are more Hebraic (Jerusalem).

Time: Biblical days

Author's Note:
Songs are not prevalent in this version. However, this is
an integral part of the play...it can be a musical. The
dancing can be more elaborate. It has been deliberately
simplified for amateur productions. Acrobats, sword dances,
jugglers, magicians can be added to court entertainment.

The scenery described in the script need not be followed.
We used two huge stone walls with lions' heads which were
constantly moved to become the varied locations by the ar-
rangement of the walls, indoors and outdoors. No curtain.

ACT ONE

SCENE ONE

IN FRONT OF CURTAINS.

MORDECAI (A MIDDLE-AGED, SWEET-FACED MAN WITH A SENSE OF HUMOUR IN FLOWING HEBRAIC COSTUME) Good afternoon, everyone. I should like to introduce myself. My name is Mordecai. I am what is known as a philosopher. Do you know what a philosopher is?

CHILDREN No.

MORDECAI It's a big word. And even a bigger thing to be...than a word. It is a person who thinks. He may think about good and bad...about people...about life...and afterwards he comes to a point where he must decide <u>what</u> to believe. <u>You</u>, my children, I want you to think about what is good and what is bad. And when you decide whether one thing or another is good or bad, you'll become a philosopher too. You, my little one, tell me how old are you? (CHOOSING A CHILD FROM THE AUDIENCE)

CHILD   Seven years old. (OR WHATEVER AGE HE MAY BE)

MORDECAI Good. Seven years old. Tell me, if I had a handful of sweets...and you were hungry...if I gave you the handful...would you eat them all or would you share it? Think and answer me, honestly.

CHILD   I would share it.

MORDECAI That is a wise choice. You have thought, decided and you know right from wrong...good from bad. Now my little philosopher go back to your seat. Remember, you are all philosophers. Are you all comfortable? <u>Good</u>. Because I want you to listen to a story which I have come to tell. It happened many centuries ago in Biblical days...in a country far, far away called Persia. There was a King, handsome and strong, named Ahasuerus. It so happened that this handsome King had a beautiful Queen named Vashti. Her beauty was so rare...you know what rare means? Very difficult to find. It seems not only was her beauty rare, but she herself was rare, very difficult to find. Just when the King wished to exhibit her, to show her off, to some visiting Princes, she would disappear. As a result, the King decreed that she was no longer Queen and was banished from the country. It was a lesson to all women all over Persia, who might be disobedient to their husbands. You are very blessed today. No one gets banished for disobedience, do they?

CHILDREN No! Yes!

AD LIB HERE ON PUNISHMENT, THEN...

MORDECAI So began the search for a new Queen. It didn't matter who she was or where she came from. All that mattered was that her beauty had to surpass the former Queen Vashti. From far and wide young women came to be seen, each one hoping they would be chosen. Now as it happens, I am not a good-looking man. Am I?

CHILDREN No!

MORDECAI But it is not for me, a philosopher, to be good looking. However, I have a niece. She is exquisite and even philosophers may try to enter beauty contests which can bring such
rich rewards. I'll call for my niece and tell her. Shall I?

CHILDREN Yes!

MORDECAI Very well, I will. But no one must know she is my
niece. I'm telling you all, here and now, a great secret. She is
my true niece, my brother's daughter. But you mustn't tell
anyone. Shhh. Esther, (VERY SECRETIVELY) Esther come here!

 MUSIC. **ESTHER** APPEARS. SHE IS POORLY DRESSED BUT HER EX-
 OTIC BEAUTY SHINES THROUGH.

ESTHER Uncle what is it?

MORDECAI (QUIETLY) Sh. (LOOKS ROUND TO MAKE SURE NO ONE IS
WATCHING) From now on you must <u>not</u> call me Uncle. You must <u>not</u>
know me. You must <u>not</u> tell anyone who you are or what you are.

ESTHER But, Uncle...er...Mordecai...why not?

MORDECAI You'll go to the King's palace and there be prepared by
the Chamberlain of the King's women to see the King, who is
searching for a new Queen. Every beauty in the land may be
presented to the King.

ESTHER I...I should try to be seen by the King of Persia! But
Uncle, I am a Jewess.

MORDECAI (LOOKING ROUND AGAIN) Sh. Call me Mordecai. Don't
tell a soul you're a Jewess. Your family came from a distant
land, from Crete...if you will...which is true...a long time
ago...but still true. I know what I'm doing.

ESTHER But the King would surely ask all about me. Besides,
he is searching for a <u>great</u> beauty. My clothes are like rags for
the palace of the King.

MORDECAI You're a great beauty, Esther. And if you do as I say,
you will see the King.

ESTHER Then tell me, what must I do?

MORDECAI In the Palace of Shushan is a kind man named Hegai. He
is the Chamberlain of the King's women. Go to him. Tell him I
sent you. But don't breath a word even to him that you're my
niece. He'll help you. He'll know how and when to present you
to the King. Go now quickly.

ESTHER My sweet Mordecai, I'll go. But don't forsake me. I'm
afraid of the King and the palace.

MORDECAI Go and I'll watch over you.

MUSIC. **ESTHER** LEAVES. **MORDECAI** SPEAKS TO THE AUDIENCE.

MORDECAI And so Esther went to the palace...to Hegai...as I bid
her. He was very pleased. For he's a man with soul and intel-
ligence...almost as good a philosopher as I am. As I stand here,
six months have passed. Would you believe it, my children, in
just two minutes six months can pass? That is not philosophy,
but imagination. You all have such imaginations, my children.
In six months so much can happen and it did. Hegai has cared for
Esther's beauty, trained and dressed her, as a woman should be,
before such a great King as Ahasuerus. Meanwhile, the King has
seen so many women and none have pleased him. He sits alone on
his throne. (EXITS)

SCENE TWO

> MUSIC. CURTAINS SLOWLY OPEN. WE SEE THE PALACE. IT IS
> DIVIDED INTO THREE STAGE AREAS. THE KING'S COURT DOMINATES
> CENTRE STAGE WITH HUGE COLUMNS. THE THRONE IS SEMI-
> ORIENTAL. ON STAGE RIGHT IS THE PART OF THE PALACE FOR MEM-
> BERS OF THE OUTER-PALACE COURT. STEPS AND ARCHWAYS LEAD TO
> BOTH THE INNER COURT AND MAIN PART OF PALACE. ON STAGE LEFT
> ARE THE GATES WHICH LEAD INTO THE CITY OF SHUSHAN. NEAR THE
> GATES ARE THE WOMEN'S QUARTERS. AS CURTAINS OPEN TWO **DANC-
> ING GIRLS** ARE DANCING BEFORE THE **KING.** HE WATCHES, BORED.

KING   Hegai! Heralds!

HEGAI   What is it, my Lord? Has there been no one to please
your eye?

> AS THE **HERALDS** GUARD OVER HIM THE **DANCING GIRLS** HAVE
> FINISHED THEIR DANCE AND SEAT THEMSELVES AT THE **KING'S** FEET.

KING   No one. What is it that I am looking for?

HEGAI   Take heart, we'll search until you find what you want.
(SLOWLY) Oh, gracious King, I've been told by a wise old man of a
most beautiful girl who comes from foreign parts.

KING   (SUDDENLY CHEERFUL) What could be more enriching than
a foreign beauty, or more challenging? Quick, send her to me.
Quick, quick I say!

HEGAI   Yes, my King. (PAUSE) She waits your attendance.

> MUSIC. **HEGAI** MOTIONS TO THE **HERALDS** TO BRING IN **ESTHER.**
> **HERALDS** EXIT AS **KING** WAITS IMPATIENTLY. ENTER **HERALDS** WITH
> **ESTHER,** BEAUTIFULLY DRESSED AND GROOMED. SHE TREMBLES WITH
> FEAR AS SHE IS BROUGHT BEFORE THE **KING.**

KING   Come here. Don't be afraid. (ESTHER SLOWLY APPROACHES
THE KING) Tell me your name.

ESTHER   (EYES DOWNWARDS) I am called Esther.

KING   How sweetly she speaks.

HEGAI   Yes, my King.

KING   (IN LOVE) You're very beautiful.

ESTHER   Your Majesty...is kind to say so.

KING   (TO HEGAI) Isn't she humble!

HEGAI   Yes, my King.

KING   Where do you come from?

ESTHER   From an ancient island.

KING   What a delightful mystery. Where are your family?

ESTHER   Dead, my gracious King.

        HEGAI HINTS TO HER ALL ALONG.

KING   It doesn't matter. I've a kingdom to give you in its
place.

ESTHER   (GASPING) My King.

KING   A King can give many things.

ESTHER   Oh yes, Sire.

KING   Hegai, take her to the women's quarters. Find her
handmaidens and be sure she's treated as befits our new Queen.
(HE SMILES SUMPTUOUSLY) A week of festivity is to be declared...
celebrations for the King's Wedding. I've found my new bride.

ESTHER   (SPEECHLESS WITH JOY) Oh, my Lord. (BOWING) My Lord.
How can such honours be bestowed upon me?

KING   Go now...be groomed as a Queen and everyone in the
kingdom will rejoice.

        MUSIC. HERALDS EXIT WITH ESTHER.

KING   (DEEPLY IN LOVE) Hegai, isn't she lovely.

HEGAI   Lovely, Sire.

KING   Isn't she exquisite.

HEGAI   Exquisite, Sire.

KING   Isn't she delicate and soft as the rose of Sharon, as a
lilly in the field?

HEGAI   Delicate and soft, Sire.

KING   Come now, Hegai. Where's the poet in you?

HEGAI   My King, you've other wives and other Queens, but this

new Queen will be the fairest, the most loving, the most grateful. She has true beauty from the depths of her eyes to her very
soul. You've made a wise choice. She'll bring new joys to you.

KING   Well said, Hegai. We have a Queen more beautiful than
Vashti.

MUSIC. FADE OUT   FADE UP

SCENE THREE

MORDECAI APPEARS ON SIDE OF STAGE.

MORDECAI   So you see, my little philosophers, he found his Queen
and she was beautiful. There was so much celebrating at the
crowning of the Queen that it lasted and lasted. Everyday was a
celebration, even after a year had passed. But life in the
kingdom is full of intrigue as well. (STARTS WALKING TOWARDS
GATES INTO...)

SCENE FOUR

IT IS DARK. TWO GUARDS ARE STANDING BY THE GATES TALKING TO
EACH OTHER. **MORDECAI** STOPS SHORT AND HIDES HIMSELF FROM THE
GUARDS AS HE LISTENS. MUSIC.

FIRST GUARD
Remember exactly what I tell you, not one detail must
be changed.

SECOND GUARD
I'll remember every detail. Nothing will escape me.

FIRST GUARD
We wait 'til it's late...very late...'til the King
retires. Then when it's our turn to take over the watch we'll go
into the King's quarters. After we are inside we can disguise
ourselves, slay the King, run out, throw off our disguise and
come in again to take over our watch. No one will suspect us.
We'll discover the King and call for help.

SECOND GUARD
Clever. You're a clever man. Do we loot the palace?

FIRST GUARD
No!! They must find nothing to suspect us. Our time
will come when the King is dead. When chaos exists. You touch
nothing now! That's an order!

SECOND GUARD
Your order is my command. Now only to wait.

FIRST GUARD
Back to our posts until tonight. (THEY LOOK AROUND AND
EXIT)

MORDECAI (STUNNED) Aha! What to do! What to do!   (WALKING
BACK AND FORTH QUICKLY) There's so little time. The King must

be saved. I'll tell Esther immediately. (MORDECAI GOES TOWARDS
THE WOMEN'S QUARTERS OF THE PALACE WHICH ARE NEAR THE GATES)
Hegai! Hegai! Come quickly, I pray you!

HEGAI   (RUNNING OUT) Who calls me and at such an hour?

MORDECAI   It's Mordecai.

HEGAI   What is it?

MORDECAI   I must speak to Queen Esther, quickly.

HEGAI   You? Speak to the Queen?

MORDECAI   (QUIETLY) I've overheard a plot to kill the King. I
must tell the Queen immediately! It must be stopped before it's
too late!

HEGAI   (LIKE A FLASH OF LIGHT) I'll find her at once...only be
careful. You must not be seen with her. (EXITS QUICKLY)

MORDECAI   I'll take care. (HE WAITS. ESTHER APPEARS)

ESTHER   (WHISPERS) Mordecai, where are you?

MORDECAI   (SECRETIVELY) Come near to the gates.

ESTHER   (HASTENING TO THE GATES. WHISPERING) Mordecai? What
catastrophe brings you here?

MORDECAI There's little time. Go quickly to the King. Tell him
there is a plot against his life. He is to be attacked by his
two night guards, tonight. Tell him I've told you so...only if
he's well-disposed towards you. Hurry, hurry! Before the
change of guards!!

     MUSIC. **ESTHER** DISAPPEARS.

CURTAIN

END OF ACT ONE

ACT TWO

SCENE ONE

     MUSIC. CURTAINS OPEN ON PALACE. THE **KING** IS RESTING ON HIS
     COUCH IN THE INNER QUARTERS OF THE THRONE ROOM. THE **HERALDS**
     ARE FANNING HIM WHILE A **HANDMAIDEN** HOLDS THE SCRIPTURES
     WHICH THE **KING** HAS BEEN READING. HEGAI STANDS AT THE HEAD
     OF THE STAIRS UNDER THE ROYAL ARCHWAY VERY EXCITED. HE
     WAITS UNTIL THE **KING** HOLDS OUT HIS GOLDEN SCEPTRE WHICH
     GIVES HIM LEAVE TO SPEAK.

HEGAI   My King...my King. Excuse my intrusion, but it's urgent you see Queen Esther, immediately. There's no time to
waste.

KING   Bring her in then.

ESTHER   (ENTERS. RUSHES TO THE KING AND KNEELS) Oh, my King, your life is endangered. Tonight the two guards who are to stand watch, plan to murder you.

KING   (JUMPING UP IMMEDIATELY) What?

ESTHER   Sire...

HEGAI   (INTERRUPTING) It's the truth.

KING   Esther, (RAISING HER UP) have no fear. Your warning gives us time to stop the murder and catch the villains. Now tell me how you discovered the plot?

ESTHER   A learned man who sits by the gates of the palace, Mordecai by name, overheard the guards and rushed to tell me so that I might save the King.

KING   It will be written in the Scriptures...the name of Mordecai, the learned man who saved the King's life. And now, my Queen, retire to your quarters. Hegai, help our fair Queen Esther.

ESTHER   God save my King.

MUSIC. THEY EXIT AS THE **KING** SUMMONS HIS **HERALDS** TO TAKE THE LARGE SPEARS AND SHIELDS.

KING   Heralds, you have overheard the murder plot. You know what must be done.

THE **KING** GOES BACK TO THE SCRIPTURES AS THE **HERALDS** IN A SWORD DANCE KILL THE TWO NIGHT **GUARDS** AS THEY ENTER.

SLOW CURTAIN

MORDECAI (COMES OUT IN FRONT OF CURTAINS) A famous man is now talking to you. My name was put into the Scriptures. The King, of course, was saved and I am a hero now as well as a philosopher. (QUIET MUSIC) Meanwhile, the entire Court is rejoicing at the triumph of Esther and the King. (EXITS)

SCENE TWO

MUSIC. CURTAINS OPEN SLOWLY ON THE PALACE. **ESTHER** AND THE **KING** ARE SEATED AT A BANQUET TABLE IN THE OUTER COURT. **HAMEN** A BIG, UNPLEASANT LOOKING MAN DRESSED IN ROYAL COURT ROBES SITS AT THE END OF THE TABLE. **HEGAI** STANDS IN ATTENDANCE AS USUAL. THE **HERALDS** STAND GUARD AS THE TWO **DANCING GIRLS** PERFORM BEFORE THE **KING** AND **QUEEN**. SOFT MUSIC ON A HARP IS HEARD ACCOMPANIED BY A SOFT FOLK SONG. THE **KING** AND **QUEEN** LOOK ON WITH PLEASURE. WHEN THE DANCING STOPS THE **KING** FEELS SO CARRIED AWAY, HE QUICKLY TAKES HOLD OF THE **QUEEN** AND STARTS TO DANCE. THE **HERALDS** PARTNER THE **DANCING GIRLS** AND THE WHOLE COURT NOW DANCES A PRODUCTION NUMBER. THE **KING** HAS EXHAUSTED HIMSELF.

KING   My, oh my, where has my breath gone.

ESTHER   (LAUGHINGLY) Shall I go and fetch it back?

KING   But where will you look?

ESTHER   Oh let me see...it might be in Hegai's sleeve. (SHE LOOKS PLAYFULLY) No...it's not there.

KING   I can barely breath. (KING SITS AS HERALDS AND DANCING GIRLS FAN HIM WITH LONG STANDING FANS) Oh, that's better. Come my mystery Queen, sit next to your King.

ESTHER   Oh, my Lord, how wonderful it is to be Queen. How happy...deeply happy am I to have you for my husband.

KING   Your sweetness grows each year, my Esther. Tell me what new jewels shall I give you. Ah, Hamen, bring me the jewel box.

HAMEN   (WATCHING BUT NOT PARTICIPATING) Yes, my King. (BOWING IN QUIET ANGER) Your bid is my command. (HE EXITS TAKING THE HANDMAIDEN WITH HIM)

KING   (HERALDS ARE STILL FANNING) Esther, my Queen, dance for me.

ESTHER   Will it please you, my Lord?

KING   Indeed it will.

ESTHER   Then I will dance.   (MUSIC. SHE DANCES A TRADITIONAL DANCE. WHEN SHE IS FINISHED, HAMEN AND THE HANDMAIDEN ENTER)

HAMEN   Sire...your jewel box.

KING   (TAKING THE BOX AND OPENING IT) Now what shall we choose? (HE LIFTS UP HEADPIECES, NECKLACES, EARRINGS, ETC. THE HANDMAIDEN IS ORDERED BY THE KING TO DRESS ESTHER WITH THE JEWELRY WHICH MAGNIFIES ESTHER'S BEAUTY) You are my pearl...my ruby...the jewels never adorned a more beautiful woman. This precious box and all it contains is for you. (HE GIVES IT TO ESTHER)

ESTHER   Oh, my Lord, you're too generous!

HAMEN   (SPEAKING PRIVATELY TO THE KING) Please don't be displeased, my King, by what I say. But as one of your lowly Courtiers, interested only in your welfare, isn't such a generous gesture, worthy of the Queen's beauty as it is, isn't it a trifle over-generous. We must ensure the wealth of the palace for our protection, for our armies. One of those jewels can supply enough weapons for the entire army.

KING   You speak in good faith, Hamen, and I'll reward your goodwill. You shall become my Chancellor. But as I reward you, so must I reward our Queen's beauty. The jewels are hers. We're rich enough in Persia.   The King's jewels will never purchase weapons.

HAMEN   (BOWING, OVERJOYED AT HIS NEW POSITION) My King is as wise as he is generous. The Queen's beauty deserves such rich-ness.

KING   Thank you, Hamen. And now my Queen, come let me show you the new orange trees in the garden. (THEY EXIT)

HAMEN   (OVERWHELMED WITH JOY) Heralds did you hear? I am now the Chancellor of Persia. (THEY BOW TO HIM) Now everyone must bow down to me. Announce me, Heralds, as I leave the palace, throughout the streets of Shushan. Announce the Chancellor of Persia, Prince of Princes, Hamen!

> MUSIC. THE GUARDS GO BACK AND FORTH ACCORDING TO **HAMEN**'S IN-STRUCTION, FINALLY STOPPING IN FRONT OF **HAMEN**. A CONFUSING AND COMICAL MOMENT. THEY LEAVE THE PALACE. LEADING INTO . . .

SCENE THREE

> THEY WALK 'TIL THEY REACH THE GATES WHERE **MORDECAI** SITS READING HIS BOOKS. THE **HERALDS** ANNOUNCE, "THE CHANCELLOR OF PERSIA, PRINCE OF PRINCES, HAMEN". **MORDECAI** GOES ON READING HIS BOOKS, NOT PAYING ANY ATTENTION. **HAMEN** IS FURIOUS.

HAMEN   Old man! Bow when Hamen is announced.

MORDECAI   (LOOKING UP PREOCCUPIED) Who goes by that I must bow?

HAMEN   Hamen.

MORDECAI   Greetings, Hamen.

HAMEN   Get up and bow to your Chancellor, the Prince of Princes.

MORDECAI   One bows only to the King. You know as well as I that you are not royalty. You are no Prince.

HAMEN   (MORE FURIOUS) I've been made Chancellor of all Persia today by his gracious King. Everyone must now bow before me...all the citizens of the kingdom.

MORDECAI   I am not a citizen.

HAMEN   (TO THE HERALDS) Is that true? He's not a citizen?

HERALDS   No, he is not a citizen. He is a Jew.

HAMEN   You've offended the command of the King. You and all your people will suffer for it. You will all perish.

> MUSIC. HE EXITS WITH THE **HERALDS** WHO CALL OUT HIS NAME AS CHANCELLOR OF PERSIA, PRINCE OF PRINCES, **HAMEN**.

FADE OUT   FADE UP

SCENE FOUR

> HAMEN AND THE KING IN INNER COURT.   THE KING SITS ON HIS
> THRONE.

KING   What danger, Hamen, has so suddenly come upon us?

HAMEN   It is a long and secret plot, oh King. Within the
walls of this very city, live a people who are called Jews.
They're not citizens and therefore claim no loyalty to Persia.

KING   We'll give them citizenship and in that way avoid any
possible danger.

HAMEN   But they do not wish to be citizens.   They claim loyalty only to themselves, as Jews, obeying their own rules and
laws.

KING   Why is there danger only now?

HAMEN   I've gone through the streets of the City, calling for
loyalty to the Crown and aid for our armies. The Jews have
answered that they owe no loyalty to the Crown...no support to
our armies. They are forming armies of their own to conquer Persia.

KING   (IMPATIENT) But why should they form armies so suddenly?

HAMEN   A new leader...they're ready to try their strength.

KING   Are you absolutely sure?

HAMEN   My King, upon my oath...my very life...I am sure.

KING   And who is this leader that has caused us this up-
heaval?

HAMEN   His name remains a secret but I will find him, if with
the King's help, a commandment is issued.

KING   Hamen, a divided house contains evil and pain. To sign
a commandment that will divide our house requires thought.

HAMEN   And while we think, Persia and you, my great King, may
be destroyed. Make this your commandment, seal it with your own
seal; that all the Jews in all of the provinces of Persia are to
be destroyed. Then ten thousand silver talents will be given to
those in charge...which I myself, as Chancellor, will pay. All
the possessions of the Jews will be given to the King's treasury
to make Persia richer.

KING   You are a dedicated man, Hamen. I shall decree this
commandment. I will give the ten thousand silver talents to you
for all those in charge. (HAMEN REALISES THE FULL EXTENT OF HIS
POWER)

HAMEN   My King, I live only to serve you!

KING   Heralds! Inform everyone in the palace of the King's
new decree. Hamen, your King has spoken. Go, tell the citizens
of the King's new commandment!

     MUSIC.   HERALDS LEAVE.

               FADE OUT   FADE UP

SCENE FIVE

     MORDECAI, IN SACKCLOTH AND ASHES OUTSIDE THE GATES, IS SADLY
     WALKING BACK AND FORTH. TO AUDIENCE.

MORDECAI The King doesn't understand what he has done. It's
the work of Hamen and his false pride. But what to do...what to
do. Think. Think. You are a philosopher, a wise man. But what
can I do?

HEGAI   (APPEARS FROM HIS QUARTERS, SEES MORDECAI AND GOES TO
HIM) Mordecai, you're grieved, deeply grieved. What is it?

MORDECAI You know the new decree of the King. I must stop it or
I and all my people are destroyed. Hamen has done this deed because of me. But how...how can I undo his evil work, Hegai?

HEGAI   Perhaps through Queen Esther. You once saved the
King's life. Maybe she would help to save yours.

MORDECAI Go, I pray you Hegai, tell Esther what has befallen.
Tell her I have said this to you. That she must go to the King
and beseech him on behalf of the lives of the Jews. She must
tell the King the whole <u>truth</u>. She will understand. Go now,
Hegai, and may the Lord bless you.

     HEGAI HASTENS TO THE PALACE AS MORDECAI PACES BACK AND
     FORTH. HEGAI GOES TO THE QUEEN'S QUARTERS AND WALKS OUT
     WITH HER TO STAGE RIGHT IN THE OUTER PALACE.

HEGAI   Those were Mordecai's very words.

ESTHER   But Hegai, you know I've not seen the King these past
thirty days. Should I go to the King without his consent? If I
displease him by such an act, he might behead me.

HEGAI   My Queen, quickly, go speak with Mordecai and I will
give you my cape as a disguise.

ESTHER   Hegai, I beg you, no one must know of this. Give me
your cape and I will go. (HE PUTS HIS CAPE AROUND ESTHER)

HEGAI   You may trust me, Queen Esther. Only go carefully; no
harm must befall you.

ESTHER   Wait for me in my Chambers, Hegai. Keep watch 'til my
return! (SHE GOES OUTSIDE THE GATES TO MORDECAI. HEGAI EXITS)

MORDECAI Esther, Queen Esther, thank God, you've come. Now you
must act as a true and great Queen. A Queen of your own people.

You must go to the King and beg mercy or we shall all perish.
The name of your house will perish. There will be no salvation.

ESTHER   But should I displease the King I will not be able to
speak for my people and only succeed in my own death.

MORDECAI   It was destiny that you were chosen Queen! Now destiny
calls you to be Queen of your own people. For you too will
perish by this decree. The King would soon find out that you are
a Jewess. If Hamen discovers anything about you he would be the
first to tell the King. Power...great power is now in his hands.
Even as I stand talking to you he's building a gallows for me.
We've come to the point where there's no turning back. If you
are to die at least die as a Queen should.

     MUSIC.

ESTHER   Uncle, I am a Queen. Never before have I felt so much
a Queen...a Queen of my own people. Mordecai, go forth and speak
to my people. Tell them to fast three days for me...and I shall
go to the King. We'll see if we perish or live.

CURTAIN

END OF ACT TWO

ACT THREE

SCENE ONE

     MUSIC. CURTAINS OPEN ON ESTHER'S QUARTERS WHICH CAN BE
     FIXED IN THE OUTER PART OF THE COURT. CURTAINED EFFECTS
     PRODUCE A FEMININE YET ROYAL ROOM. ESTHER IS BEING AIDED BY
     THE **HANDMAIDENS** AS SHE IS DRESSED, COMBED, BEJEWELLED. THIS
     IS A MIME ALL SET TO MOVEMENT. ALMOST A RITUAL KIND OF
     DANCE AS **ESTHER** IS BEING DRESSED.

ESTHER   Not a hair must be out of place. Every jewel must be
perfect. Do you hear me?

FIRST HANDMAIDEN
     Yes, Oh yes, my Queen.

SECOND HANDMAIDEN
     Just as you say, my Queen.

ESTHER   Our lives depend on this.   This is no woman's friv-
olity.

     HANDMAIDENS CONTINUE THEIR DANCE-LIKE MOVEMENTS IN DRESSING
     THE **QUEEN**, BUT NOW WITH MORE DESPERATION IN THEIR MOVEMENT.

FIRST HANDMAIDEN
     You are perfection.   (STANDING BACK AND LOOKING)

SECOND HANDMAIDEN
     Never have you looked more beautiful.

ESTHER (TURNING AROUND AND LOOKING INTO THE MIRROR NOT WITH GIRLISH DELIGHT BUT WITH REGALITY) Yes, I am as a Queen should be. (TREMBLING) Dear God be with me now. I beg you please do not take away from me and my people all that you have given. I shall be humble to you forever. Grant me this day, oh Lord, and I shall be worthy of it.

SHE STANDS PRAYING WITH HER **HANDMAIDSEN.** MEANWHILE DURING THIS SCENE OF **ESTHER** THE **KING** HAS BEEN READING THE SCRIPTURES IN THE INNER COURT. HE IS RECLINING ON A COUCH AS THE **HERALDS** AND **HEGAI** STAND WATCHING.

KING For some reason I cannot rest. I must read again and again the attempt made on my life. It was a man named Mordecai who saved me. Tell me, Hegai, how did I reward this man?

HEGAI Your Majesty there was no reward. It was his duty.

KING Strange that I didn't reward this man. As for duty, Hegai, it was the duty of the guards to protect me, not to take my life. No, this was ingratitude on my part, and ingratitude is unforgivable. I must honour this man named Mordecai.

THERE IS A SUDDEN KNOCKING UPON THE DOOR TO THE INNER COURT.

HERALDS Who goes there?

HAMEN It is I, the Chancellor, Hamen. I've come on urgent matters concerning the King.

KING Allow him to enter.

HERALDS OPEN THE DOORS FOR **HAMEN** TO ENTER. HE WAITS FOR THE **KING** TO HOLD OUT THE GOLDEN SCEPTRE. THE **KING** DOES SO AND **HAMEN** ADVANCES TO THE **KING.**

HAMEN (BOWING) Forgive my intrusion, oh mighty King, but I have...

KING My good Hamen, I was about to call for you. You've come just in time.

HAMEN I am overwhelmed to please you.

KING Now Hamen, I should like to pose a question to you.

HAMEN (INTERRUPTING) Excuse, my gracious Lord, the interruption, but may I speak of the urgency...a gallows has been built...

KING No wait, Hamen. For my purpose is far more important. Tell me how would you honour a man who has saved your life and whom you have neglected to honour?

HAMEN (THINKING IT IS HE WHO IS TO BE HONOURED) My Lord, I would honour a man who has done this for me by dressing him in courtly robes. Then I would have a procession for him through the streets of the city and proclaim him a hero, the saviour of the

King. Afterwards he would have the highest honour at Court.

KING   (DELIGHTED) Wisely said. So shall it be, wisely done.
Hamen, find the man named Mordecai, and do exactly what you have
just said to honour him. For this is the man who saved your
King's life.

HAMEN   But...but...my King...Mordecai...the gallows...Mor...

KING   Not a word, Hamen. Find the man, Mordecai. Bestow
those honours upon him. I'm ashamed to have waited so long.

MUSIC.   FADE OUT   FADE IN

SCENE TWO

> ESTHER HAS FINISHED HER PRAYERS AND BEGINS TO WALK PRAYING
> AS SHE GOES TO THE INNER COURT READY TO FACE HER DESTINY.
> SHE ARRIVES AT THE DOORS OF THE INNER COURT. SHE OPENS THEM
> HERSELF WITHOUT CALLING FORTH AND STANDS AT THE OPEN DOORS
> BEFORE THE **KING**. HE DOES NOT TOUCH THE SCEPTRE BUT STARES
> AT **ESTHER**. HE IS ENTRANCED. SHE STANDS AS A **QUEEN** AN-
> TICIPATING HER FATE. FINALLY, SLOWLY, THE **KING** HOLDS FORTH
> THE GOLDEN SCEPTRE. **ESTHER** BURSTS FORTH, THE GREAT BURDEN
> HAVING DROPPED FROM HER SHOULDERS.

KING   What is it that the beautiful, Queen Esther, wishes and
it will be granted her to half of my kingdom.

ESTHER   (NOW BESIDE THE KING) I wish only to see you my Lord
and to prepare a banquet for you and Hamen alone in my chambers.
I've not seen my Lord, these past thirty days and I fear I've
been forgotten.

KING   Oh, Esther...you are above all my other Queens. We
shall come to your banquet and I'll feast my eyes only on you.

ESTHER   My Lord, your Queen has been made happier than she has
ever been. I beg leave to prepare for the feast. (EXITS WITH
KING'S APPROVAL)

KING   (TO THE HERALDS) We must tell Hamen of his invitation.
This is a day of many celebrations.

> MUSIC. IN A ROYAL PROCESSION-LIKE MOVEMENT THEY EXIT.

FADE OUT   FADE IN

SCENE THREE

> ESTHER HAS RETURNED TO HER QUARTERS. THE FOLLOWING SCENE IS
> ALL DONE AGAIN IN MIME MOVEMENT. THE **HANDMAIDENS** MOVE IN
> THE TABLE AND CHAIRS OR PILLOWS AND SET THE BANQUET.   IN
> THIS MIME-DANCE THE SCENE IS SET AS **HAMEN** AND **KING** MAKE
> THEIR ENTRANCE. THE **HERALDS** WAIT OUTSIDE.

ESTHER   (BOWING) My Lord, my gracious King. I humbly serve you.

THE **KING** AND **HAMEN** ARE SEATED BY THE **HANDMAIDENS** AND THEN IN
DANCE-LIKE MOVEMENT THEY BEGIN TO SERVE THE **KING**, THE **QUEEN**,
AND **HAMEN** THROUGH THE FOLLOWING SCENE. **HEGAI** STANDS IN AT-
TENDANCE.

HAMEN   Fair Queen Esther, I'm most grateful to be received by
you. (ESTHER NODS ACKNOWLEDGEMENT)

KING   Remember, Esther, when you were first crowned Queen,
how a man named Mordecai saved my life? I never rewarded this
man. But today he was honoured by a procession through the
streets of Shushan, proclaimed a hero and will hold a high position in Court.

ESTHER   (FILLED WITH JOY) Oh my King, you are kind, you are
just!

KING   I knew this would please you. And now Queen Esther
what is it that you wish and I will grant it to half my kingdom.

ESTHER   I seek your love...

KING   I've not forsaken you, my comely Queen. Tell me what is
it?

ESTHER   Oh, my King, I have such grief in my heart.

KING   Tell me, my dove, and I shall carve out the grief and
fill it with joy...only tell me, my Esther.

ESTHER   Would you, my Lord, see me dead?

KING   See you dead...never!

HAMEN   Good Queen...never!

ESTHER   And yet it is you, Hamen, who would do so!

HAMEN   I? Never...never my Queen!

ESTHER   You are my enemy and would kill me.

KING   How so?

ESTHER   My Lord, by Hamen's commandment I would be killed. For
I am a Jewess and Mordecai is my Uncle.

KING   But I have honoured Mordecai and you are my Queen.

ESTHER   By the commandment, all Jews are to be killed. I beg
the King to revoke this commandment. Hamen requested it only to
harm Mordecai. He even built a gallows for Mordecai's head.

KING   (IN A FURY) You did this Hamen? Without my consent?
The commandment was decreed because you swore the Jews were disloyal and unlawful. I command an answer.

ESTHER   Where, oh King, have I or my people been disloyal or unlawful?

HAMEN   I beg you, Queen Esther, I meant you no harm. Please
help me.   You are favoured by the King.   (HE GOES CLOSE TO THE
QUEEN)

ESTHER   You meant harm to my people and to my Uncle. You were
not so humble with your power.

KING   Do not plead with the Queen, Hamen, you have aroused my
fury.   I'm a generous man, a tolerant King, but you have misused
the power entrusted to you.   You would have murdered behind the
King's back! Heralds! (THEY IMMEDIATELY ENTER) Take our Chancellor to the gallows he so carefully built for Mordecai.   Call
the Executioner.   On this day he'll reap his just rewards.
(MUSIC. THEY TAKE **HAMEN** AWAY QUICKLY) (TO **ESTHER**) Oh, Esther, I
gave power to Hamen without knowing how he would use it and now I
must sit in judgment on myself as well.

ESTHER   Merciful King, you've destroyed my enemy but now
protect us from this dreadful commandment.

KING   The commandment has my name and seal.   It can't be undone.   But a decree must be made. Hegai, summon Mordecai.   We
need his wisdom. (MUSIC)   The house of Hamen will be destroyed
forever...his evil stamped out...

ESTHER   My Lord, I thank you for myself and all my people.

> **HERALDS** PROCLAIM **MORDECAI**.   **MORDECAI** ENTERS NOW IN COURTLY
> ROBES.   HE BOWS TO TO THE **KING**

KING   Welcome, Mordecai.   You know Hamen has been hung for
his treachery and I have honoured you as my loyal subject.   If
your people serve me as you have, your King will be well-served.

MORDECAI My King, I thank you for the honour you've bestowed
upon me.   On behalf of my people, we pledge everlasting loyalty
to the King of Persia.

KING   Now Mordecai, I have summoned you to write the new commandment, one that will change the villainous decree of Hamen and
save your people.

MORDECAI The only decree possible my Lord is to allow the Jews
the lawful right to defend themselves against any attack in any
of the provinces of Persia.   This must be known all over the
kingdom and when your name and your seal are seen many will be
afraid to attack, others will understand the King's intent. That
is my decree.

KING   So be it, Mordecai. Write it down and I shall sign and
seal it.   You'll become my trusty Prince of Princes, Mordecai...
To you I give the House of Hamen, to be now called the House of
Mordecai.

ESTHER   And for all of us, on this day when Hamen cast his lot,
his Pur, remember he was destroyed instead.   Let us call this

day, The Feast of Purim. So sing, dance and rejoice in everlasting peace.

    MUSIC. ENTIRE CAST DANCE IN CELEBRATION.

CURTAIN

END OF PLAY

THE DIFFERENT
LOCATIONS FOR
'THE CROWNING GLORY'
COULD ALL BE
SUGGESTED SIMPLY
BY DIFFERENT
ARRANGEMENTS OF
BASIC FURNITURE
AND TWO GIANT
'STONE WALLS.
WITH LIONS, OR
LIONS' HEADS
ON THEM.

MORDECHAI
ESTHER
HAMAN
HANDMAIDEN

KING AHASVERUS
ESTHER
HAGAI

LIST OF PROPERTIES

THE EMPEROR'S NEW CLOTHES

Apron
Tablecloth
Hand fans
Two pairs of spectacles
Crown
Processional robe
A canopy of silk supported by four decorated
poles, used for King's Procession

SLEEPING BEAUTY

Crowns for King and Queen and Sleeping Beauty
Royal cloaks (King and Queen)
Fairy wand
Fairy crowns
Red fiery wig for Barbel
Spinning wheel
Dough
Rolling pin
Mop
Cream pie
Pots and pans
Spiderweb front curtain
Feather stole
Lorgnettes
Monocle
Plumes for the hair
Hand fans of lace or feathers
Swords
Goblets
Cradle
Comb
Hand mirror
Huge and decorated wedding cake

CINDERELLA

Cut-out PIANO, on which are
Glass slippers

PIANO STOOL, on which are
Silver tray
Silver cream jug
Dust cloth

TABLE, on which are
3 cups and saucers
1 plate with scones
Silver teapot
3 table napkins (serviettes)
Fan
Silver sugar bowl
Silver sugar tongs

Letter holder
3 letters - one to be read
Jam jar
Knife
2 spoons

Bell
Plate with crumpets
Special delivery letter
Pumpkin (breakaway)
Chiffon scarf
4 British hand flags
Scales of justice
Spear
2 fans
Cinderella's dress

THE LITTLEST TAILOR

Fly swatter
Cheese
Deck of playing cards
Lanterns (1 or 2)
Shotgun
Rope
Ribbon with 'Seven AT ONE BLOW'
    stitched or painted on it
Scissors
Sign 'DINER'S HOUSE'
Tree stump
Twigs
Cut-out bird
Cut-out alligator

ARABIAN NIGHTS

4 swords
Feathered canopy
2 pieces of light blue silk or similar fabric, 8 feet long
Pillows
Books
3 huge oranges (constructions)
Brass jug with a stopper
Flower (Tiger lily)
Thistle
Goblet

PETER AND THE WOLF

Samovar
Tray
Glasses for 10
Books
Dusting cloth
Tea towel
Handkerchief
Rope
Pince-nez

Waistcoat pocket watch and chain
Russian student's cap
Black Homburg hat
Cup for Duck

ALICE IN WONDERLAND

Bottle (labelled INK BOTTLE)
Huge pocket watch (cut-out)
Huge cut-out of a teapot
Cut-outs of red hearts
Table top covered with huge decorated table cloth
which will cover an actor six feet tall

PINOCCHIO

High hat (top hat)
Flower
Glasses
Book
Red wig
Black cloak
Nail file
Apron
White wig
Whip
Crown
Fairy cape
Feather
Wand
Short pants
Trunk

THE RED DRAGON

Crutches
Small scrawny Christmas tree
Christmas lights for tree
Christmas decorations
Christmas presents in boxes
Wrapping paper and ribbons
Teapot
Teacups and saucers
Plates and cutlery
Toast
Kippers
Sugar bowl and milk jug
Books
Pencils
Paper
Sword

MR. EASTER BUNNY

High hat (top hat)
Cups and saucers
Teapot
Sugar and cream bowls
Tablecloth

                    Easter eggs
                    Bolled eggs and toast
                    Maypole
                    Ribbons
                    Flowers

CROWNING GLORY

                    2 peacock feathers (gigantic fans)
                    2 black cloaks
                    Jewellery box
                    Jewels (necklace, bracelets, earrings, headpieces etc.)
                    Goblets
                    Hand mirror
                    Table
                    Banquet food
                    Plates
                    2 swords
                    1 sceptre
                    2 spears
                    2 helmets
                    2 shields
                    Scripture book (large scroll)
                    Small scrolls

www.ingramcontent.com/pod-product-compliance
Lightning Source LLC
Chambersburg PA
CBHW051501030726